The Interpreter of Silences

The Interpreter of Silences

JEAN McNEIL

McArthur & Company

Toronto

First published in Canada in 2006 by
McArthur & Company
322 King St. West, Suite 402
Toronto, Ontario
M5V 1J2
www.mcarthur-co.com

Library and Archives Canada Cataloguing in Publication

McNeil, Jean, 1968-
The interpreter of silences : a novel / Jean McNeil.
ISBN 1-55278-563-7
I. Title.
PS8575.N433I68 2006   C813'.54   C2005-907830-8

Design and composition by Tania Craan
Printed in Canada by Transcontinental Printing

The publisher would like to acknowledge the financial support of the
Government of Canada through the Book Publishing Industry Development
Program, The Canada Council for the Arts, and the Ontario Arts Council for
our publishing activities. We also acknowledge the Government of Ontario
through the Ontario Media Development Corporation Ontario Book Initiative.

10 9 8 7 6 5 4 3 2 1

Acknowledgements

The author gratefully acknowledges the support of the Canada Council for the Arts in the writing of this book. Thanks also to Euan Thorneycroft at Curtis Brown in London, and to Marilyn Biderman in Toronto, who read an early draft of this book. Rex Tasker in Musquodoboit Harbour, N.S., was helpful in shedding light on the strange habits of eels; thanks too to June Tasker in Halifax for her hospitality and support.

That was the strange unfathomed mine of souls,
And they, like silent veins of silver ore,
Were winding through its darkness.

Orpheus. Eurydice. Hermes.
—Rainer Maria Rilke

Who knows how long they brew there, under a vat of weed, before they spiral to the surface. At this stage they are embryos, suspended inside a transparent sac buoyed by droplets of oil. Then they are sieved through the mesh of Sargasso, gripped by currents that will deposit them in the soupy jungle waterways of Guyana or in Lough Neagh, Northern Ireland, or anywhere in the river-frayed coastlines between.

For months they are only scraps of transparent gelatinous flesh, no bigger than a thumbnail. They float, thickening, until they resemble tiny chevrons. By the time they reach the island they have lengthened and look like thin hairs dotted on the ends with two tiny black eyes. This is the first of several mutations: throughout their lives they will change colour and shape several times, even the composition of their blood.

They will arrive and leave at night, entering the island's salt lakes through a bight, wrung in the currents that swirl around the stanchions of the Seal Island Bridge. They taste the sudden drop in salinity and know they are home. Although they have never seen this before, there is also something familiar about the single halogen light and the two concrete fingers pointing into the lake in a V, the coal-black water, the shattered hulk of a ruined ferry.

She is standing on the shore beside the ferry with her father. He is pointing southeast, in the direction of the Sargasso Sea. She is twelve years old and her father is explaining that the eels will return there to die. In his voice is the rough note of satisfaction produced by inevitable truths. Less than you might imagine separates him or her from these creatures, he says; like them we will return to the nowhere from which we came. There we will start again. We are on a loop, he tells her. Time is repeating itself endlessly, we are repeating ourselves.

Above them, close enough to see the severe hook of its beak, a bald eagle spirals, its four-foot wingspan titled on thermals.

She is only twelve years old — what does she know about time? Even so, she thinks, I don't want to be part of this rigid continuum. She thinks, let me be the one to break the cycle.

CHAPTER 1

She thinks of it as a recurring dream, not because she has it often — in fact, she has had it only four or five times in all the years she has been away — but because each time it is exactly the same.

She stands on the lip of the hill under a bleached and uncertain sky. The cabin is tucked away, just beneath the brow of the hill, surrounded by piles of ash-coloured snow. It has the vaguely sinister look of fairy-tale illustrations. Then she walks down the hill with gelid, half-paralyzed limbs, slipping toward an unannounced precipice. Within the dream she is aware that she is trapped in its folds, and that there is nothing she can do about it.

Then her hand is on the door and she is inside calling his name, but the cabin is only a knit of spider webs, the stove is cracked in two as if by an earthquake, the light-switches have been ripped from the walls by the teenaged robbers that prey upon the island's forsaken houses.

She circles the rectangular space that serves as the living room and kitchen, calling his name, fear fluting her voice. She slowly becomes aware of a figure seated at a kitchen table studded with tiny pyramids of termite dust. She turns toward it. It is him, sitting alone in a dank corner. He is skeletal, but still alive. He looks at her with emaciated eyes.

Even in the late-morning sun, the salt lakes retain the lead hue of winter. They are ribbed by thin black waves, like a mackerel's back. It is early May and the last of the old ice is unlocking its fists. The thawing ground is strewn with survivors of the yearly permafrost: a Baxter's Chocolate Milk carton, its brown swish bled to yellow, a couple of pennies hollowing the ground in perfect circles, carpets of sodden pine needles, their stale menthol scent. It was hard to believe that one day soon this unlovely spring would become, almost overnight, a hesitant yearning toward summer.

She had asked the taxi to leave her at the bottom of the road; she would walk the quarter mile uphill to the cabin, her wheel-case-backpack hybrid digging into her ribs as she scraped through gravel and slush. The taxi itself was a car of the ilk she hadn't seen in a long time: a single bench for a back seat, a long square hood, a rear hubcap rattling loose. What were they called? Impalas, Reliants. A gas guzzler, a remnant from the Eighties, maybe even the Seventies.

Her clothes still have the frigid, gassy smell of the strato-sphere. She had flown in that morning in a cold plane that had been parked on the tarmac all night. From the plane she had witnessed a land still levering itself out of the shocking devas-tation called winter: glacial lakes, boggy taiga traced by thin veins of mining roads, flatlands corrugated by drumlins. Stewardesses dole out overbrewed coffee and dry croissants while she watches as Northern Quebec turns seamlessly into the thumb of the Gaspé, then the black matted forests of New Brunswick, the thin waist of Tantramar.

She had two hours' wait in Halifax airport. It had been renovated since the last time she had passed through and now sported sleek vinyl couches and large-scale photographs of lobsters and fishing shacks, mounted on lightboxes. She watched a woman wearing suede ankle boots tapping into a laptop as a Continental Airlines jet materialized in the win-dow behind her.

Then she is on another, much smaller plane, skirting the moraine coast of the peninsula, then over the Canso Strait. Minutes later the lakes appear as a swatch of velvet blue cupped in the palm of the island. The plane dropped closer to a salted, carbon land and its acid barrens, muskeg, black pine forests. Then the seatbelt sign flashes on and the land rises to swallow her.

"Who is it?"

"It's me, Dad."

"Who the hell is me?"

His face appears on the other side of the screen, dark and woven with mesh.

"Hi, Dad."

"What in the name of God are you doing here?"

"I've come home to see you."

His eyes narrow. He makes no move to open the door.

"Did Maureen send you?"

"She called me, yes."

"Christ Almighty."

She puts out her hand to open the door.

"NO!" he shouts. "I mean, hang on a minute. This place is a dump. I've got to do some cleaning."

Through the mesh she sees him swivel his gaze around the room, run a hand through his hair.

"It's okay. I'll do the cleaning. Just let me in."

He makes no move to stop her so she swings open the door. The smell hits her first, the woody, static smell of childhood: candlewax, kerosene, fish, woodsmoke.

Is it her imagination or is he smaller? He seems to have shrunk, although from the inside. Otherwise he is the same: a mop of unruly hair, somehow unseemly for a man of his age, still dark although laced by strands of grey.

"You look good," she ventures.

He eyes her case, Bottega Veneta. She had bought it at discount in a warehouse sale on the outskirts of Florence.

"That's a big case you've got there."

It could have been bigger, but she declines to say. She had

acquired her packing habits from Caroline and other members of the fashion tribe, all confirmed heavy travellers, packing *body lait, lift minceur,* perfumes and multiple pairs of shoes even on short trips. But for this trip she had packed like a Marine: get in, get the job done, get out.

She pokes her head through the door into what had once been her room, and then yanks it back in shock. It is preserved as the day she left, a museum to her departure. The Periodic Table of Elements still tacked up above her bed. Beside it an old *National Geographic* foldout map of the world; Yugoslavia is intact, the Soviet Union a giant red stain. A pelt of dust coats the frame of her print of Alex Colville's painting *Horse and Train*, the dark horse still visible through a sieve of dust, its ears laid back, hindquarters churning, running straight into the path of an oncoming train.

"You could have at least cleaned it."

"What for? You were never coming back anyway."

It is so like them, she thinks, to trade rebukes straightaway.

She shoves her bag on the bottom bunk — he has also kept the bunkbed Anita and she shared — and goes to inspect the living room.

The cabin had always been rustic, the kind of place better-off people would keep as a summer cottage. They had running water but no central heating, apart from an ancient iron stove that had been manufactured in Sackville in the Thirties and whose white enamel had long ago soured to an oyster hue. It sat like a Sumo wrestler between the kitchen and the living room, disseminating the cabin's seaweed smell. It had never broken down, but if it had they would have been reduced to burning wood in the middle of the living-room floor or huddling next to the rank kerosene heaters her father had kept around in case of an emergency.

The kitchen table was two planks of wood with benches on either side. A blue-and-red china cabinet still occupied most of the living-room wall. Inside it is dusty china, unused for at least ten years, with its pink nymphs and brittle teacups. A tan-and-orange check chesterfield, a relic from about 1972, occupied most of the living room. She guesses that the same musty boxes of Scrabble with half the letters missing still lived underneath it.

The door to his bedroom is ajar. She catches a quick glimpse of a row of postcards tacked above the bed in his spartan room, trying to remember the circumstances of their sending. A limelit Venice, the bulbous egg of Sacre Coeur, the harsh Aztec sun of Mexico.

She drifts back to the kitchen. Beside the stove are plastic milk crates full of bags of dried pasta and rice and a few spice bottles so old their labels have faded to mere outlines: oregano, basil, bay leaf. Above them three pots are nailed to the wall, along with several heavy iron cooking utensils of unknown use, now covered in a caustic rust. In a Dole Pineapple cardboard box are stacked issues of *National Geographic, Scientific American, Reader's Digest.* Anita must still be sending him subscriptions to these magazines for Christmas gifts, just as she has done for years, to help keep him in touch with the world.

He stands a few feet away, his back toward her. He seems to be chewing on something. She realizes it is words: he is turning them over and over in his mouth, trying to choose which ones to eject.

"I don't want you to see me like this."

"Like what?"

"Don't treat me like an idiot. I always said the only reason you'd come back is to come to my funeral so I guess I'm as good as dead."

He sits down heavily on the bench that rimmed the kitchen table.

She takes a step toward him, her hand reaching out for his shoulder, but she stops just short.

"I'm not here because you're dying."

"Why the hell are you here then?"

"I'm here to see you."

His eyes travel up to meet hers; they seem to come from a long way away. They are still the light brown eyes he always had, quite unlined, considering he spent most days outside. The look in them is not sharp enough for reprimand, not blurred enough for sadness. She doesn't know what to call it.

"You never wanted to see me. Not once in your life did you ever want to see me."

She sits down opposite him, mirroring his posture, her elbows on the dusty kitchen table beside two mugs and an empty box of Red Rose littered with the black dust of long-dried tea leaves. She tries not to notice that the mugs are netted with mould.

"That might have been true at one point," she concedes.

She is conscious of how her voice has changed in the few minutes since she walked through the door. Now it is low, reassuring, the same tone she remembers hearing her aunts, her grandmother, use to placate drunken or disappointed men. It is a voice she didn't know she possessed, until now.

She reaches out to put her hand on his arm. He says nothing, but neither does he flinch.

They sit there facing each other in silence until a cloud swallows the sun, pouring a false twilight into the cabin, and she rises to turn on the light.

"So how are you getting on?"

Duncan gave her a shy, evasive smile — a young smile on a sixty-five-year-old face.

"Not too bad. What's that you got there?"

"A bicycle. Remember them?"

"What're you doing going around on that?"

"My father killed the truck. I was hoping you could get some more air in these tires. I've got to get to Indian Bay and back."

She followed him into the garage.

"I guess you won't see too many changes around here," he said. The body shop was shut; Duncan hadn't used it in years. A dusty windowpane looked out into its empty cavern from his office. The hydraulic hoists that would raise a car delicately on four elephant legs were still intact, as was the fume of rubber and stale grease. Sloppy oil stains on the walls damp corners in which tiny mushrooms grew. Duncan was forever trying to get rid of them, but they just sprouted up again.

It had been eight years since she had last seen him, but to her eyes he was identical to the version of the man he had been when she worked for when she was a teenager. Duncan was one of those men whose changes were so subtle as to be glacial. He was still that tall, sturdy character, with the light blue eyes and long rectangular jaw of the Norseman.

"So how are your kids?"

"Oh, they're doing all right. I've got grandchildren and everything now. Never see them though."

Duncan's wife had been dead — breast cancer — for nearly twenty years. His children had scattered all over the place. One was in insurance in Manitoba, another was an engineer and lived in northern California, both responsible family men, providers for their sluggish children, both of them balding, even though their father had retained his thick, glossy hair. Duncan had shown her photos once, on one of her rare trips back; snapshots taken in living rooms of boxy houses under the flat light of the Prairies or the vindictive clouds of coastal California, studio photographs of the children on the walls, thin trees too young to cast any shade planted in the yard.

"And how's business?"

"Not so good. I tried to sell up a couple of times but it looks like they've got all the franchises they want around here. There's two on the other side of Indian Bay."

She nodded.

"I saw."

Garages owned by other Duncans had been bought by Ultramar, now corporate yellow-and-blue, three eager young men attending the forecourt.

"To tell you the truth I'd like to retire, but I can't afford to."

"Why don't you hire someone to take over?"

He placed the air valve on her bicycle tires and a scream of air escaped. "Tried that too. Nobody would have it. They think I'm a lost cause around here. Some people buy their gas from me out of pity. They think I don't know that, but I do."

She stole a look at his bent, capable hands, the same hands she remembered from the summers when she'd worked for him minding the cash register while he pumped gas, selling packs of Craven "A", du Maurier, Player's, dispensing ribbed glass bottles of Fanta, Sprite, Teem. In the summers she sold Freezies, Fudgsicles, Popsicles; in the winter cans of Valvoline, plastic jugs of antifreeze. Sometimes Duncan would leave her to mind the shop while he ran into Indian Bay for more oil or milk. She liked being left alone with responsibility, with gas pumps, the till float, the taut cellophane on the packets of cigarettes, cars pulling in off the Trans-Canada, headed to Sydney, to Halifax or even the States, their prosperous-looking occupants, men in Ralph Lauren shirts, bored children, their feet propped up on the back seats, reading *Tintin*s spread across their knees.

Strange business, her father's sister Maureen said, audibly and deliberately to anyone within her earshot. *A sixteen-year-old girl spending all her days with a fifty-year-old man. That'll start tongues wagging.* She and Duncan really did strike a rhythm with each other; they could sit side-by-side without speaking happily, making idle observations about the sunburned couple in the car from Saskatchewan that had just come through. Sometimes they played cards to pass the time. Duncan had never been improper, nor had he assigned to her the easiest role available, that of daughter. No, if she had to classify it she would say he had treated her as a friend, and this had taught her something valuable and which she took forward into the rest of her life: that a fifty-year-old man and a sixteen-year-old girl could be friends.

"Did you hear they've rented John R's old place?"

"I thought it was sold."

John Rory's was the house next to the cabin. It was an unexceptional farmhouse, but she could imagine it had a certain clapboard charm, at least for visitors. Someone had painted it recently, a cream colour which would withstand the brunt of no more than two or three winters before peeling. The old barn had escaped renovation and stood next to the house like a mute companion, its shingle bleached to the same faded denim as the local roads.

"No, his sisters own it now," he corrected her. "They live in Sydney; they rent it out every summer. You'll be neighbours. Some people from New York. I hear they got something like nine hundred US a week out of them."

"Nine hundred US." She shook her head.

"People are paying stupid money for land around here now. Some American bought a piece of bare shore up at Skir Dhu for over a hundred thousand. There's not even a house on it. Then there's the Germans. They own most of the land over Dundee way now. You should see their satellite dishes, picks up their German TV. Donny McKenna goes over to a German's house one night and said it was all sex. Even on talk shows people were naked." Duncan didn't sound scandalized so much as bemused.

"What do I owe you?" she asked.

Duncan stared at her, quite shocked. "You've got to be kidding."

"Sorry. I just thought…"

"Well, don't think."

He set off into the garage. She followed, uselessly, suddenly miserable at her gaffe.

Duncan went into his office next to the body shop, a chaos of unfiled receipts and invoices; a blizzard of business cards and scraps of paper with the numbers for automated weather forecasts was taped to the till.

"I could give you a hand here," she said. "I could help you modernize."

His shoulder pivoted toward her, but she couldn't see his face. "What do you mean, modernize?"

"Put things in order, introduce something new, something to attract customers. You know, the tourist trade."

"You'll be busy enough with your father by the sounds of it."

"Not so busy I can't come down here one a week."

"We'll see."

We'll see, she knew, meant *no*.

They went outside. The traffic sounded suddenly too loud; tractor trailers passed at a hundred and twenty kilometres an hour, their engines groaning as they geared down for the turnoff to Indian Bay. The stream of traffic was already punctuated with trailers and the odd camper van, advance parties of what would soon become flotillas of vehicles sporting licence plates that had fascinated her as a child. She had made a game out of them, making inventories of the states and provinces that passed through Duncan's garage: Saskatchewan's golden puff of wheat, the spindly flamingos of Florida, the mercenary thrust of New York's Statue of Liberty, Quebec's plangent motto: *Je me souviens*.

"I would have done the same, you know, if I'd had your advantages."

She turned to him, not quite sure if she had heard him correctly. She wondered which advantages he was thinking about. Youth, maybe, a reckless sense of possibility. He must know she never had any money. She smiled to show she hadn't taken it as a rebuke for not having come back in all these years, although perhaps it was.

A car pulled into the forecourt. Duncan wiped his hands on his overalls and went out to serve the driver. She hovered there for a minute, watching from the side of the building as a young-looking man with dark hair and glasses rolled down the window. *What can I get you today?* she heard Duncan's stranger-voice say. The man in the car counted US dollar bills, leaning his forearms on the steering wheel.

She mounted the bike. When Duncan's customer had left she would go too. For some reason she didn't like to be observed, even by total strangers, when she was cycling. Everyone who lived year-round on the island did it, looking boldly through the windshield as they passed cars, tracking friends and neighbours by their vehicle; it was habit, almost instinct. She could hear people as they whizzed by in their Fords or Nissans, *That's Alistair's daughter, home for the summer. Poor thing, look at her on that hill. She must be exhausted.*

The stranger drove off. She forgot to get a look at the licence plate. He was probably a tourist; his glasses were too sophisticated for him to be a local.

"See you later," she called to Duncan, and pedalled out the driveway.

The road to Clam Harbour is a ribbon of frost-shattered asphalt, bleached by sun and salt to an attractive light denim. It cuts through a black corridor of spruce to open onto shimmering fingers of lake. The road is hemmed by a gravel shoulder where tufts of weed grow, clover, thin red runners of wild strawberries that spread themselves across the bank like capillaries, dark blotches of blackberry bushes. Stale meltwater lines shallow ditches on either side of the road, matted with algae.

She passes two boys on bicycles, their faces streaked with dirt. *That's where Glenn's car went over the bank and into the water!* they call to her, their voices sheared with the drama of disaster. *He died right away! No he didn't, he drowned trying to push open the door! Did you see the dead porcupine?* Yes, she had. She had been obsessed with roadkill once: squirrels, skunks, porcupines, their entrails dried by the sun until they are only a cranberry stain on the tarmac.

At the top of Chimney Hill she stops to rest. This is the stretch where moose frequently straggle out of boggy woods to cross, just before the turnoff to the old dirt road that leads to Surprise Cove and the gypsum sinkholes. She had mapped the road closely on years of walks. She would set off, accompanied by her father's dog-of-the-moment, to return hours later. *I don't know what you get up to,* her father would say. As she got older she sometimes allowed him to believe that she had spent the afternoon watching videos and drinking beer in some friends' rec room, as any normal teenager would do.

She stands, a leg on either side of her bicycle, drinking in a watery sun. No traffic passes. Only a few families live along the Clam Harbour road now, it has never been resurfaced properly, only potholes filled in, fractures padded; over the years it has acquired a precipitous camber in places, so that driving it at any speed is akin to being on the Tilt-a-Whirl. Her father had told her of summers when cars were lined up all five miles to the Trans-Canada turnoff, waiting for the ferry. In the years before the bridge was built the ferry from Clam Harbour was the only link between east and west flanks of the island. Gas stations like Duncan's had flourished then, as had the long-shut convenience store near the ferry.

The ferry is there still, slowly dissolving in the dock, pitted with holes. The crossing is still marked on old road maps, and the occasional tourist could still be found driving down the road, executing messy three-point turns in what used to be the loading area, cars full of wide-eyed strangers staring out at the few houses straggling alongside the road, faintly shocked. *Is this all there is?*

The road is a dead end. In case anyone is in any doubt of this a rusting NO EXIT sign stands next to the ferry. A gravel road curves up the hill, past Celyn's house, John Rory's, leading finally to their cabin, the last house on the road. Beyond their cabin the gravel road becomes a rough track, barely negotiable with a four-wheel drive. It runs along the eastern flank of the mountain to emerge next to the bridge and the Trans-Canada, but more often than not it is blocked by a storm-lashed tree or a swollen brook.

She hoists herself back on her bicycle and pedals down the road, past the burnt-down house that gives Chimney Hill its name. It is one of many abandoned houses in the area, slowly being eaten alive by woods and weeds. She can still make out the form of an old kitchen stove, now rusted into the shape of an open clam, and a spindled bed frame blanketed by wildflowers. She is surprised at how hungry her eye is for the detail of a place that she has so deliberately tried to forget. Her ear tunes itself so effortlessly to an old frequency: the wind breathing in tandem with the land, the uninterrupted news of silence.

Eve arrived back at the cabin to find her father pacing in the living room.

"What's the matter?"

"Somebody phoned for you. Some feller."

"Did he leave a number?"

She waited as he rummaged in the living room for the scrap of paper. He presented it to her. On it was her own phone number.

She wanted to turn to her father and say, "That's my husband." *Husband.* She let the word take its heavy place in her mind, like an overweight person stuffing themselves into a too-small chair. Such a strange word, she thinks, not for the first time. It is not quite modern, strict and cosseting. It might sound like a vindication, or a lie. In the end she said nothing, just picked up the phone and dialled the number.

Hi, you've reached Eve. I'm away for the summer but can be reached at — her answering machine voice, a tone she had parsed from listening to other people's machines; the breathless, offhand voice of the successful urban professional.

"Lew. It's me," she nearly whispered. "I hope my father didn't scare you. I'm in tonight, so give me a call." She hung up, but something — some small doubt or uncertainty — kept her ear to the receiver, listening to the metallic buzz of empty space.

Llewellyn strikes an itinerant posture on the edge of the bed, his arms spread impatiently among piles of her clothes, legs jiggling.

"You always said you wanted to take a summer off and just read all the books you always meant to read." He waits for her response. "It'll be a great break," he adds.

She is thinking, *You seem eager for me to be gone.*

"You look tense."

"Of course I'm tense. I'm going away for four months. I don't know when I'll be back. I don't know what's going to happen."

Outside, a cobalt sky, dark tors of thunderclouds. Elms are embroidered with new buds.

"I thought this is what you wanted."

The expression on his face is untroubled. Her husband insists on seeing the advantage in everything that happens, no matter how much imposed from the outside, no matter how much beyond his control.

"It's not what I want. I've got to do it."

He splayed himself, even more extravagantly, across their bed. "But you'll get something out of it," he said.

This summer would pass, uniquely, without wilting in the streets of Chinatown, harassed by skyscrapers smug in their verticality, by Caroline's customers, the intricate demands of Russian or Taiwanese nouveaux riches with a shaky command of English: *I said no turquoise. Can't you make it more rich-looking?* Her thinking, *The word you need, Madam, is* opulent.

She would be suspending her life for four months; who knew if it would be there when she returned? In her absence others — perhaps even the people she thought friends, perhaps even Llewellyn — might gather over her spoils and pick at them. For some years now she had had the kind of life that other people thought desirable. It was her first experience of being on the right side of jealousy, and she found she liked it there.

"You don't know what it's like," she said.

Llewellyn had never asked her many questions about where she came from. And if he did, what would she say? Would she tell him about the real content of her life as it had been? From the beginning she had understood that Llewellyn would not tolerate being in close proximity to a particular corrosive brand of sadness. He would shy away from it, and from her. Anyone with any sense would.

It seemed enough for both of them that her husband should know where she was from, geographically, that she had a father and a sister she hadn't seen for years, a mother dead. When she had first imparted this information she had watched him receive and then discard it almost immediately, as if to say, it doesn't matter. *You're here now, with me.* This was Llewellyn's message, and the one which the city of instantaneous gratifications they lived in seemed to confirm, the Bloor Street mavens and their hunger for Italian shoes, the film "development people" devouring bruschetta in sidewalk restaurants, the hard-faced gourmands in the St. Lawrence Market on Saturday morning, on the hunt for organic Mexican dark roast: the point was to take pleasure in the present, to siphon it fully of all its riches. Take everything possible from the moment, the city seemed to insist; the moment is all you have.

CHAPTER 2

"I don't know how you can stomach this newspaper every day."

She held up the front page for him to see. WHALE CARCASS TOWED BACK OUT TO ATLANTIC was the top story in the local section, followed by DEVCO SALE WOULD SAVE 500 JOBS.

The newspaper was stocked with stories of local boys coming home after years in the wilderness — Quebec, Alberta, the Northwest Territories — it didn't matter; they lost their jobs and slunk gratefully home. NO PLACE LIKE HOME, SAY UNEMPLOYED BROTHERS.

"What's the matter with it?"

"It's all so local."

Her father shrugged. "Well, this is a local kind of place."

"It's all about unemployment."

"This is an unemployed kind of place."

She studied him to see if he was cracking a joke, but his face was impassive. Then again, she had never been able to read her father's emotions on his face. His manner had always been of a mild, unstudied inscrutability. Somehow he had resisted the island's unspoken edict among men of his age and background, that he be a "character" — a wild man, reelingly drunk, a sweet crooner, a do-gooder who turns mean at the full moon, a joker. He lacked a lyrical turn of phrase, he resisted making ribald comments about politicians or Quebecois separatists. He bored Eve to tears as a teenager. She had always thought it just an expression, bored to tears, until one day she came home from writing her final English exam, exhilarated with relief, and he said a few words about the price his catch had commanded and sunk his face into a cup of tea. She'd gone to her room, sat on her bunk, and cried — not out of frustration or disappointment, she was sure, but from sheer, pounding boredom.

She coveted the fathers and the anecdotes about them other girls had to tell. These men were like the Greek heroes they studied in History class; she imagined them in frozen, mythic postures. Take Charlene Aucoin's father — her best story was Dad and the Buddhists. Her father picked up a couple of unsuspecting hitchhiking Buddhists who were thinking about opening a bakery in Indian Bay and drove them around the Cabot Trail. They didn't understand that Dad just drove them for the hell of it, Charlene said. He wasn't even going that way. He drove with a forty-ouncer of rum stuck between his thighs, glancing in the rearview mirror each time he took a swig, on the lookout for *them RCMP cocksuckers*. Those poor Jesus Buddhists, she can remember Charlene saying. They hightailed it back to the mainland, of course; but they must have got something out of the whole episode because they sent her dad a postcard from Halifax saying they'd opened a bakery on Robie Street.

Then there was Jennifer McKenzie's father, who single-handedly scandalized a group of cottagers from Ontario by rowing up to them as they were frolicking in the lake and doing a striptease in his rowboat. He got down to his drawers and his rubber boots before firing up the outboard motor and zipping away. "He wasn't even drunk," Jennifer said. "He was just mad at all the racket the cottagers made with their barbecues and their lawnmowers."

If she had had such a father she would have been a vivid, popular character like Charlene or Jennifer, she reasoned. And so the weight of blame accrued.

"So how's business?"

He took off his cap. His unruly hair cascaded over his forehead until he snatched it away.

"I don't think I'll see another season."

"Why do you say that?"

"Because I'm fed up with the whole business, that's why. All them guys down in North Carolina and New Jersey got it sewn up. I can barely get the dealers to come up here for what I give them. If I had a refrigerated truck I could take them down to Halifax and put them on a plane for Holland. But how the hell am I going to raise the capital for a truck? So they come up here and offer me their pitiful prices. I could sell rights to fish my weirs to Frank Haslam down in Musquodoboit. He's got the contacts to ship them to Montreal."

"Do you really want to do that?"

"What else is there? Fishing's big business now. Those guys out there off Cape North, they've got two-hundred-thousand-dollar boats. You're either doing it in a big way or you're not."

She knew there were things he would not tell her, that for years he had signed on for pogey in the winters, as did many fishermen. Only those with crab and lobster licences could afford to live year-round off their catch.

"You wouldn't sell some land?"

"I don't know." The words wheezed out of him. He clasped his hands, unclasped them. He gave them a look as if he'd never seen them before. "What else can I do?"

She felt a sharp apprehension. She had expected her father would always be the same, she realized; she had relied upon it, perhaps so that she herself could metamorphose with impunity, so that she might have something to measure herself against.

He pushed himself away from the stove. "Let's find out what's wrong with me, then. Get it over and done with."

"Really?"

"Why the hell not?"

"When?"

"Whenever you damn well want. That's what's going to happen anyhow, isn't it? You'll get your way. Just like always."

"What *always* are you talking about? When have I ever had things go my way?"

He turned so quickly, so gracefully, like a pirouette. The

movement sparked something inside her and suddenly she heard her mother's voice. *It was the way he walked that first made me notice him. Not really a man's walk.* When had she told her this? Or was it something she had overheard, those nights spent eavesdropping through the hole in the kitchen ceiling.

"Where are you going?"

Her answer was the sound of the door slapping shut. She heard his footsteps recede. She had forgotten her father's hit-and-run conversational style; he was a guerilla fighter, raiding outposts, taking up sniper positions before disappearing.

Without him in it, the room seemed not to want her there. The walls literally frowned at her. A twilit silence began to lap against the cabin. She heard a hollow, looped cry of some creature she could no longer identify.

She tried to shake off a spooked feeling and failed. She felt a sudden desire to be on the move, to be walking anywhere. But where was there to go? Whenever she felt hemmed in at home she could just set off down Queen Street and walk east, a voyeuse spying on the couples and groups sitting at sidewalk restaurants and bars. Here there was only the gravel road, the ferry, the shattered asphalt ribbon leading into its dark mouth.

She tried to read. She picked up the newspaper again. Her father had circled the weather forecast in red pen, for some reason. *Rain likely tonight.*

"Look what the cat brought in."

This was exactly how Celyn greeted her as a child. She had trudged up this same path countless times then, to play with Celyn's children. They had entire bookshelves of hardbound children's books, castles and car garages made of plastic, wooden toys with stickers announcing they had been handcrafted in Vermont. She would go back to the cabin, her three books, the dusty board games she lacked a partner to play with.

"I've been waiting for you," Celyn held the door open. On the floor were the same rugs Celyn had woven fifteen years before, with tartan patterns. Neither Celyn nor Bob had a Scottish background.

"Where's your loom?"

"Oh that thing," Celyn laughed. "I got rid of that years ago."

Celyn was still that pretty, deeply pleasant woman she would always be, barring some terrible catastrophe. She had a thin, symmetrical face, stern light blue eyes whose irises were ringed with a darker hue, making them look as if they had been drawn in outline first. She had always been the most balanced person Eve had known growing up; then she had been a confident, pretty young mother. Eve had thought it a deep mystery how someone like Celyn could end up in Clam Harbour. She was American, from the Connecticut suburbs. Celyn's father was a lawyer; she had grown up in a big-boned house made of brick, with two neat white columns standing sentry on either side of the door — Celyn had shown her pictures when Eve had been fifteen or sixteen and voracious for news from the outside world.

Celyn had married a rich man, or rather a man who went from being a rebellious Sixties-generation student to being a banker, apparently from one day to the next. Bob was from Massachusetts and spent half the year in Boston where he worked as an investment banker, coming back to the island in the summers. Celyn lived on the island year-round. They had opted for Clam Harbour as a place to bring their children up until high school, after which they were promptly sent to the best universities in the States.

"When were you home last? I can't remember."

"Must be eight years ago now. For a long time there didn't seem much to come back to."

Celyn nodded. "It's not exactly an international hotspot here."

"There was a point when I was travelling so much I couldn't face getting on a plane."

Celyn gave her a long, low look, fringed with an obscure disapproval. Perhaps Celyn knew very well that the exhaustions of being a cosmopolitan were not at all the reason Eve had stayed away. Perhaps she thought she was bragging.

"Well, it's good you're back now."

"I don't know if it is or not. But I had to see for myself."

"You're going to get him checked out?"

"If he'll let me. What do you think of McIntyre?"

"The GP? Well, he's no brain surgeon. He's keen on sailing. He bought a boat last year and spends a lot of his time out on the water. I get the feeling he's putting in time until retirement. He'll probably refer your dad to a specialist straightaway, after he's done all the basic tests. What's Anita doing about this?"

"I don't know."

"You haven't spoken to her?"

"I don't want to bother her."

She saw a frown slide over Celyn's face. This expression was more clear in its meaning: *She hasn't even called her own sister.*

"I'll have to buy a car."

"What's the matter with your father's truck?"

"He did something to it. Water in the oil sump, or oil in the radiator. I can't bear to bring myself to look. All I know is that it's past repair."

Celyn leaned back against the stove and crossed her arms over her chest. "He's that absent-minded? Well, I'd do it soon. You'll kill yourself biking into Indian Bay every day."

"Although if I buy a car, there go my savings."

"Well, you'll just have to do it."

Celyn's voice was sympathetic but breezy. Eve wasn't sure Celyn had ever come up against anything truly insurmountable. Her lawyer father and her husband's salary would have always protected her from the vagaries of inadequate savings and second-hand cars.

"So how are Sarah-Jane and Felicia and Robert?"

"Robert got married two years ago. He's in Santa Fe, biochemical research. Sarah-Jane's just got tenure in oceanography at Washington State. Felicia's still in New York. She's with the permanent secretariat now. She just spent six months in Mauritius, or was it Mauritania? Do you know she's learning Mandarin? They say that's one of the toughest languages to master."

An old panic grabbed Eve by the throat. She had worked so hard to get out of this place she had forgotten to aspire to being a scientist, a lawyer, a UN functionary. She was thirty-four; she had had a husband and a job that allowed her to travel business class, but she hadn't made herself indispensable to the world.

"Did you hear John R's place is rented for the summer?"

"Duncan told me. It's funny Dad hasn't mentioned anything. Then again, he doesn't really talk these days."

"He must feel devastated." Celyn said the word so that it emerged dismembered: *dev-as-ta-ted.*

"I know. I never thought I'd have to deal with anything like this. I mean, cancer, or something like that maybe, a physical disintegration…"

The truth was, she had never thought she would have to deal with any kind of falling apart, not even her own. She found that she didn't actually believe illness led to death, that death would not always be quick, a turn of events, and suddenly you were no more.

Celyn nodded. "I know. None of us do."

She said goodnight and left, walking the neat gravel path to the bottom of the hill, mentally preparing herself for the transition to the smoky cabin. As she walked she realized Celyn hadn't asked her anything about herself — about her job, about her marriage, or whether she had had to leave anything of significance behind. Perhaps she already knew these things through the efficient local grapevine that made questions of this sort redundant. But more likely it was a lack of curiosity. Celyn was kind, yes, a thoughtful, caring person, Eve considered, but she lacked a certain curiosity about the depths of other people's character and experience, had no real interest in plumbing them.

For years Eve had played a game with herself in which Celyn was her mother, but her house was too small, and the man down the road was so lonely, she had been sent to keep him company. After all, the children's books she read were full of such stories: the extra, accidental child who had to be farmed out to someone else. At the same time, Celyn and her family were to be watched, studied carefully, as if they were a renegade species on the way to becoming dominant. Their habits would have to be parsed, so that she could protect herself from their greater power.

Celyn's house had been Eve's initiation into adult life with its flower-power permissive parents, the parties they hosted that cut across class and geographical divides, investment bankers from Boston and liquor store cashiers from Indian Bay, drinking and dancing together. When she and Felicia turned fifteen they had been allowed to join in, even to drink in the house, *in recognition of your incredible maturity.* Celyn's laugh was warm but contained an edge of some complex, rueful knowledge. It was exactly the way she imagined mothers of teenaged daughters should laugh.

At one of those parties she and Felicia had gone to bed after midnight, only to wake an hour later to the sound of Celyn shrieking.

"What do you mean you're *in love*? How can you be in love with a fucking *librarian*?"

Bob's voice said, "Just calm down, now, will you?"

They had tumbled out of bed and peered down the stairs into the living room to see Celyn hitting her husband with a plastic fly swatter, before turning it on herself. She had to be disarmed by a young, quite beautiful woman Eve recognized as a librarian at UCCB. The librarian managed to pluck the fly swatter from Celyn's hand, brandishing it in the air above their heads while Celyn leapt for it. "Gimme that. He's my goddamn husband. I can hit him if I want to." Like a drunken ballet corps, the fly-swatting trio tilted in unison.

The sound of the fly swatter stayed in her ears as she tried to get back to sleep, the gentle but brisk flap of plastic against skin. She had almost forgotten now how awful it was to be a child witnessing adults in anguish. She remembered waking up an hour later and going to the kitchen for a glass of water and finding Celyn, Bob and the librarian sitting at the table, drinking a bottle of scotch.

And here they were, still together. Their house showed no signs of these squalls of emotion, nor any other scars.

She turned off the flashlight and walked along the road in the dark, scuffing loose shale, sending little showers of stone rolling downhill. She jumped as something sprung across the road only twenty yards ahead, and then disappeared with a crash into the thicket. She stopped, her heart beating. Why should she be so afraid of a deer? When she was growing up in the cabin seeing a deer on their land had been as remarkable as seeing a fly. Now, though, she stood stock-still in the night, marvelling at the brief flash of fur, its tawny smoothness, the liquid alarm in the deer's dark eye.

∿

Three girls stand balanced on the concrete edge of the ferry dock. Eve, her friend Sally who is more robust and wants to be the first to jump, and small, dark Roberta. In the coming autumn Roberta will move with her family to Alberta, and Eve will never see her again.

Below, indigo water, rust-coloured clumps of seaweed, tendrils of eelgrass, the mauve blotch of a jellyfish. Her friends are waiting to jump behind her, jiggling, adjusting their goggles. She wears a one-piece bathing suit, goggles which she holds tight over her eyes as she tries to keep them from flying off on impact.

The water foams to yellow, air bubbles, thin tentacles of eelgrass, nests of kelp that feed them on the stony lakebed, purple bruises of starfish. On impact she remembers that her mother is dead. She has been in the ground now for six, seven months.

The water feels heavy. Instead of buoying up, she is sinking. She opens her eyes inside her goggles. The eelgrass swirls, sinuous, medusa-like. It is the light auburn of her mother's hair. Two or three feet away, the water foams to ermine suds. A ball of young silver eels, threading in and out of each other, tangled, a dozen or more of them, somersaulting through the water surrounded by a pearly foam of slime. She rises to the surface gasping, her goggles flooded by panic, and swims away.

CHAPTER 3

"Oh. Hi!" The voice, deeper, more assured and measured than she remembers, strikes her like a light blow.

In the end she forces out an identical *Hi!* followed by an awkward exclamation point.

"Is Dad around?"

"He's here somewhere, just a moment." She hands the receiver to her father. *Anita*, she mouths.

"How's it goin'?" Her father's voice is transformed. Its centre is still gruff, but its edges are trimmed with honey. Anita's voice leaks through the receiver. "Not too bad and yourself?"

She goes outside. The afternoon is waning. Already the smoky blue light of a late-spring evening hems the woods. An indistinct disappointment gathers inside her in small stony pools.

She hears the screen door slap shut behind her. "She wants to talk to you."

She takes the receiver, puts it gingerly to her ear.

"So you haven't even taken him to the doctor yet?"

"Not yet, no, but we have an appointment."

"You've been back two weeks."

The teenaged rebel slunk out of her and said, "More like three."

"Well, isn't that just dandy!" Anita said several words in rapid succession that Eve chose to not quite hear, but she knew they amounted to this: If Anita had been on the case, she would have had him in the doctor's office within a week, in hospital in two.

"He doesn't want to go."

"Well, force him to."

"How? You tell me. The more you try to force him to do something, the more he finds a way to slip out of it."

"He could wander off into the woods. He could burn the place down, with both of you in it."

"Okay," she said. "I'll try."

"You do that."

You do that. Had her sister always spoken like this? Tart, matriarchal. Then, she hasn't spoken to Anita in three or four years at least. Although Anita has kept her on her personal email list, forwarding her circular emails with subject lines like The Positive Side of Life, A Smirk of Wisdom, Girl Power. The messages feature babies or dogs in amusing situations; others are about freak weather events that hit the Maritimes; they come with jpegs of snowbanks and flooded valleys.

She sat down in the long spring grass, which fanned out around her. She pulled a blade, which squeaked in protest. She put it between her teeth to chew on. It tasted young and sour.

Behind her in the cabin she could hear the sounds of her father's conversation, grunts followed by explanations. *You don't say. Well I'll be... That just goes to show.*

He came out onto the doorstep, a slightly defiant look on his face. "We're going to see Anita."

The dread at seeing her sister, the quality of it, is quite indescribable. It has a glacial aspect; it has been inching toward her for years.

"Why?"

"Because she wants to see you, that's why."

"She doesn't want to see me, she wants to see you."

"Now don't be like that," he said. "Your sister loves you."

They drive the old road to Indian Bay along the lakeshore. It winds around inlets choked with cigar-shaped reeds, huddles into sudden clefts, and then opens out to a fine view of the Malagawatch peninsula and the needle point of Seal Island.

"MacGregor'll have good hay this year." Her father pauses

significantly, as if he is about to make some sweeping observation, but he is silent. The farms she remembered were all there, fields cleared for hay. But the Holsteins that had once grazed there were gone. Instead an older man on a little red buggy lawnmower sawed up and down the hill, white knees protruding from his canvas pants, a sunhat on his head.

The road has other admirers; in front of them a wide-hipped sedan with New Hampshire licence plates, an early tourist arrival, crawls at a near-stationary speed. She is grateful for the chance to admire a view that on her bike is only a hazy backdrop to straining hamstrings.

"Bob Swann's painted his house orange." Her father made a tsk-tsk noise. "Look, Mary MacEachern's back from Halifax. Her chemotherapy must've gone all right."

"How do you know she's back?"

He gives her a look: *What kind of question is that?* "Her son Keith's car is in the drive. He drove her down there."

The Bayside Clinic doctor was still in the same office he had always been in, two streets up from the lakeshore, next to the Co-op. She entered first, her father's reluctant shuffle trailing behind her.

The doctor rose to greet them. There was a faintly sweet, minty smell to him. McIntyre's glossy black hair had hardly greyed, even if its sheen was dulled. His glasses perched on a nose made hawkish with lines and droop.

Her father lowered himself into the leather-look chair on the other side of the doctor's desk. She took up a position to the side. Behind her was a bookcase. Huge tomes bound in navy and chocolate leather thundered knowledge from the shelves, covered in a thin film of dust. On the table behind McIntyre's desk were two family portraits; one a studio shot with a blue background, the other in a sunlit place. She leaned forward and caught the unmistakeable outline of the Disney World castle in the background. In both photographs three blond women, his wife and two daughters, flanked a younger version of the doctor.

"Alistair. We don't see you here very often. When was the last time? Over five years ago. Suspected gallbladder stones, I seem to remember."

Her father cleared his throat. "Don't take this the wrong way, but I don't like to see doctors any more than I need to."

Her father pursed his lips, seemed to be about to say something more. Both she and McIntyre leaned forward. Her father retracted his lips. He raised his shoulders and then let them fall. This odd shrug was accompanied by the sound of air being forced through his nostrils.

A silence rummaged around the room. From the other side of the door came the sound of women laughing.

"She...," her father's hand jerked out sideways in her direction, "brought me here."

The doctor nodded reasonably. "Is that right?"

"She...," the hand again, "seems to think I've got memory trouble."

"His sister called me because she feared for his safety," she clarified. "She said he was going to burn the cabin down, or get lost."

Her father's face came swivelling around toward her. "How in the name of Jesus would I get lost on land I've owned for the past thirty years?"

Now it was time for her to purse her lips. She was picking up her father's gestures again, like an understudy. "My father started a fire in March. Inside the cabin. My aunt thinks it was a candle."

"It wasn't a goddamn candle. My sister just wants me locked up."

"You're having trouble remembering things, sequences. What you did yesterday, what you did last, what you'll do next."

Fear seeped into her father's face as she spoke. As soon as she registered it, she had to look away.

"Well, there's some nights I don't sleep a wink. It's probably because I've spent the last ten years on the nightshift."

"You're still fishing them eels?" the doctor asked. People had always said this, she noticed, *them* eels, as if either the eels or her father were miscreants.

"Not that there's many left."

"Well!" The doctor threw up his hands, as if there was nothing else for it. "Why don't we run some tests." It was less a question than a statement. "Then we'll know for sure."

Her father was up and out of his chair before she had even absorbed the word. *"No."*

"What do you mean, no?" She glared at him. "That's why we're here. You agreed to come here with me."

"Well now I'm changing my mind." Her father turned to the doctor. "Listen, McIntyre, this isn't against you, but if there's anything wrong with me I'd rather just be put down like an animal than to go through all that."

The doctor was looking at her meaningfully. She realized he had forgotten her name.

"Eve."

"Eve. Could you stay here for a few minutes? Alistair, listen, we'll be right with you in the waiting—"

"I'm not waiting in no room while youse two talk about me on the other side of that door." Her father forgot his grammar when he was truly angry. "I'm going down to buy some cord in the Home Hardware." On the way out he tossed her a sullen look.

She sunk into the chair her father had just vacated, her back bowed, staring at her knees. She resisted the urge to hold her head in her hands.

"How long has this been going on?"

"No-one knows. He hardly sees anyone. My aunt only found out when she dropped by and saw the scorch marks on the wall from the fire. Most of the time he's absolutely fine. Then he'll come into the kitchen and ask where he's put the hammer when I saw him walk out the door with it only two minutes before. He'll sit for a long time just looking out the window. He never did that before. He was always on the go."

The doctor looked away, a remote look she recognized and dreaded on his face. "Well, I'll make you an appointment at the regional, if you think you can get him to go. I'm set up to do bloodwork here, but you might as well do it at the hospital. They've got the lab right there."

"I'll try."

She heard the defeat in her voice. What she meant was, *I don't think he loves me. I know he doesn't trust me.*

She thanked the doctor, and tried to smile. But the smile sat leering on her face. There was nothing to smile about, really. As quickly as it had appeared, she folded it away.

She decided to leave Celyn's truck in the parking lot and walk. The town had changed little over the years. Indian Bay had always possessed the static, poised quality of small-town beauty queens, waiting for the inevitable admiration. It consisted of three or four wide streets named after the trees common to the area: Maple, Chestnut, Elm. On them a drugstore, a bank, a real estate office and hardware store were lined up, freshly painted, as if for inspection. The grandest of the houses were long ago turned into craft shops. As a child she had spent many hours drifting through the living and dining rooms of these wide-hipped houses of former gentry, fingering seals sculpted out of stone sporting little caps of Nova Scotia tartan, polished sand dollars, owls carved from driftwood and oven mitts in the shape of lobsters.

Indian Bay's calm waters, protected from the wind and waves of the widest part of the lakes by a forested island, were a haven for sailboats and yachts. It was only late May, a month before the American yachties usually turned up, but already the bay was crowded with sailboats, the sun glinting painfully from their white fibreglass, sitting like prim storks amid the squat Cape Islanders. The Cape Islanders were likely recreational boats now, as were two large three-masted schooners that competed for the tourist trade.

The Yacht Club had been transformed from its original shack into a glassy structure with a restaurant and offices. The Yacht Club was for visiting Americans, wealthy mainlanders or the island's captains of industry: the building contractors and their families, the automotive dealers and the dentists. These people had the same last names as Eve and her father, but still managed to look like another species, standing on the decks of their boats with their thin-soled deck shoes, their hard brown legs encased in canvas shorts. Eve has never set foot in the yacht club.

In the Home Hardware store she asked the cashier if she had seen him.

"I think he's in the hosepipe aisle, dear."

Sure enough, there he was, frowning into coils of green plastic. "There's so many lengths," he said, when he saw her.

"Want an ice cream?"

His watery eyes betrayed surprise. "Sure."

They went to the ice-cream counter in the drugstore, the same drugstore where, as a terminally bored teenager, she had idled, surreptitiously reading *Vogue* and trying on lip gloss.

They took their ice creams down to the lakeshore. Her father licked his exceptionally slowly, so that it dripped down its fingers.

"You're taking your time over that ice cream."

"I was just trying to remember the last time I had one. Your mother used to buy me ice cream."

His face betrayed no expression at all apart from that concentrated but baffled look, as if he were trying to catch the tail of some animal that was disappearing around a corner.

On the way home they passed the museum built in homage to the famous American inventor who summered in Indian Bay. He had worked on his prototypes in a wide-girthed house parked hawkishly on the edge of the peninsula. As a child she had passed many hours in this museum, heat-stunned summer afternoons spent staring at photographs of sepia-coloured men and women in black coats fitted close to the waist, leather ankle boots on their feet, slipping and sliding on the ice as the inventor and his friends struggled with prototypes of flying machines. The contraptions themselves looked like giant wooden models of dragonflies. In these photos were elements — more elegant for sure, but still familiar — of her own childhood: cold, remote winters, large houses barely kept warm by ancient stoves, ecstatic dogs chasing grouse and gulls, skidding across the icy bay on their claws.

In the cabin her father goes to sit at the card table without even casting a word in her direction, their moment of intimacy with the ice-cream cones evaporated by some unspoken command of his; she wishes she were the one mapping these boundaries, deciding which understandings would last and which would not, but this is not her environment anymore. She is not in control.

She decides to absent herself, sitting on the step with a bottle of beer, fending off precocious early-summer mosquitoes, the storm windows they had removed a week ago stacked against the cabin's flanks. Darkness falls, although it is less a darkness than a cloaking in blue silk, the sky and the sea retaining a silvery light while the mountain is soaked in night.

Inside he has turned on the light. She can see his silhouette clearly in the window, denuded now of its extra layer, his chin in his elbow, contemplating his evening solitaire game.

She wanders through the garden. Her father used to love to garden; as a child they had had an exotic flower garden, and every fruit and vegetable: huge pumpkins, watery pansies, a regal plum tree. Now his garden has the mistaken beauty of a ruffian's Eden, he has let it get out of hand. The father she knew was deft with the pruning shears, even ruthless. She is awed by the prowess of a single peach-coloured rose. It gapes and folds, shamelessly lovely. A vivid clump of rhubarb, a bees' shattered hive. Ribbons of cool air flutter through the remains of the day's heat. She watches as a single star punches though the gathering mesh of dark. The nights are still cool — "snappish" her father calls them — but the days have begun to inch up into the mid-twenties. This is her favourite season, the elongated twilights of early June. No-one should get sick or die in summer, she thinks. Summer should be an amnesty, a renewal.

We're going to have to say goodbye. Her friend Laura, their last meeting before Eve leaves the city; Laura is leaving too. She is a publisher, and half American. She is moving to the States at the end of the summer to take up a job with Rutgers University Press. They meet in a coffee shop. Laura's dark hair and large, glossy brown eyes are framed beautifully against the maroon interior. Laura is approved of by life, to the extent that colour schemes and interiors seem to willingly collude with her. They swirl their lattes to a muted sound of gently deflating foam. The coffee shop is too hectic and air-conditioned for a final meeting. Eve pulls a sweater tight around her shoulders.

Laura and Eve have known each other for eleven years now, since they met in their Eng Lit 300 class at Victoria College. There will be no more dinners together, no more weekly film outings. Laura says, *We're going to have to say goodbye* and while her gaze is serious and rueful there is something eager in the finality in her voice. Eve doesn't say so because she knows Laura is an interesting, dynamic, positive person. Her life has shown her that this mental attitude attracts what she needs and deserves. *There is a time for everything,* Laura thinks: for friends, houses, lovers. She finds it easy to move on. Eve thinks she can hear the sound of snipping — of some firm and fast fabric, or metal, being cut. Laura is cutting the wires that have bound them for over ten years. *Snip, snip.* Laura puts on her Walkman and leaves the air-conditioned coffee shop, walking into the sun, which was setting, as it sometimes did, square in the middle of Dundas Street.

Eve turns to see her father framed in the window, sitting at his card table, his back bent in concentration. Will they make themselves similar, she wonders, just as they did through those years she lived with him, two conversant shadows becoming a mirror. How his gestures became her gestures, how she absorbed his expressions and mannerisms and mimicked them like a carnival puppet. The pursed lips. Hands running amok in his hair at times of crisis. Will she use his words, remnants of Gaelic and old farm-talk, local words no-one apart from islanders understand, except of course the people they had come from, other islanders across the ocean: *furach,* the coldest part of the winter; *groomach,* overcast, *slancha va!* A glass raised in good health.

It is just a place, she reminds herself. It doesn't carve out your destiny. It isn't grasping you, hauling you inside it. Places are neutral; they are just where you decide to be for a while. That's all.

If he's got it, then he'll have to be taken care of.

Llewellyn is instructing her in cause and effect. She is in her apartment, packing, Llewellyn and his poised-to-leap posture on the bed. Where will he go, once she is gone? Perhaps nowhere: just to work, to the coffee place on the corner, to buy flowers. Or maybe she will return to find the apartment denuded of his shoes, his suits. He will have a job with CBS, NBC, PBS.

You'll need to arrange for him to be in a home. You can come back. It's bad, but it's not going to affect your life.

I'm not worried about it affecting my life. I'm worried about what he stands to lose.

What do you mean?

He'll lose his house, his land, his mind, himself.

But that happens to everyone, Llewellyn says. *Eventually.*

Some tender and compromised part of her rebels against this. Her husband is too sink-or-swim. This is linked somehow to his insistent optimism, but also she is suspicious of this capacity of his to accept reality as it is, without fight or regret.

The amber light of evening gathered between the trees, on the flank of the mountain, a dark cascade. She inhales a breath of air laced with the kelpy brew of a warming ocean. In the last light of the day she watches a bald eagle loop lazily over the lake, its wings scratched across the sky like a scar.

A light came on next door. Whoever they are, these summer people who have rented John Rory's, they'd arrived early. Most didn't show up for another ten days or so at the earliest, when school let out. They had rented a four-bedroom house; they were certain to have children.

Over the past few days signs of habitation had been multiplying, but they were useless clues as to the number and inclination of the summer neighbours — an empty Styrofoam cooler in the driveway, meltwater sloshing in the bottom, dismantled tents out to air, where they ossify in the sun. A makeshift curtain has appeared on the kitchen window, the one facing the road. The material is sheer, almost gauzy. Nice try, folks, she thinks, but there's no privacy here, curtain or no curtain. The house is close enough to hear voices, but not a peep. Good, she thinks. Quiet people.

CHAPTER 4

In the years to come when she would remember her first meeting with Noel, the experience would refuse to cohere, insisting on remaining in separate broken memory frames: the broken step, the silver glint of a spanking new espresso maker he had brought with him, obviously untrusting that such a contraption could be bought in Cape Breton, a wing of dark hair, the lanky, nonchalant way it draped itself over his temple, a buzz of happiness, instant and mysterious, but also a sense of a fleeting, nearly insubstantial perception, which she immediately chose to discard.

She struggles to recall another instance in her life in which she arrived at a moment only to find that she had been expecting it, although until that point she was unaware she has been waiting for anything at all. In the cold light of day her meeting with Noel was inauspicious and bland. But in her memory it is cast in a moody, nearly submarine light; the sort of light that picks up the edges of things, sets them to shimmering.

She managed to knock, just before the wood groaned and then sprang away beneath her. Her ankle went through and touched ground. She was trying to right herself when the door opened.

She looked up into the face of the man she had glimpsed at Duncan's garage earlier that week. She registered dark hair neatly receding in two smart wings on either side of his forehead, an elegant pair of glasses that failed to obscure serious brown eyes.

"I'm so sorry, it looks like I've broken the step." She extracted her foot and stood upright. She extended her hand. "I'm Eve. My father lives next door."

He returned her smile, although with the merest of hesitation, and then took her outstretched hand.

When he said no more she asked, "How long are you here for?"

"Until Labour Day."

"That's good, spending the whole summer."

"Is it?"

"It's good to see the whole summer here. So many things change."

"Like what?" His tone was polite, interrogative, although he was frowning slightly. Maybe he wasn't interested in the trajectory of the local summer.

"The berries, the growing season, the length of the days. The water temperature. By early September it's just about warm enough to swim."

Her last comment elicited a rueful smile. "I heard the water was cold."

She became aware that she was still holding the jar of jam. She thrust it at him. "We thought you might like some jam. My father makes it."

He took the jar with both hands. "That's kind." His voice betrayed real surprise. He took a step back and opened the door. "I'm sorry, we're standing here on the step. Do you want to come in? Actually, could I ask you a favour? I need a hand with something."

"Sure."

"I'm Noel, by the way." He didn't hold out his hand, as they had already shaken hands, so she merely smiled and said *Hi*.

"My girlfriend's coming in ten days. She couldn't get away any earlier. She's studying for her law exams. She really needs to be quiet."

She nodded. Message received and understood. "This place is good for quiet," she said.

She stepped across the threshold into John Rory and Eileen's kitchen. The yellow linoleum floor was preserved intact, the glassed cabinets still held the china she remembered from countless cookie-eating sessions. Here she was, standing in the same

kitchen she had stood in as a five-year-old, a fourteen-year-old.
Now she was thirty-four years old and talking to this stranger.
What was he doing in their kitchen? Where had John Rory and
Eileen gone? She looked up to find his eyes on her. In them was
a watchful, intelligent expression in which a natural scepticism
was only just held at bay.

"I was just taking it all in. I used to come here as a child all
the time," she explained. "But I haven't set foot in the house for
ten years."

"Can I get you a cup of coffee?"

"No, please don't go to any trouble."

"No, I'm making some for myself."

As he spooned coffee from a tin can she got a better look at
him. He was wearing a checked blue-and-red shirt and dark blue
jeans. His glasses gave him a slightly bookish air, but he moved
as if he were used to being physically decisive. He had a broad,
square forehead from which the rest of his face tapered delicately. His face was clear and olive-toned, but his brow was hemmed
with milky freckles. She had noticed his eyes from the beginning
— they were so dark they were reflective; she could see herself
mirrored in his irises. His eyebrows had a downward cast which
gave him a very slightly disapproving look.

"You don't mind being here by yourself?" she asked.

"It took me a few days to get used to the quiet at night. You
can read a lot of things into silence." He shot her a smile that
transformed his face into something temporarily playful, even
mischievous.

"Although there's usually nothing there," she said. "At least
that's what you hope."

He clicked the espresso maker shut and put it on the burner.
"I do find it spooky sometimes. I was just thinking the other
night how I've lost the knack for being on my own in the middle
of nowhere. It never used to bother me." The careful, nearly
evaluating expression had settled back onto his face, as if he
were reining something in.

"I'm home for the summer to visit my father. Normally I live in Toronto. Where do you live?"

"New York City, although we're just about to move upstate. I'm getting to the point where I find the city too much, even though I love it in other ways. I suppose it's a compromise." The way he said this, distanced, a little resentful, made her think he might not be well acquainted with compromise.

They fell into a silence, apart from the gurgling of the coffee maker.

"Do you know much local history?" he asked, after a minute.

"What kind of history?"

"Anything — the settlers, the indigenous people. Why Gaelic has survived so well, where the French population came from."

"Some. Why?"

"I'm really interested in small places, places with distinct cultures. I'm curious about how small places manage to resist becoming like everywhere else."

"You mean how they resist the normalizing forces of globalization." She paused. "I think we'd probably welcome global capitalism if it ever took any notice of us."

He laughed. "You know, I'm still trying to get a handle on why Canada is so different."

"Different from what?"

"From the States. Everything seems so similar — it looks the same, really, but yet it's completely foreign."

She nodded. "A lot of Americans wonder about that."

"What do you think it is?"

She felt empowered by his open, genuine expression. "Well, there's the usual suspects: a parliamentary system, the social contract — based on European socialism more than frontier capitalism. But I think it's that Canadians have a nearly pathological common sense. You're not burdened by that."

Through her little speech she had watched his eyes widen, slowly and visibly. He laughed again.

"You said you need a hand with something?" She said it

politely and kindly, and also to reinforce the hierarchy: me knowledgeable local who comes bearing quaint gift of home-made jam; you guest in an unfamiliar environment who is already making too many assumptions about its governing reality.

He registered her tone with a very slight stiffening of his body, as if he were snapping himself to attention. "There's a couple of rooms up in the attic. My girlfriend might want to use the attic as a study. I'm sure the view is amazing. Do you think that would be all right with the owners?"

"I can't see why not."

"There's just one thing." He gave her a sheepish smile. "I can't find the stairs."

"Oh, they're the kind you have to pull down. They're not really stairs, more like a ladder. I'll show you."

They mounted stairs of the old house, each step creaking under their weight. She remembered the doorstep. "I'm sorry I crashed through the step," she said. "I'll fix it for you."

"No, don't worry about it."

"No, please," she insisted. "Otherwise you'll be stepping around it all summer. You might even sprain your ankle. It'll take me a minute. We've got tons of wood lying around."

"Are you a carpenter?"

"No, but I know how to nail a few planks of wood together."

She caught the defensive tone in her own voice in the same moment that she saw he was looking at her hands. Involuntarily, she followed his gaze. They were a mess. Crescents of dirt nestled beneath her nails from when she'd weeded the garden that morning. She felt suddenly conscious of her appearance. Certainly, she hadn't dressed to impress: she wore a jean jacket over a light blue shirt and dark blue linen drawstring pants. Her hair was scraped back and held in a plastic clip. She wore no makeup, not even lip balm. She ran her tongue along her lips to find them, as usual, dry and chapped. Then again, why was she worrying how she looked? This man could see her playing solitaire in the cabin in the middle of the night (a recent habit) from his window. They'd probably run into each other jogging down the road in the morning; he would observe her trying to explain away her father's increasingly erratic behaviour. There would be no beauty contests here.

They stopped in the upstairs hallway. Lining it were five sepia photographs framed in dark wood. In them tight-lipped people stared fixedly at the camera.

"I spent half of yesterday staring at these photographs. I suppose they don't seem that interesting to you."

"I used to spend whole afternoons looking through my father's pictures."

She smiled. He smiled back. In the moment between the exchange of smiles a forceful clarity nudged its way into her consciousness. She perceived there was something at once vulnerable and exact about him. He seemed to have a natural confidence, but a larger uncertainty hovered in the background, like a figure just outside the frame in a photograph. It was as if the moment and its clarity gave her back her instant impression of him, when she had greeted him on the doorstep but which for some reason she had banished: that he was a confluence of opposites, of vulnerability and prowess, certainty and hesitancy, so that in him they might be indistinguishable.

This instant understanding was accompanied by a strange echo of familiarity. It was somewhere inside her, it was of her.

"It's been a long time since anyone has lived in this house year-round," she said.

"I guessed. It has that empty house feel. As if it's waiting for me to fill it. It almost seems to expect something from me."

She stared at him, quite amazed. He had hit some forlorn note inside her, dulled by disuse, and set it to ringing. "It's good they painted the walls," she said, partly to drown out this sound. "They used to be dark green."

"I love the colours of the land here. Everything looks faded."

"I know, the whole place looks like an old pair of jeans. I used to wonder if it was because the land is so old, geologically."

"Really?"

"These are the last of the Appalachians." She threw her hand toward the kitchen side of the house, which backed up onto the mountain. "They're the oldest mountains on the continent and Cape Breton is the end of the chain. The island used to be on a major fault line. You can still see it in places, although you have to go to the mainland. The geology here is really interesting, lots of metamorphic rocks. Up Cape North way the rock corresponds to Europe's — it's the same rock you find in Scotland or Norway — but most of the island is geologically of the Americas."

She looked up to find he had fixed her with a curious stare. "I studied Geology at university," she explained. "I tend to ramble on about it."

A lime light filled the hallway, filtered through tinkling poplar leaves, their edges trimmed with silver. It was a cool bower light, sprung not from the sun so much as an underground source. She felt it seep into her, as if it were destined for her body and not the room.

They seemed to become aware, in the same moment, that they had been standing on the landing in silence.

"The stairs..."

"They're here." She bounded into action. "See that hook in the ceiling... that's how you get them down. We need to find the pole with the latchkey."

They separated to scour two empty bedrooms for the wooden pole. Finally she found it shrouded in a tube of dust inside one of the closets.

He raised the pole aloft, sending a shower of dust onto his glasses. He lowered the pole and removed his glasses. He turned his bare eyes toward her; shorn of their glasses, she saw that they were very dark, their edges gleamed with violet so that they looked almost purple.

"Let's try this again." He hooked the pole and latchkey into the ring and pulled. The trapdoor came away with a whine of springs and rust, folding the stairs down and scattering dust particles in their hair.

He put his hands on either side of the stairs and shook them to test for stability. He started up and she followed him into the attic.

It hit her immediately, just as when she had stepped into the cabin for the first time in eight years: the smell of old houses — sun-warmed wood, a hint of wool, like the old blankets woven in PEI, dark grey marled wool with yellow satin trim, which she found indeed still lay stacked in the attic cupboards. Dust. Something sharp and astringent, but plantlike: heather, or nettles.

From the attic three small windows looked out onto the lakes; grey curtains hung limp over them, black-hemmed with mildew. A double bed and a narrow cot were wedged between them; the only other furniture was a solitary dresser and chair, covered with white sheets. Everything was coated in an inch-thick pelt of dust.

"Let's get some air in here." She struggled with the windowsill. Finally it gave way, setting the sheer curtain shuddering in the wind. Then they each took a sheet and shook them, releasing a dust storm. As the sheets floated from their hands, wave-like, trembling, she was seized by a vision. She had to put the sheet down.

"What's the matter?"

"I just remembered. This is where Malcolm used to sleep."

"Who's Malcolm?"

"He was John Rory and Eileen's second son. He was born... well, retarded is what they used to say. He had learning difficulties."

She had only met Malcolm once or twice before he died. She was nine years old; Malcolm must have been about twenty-eight. She remembered the tall, powerful-looking man she'd seen lying on the cot, in the same room where she stood now. He had had blond hair and a square, rugged face. She said, *Hello Malcolm*, as she had been instructed to do, but he just stared out the window.

"What happened to him?"

"He died. He was only twenty-eight. He loved to lie there—" she pointed to the narrow cot, "and watch the curtains flowing in the breeze. He did that all day long, watched them blowing in and out."

"That's really sad."

She found it annoying, Noel's gosh-golly frequency of speech. But at the same time she heard the sincerity in his voice, saw the utter concentration on his face. "There are a lot of sad stories around here," she said.

He coughed; his eyes had turned bloodshot. "I think the dust is getting to me."

"We'd better go down."

They bundled up the sheets in their arms and climbed down the stairs.

The evening turns stormy. An urgent rain drums on the roof. Her father plays solitaire by the screen window. Eve sits on the chesterfield reading a *National Geographic* article about Japan. The photographs are typically triumphalist; they suavely invite wonder and awe. A photo shows the cacophony of skyscrapers in modern Kobe; next to it is a wooden palace fringed by jasmine and cherry blossoms, like a giant bouquet. The faces of the Japanese faces are impassive, like masques.

The Japanese consume 100,000 tons of eel flesh a year, the article reports. A section on food details how the Japanese prepare eel. *The eel should be pinned through the head, while still alive, to a wooden board.* A picture shows the eel's back being unzipped with a single cut of a knife, then spread open, lilylike, for the guts and the backbone to be taken out. *It should then be cut into thin strips to be skewered by thin bamboo.*

The depth and density of their brown.

The thought places itself, effortlessly, among the pictures of crucified eel. She has seen caramel-coloured brown eyes before, but his are dark and lapidary. *Obsidian.* That is the word — a volcanic-glass brown, at once viscous and watery. But for that violet ring around his irises she might not know where his pupils stop and the iris begin. They are candid eyes; they would never be bought, or influenced easily. Also, they have a reflective quality, as if they would bounce your desires straight back to you if they did not find favour. A word, archaic, possibly inappropriate, steals into her head: *Levantine.* He probably has some Jewish or Hispanic in his background, or both.

Even with the spinal cord severed and the cooking begun, chefs have reported the eel-flesh moving, or convulsing — such is the tenacity of the eel's nervous system.

Tears welled in her eyes. Her father would say, *There you go again, treating every creature like it's human. Who knows if they hurt?*

"You were over there a long time."

She looked up. Her father sat with his back to her, hunched over his cards. He wanted to see the attic but he didn't know about the folding staircase.

"He's a young feller. Why couldn't he do it himself?"

"I told you, he couldn't find the ladder."

"Don't let them take advantage of you."

"I didn't. He was friendly. He made me coffee."

A sceptical sound, halfway between a grunt and a laugh. "Before you know it they'll be over here every time they have a leaky pipe. Which'll be often in that place, mark my words. They think we've got nothing better to do here just because we don't fool around with computers and that crap."

This is the characteristic she likes least about her father. He brought her up to be on the lookout for condescension and usury, and it has taken her years to shake off the suspicion that everyone is poised to take advantage of her. This was a poor-man's tactic, of course, a defensiveness arisen from a part of the world that has been used up and thrown on the scrap heap.

"Dad. He said thank you."

Such serious eyes. Although new, as if they had just been poured into him. From time to time as Noel was speaking she thought she saw a flash deep inside them, like a reflex that seemed to harbour, at the core of its jolt, an evaluating quality that could pass judgement as easily as register approval. What does he do in the world, to have developed that evaluating eye?

I know how to nail two planks together. She winced at the memory of her voice. He was trying to be solicitous and helpful and she had knocked his goodwill on the head. This was the defensive, capable tone she habitually assumed with men and which Llewellyn had informed her, after they were married, was a distinct turnoff. "It's as if you're competing with me to be more manly," he would say, during their frank, no-holds-barred tête-à-têtes in which they tried to grapple with the essence of each other. "I don't want a man for a lover. I'm not trying to be *a man*," she would say.

"What're you writing anyway?" Her father had turned to face her. Behind him a completed solitaire game was fanned out on the desk.

"Just notes."

"Notes for what?"

"Notes for nothing. I write because I've got to do something in this place to stop me from going stark raving mad."

He flinches, ever so slightly, like the shudder of a bird.

She can't find it within herself to say, "I'm sorry, Dad." She can barely even call him that, she notices: *Dad*. Nor has she ever called him by his first name. She puts down her pen and the eel article and stares out the window. The light in John Rory and Eileen's kitchen is visible through a mesh of poplars. She runs over the afternoon, her mind following the contours of the events lightly, delicately, like a wet finger tracing the rim of a wineglass.

They had talked for an hour. They had gone high into the third-floor bedrooms, the two tiny attic rooms where Malcolm had once watched the curtains flowing in the breeze. Together they had taken the sheets off the narrow beds with their rusted springs, beds that spoke of poverty and childhood. They had shaken out the sheets and laughed and she had been amazed at how, after less than an hour spent in his company, easy it had been to laugh with a stranger.

CHAPTER 5

Memory travels farther at night. Noel can feel it barrelling toward him, hugging the curve of the earth to arrive under the cover of darkness. He knows this because during the days he is immune.

He sits at the kitchen table, the black eye of night framed in the window, staring at him in rebuke. Somehow he can't make a start; even the thought of picking up the first photograph fills him with torpor. He has kept them in a dusty shoebox, negatives poking through ripped envelopes. Rachel didn't know he had brought them, although he could imagine her reaction when she found out, as she eventually would. *I thought you were moving on.* He would tell her he had brought them so he could finally put them in order, allocate them to albums labelled with the date and place. She approved of such organizations of life experience; she had eight albums and a raft of scrapbooks that she had kept since she was a child. Noel had bought five albums in the drugstore in Indian Bay, clearing them out of their entire stock.

He looks out the window, avoiding his reflection. *Why have you done this?* He talks to himself like that, often: addressing himself as you. He suspects many people do, but also that there is something wrong with it, that a dangerous dissociation is taking place, a failure to take responsibility for himself: *Why have you deliberately brought yourself to another place with a licorice night, so glossy and thick it has to be chewed through?* Two days of solitude have already changed the rhythm of his thoughts. They are no longer frayed at the edges by responsibilities, expectations, the emotional equivalent of milk and newspapers he forgot to pick up at the convenience store. Now they are gravid, accusing. His thoughts speak to him like fathers.

He imagines his life as it would be if he had stayed in the city, working through the summer. By June the mornings are already hemmed by a lemon haze of heat and pollutants. He walks to his office at the tail end of Broadway on scorched pavements, harried by hot gusts of canyon wind. He is someone who relies upon pattern, routine; he doesn't feel at all stultified by the idea of doing the same thing, day after day. He is aware that his simple routine of subway commute, morning coffee, reading the papers of whatever country he is working on at the moment on the Internet is a kind of soporific; it allows him to be adventurous, even chaotic, in the rest of his life.

He finds it reassuring that he will emerge from the subway at the NYU station, buy his coffee from Guido at the no-name deli. That he will catalogue the crushed vegetables baked by asphalt, which is also garlanded by discarded flowers from the florist across the street, the customers emerging from the shop's cool bower carrying bouquets in front of them, arms outstretched, like trophies. Also the mustard fume of thunderstorms, wisps of air-conditioned air, walking through scythes of hot, cool, hot. Slim wedges of sky, the startling angles produced by skyscrapers, the Trade Center towers looming over him, two trim silver-blue plinths.

He loves this vertical city, but at times he considers it might be no more than his personal departure lounge. He comes and goes, sucked onto escalators, into corridors, the frigid lozenges of airplanes, countries where there are no skinny muffins and two-percent lattes, no chilled punnets of blueberries at the corner deli, no ginger lemonade. He wants this deprivation and this velocity to always be part of his life; he harbours no fantasies of farmhouses upstate or in Connecticut, although Rachel does. This is what happens when you consent to be married, he considers: another person's dream becomes your own, whether you like it or not. Your future might become something you acquiesce to inhabit.

Although they are not married, not yet.

This was another sly, sideways doubt. Lately they had been stealing underneath the threshold of his mind. Why not admit it: he misses the city, his routine, the pathetic air-conditioning system they are waiting on a grant from the Ford Foundation to improve, his pen so sweaty it slips from his fingers. He has forfeited what he intends to be his last summer at Global Witness, his last summer in Manhattan, to sit in this farmhouse on the edge of the Atlantic Ocean. He doesn't know why.

The face in the photograph is quite light-skinned for a country of dark people. A moist face, shimmering, pliant skin. That face had been in the world thirty-one years, his own age now.

He has never before been haunted by anyone's memory, although he knows of the affliction from friends, movies, novels. Nor has he ever suffered flashbacks. The timing perplexes him. Why is it happening now, four years later?

Accompanying the face is another memory, of empty, quiet nights, as if the air had been sieved of the normal nocturnal sounds of cities, no dogs barking, no random shouts of acquaintance or warning from the streets. In fact there were no dogs; they had been killed by the Patriotic Front Army as it advanced through the country, squaring off against Hutu Power. The dogs had been eating the thousands of dead, so they were shot.

The smell of banana beer, sweet and leafy. They had drunk a beer each at least every night they were on the road. On the last night they were together they had switched to the bottle of whisky he had bought in the duty-free in Brussels.

It was a tense year; although three years had passed since the genocide, there was still violence, acts of terror, disputes over property as the country absorbed a returning population, among them *interahamwe* — the *genocidaires*, and Hutu Power bully boys who had manned roadblocks or rounded up villagers for a spot of slaughter.

At times he can't remember what he wrote in his reports, what he concluded. Certainly he hasn't read them since they were published. He wonders if he isn't taking himself seriously enough, if this is a sign he is not fully engaged in his job. Not that his memory isn't acute but rather it has collapsed into sensory impression — perhaps, he reflected as he looked out the window of the old house, the square of resolute night it framed, that was all memory was: impressions, gathering and dissolving, slipping through fingers like sand.

He remembered the nights best, drinking, laughter, decompressing at Chez Lando's, how when there was no moon he couldn't even see his own hand held out in front of him. Soundless nights, long candlestick fingers wrapped around a dusty bottle of banana beer, time congealing around them, the uneasy sense of expectation he had, that time playing with him, with all of them, that something was coming, something that he would later tell himself he could have predicted. These might have been the last fully happy days he had lived, simply because they were from a time before he even had cause to think in such terms: fully happy, questioning his reactions and understanding, measuring the satisfactions and pleasures time granted him. But in those days he preferred to simply work, and drink, and talk to his colleagues, to Alexandre, and this was how he passed those long, slow, satisfying days of his life.

"They say that's the third one this year."

"Third what?"

"House burned down. Well, this time it's a barn." She showed her father the headline. THIRD ARSON ATTACK THIS YEAR FOR NORTH SHORE. "I can't believe it's still happening. Is it still only up in Ingonish?"

"I guess."

"But it's been going on for years."

Ever since she could remember she had heard of random burnings, usually up Ingonish way, always unoccupied. Occasionally, places were burned in Tarbert or Indian Bay, on Seal Island or in Boisedale. No-one knew if it was one person or several carrying out the attacks. They always happened in the dead of night; there were never any witnesses; they were made to look like accidents; indeed the police and fire departments and the insurers who investigated them often decided on an open verdict.

"You think they'd have caught the guy by now," she said.

She finished putting the dishes away. She had to shake off an incipient chill. To think you were being watched by someone who wanted to burn your house, just as the bobcats watched the owners of ducks and chickens from the gnarled hem of the forest. When you left the house, they pounced.

Her father stood up. "I'm going to have a look at Harold." He reached for his raingear that hung, as it had done for her entire life, from a hook on the kitchen door.

"You've still got him?"

"Come down and see for yourself."

She looked out the window into a wet angora sky. "I don't know."

He tossed her a testy look. *You think that's bad? Boy have you gone soft in the city.*

She went with him, more out of determination to prove him wrong than any real desire to see her father's pet. They took the path through tall pines, a soft crunch of moss under her feet, the wet mulch of the forest floor, a mint smell of balsam. She followed him down the hill in a driving rain, pursued by the empty dull groan of wind sieving itself through trees. It was a strange aural effect; she had never heard it anywhere else. As a child she had taken it for the moans of ghosts.

"Your mother used to hate this walk," he said.

Her mother had hated everything about the cabin. The first hot days of summer, mid-June, packing up the house to drive over the bridge, then the mountain, to the cabin on the other side of the lake. Anita teaching her to throw rocks in the hollow of the concrete culvert. The rock slicing through the air, the hollow ping as it landed deep under the road.

I don't know why we have to drive all the way over the mountain just to sit on the other side of the lake.

Fishing's better.

For Christ's sake, Alistair. It's exactly the same fish. Why don't you take us to Florida and then you'll see some different fish.

There was no argument about going to the camp. He had been brought up that way; summers were always spent in camps, which were really shacks he and his brothers had built to sleep in when out fishing or hunting. The game wasn't really any better at the camp, but at least they escaped from their mother's rigorous eye.

Her mother coming to stand behind them, watching them throwing rocks in the culvert, blowing smoke through narrowed eyes. *Your father drags us across the lake because it gives the illusion we're actually going somewhere.*

The station wagon smelled of fishing tackle and cigarettes. They sat in the very back, where children wouldn't be allowed to ride these days without seatbelts, among rogue screwdrivers and boxes of waterproof matches. On the way to the cabin they stopped in at the Seal Island Motel where her mother did shift-work. She and Anita would be allowed their first ice creams of the summer, the waitresses like nurses in their white uniforms. Both of them carrying the cones back to a too-hot car, the ice cream wilting instantly in a blast of heat, tacky fingers. Then riding over the mountain with their necks sticking out the rear window, tongues licking the air, like dogs.

So began a season of rainy-day puzzles, thrice-done crosswords and plastic hand-held pinball machines. Their mother disappeared for hours; they would find her down at the shore, sitting on a piece of driftwood, smoking and staring out into the lakes. She and Anita would surprise her there, and in return she gave them a vacant, startled look.

What are you two doing here? Go and help your father.

Help him do what?

It wasn't just that Anita was old enough to be saucy; she had never been in thrall to their mother, she seemed to keep a part of herself reserved for her alone. Besides, they both knew their father would never accept any offer of their help. *You just do as you're told.* Anita and her racing each other back through the woods, tripping on roots.

The velocity and completeness of the memory disoriented her. She realized they had arrived at the shore and that her father was speaking to her.

"Wait 'til you see. I put spruce boughs and stones and some twigs inside. Makes him feel more at home."

The tank was raised off the ground by several sheets of plywood. He had fashioned a birchbark windbreak around the tank and lined it with boughs, to keep the water from freezing in the winter. A plastic tarp lay open on the ground. He bent over and lifted it, shaking rainwater from its folds.

"Some nights I cover him up so he won't see the moon."

"Has he tried to escape?"

"Oh, about seven times now. It's his time. Last year he just about made it. I found him in the grass about twenty feet down the riverbank."

Part of her will always revolt at the sight of them. She had to steel herself to accompany her father on those nights, weirs and eel boxes thick with thrashing snakes, the soapy froth created by their rubbings against each other. She watched him slice into their hide, tough as rubber tires, was forced to watch the way they keep on writhing, even when their guts are lying on the cutting board like so many dishevelled ribbons. He disembowelled them while still alive because there is no way to kill them, other than to put them in the freezer. Even that merely stunned them into dormancy. When he slit them open, they torqued back into life with a single thrash.

She peered into the tank. The smell hit her first: salt-soapy, slightly medicinal — not dissimilar to the dank petroleum smell in Duncan's garage. For years, when her father would come in from a night's work and wake her up for school, this was the first thing she smelled.

Harold was lying at the bottom of the tank, straight as a board. He had the cylindrical, thick body of the adult eel. The ridge on his back looked sharp, as if it would cut her, if she touched it. Floppy gills fluttered on either side of his head.

"He's huge."

"I give him minnows and mussels. He even had a go at some lobster bodies."

"Don't you think you've kept him confined to this box for long enough?"

"For Christ's sake, Eve, he's an eel."

"Just because he's an eel doesn't mean he can't feel things."

"He can feel things, sure. But he doesn't think: somebody get me out of here, I've been trapped in this goddamn tank for ten years."

"How do you know?"

"Look, he's still got the scar." He pointed to a ribbon scar on the eel's neck. "That's where he got bit as a youngster, when he was caught in the weir. A muskrat came in and took a little chunk out of him."

She couldn't help herself. "Why don't you just let the poor creature go?"

"You're still the same sentimental thing you always were."

"Who's being sentimental here? You keep a pet and kill the rest of them."

"I kill them so I can eat. If I didn't have to eat, I wouldn't kill anything." He wouldn't meet her gaze; instead he addressed himself to the mute façade of the forest. "If you were starving, you'd lose your feeling for them quick enough."

"Yes, Dad, but I'm not starving."

Then again, maybe she was. Hunger is a state of mind, she reminded herself; for all she knew she might be at the beginning of an internal famine.

He was sawing wood now, beneath the tarp he had strung up between two low alder trees to keep his wood dry. Bent over, she could see the outline of his spine through his woodsman's shirt.

He seemed younger to her, every time she saw him, with his unweathered face, so unlike the washboard faces of other fishermen in their sixties. What wrinkles he did have were to be found in unexpected places; when he smiled they appeared on the edges of his eyes and drooped downward, suspending his expression between happiness and regret.

His father, her grandfather, had been called Black Donald on account of his dark eyes and hair the colour of squid ink; he was one of the True Celts, her father had told her. These were dark-haired people, small in stature, quick and flexible. They had an untidy, macabre sense of humour and didn't like to be crossed. According to her father, who had heard it from his own father, their people were good on the sea and more comfortable in the company of animals than that of people. There had been plenty of her father's sort of man on the ragged western isles of Scotland, but the New Country was so much more brutal in its seasons. The small dark Celts were replaced by hale Viking Scots from the east coast, the crafty English, the almost supernaturally tough Irish. Her father might be a holdout, a remnant, of the earlier, delicate men.

Her father was always bringing home injured rabbits or foxes he'd found caught in traps. He would wipe iodine on their wounds, feed them until they had recovered, then release the creatures back into the wild only to watch them eat his lettuce. She understands that he was afraid of appearing sentimental, so he assigned that role to her even though it is he who rises at four in the morning to feed his eel, it is he who nursed the fox with the bloodied paw.

"I don't know why you just don't go." He had stopped sawing and was standing in front of her, a strange fixed look in his eye. "I don't see why you should hang around here all summer. You're a grown woman, you've got a life to live. I can manage well enough. What's the worst that could happen?"

He had caught her off guard. She shuffled her weight from one foot to the other. He stared at her in silence. He seemed to be taking her answer seriously, rather than the meek expression of confusion it really was.

"Well," he said, "I guess it's all right, for the time being."

The time being.

She thinks of time like the lake, a liquid realm, one of many depths. What would it be like to live without memory? Wouldn't time, too, disappear? You didn't so much move through it as dove and surfaced. She has a quick, shattering vision: her father lurching from moment to moment, hopping from one isolated craggy peak to another, trying to ignore the airless gulf between. On each of these temporary citadels he tries to construct ramparts, passageways, the bare walls of rooms for himself to inhabit, but within a second or two he is compelled to move.

She pictures him settling in new houses only to find that he has to go, gathering up belongings he no longer even recognizes as his own. He will enter a wintering landscape that will become progressively more stark. The trees, rivers, stones of his mind will disappear one by one, until the sky and the water are also gone. He will stand exposed in this empty land, a lone naked figure, his mind tangled, shreds of identity flapping from him languidly, even decoratively, like ribbons in a breeze.

A horse the dark hue of muskrat pelt is running, ears back, hindquarters churning, toward an oncoming train. They are on the same track, only minutes from collision. In the dream he is the horse, or inside the horse, and nothing can stop him. He is only seconds away from impact. The train becomes larger and larger until it runs straight through his eye and he is inside it, horse-flesh exploded, a bodyless, boundaryless creature, encased in iron.

The dream is about the painting in Eve's room, of course: *Horse and Train.* He wants to take the print down but it is a remnant of her presence in the cabin. Eve wouldn't know about the years of afternoons when he lay down for a rest in her narrow bed, trying to imagine where she was, what she might be feeling. If only he concentrated hard enough, he might be with her, although he would loiter unnoticed, just outside the frame. He lay in that nameless point in late afternoon he thinks of as the bottom of a pendulum's arc: a wasted, static moment, the time of day he feels least substantial, quite unreal. *What does a teenaged girl take to in such a painting?* he would wonder as he stared at the print, with its dark inevitability, the terror and mystique of the coming confrontation, the certainty that there will be a vanquisher and a vanquished.

From the day she was born he had known she would leave, and that it would be years before he saw her again. He knew this with the certainty of a dream he still hoped would not congeal into reality. He knew his daughter would catapult herself into the world in a way he had never risked. For years he would hear from her only through the occasional stilted telephone call, and cryptic postcards. When he heard less and less of her he gave up these afternoon sessions of attempted telepathy, and went back to lying down in his own bed. He tried not to fear for her but of course he thinks of her as a child, his child, still: raw, unfinished, driven by obscure compulsions. She would never think as he would, on consuming streets of Venice, Mexico City, New York, thinking, *Where are my people?*

And Eve, she is not in New York, for once. She is here, lying on a bunkbed on the other side of a plywood partition, stupefied by the eventlessness of life in the cabin. Summer has only started but already she is becoming browner, harder. She is the cod fillets he used to dry in nets suspended between two birch trees behind the house as in a giant hammock, their skin brown and pitted with salt.

She is thirty-four and she finds she wants, more than anything, to look like a boy. Perhaps she really wants to be a man. To be light, hollow. Soon she will cut her hair and when people pass her on the highway in their muscular Jeeps and Fords, they will say, was that a boy or a girl we just passed? *Boy, girl.* How wonderful it would be, to inhabit that borderland between the genders. Even if she is long past that ephebic age, eighteen or nineteen. At eighteen she was unmistakably a girl, with her bloated thighs, her floral dresses. But fifteen years of being on the fringes of the fashion industry has made her hard and sleek, helped by potions: *lift minceur, lait restoratif.* She knows she looks much younger than her age. She is a sprite, an ageless person, not at all thick with womanly importance as other women her age she knows have become. In liquor stores where she is not known the cashier will occasionally ask her for ID and when she shows them her birthdate they will both have a laugh.

She lies in her bunkbed with her head propped up on two pillows. At eight o'clock the science program comes on the CBC. She knows the program's producer — Llewellyn was seconded to work on the show for three months the previous year. They interview a theoretical physicist, a man with an Asian name but a very American accent. He describes the universe as "soap bubbles" — pockets of time and space connected by thin corridors, which he calls wormholes. When the universe dies, as it must, when the soap bubbles collapse — he intones all this in forceful syllables devoid of rue — our only hope is to escape through a wormhole. Escape into where? the interviewer asks, into another soap bubble? No, the theoretical physicist answers. Into forever.

~

She is twelve, thirteen. Her mother has been dead for five years. She is in the Indian Bay drugstore, contemplating shoplifting, but she knows all the cashiers, they let her read the magazines. Pepsodent, Listerine, Maybelline, makeup counter smells. Strawberry lip gloss, the dusty perfume of pressed powder. She is fascinated by the women in *Vogue,* aggressively louche women with the faces of children. They even have childish names: Astrid, Karine, Molly. At university she will read a sociology textbook that asserts this is what men the world over want: childish-faced women with the correct hip-to-waist ratio.

She wants to defend her mother's beauty against these girl-women. Her mother was beautiful, everyone said it was her fate. *Fate* — what they meant was that if she hadn't been beautiful she would still be alive, and Eve and Anita would have a mother.

The kind of woman who turned men's heads. Didn't know what to do with her looks. Wasted here. She could have been someone out there, in the world. Her relatives utter these phrases in rue-stained voices. They don't realize she can hear them, in her eavesdropping position upstairs, listening through the register, the grille-covered hole in the floor that allows heat from the old coal stove to rise to the floor above.

She catches the satisfaction in their voices, their delight in learning that the Bible stories and the pioneer parables and the priests' sermons from the pulpit really were applicable to life. That the things that happened to people had a shape and a reason, and that those people could be laid to rest.

She turns the thick, scented pages. Fiji by Guy Laroche, the debauched glamour of Helmut Newton, Gianfranco Ferré, Linda Evans modelling Halston. She is unaware that in fifteen years' time she will be a bit-player in this haughty, disembowelled world. She will call Condé Nast's Hanover Square offices in London to speak with women named Miranda and Isabella, negotiate editorials for Caroline, text message Deborah Turbeville's assistant to arrange a shoot involving Louis Quinze furniture and teak escritoires.

She fields the arrowed thrust of impatience. Stealing from the drugstore, or considering theft — this too is a pre-emptive strike against oblivion. But she doesn't want to get into trouble: she has seen from other girls in school, older girls, where trouble leads: to the county court, the juvenile detention centre, the abortion clinic. She is already contemplating how to avoid the pitfalls of teenage recklessness, how not to be one of those girls who will do anything to feel alive, girls who will pay the price.

CHAPTER 6

Two tents bought new from an outdoor supply store remained to be unpacked. Before he had left he had trooped, accompanied by Rachel, to the macho, task-ridden world of Swiss Army knives and Gore-Tex and bought brand-new equipment. Portable gas stove, cutlery, Thermos, emergency blanket, first-aid kit. Rachel had insisted, and he paid up in defeat. He nearly said, "We're not going on a survivalist course, you know. It's a cushy vacation in a house that costs nine hundred dollars a week."

Then again, the last few years had dulled his early enthusiasm for roughing it. He had slept in the shells of abandoned houses in winter — grimy sheets of translucid plastic fluttering where there had once been windows, he had strung his hammock between giant Ceibas in the rainforest and swaddled himself in mosquito nets, only to be rained on the whole night. At this point in his career Noel could make a plausible inventory — really he could have written the guidebook of — the Armpits of the Universe, as he called them (although privately — to his colleagues he continuously praised their "authentic struggle," their "potential for reconstitutive peace processes"): Lagos, East Timor, the Magdalena Medio.

So they had rented this house, on the premise that he had earned it. Noel was surprised how comfortable he felt in this house with its relic smell, the cream wallpaper dotted with little green paisleys, the old linoleum in the pantry, the stone containers labelled SALT and COFFEE that were neither retro nor chic. The house seemed to be exhorting him, *live in me*. He'd taken a chance and told the neighbour this, although he knew it sounded dangerously whimsical. But she'd understood. In fact, it seemed to affect her in some way.

He was spooning coffee into the espresso maker Rachel had made him pack — she didn't like cafetière coffee, she found it too bitter. Five days to go until her arrival. She would be tired from the drive to Newark followed by a flight to Halifax, then another plane to Sydney. For him this would be a short journey, hardly meriting fatigue. He was accustomed to overnight flights to Europe, followed by eight- or ten-hour waits in departure lounges followed by a night flight to Africa. At least he could trust Rachel not to miss the plane. He was easily disoriented in airports: once he had missed a plane while mulling over which wine to buy in the duty-free. Last year while catching a flight from O'Hare back to New York he had placidly let his departure time go by, even though he could see the clock and the screens. He'd watched his flight take off while idly reading the alarming notices about the Warsaw Convention on the back of his ticket.

He was looking forward to her arrival. Not that he had been lonely. The days in the house were passing as he intended: getting the house ready for Rachel, who had instructed him to wash the bedsheets, even if he had come to them freshly washed by the owners. He had dusted the house from top to bottom, and before she came he would make sure the fridge was full. He kept himself busy doing practice runs setting up the tent, buying insect repellent and beer and camera film. No, he hadn't felt lonely at all. Maybe once or twice, when the thick shadow of the mountain seemed to press in on him at night.

Then again he hadn't expected to find someone like Eve in Clam Harbour: someone his age, educated, who had obviously been out in the world. He'd assumed his neighbours would be grizzled local-colour fishermen — not that such people hadn't turned up in Clam Harbour. But he'd also bumped into the woman from Massachusetts — or was it Connecticut? — whose kids had gone to Yale and Cornell.

The island kept surprising him. Indian Bay was a little twee, but there was little of the self-consciousness, the smugness, of summer holiday towns in Massachusetts, Rhode Island, Maine and their cannily marketed rustic authenticity. Those towns always looked like they were counting the cash of some film company after having served as the location for the next American family-in-meltdown-only-to-find-redemption movie.

Nor had he expected Cape Breton to be so gritty and removed from the rest of the world. Perhaps because there was no large city nearby, he couldn't feel its shadow cast over the place, sucking the inhabitants in on the off-season, to labour in offices and bars. Here he felt contingent, barely real, poised on the rim of a continent — almost unreachable. Exactly as he had wanted, he reminded himself. And if the shadow had followed him here, if he felt lost in nothingness, perched on the outer rim of the world, a stranger, then that was what he had wanted to feel, wasn't it?

Rachel had hardly challenged him when he decided to drive up two weeks ahead of her.

"Are you sure? Two weeks alone in a place where you don't know anyone?"

"I've done it enough times for work."

"Precisely," Rachel had said, in that summing-up way that she would put to good practice as a lawyer. "You were *working*. There were people to be talked to, reports to be written. There you'll be doing nothing."

"I'll keep busy."

He had never taken time out for himself, as Rachel had taken to characterizing it, before. He usually spent his summers honing his skills, perfecting his French or Spanish, trying to learn Arabic. He wanted to work in the Middle East, eventually. That's where everything was going to happen in his line of work.

So he had dusted the house down, fiddled with tents and camping equipment, readying them for the day when he and Rachel would hurl themselves into the wilderness. He cleaned out the Styrofoam cooler he had brought with him in the back of the car, not realizing that coolers were so much cheaper up here — he'd had no idea how everything in Canada, after you converted the dollar, was almost half-price.

He had sorted his reading material, now scattered around the living room: *The Nation, Harper's,* two-week-old copies of the Sunday *New York Times,* the latest books by Chomsky and Zinn, a collection of writings from Sub-comandante Marcos and a few theoretical tomes he was meant to read for work. He'd brought a few novels, although the truth is he found fiction soporific. He could only read a bit each night before it sent him to sleep, whereas current affairs made his mind sit bolt upright. He was more interested in learning about how the world worked than what made-up people felt. Although when he did read novels — popular but literary novels of the American condition or the American mind — he was pleasantly surprised. He found his emotions stirred at the same time, an exact harmony with intellectual learning, and the combination of the two was more powerful than he would have guessed.

An hour later he was sitting at the kitchen table, his coffee cold and untouched. All his tasks accomplished, he had run out of volition. Almost immediately the trembling had returned. Muscle twitches ran through his calves and forearms like miniature currents. How could he be thrown off track this easily, tossed back into that cold room papered with doubts?

"Everyone says people went crazy," Alexandre said. "But I think they went extremely rational. They only did what is in all of us to do."

The past is past. This was another thing people said, over and over, like a political slogan — which, he supposed, it was. He thought the opposite; it took that experience to convince him that the past was actually present, living alongside them, like a videotape running in parallel time. Killers were certainly walking in tandem with him on the street. The only difference was that now they didn't carry clubs or machetes, but this was a detail. In another dimension they were still murdering people. How could anyone draw a frontier between the past, present, future when they were only one moment sliding into another on the edge of a ragged synapse, and most of the time we are too tired or unalert to notice their fleet passing.

Where was the exact boundary of the present and the past? Noel tried to concentrate on individual moments, walking down the street, the equatorial sun a golden goblet dropped on his head. Watch the moment come, he instructed himself, see it go, feel its slide. But what was the exact point at which the moment arrived? When could you say with certainty that you were in the now, given that by the time you perceived it, *now* had become *then*.

He tried to teach himself to live in the single molten moment, to shear his mind of past deeds and corrections. Concentrate on the warm Coke you are drinking. Concentrate on Paul, whom you are interviewing, a fifty-three-year-old Hutu moderate who had hidden in his garden, then made a run for the hills and spent that night and the next day floating in a river already choked with dead bodies, trying to impersonate one of them.

"Hills ought to offer some disguise," Paul told him. "But they didn't. There was nowhere to hide. I don't know why I survived," he said, with that slow childlike grin of wonder Noel had come to recognize and fear. "I could hear the sound of machetes splitting bone. I have never wanted so much to be invisible; maybe that's what happened. I disappeared." A long pause in which they both shuddered, harassed by noonday flies. "I am a coward," Paul said. "I am alive and my wife and children are dead."

Noel was about to remonstrate with a familiar litany of reassurances: *Of course you're not a coward. You are not responsible for their deaths. You need to live your life.* But Paul had lapsed into a stony state beyond the boundaries of normal silence. This was also familiar to Noel, from others he had talked to. He knew no-one could visit them in that place; there they were alone.

His interview notes became peppered with observations that were, strictly speaking, unnecessary for his work.

Liars scratch the backs of their neck before they tell a lie.

He told the story in a whisper, as if he were afraid someone nearby would hear us.

Girl with gold earrings, thirteen or fourteen. Brings us more warm Coke. As she turns away I see a thick roll of scar tissue, stretching from one end of her neck to the other.

Then those evenings at Chez Lando, drinking "to decompress" as they all put it. His surprise as, in the middle of another grim joke, he looked down to find his own arm covered in blood. Time was dissolving in this hysterically bountiful country of goblins, *mille collines*, the thousand hills, purple hills and red earth, a landscape with the colours and texture of a bunched Mayan textile. The endless succession of intelligent, intense people he spoke to, who had seen their children murdered in front of their eyes, or gang-raped, deliberately infected with HIV.

Then the others, the many people on the far side of righteousness, but who claimed it as their own. Joseph — he smiled all through their conversation, strange chewy smiles. "No, I wasn't there. I was visiting my uncle. I wasn't in the village at the time, thank God." He already knew from surviving witnesses that Joseph had hacked an old Tutsi woman to death. Her family had fled on foot to the hills, leaving her alone at her farm. He then set upon her dog and her cattle. The woman had been his neighbour for twenty-five years; she had known him as a baby.

Eunice, sixteen at the time of the genocide, had been allowed to live but had been gang-raped by soldiers. "We will let you live," they told her, "only so that you can die a slow death." This was exactly what was happening when he met her. Eunice was nearly twenty and no more than a skeleton peppered with bedsores. Still, she was able to smile at him politely, almost coquettishly, from sunken eyes. He learned from her that those rapes were her only experience of sex. He wanted to tell her what love could be like, that sex could be a force for good as well as evil, but found he couldn't. Eunice was twenty and she was dying. Why tell her about a pleasure she would never experience?

He'd spread the photographs on the kitchen table until they formed a haphazard quilt of faces. He chose one at random. It was taken inside a dark hut hurled into a tinny light by the flash. This was Matilde, a fourteen-year-old girl he'd met in a hospital where he'd gone to interview a nurse. She had been raped so many times she needed reconstructive surgery. She later died of an infection.

Then a shot of him and Alexandre outside in the road, the mud and liquid ditches of the rainy season, squinting into the lens. Also a photograph of Paul, a friend of Alexandre's, who was killed in a road accident while he was there. Paul was a moderate Hutu who refused to take part in the massacres and who'd nearly been killed because of it. In the photograph he was smiling.

Of Alexandre he had only a handful of photographs: them in a village in the west, near Gisenyi, the volcanoes of Zaire puncturing the horizon. Alexandre at a chessboard table of white and black faces, expats and their Rwandan friends — another night out at Chez Lando. He and Alexandre, their arms loosely draped around each other's shoulders, standing in front of a mimosa tree.

What had always interested him about photographs is what they do not show: the acts that precede or follow them, arms dropping from shoulders, sighs, exhaled air, relief, kisses on cheeks goodbye. Acts, words more or less pertinent, memories. In this casual dimension the people in the picture are still alive, ordering beers, kicking footballs, wiping their glasses clean. Only frozen, captured, are they dead.

For him, the power of photographs lay not only in the memories they provoked, but in how they seemed to travel against the grain of time in a vain if persistent attempt to detain it, how they dared to propose solutions to history's errors. In fact, he considered, photographs might be the only possible riposte to the force bent on instructing us that time passing was not, after all, about the individual, but rather an era, a stage, a collective history.

He puts them down, and turns to stare out the window at the black eye of night. What is happening to him? Although he already knows. Too much internal tension, a vicious scrap between categories, a disorientation in space because he was being required to function pleasantly and competently in a place he did not want to be.

Noel thinks of his friend — his best friend he supposed he was duty-bound to call him — Arturo, saying at a Manhattan dinner party only a week ago, *I just want to get past this cycle everyone consents to be in, you know: fuck up and move on, fuck up and move on. But I guess that's life, isn't it?* The wry laughter and agreement ringing around the table. And Noel, barely able to disguise his disdain for people who make claims about what life is. Even though he was in the midst of it, Noel would never be able to say he knew what life was or was not.

It wasn't your fault. This was what the few people who knew counselled — Arturo, Rachida, his therapist. Nothing seems to be anyone's fault now, he had replied. I *want* it to be my fault. On hearing this they all backed away in distaste, even the therapist. Noel was alone, then, in a way he had never imagined, a dissident within himself, straining for release.

In the morning she found a horse in the yard.

She had woken early and tread softly past her father's room, yanking open the screen door — she'd discovered that opening it with a quick screech was more effective than opening it slowly, which elicited a drawn-out scream. Where did he keep the oil these days anyway? The father she knew had never let anything become squeaky or, God forbid, rusted.

Standing knee-deep in the long grass, dew soaking its coat, was a dirty white horse. The horse gave her a hesitant neigh, as if it knew she suspected it might not exist.

She approached it and put a hand out to touch its neck. Its coat was wet with mist, the fur grey and stained green by moss and lichen. Its eyes were bright and inquisitive.

"Hello, fella. What are you doing here all by yourself? I thought you were a unicorn."

The horse's ears quivered at the sound of her voice. She took her hand away and brushed it against her thigh, streaking her jeans with a coating of bugs and dew.

"What's happened to you?"

The horse looked away, as if to avoid her question, and stared placidly into the trees.

She went to the side of the road and yanked some thin grass. "Here," she shook it under its nose. "Bet you'd like some more of this."

The horse gave the grass a quick sniff and then raised its head with a deriding jerk.

"Be that way then."

She took a quick look between the hind legs of the horse and saw it was a mare. She cast around for a piece of rope to make a halter. She was standing with a rope in her hands, trying to decide what to do, when she heard the scuff of gravel on the road. She looked up to see Noel heading down the road.

"You're up early," he called.

"Some overenthusiastic bird woke me up at five o'clock."

"I think I heard that bird too," he said. "He's very punctual. I didn't know you had a horse."

"We don't." She pointed — ridiculously, as if there was any other horse they might be talking about — at the animal grazing beside her. "It just appeared."

She broke into a jog, startling the horse, to join Noel on the road, although she wasn't sure why she was approaching him; they could have kept up their half-shouted conversation from where she was. As she got closer she thought he looked older, somehow, more finished. There seemed to be new lines in the corners of his eyes, a new seriousness to his already intellectual mouth. She had met him only the day before but already he was changing, hardening in the same way ideas cohered after a certain amount of study.

"Where did it come from?"

"I don't know. There's no-one around here who has a horse. At least not that I know of. There are no farms on the road. She looks like she's been in the woods for weeks." Eve frowned. "It's uncanny."

He was giving her the same intent look he had given her when they had stood in the kitchen, as if she were something to be studied.

"You know, you don't speak like people here."

"I know. I've lost my accent."

"I don't mean your accent. It's the words you use."

She looked down at the ground, in part to get away from his inquisitive gaze. He was curious, this man, and a listener. She felt sure he wouldn't come in for the usual wife's complaint: he never listens to me.

"Did you get the attic cleaned out all right?"

"Yeah. Rachel will be really pleased to have a study. Just wait till she sees the view." He shook his head in admiration.

The slap of a door and a sudden gush of water from the cabin signalled her father was awake.

"My father will have a fit." She made her voice gruff: "Where'd you get that goddamned horse?"

"Your father doesn't like horses?"

"He doesn't like change."

Noel's face lurched into a smile. She had noticed his expressions seemed to stutter back and forth, like switches being flicked, without any preparation. It made him seem younger than he likely was, and guileless.

"Do you think you can find the owner?"

She shrugged. "We'll put the word out with the RCMP."

"What's that?"

"The police. They can add her to their missing-horses file."

This elicited another quick-change smile.

"We're going to visit my sister today." As soon as she said it, she thought, *Why am I divulging this? What does he care?*

"Where does she live?"

"Glace Bay. It's near Sydney."

"I haven't been yet."

"I haven't been for years myself. When we lived on the other side of the lake we would go every week."

"You used to live over there?"

She pointed across the lake to where a lone white house stood in a clearing between dark phalanxes of forest. "We lived there until I was eight."

"Why did you move here?"

"My father had to sell the house. He'd already built this place as a fishing cabin. It was the only place we had to go, so we moved here. I used to try to swim back across. My father would come in the rowboat and haul me out of the water."

She had meant to elicit another of those lurching smiles from him, but he only looked at her with concern.

"I guess you didn't want to be here."

"I guess not."

He looked away from her. Some awkwardness had stolen over him. "I'd better be going."

She watched him walk down the road, past the NO TRES-PASSING sign. The signs were new; they had been nailed to trees by outsiders who had bought up the land running down to the shore from the abandoned road. What were they going to do, shoot her? She had always walked the trails through these woods. When she was sixteen she had cut a trail herself up to the top of the mountain, three miles long, most of it uphill. She knew the land from top to bottom, where the rivers began, what parts were swampy, the numerous brooks that coursed down the side of the old mountain like so many veins on the back of a hand.

Then her father's voice, just in time for Noel to catch it, she calculated, as he made the turn in the road.

"Eve! What's that goddamned *horse* doing in the yard?"

* * *

Open May 'til September: the sign on the door of Kay's Lobster Hut was a familiar one in Indian Bay. The restaurant was a low-slung white building two streets up from the lakeshore. It advertised itself mainly to the bay, where visiting yachtsmen could hardly miss the giant wooden lobster on the roof, black eyes bulging, claws held aloft, as if in self-defence.

The door squeaked and opened to display a lobster tank. Inside, lobsters grappled with each other. She catalogued the familiar restaurant bric-a-brac: pads of bills, credit card swipe machine, toothpicks, bowl of post-lobster mints.

"Hello?"

No answer. Behind the reception a swing door drifted open and shut in a breeze. She inched toward it. Just as she was about to swing it open, a small, neatly dressed woman emerged from behind it.

"Can I help you?"

"Do you have any vacancies?"

"Come again?"

"Jobs... if you've...." It had been so long since she'd had to ask for a job.

"Oh." The woman wouldn't quite look Eve in the eye. "No. Not really."

"Not really?"

The woman sighed. "The fact is, I've got a bit of a problem with staff, but it's recent — just a few minutes ago, in fact. I haven't had a chance to think what I'm going to do about it. Listen, let me talk to... to someone. Can you have a seat for a minute?"

She sat down and stared at the Nova Scotia Tourism Board posters on the wall: Peggy's Cove, the Cabot Trail, Cape Blomidon — drastic promontories lit by shards of sun, shrouded in salt spray. The dining area sported red vinyl chairs neatly parked at twenty-odd Formica tables covered with plastic tablecloths. She gazed at the ketchup bottles, plastic bibs, the lobster forks that looked like giant tweezers. This had all been fun when she was a kid and they would go out to a restaurant once a year for a lobster supper.

The woman returned.

"It looks like I'm short a girl."

I'm not a girl.

"That's great."

The woman's name was Bonnie. A slim diamond grasped her fourth finger. She had managed Kay's for the past three summers, she told Eve, after working there as a waitress each summer since she was eighteen, which might not have been that long ago, it occurred to her, even if Bonnie already had that stolid, confident-matron air about her. She probably had a couple of kids already.

"You'd be surprised how many youngsters go to the mainland for summer work," Bonnie explained the staff shortage. "This is the kitchen. And this is your uniform."

"Uniform?"

"Oh, nothing special. You should wear black shorts — we don't provide those — and sneakers, we don't provide those either. Here's your shirt." Bonnie held up a red polo shirt with Kay's Lobster Hut splashed across the chest in yellow writing. Where the little horse and polo player usually appeared was the same defiant lobster that graced the rooftop sign.

"You'll want to wear this when you're clearing the tables." Bonnie held out what looked like a plastic bib, the ubiquitous lobster splattered across it. "Lobster can be a mess, you know," she said. "At the beginning we'll give you just a couple of shifts a week, so you can get your legs."

"I've waitressed before." Eve declined to say, *at some of the top restaurants in the country.*

She took her Kay's Lobster Hut shirt and folded it onto her bicycle rack. She threw a leg over the saddle and hopped on. She had to buy a car by next Wednesday, her first shift; she'd never survive the bike ride in and back and do a six-hour waitressing stint on top.

On her way home it began to rain. She ducked into Duncan's garage to let the downpour pass. He tossed her a greasy towel.

"Look at that calendar," she pointed to a heap of paper, frayed at the edges, long ago dropped to the floor. "What's the date on it? January 1988."

As a riposte, Duncan said, "Too bad about your truck."

Duncan had come the week before to take a look at her father's truck and had pronounced it clinically dead. The engine was ruined, thanks to her father's mistake. *Not even worth the money you'd spend putting a new engine in it,* Duncan had said.

She'd have to get Celyn to drive her into town that weekend and she'd buy a second-hand car on the spot.

She pedalled out the driveway, amazed and slightly scandalized at how she had acquired a new full-time life, and so quickly. Between her new job, the inevitable future visits to Dr. McIntyre and her father's dilemma she wouldn't have much time to examine the chord that had started up inside her, deep but also breathless, not unlike when the wind picked up on the lake. It was a clarion, transitional sound, like the foghorn at night, or the forlorn call of a loon.

"I don't have much time to talk," Llewellyn began. This was not unusual — he was on deadline at this time of day.

"How's work?" she asked.

"Crazy as usual. We're doing this piece on the cod stocks."

"About how they're exhausted?"

"Just a little tired. That's what they tell you in Newfoundland. That's what they want you to believe. Plus some political scandal in Saskatchewan, if that's actually possible. Christ, everything in this country is such a non-event. When am I going to blow this Popsicle stand and get a real job?"

She wished she shared this conviction and the drive and ambition that fuelled it. She wanted to say, *You can go to the States and get a job. You can go anywhere.*

She listens to him tell her about the difficulty of finding someone outside the government fisheries ministry to talk on the record about the latest scientific theory to explain the demise of the cod, about the unreliability of eyewitness accounts in general. As he speaks in his familiar jokey, fey, but utterly competent, news editor's voice, a strange effect overtakes her. Suddenly the cabin becomes small; it recedes to a tiny thing, like a room in a toy house.

She pulls away from it, and even further, until she can see her and Llewellyn. They are also faraway, not so much seen through the wrong end of binoculars, but no— they are on TV. That's it, they are a couple in a television documentary about modern life and the pressures it puts on relationships. In the documentary it is winter, last winter in fact, which is only six months ago but already it has the poised, hollow feel of another era.

On the television screen she sees them moving through a pallid city, bank towers breathing through their tops, plumes of smoke into a crisp linen sky, Llewellyn reads *Toronto Life*, scouting out the latest restaurants. Trattoria this, bistro that. *I am such a foodie,* he says. She is becoming resentful of this diminutive, consuming word. They go to restaurants where they eat mysterious substances wrapped in banana leaves, nouveau tamales, yucca fritters on the side, grilled crab, various kinds of aioli: mint, basil, lemon. The beautiful, responsive waitpeople, their dextrous anticipation of desires, bearing fettuccine with scallops, artichokes and harissa, grilled blue corn soup with soured cream. Llewellyn tells her the daily storyboard, some British guy who has pitched up in Vancouver with no passport and no memory after being robbed in Toronto. His amnesia is real; he is at the end of his tether. He will kill himself unless someone tells him who he is.

Then home, a snowstorm, the Bathurst streetcar, vinyl roofing. She tries to pan out, as if she is in charge of this celestial camera, to reveal what actually surrounds them. The winter-still lake, chemical works standing sentinel around it all the way to

Buffalo, the hasty suburbs. Llewellyn talks about the waiter, he guesses Armenian, or Greek, those black eyes; then his father's photos, their trip to Indonesia, his plans for the future. I could work for CBC for the rest of my life, or go to the States, make real money. Of course, she tells him. The world is your oyster. You can do anything.

Meanwhile her life is a shifting patchwork of countries, textiles, minerals, products. In the past four years she has done it all: illegally sourced stones, open-pit mining, fashion journalists, the requisite temperamental photographers, minor forms of bribery, Fair Trade, Unfair Trade. She struggles to conquer a subtle guilt she felt while travelling, that she should be more awed by what she sees around her. But the beggars are only beggars. Thin dogs, puddles. The beach is beautiful but beauty fatigue has set in. Another Chanel lipstick bought in the duty-free, more frequent flyer points racked up, the pleadings to a God in whom she only believed when she was frightened — please don't let me die on this flight through the stratosphere, please keep my soul aloft. She longs for her espresso maker and her hot Trinity Bellwoods flat, but the graphic prosperity of the city alienates her; she can't help thinking that real life is lived in more messy, exigent places. She is never quite content anywhere.

Lately a cunning indifference, even a lassitude, has stolen into her life. It has crept up when she wasn't looking and swamped her. Her arms and legs feel heavy, as if she is trying to walk in a swimming pool. She is only another person, an insoluble mix of pride and fear, driven not by dignity but by a need to shore herself up against imagined raids on her precious self, her security. She is intelligent enough to know that this is a privated place, and that great vistas, sunsets, panoramic glass, the very landscape of possibility, exist just somewhere beyond its ramparts. But how to get there?

"You sound tired," she said, even though it was she who was exhausted.

"Yeah," Llewellyn sighs. "I've been up all night."

She was waiting for him to ask her about her father, her feelings. She had an entire speech prepared: about the weird sense of unreality that has overtaken her, how life can change so quickly, she is a nickel-and-dime waitress, how she can't ever remember having made a decision not to understand her father but this is what seems to have happened; she can no longer decipher the cryptic homilies in which he and others on the island speak, *you never know, what goes around comes around,* when an authoritative — no, bossy — voice cut in.

"...that link-up from St. John's."

A hand muffled the receiver. She heard the murky outlines of conversation.

"Sorry." Llewellyn came back on the line. "That's Susannah. With an '*h.*' My new senior producer."

"Let me guess how that's going."

"Exactly. Listen, we're on air in twenty minutes."

"It's okay," she said. "I'll let you go."

Summer announced its arrival in a hundred occulted ways: sphagnum rose and plumped, slope bogs and their tannic waters the colour of tea began to drain. Fireweed and black knapweed flowered on roadsides, the brush at the edge of fields revealing the droopy radiance of the shy blue iris, of the tawny daylily, of bunchberry and yarrow. Cloudberry bushes embroidered with buds, muskeg steeped in a lengthening dusk.

Lupines began to appear on the roadside, pink flowers in acidic soil, blue in alkaline — "nature's litmus paper," as her Grade Twelve Biology teacher had said. Stately, Crete-shaped clouds began to appear in the sky. Flocks of gulls foamed overhead, enraptured by the arriving flotillas of sea trout and glass elvers.

More than anything these porcelain June mornings signal that the summer has begun. In a couple of weeks, she knew, the character of this year's summer would congeal. It will either become rainy and cool, harried by the Atlantic fogs that sometimes blight the island, or it will intensify into a jewel of a summer, spare and clean and hard.

~

Anita leaves in the summer: Anita is twenty, Eve is twelve. On Anita's last night in the cabin Eve sits outside in the damp grass with her arms around the dog, watching her father and sister moving around inside like shadow puppets, their silhouettes projected on the walls by hand-held kerosene lamps that wink as they move from room to room.

She is patrolling for signs of desertion, even though she knows it is imminent. Anita has met Lloyd; they are engaged, although Eve herself has only met the man twice. She watches them moving from room to room, striking newly itinerant poses, inhabiting dark crevasses of the odd-shaped rooms.

Soon Lloyd will come and drive Anita away. She should be starting to dream of a man who will take her away, but already she suspects she will have to be both mother and father, man and woman for herself. Some people are fingered by destiny, picked up and transported; others have to pay their own passage.

The next day Lloyd drives up. He has a small house in Glace Bay inherited from his coal-mining uncle; he has cable TV and a microwave. Eve returns from one of her exploratory walks to see them driving away down the road. Anita can surely see her in the rearview or side mirror, but she doesn't smile or wave. Anita has learned her lesson from their mother, and learned it well. She sits in the passenger seat and stares straight ahead.

The autumn after Anita leaves, a famished stray dog comes onto their land. It tries to eat an eel he finds in the grass. Savaging it, taking twenty minutes to die. The dog didn't know he was up against a living cord of steel. Anita is in Glace Bay with Lloyd;

her father is having a drink with some buddies of his in Indian Bay. She cowers alone in the cabin at the sounds: the dog's primeval, ruthless growl, the torque and thrash of the eel. She wants to go out and stop it but she is afraid the dog will turn on her. She goes out anyway to try to scare if off and sees thrashing, slime, the dog's muzzle wet with blood. A few hours later the dog is dead. Eel blood is toxic. She is amazed that the dog does not know this instinctively. Maybe it was so desperate it didn't care. When her father gets home he buries the dog on their land, just below the cabin.

CHAPTER 7

The highway was decorated with new, righteous signs. DRI-
VING WITHOUT YOUR SEATBELT IS AGAINST THE LAW.
DO NOT DRINK AND DRIVE, and, somewhere near the
turnoff to Kempt Head, JESUS SAVES. Other roadmarks were
unchanged: The Seal Island Motel, the Irving Gas station in
Big Bras d'Or, the tours to Puffin Island announced by a giant
billboard puffin, the Lick-a-Chick near the exit to Sydney
Mines. At the wheel of Celyn's spare truck, her father dozing
and silent beside her, Eve feels free for the first time in nearly
a month. No customers to be professionally perky to at the
Lobster Hut, no father to bicker with, only the roadside pha-
lanx of silent spruce. Gaps in the trees reveal occulted lakes.
Ribbons of trees interwoven with the blue of lake: trees, lake,
trees, lake, the sun sieved through them. They pass Round
Lake, where she had learned to skate in the winters and swim
in the summers, although it was plagued by leeches. She had
pried them off her legs with salt, hearing the pleasing sound as
they unstuck themselves, a miniature suction, like a sigh.

They pulled in at the Mayflower Mall. Her father went to
Sobey's and she went into a drugstore. She tried to avoid the
magazine rack but ended up flicking through *Vogue*. Three
young men were rifling through a solid bay of chocolate bars in
the aisle behind her. *The mackerel he pulled off his line, you'd
never believe it. Holy Jesus Christ. That's fuckin amazin, Wally.*

25 Best-Dressed Women of the Year, pedicures, highlights.
She turned to the catwalk-report pages to scour for Caroline's
creations, although few apparel designers put jewellery on the
catwalk. The more ostentatious designers used Caroline's work:
John Galliano, Dolce and Gabbana. As always her eye was

drawn to Narciso Rodriguez's work, whose simplicity she admired, to Matthew Williamson's Indian silk colours, to Ben de Lisi's shapely plinths.

Where's the goddamn O Henry bars? Got a hangover like a marching band playing in my head. Marching band. That's a good one. What was that fuckin metal band we heard over in Port Morien. What was their name, Annihilation? I think it was Apokalypse. With a K.

Their bass player wasn't very good. He missed a couple of entries, one of them said, his voice suddenly grave, even intellectual.

She scoured the pages, cataloguing patterns and fabrics: Missoni and Pucci, whom Caroline referred to as One Idea Designers, albeit incredibly successful ones. Anya Hindmarch bags, the usual coquettish Jimmy Choos, the Zulu posture of increasingly adolescent models — her eye drank in the familiar excess of beauty, the opulent concern for form.

Eve paid for the magazine with a furtive air, as if she were buying drugs, and shoved it in her bag.

They drove on, her father directing, as Eve had never seen Anita's new house in a suburban-style crescent outside town.

"Everything brand-new, them homes," her father whistled. "D'you know the plastic wrapper was still on the bathtub when they moved in?"

Glace Bay was less scrubby than she remembered. The houses were small but prim, with neatly mowed lawns and decorative butterflies pinned on their outsides, freshly painted verandahs, spanking new gas barbecues perched on back decks.

Anita lived on Birch Crescent, actually a circle with three houses rung around its perimeter. They were in the driveway and Eve had shut off the engine before she knew it. She had no time to prepare herself and it came upon her like a gust of wind, the shock of her sister, or a version of her, standing on the doorstep.

She was so *trim*. At twenty-one, twenty-two Anita had been on her way to being a Rubenesque creature, warming bottles of milk and changing diapers, apples for cheeks, huge workaday hands gripping beings who were the flesh of her flesh. Now here she was, slim and dressed in a pale blue shirt, a tight-fitting jean jacket. Eve took in the details of Anita's face she had forgotten: the slight drift in her left eye, the faintest of scars on her chin where their father's most volatile dog had tried to take a chunk of her chin when she was a baby. She had a sophisticated haircut, crisp but wispy, accentuated by reddish highlights. She looked like a match that could be struck and lit.

From the house charged two children. Her youngest boy — she struggled to remember the name. Was it David? — gave her a frank stare.

"Are you Eve?"

"That's right."

"Are you my aunt?"

"I guess so."

David didn't look like either of his parents. He had a dreamy expression and light brown eyes. As she looked down on his questioning face, she thought, *he looks so new*. She rarely encountered children, never at work, hardly ever in her Toronto neighbourhood. Out of the corner of her eye she saw Anita throw her arms around their father, who leaned stiffly into the embrace.

"You're staying for supper, aren't you? Lloyd bought some steaks." They still hadn't greeted each other when Anita took them inside, passing through a porch stuffed with Black and Decker power drills, Bauer skate boxes, two-litre bottles of Fanta, a deflated inflatable swimming pool.

Lloyd was sitting on the chesterfield, watching TV. David yanked Eve into the room. She hadn't seen her sister's husband in eight years. He had aged well; he was still the tall, dark-haired man Anita had married after a string of rapid boyfriends, nearly twenty years ago now.

Lloyd put down the remote control and rose from the chesterfield.

"Hello there." He ran a hand through his hair, didn't quite look her in the eye. In that evasion, she knew, lived Anita's censorious judgements, years of them. Never comes to see Dad. On her own trip. Good at looking after Number One. Never even sends the kids Christmas presents. Lloyd couldn't be expected to be hail-fellow-well-met, she reminded herself, and settled into a matching awkwardness.

"How are you keeping?"

"Good, thanks. Good."

"The kids look good."

He nodded. "Kelly'll be around later. She's at soccer practice."

Of course, Kelly. How old would she be now? Fourteen?

"How is Kelly?"

"Oh, she's a wild child," Anita said from behind her in that breezy, reserved voice Eve knew Anita kept for strangers or people she didn't much like. "I keep telling her it's going to end up in tears or the maternity ward, but she won't listen."

"We're going to look at the shed," Lloyd said. "Alistair wants to borrow the power saw."

She followed Anita into the kitchen. "So what's going on with Kelly?"

"Boys, that's what's going on."

"Have you told her…?"

"Of course I've told her. I've practically taped condoms to her forehead." Anita spread her hands on the counter, as if to balance herself. "It's the same with all girls her age. I must have been like that myself, once." A distant, censorious look settled on her sister's face, passing judgement on that silly, unformed previous version of herself.

They are still present, instantly and intact, the qualities in her sister Eve has always stiffened against. The breezy, not entirely friendly, manner. Perhaps this is a mother-manner now, developed after years of coping with unceasing demands and tricky questions. Although Anita had had it as a teenager — this air of independence, of not really needing people to like her.

This quality had guaranteed her sister's social success, had drawn Anita boyfriends and a husband by age twenty.

An old thought ambushes her. *My sister is strong and I am weak.*

Eve had folded tightly into a kitchen chair, her hands screwed together on her lap. Eve had put on her best casual clothes, a pair of Joseph black trousers and a ribbed, fitted, grey V-neck cotton shirt. It has just recently become warm enough to wear sandals — a pair of medium-heeled Campers bought in Barcelona were on her feet. She made a mental note to get Llewellyn to mail her additions for her wardrobe from Toronto next week.

"You look thin," Anita said. "You look dressed up."

"Well, I'm not."

Anita still wore the tiny gold cross on her neck. The last time Eve had seen her she had pointed to it: *What's that? Are you going all religious? It's my solace,* Anita had replied.

"So, how is Dad?"

"He's not the man I remember."

"Of course he isn't." Anita leaned against the counter, fixed her gaze somewhere beyond Eve's shoulder. "That's why I want him somewhere safe. I want him out of that cabin. He shouldn't be alone at his age. I know what he went through, now, bringing us up. How hard it was for him. Kids teach you that. I can't imagine how he ever did it, a man on his own with the two of us."

She had meant to let her sister have her say about children and the sacrifices they required.

"Do you seriously think I can't empathize with him because I haven't got kids?"

Anita pursed her lips. For a second, she looked exactly like her father: that same stubborn posture that was as mental as physical, as if they had both been born for the express purpose of facing down an unpleasant question. "All I'm saying is it puts things in perspective."

Eve felt a surge of restlessness. She wanted out of this kitchen with its yellow-and-green colour scheme, out of the boxlike house, cladded with insulation against the zero winter always hovering on the horizon, out of the island with its clusters of similar houses ranged around frost-shattered rocks, tar ponds, chemical plants, glittering underground pockets of untapped coal.

"You know, there's such a thing as imagination. It means you don't have to experience everything personally in order to understand."

"It's good to see you're still patronizing. I was worried you might have changed." Those eyes again, blue and resilient, fracturing her into her component parts. *Eve uses the people around her for fuel to stoke her emotional furnaces. Eve has chosen to labour in the trenches of vanity and ornamentation because she can't face up to real life.* In a sense this reprobation wasn't personal; although Anita's suspicion of her was supposedly grounded in her character, she had no doubt that Anita might have held the same opinion if Eve had stayed, married, become pregnant, had a ten-year-old boy to drive to hockey practice by now. The exhaustion and disappointment flipped back on her, like a horse she had been riding and trying to control, but which had finally reared up and dumped her.

She couldn't imagine finding the words to tell Anita about the effort it had cost her, how she was still reeling from it: university, the carousel of bad apartments, two jobs to keep her going, up until 3 a.m., exams, solitary lunches eaten in Vietnamese restaurants, arriving at parties where she knew no-one; eventually Lew, designer beers, film festival premieres, fashion junkets to the Caribbean, the shifting, ambiguous terrain of urban friendships, people coming and going as in a giant departure lounge. *My mother is dead.* No-one asking, *Who's yer father, dear?* Negotiating with the peculiar hunger sprung up inside her, to not be herself. To be someone else, but who? To be released.

"It's time Dad was taken care of by someone," Anita was saying. "He brought us up practically alone, now he's been alone in that cabin stinking of seaweed and kerosene and God knows what else for over ten years."

"He seems happy enough."

"It's not a humane way to live." Anita said humane as human.

"He doesn't want to move."

"For the love of God, Eve, that's because he's used to it! He doesn't know anything different; he can't even remember what it's like to have company. One of these days he's going to lose his marbles. That's what's happening, isn't it?"

"I don't know if it is or not. He's absent-minded. He sleeps at odd times of day and then stays up all night. He doesn't seem to care about anything."

Anita shook her head. "That's it. He's losing it. He was never like that, not even after… after she died."

"I know."

As if by a silent accord, she and her sister had maintained the name taboo assigned to their mother. Since they had both been adults they had never spoken her name.

David came in and threw his arms around his mother casually. "Mom, can I watch TV?"

"If your father says it's all right."

David about-faced to find his father. "Dad!"

She watched as he trailed into the living room. She realized she knew nothing of these everyday negotiations of families.

She felt dizzy. She tried to get up, and then had to sit down again immediately.

Her sister watched her rise, and then wobble. She stared uncertainly for a second. Something won an internal struggle. "What's the matter?" Anita said. "Are you okay? You look pale."

The kitchen had receded to a tiny version of itself, like a doll's house. Eve felt small, too. She felt herself shrinking away to nothing.

"Here, let me get you a drink of water."

Cool water slipped down her throat.

"What's the matter?"

"I don't know. I felt like I was going to faint."

Eve couldn't say what was happening to her, only that it was something to do with what she had just witnessed: her nephew, his mother, arms, a sleepy embrace. Then another thought, rising from within her gaining mass and velocity as it surfaced: *I have never looked at Llewellyn and thought: I want your blood, I want your flesh, I want to see you in my children.*

"Well, if it isn't Herself, home for supper for a change. Kelly, come and meet your Aunt Eve."

Anita spoke as if they had never met before. It was true she hadn't seen Kelly since she was seven years old. She remembered her as a bright, inquisitive child, given to crawling all over visitors. Yet she also had seen in those strangely independent, even lonely, seven-year-old eyes that Kelly didn't seem to need the love that came to her. Once she had taken her to the corner store to get Popsicles, the summer before she left for Toronto. She remembered the look the woman at the store had given Kelly as they approached the counter. It had struck her at the time — wary, even a little afraid. The way an adult would look at another adult.

The person who walked into the room now was another version of that watchful, slightly clinical girl. She was dressed in a white blouse and blue jeans. She was slim and blonder than Anita, with her hair cut geometrically and short, almost boyish. Underneath the haircut was a replica of her mother's face.

"Hi, Aunt Eve. Hi, Mom." She put down her bag on the chair and then flopped into it.

"How was your last day of school?"

"Really boring. So what's on the agenda for this afternoon?"

"Grandpa and Aunt Eve are staying for supper."

"Eve," she said, trying not to sound annoyed. "Just call me Eve."

Kelly's eyes flickered with interest at the hint of conflict. "Want to see my room? Mom says you work in fashion."

"I make jewellery."

"She says you know fashion people."

"Well, I suppose."

Kelly's bedroom was of the studious ilk: no heartthrobs or pink frills. On her bookshelf was a complete set of *The Canadian Encyclopedia* and a Collins dictionary.

"So is that what you want to do forever, work in fashion?" Kelly asked.

"I don't know."

The girl flopped down on her bed. "I'm trying to figure out what to do, and I'm just wondering if I have to choose forever. You know, these guidance counsellors going on about how you have to make an informed choice about university, how what you do now will *affect your whole life*." She rolled her eyes.

"I don't think it works like that anymore. You can choose to do lots of things."

"So what would you do, if you could choose?"

Eve hesitated. She was unused to being asked such direct questions. Maybe this is what people meant when they said children keep you on your toes.

"Be a writer, I suppose. Write books."

"What kind of book?"

"My kind."

Kelly smiled. "That sounds great. Would you write a book about here?"

"I don't think so."

"Why not?"

"I don't know. I just wouldn't."

Anita appeared at the door. "What are you two doing?"

"We're just talking about boyfriends—" Kelly said it in a fobbing-off voice.

Eve watched her sister deflate slightly. "Supper's almost ready."

"She looks like a boy, don't you think?" Anita hissed.

"No. Not at all. Why do you say that?"

"Her hair's too short. There's girls like that in her school. You know."

"Girls like what? You mean lesbians?"

Anita shuddered. "Thank God there was none of that when we were growing up."

"Yes there was."

"Who?"

"Elizabeth McCracken, for one. Michelle Firestone."

"Were they?"

"Oh come on."

Anita frowned. "You never did anything like that, did you?"

"No," she lied.

She forgets that supper is early in Cape Breton; by five-thirty they are eating and by seven they are on their way, hugs in the driveway, she and Anita skirting a goodbye just as they had avoided a definitive hello, Lloyd hovering in the background, a strange anxiety poised on his visage, that shadowless fear seen only on manly men's faces.

When they were near the turnoff to Big Bras d'Or, her father piped up.

"I had a talk with Anita."

She glanced at him. He was looking straight ahead, his eyes fixed on the highway.

"I'll go to the hospital."

"All right."

He turned his head to look out the window. She swallowed her hurt. He was treating her as if she were his jailer, his persecutor. Then again, maybe she was.

This had been the purpose of their visit, arranged via a stark telephone conversation between Anita and herself: that Anita should take him aside, and convince him to go for tests. It was the first time since she was a teenager she had colluded with her sister against their father. Commiseration ought to have brought them closer, but instead of the huddle of a shared secret their dealings with each other remained cool and explicit.

"Why don't you invite him over for a drink?"

"Who?" Even though she knew who.

"The young feller next door. He's on his own, isn't he?"

"For a few more days."

"Well, get him over. It's the neighbourly thing to do."

"But you'll sit and talk with him for ten minutes about fishing tackle and then go to bed."

"What's the matter with that?"

His question didn't require an answer, and so they drove in this logical silence for the final fifteen miles.

"Some journalists are vultures."

Alexandre's English was eerily perfect. He had learned it by listening to the *Teach Yourself English* programs on the BBC World Service, he told Noel, and by reading the odd book he could get hold of through the Jesuit school at Gisenyi. *It ought not to be possible,* Noel thought, *such flawless if rigid English from a radio, but here was Alexandre as proof.*

"They just want to see the blood, the drama," Alexandre added. "It makes them feel more real in their own lives."

Noel nodded cautiously. He'd heard such opinions expressed before, although the humanitarian nature of his work had always allowed him to exempt himself from these punishing assessments of *Internationals,* as Alexandre called them.

They wove in and out of cloud-shredded hilltops, passing through curtains of fine rain that would suddenly and mysteriously dissolve into scythes of sunshine. The carmine soil of the country was corrugated with crops; corn, beans, sorghum and sweet potato, pine-green clumps of coffee bushes, groves of avocado studded with orange bougainvillaea. And everywhere fields of a shimmering, almost plastic, green.

Noel had never seen such an intensively farmed place. Every

parcel of land was under cultivation. This was part of the problem: too many people, not enough land. Young men needed land as status in order to marry, but they ended up labouring on other people's plots, or unemployed. Alexandre had been one of them, at least until he had been given a scholarship to technical college.

Noel had inherited Alexandre as his Kinyarwandan translator from Elise, his predecessor. Elise was in the northern part of the country now; he had been assigned the west. Alexandre would not go to the north for some reason, so he stayed with Noel.

He glanced at the profile in the passenger seat. Even Noel could see in it a classic Tutsi profile, although everything he had read suggested that Hutu, Tutsi and Twa were no longer real racial or ethnic distinctions in Rwanda, rather ones of class. Alexandre was ectomorph-thin, fairly light-skinned, with large, intelligent eyes. He had a delicate, nearly girlish quality, down to the narrow tips of his fingers and their perfect nails. There was a gentle sashay in the way he moved, interestingly combined by a carefully wrought tension, as if the thinnest cord of wire were running through him, protruding from extremities, knitting his resolve tighter. Noel always liked to work with alert, intelligent people, and he thought it absolutely true that these characteristics could be discerned in the way someone walked.

"How many years did it take to build the Chrysler Building? Could you explain to me why America continues with its embargo of Cuba? Why do you persist in growing genetically modified corn when Europe won't touch it? What is the real US external debt, and exactly how many is a trillion?" Alexandre was hungry for knowledge of the world the way others in his country were hungry for cars and television sets. He kept up this staccato fire of polite, ravenous questions until Noel had to admit he didn't know all the answers.

Alexandre had been educated at a Catholic mission school in Gisenyi, and then he managed to get the Fathers to pay for him to go to technical college in Kigali.

"I had no business being a seminary schoolboy," he explained to Noel on one of their drives. "I didn't believe in the religion for a second. I saw immediately that it was a— what is that word? It is a building word." He frowned, and then his face lurched as he retrieved it. "*Cladding*. It is a cladding for power. That's all."

Noel glanced at him; he imagined Alexandre at eighteen, wading though catechism classes, surrounded by obedient boys, keeping his silence because the charity of the Fathers was his only way out.

Alexandre beside him in the dusty Toyota, one arm kept out to wave to people. So often he pointed out things Noel himself missed. "Did you notice that old man made no mention of his family? That is because they are all alive and well. They are all killers, even his little eight-year-old nephew. He was seen with a machete, being taught how to slice open a woman's belly to see if she was pregnant."

Alexandre had been in France for two years on an expired student visa, he had told Noel. That was where he had spent the genocide, returning to Rwanda in August 1994. "I had to come back, I felt compelled," Alexandre explained. "Although now that I am back I think only of leaving again. It was the biggest mistake of my life. Now I am trapped here." At this Alexandre had smiled, as if making mistakes gave him a kind of satisfaction.

"Alexandre, my translator, is thirty-one," he began one of his emails to Rachel. They had gotten together only six months before he had to leave, and he was assiduous, at least in the beginning, about writing to her. "He's very correct, even severe. He is the last surviving member of his family, which used to number forty-two, apart from two first cousins, both under the age of ten. Alexandre is their father now.

"We go from village to village, interviewing people about the resettlement program. The government wants to change the social structure of the country and settle everyone in villages.

People here are used to living out on the hills, in little more than huts, surrounded by their fields. The government forces them to destroy their houses and move to the *imigudugu*, government-sponsored villages. It's a forced resettlement program, of course, everyone knows that. We take people's testimonies about how they are forced out of their homes. Everyone knows we are here, but there's been no direct threats yet. It's strange, I'm so unused to it — not being threatened, or at least warned. It makes me nervous.

"People here are so tired of fear. This is just another thing to fear: will the government move me before my potatoes are ripe? I met one old man whose neighbour had been fined twenty-one thousand francs — a fortune for a farmer — because he wouldn't leave his potato crop. 'At least they didn't shoot me,' he said."

Rachel listened patiently to these anecdotes during their few, hysterically expensive, long-distance phone conversations, throwing in judgements, commiserations. She never asked him how he felt. This was something of a relief, because he tried so hard not to feel anything in particular, seconding emotion to a kind of alert observant stance, to become a collector of details. He spoke with men and women, peasants and community leaders, lawyers in the city, with government functionaries. In the first three weeks he must have talked to two hundred people. A few stood out in his memory: Joseph, whose home he had built with his own hands after the genocide, and which the government ordered him to destroy; Silas, a Tutsi lawyer and one of only a third of lawyers in the entire country to have survived; Hutu brothers Gerard and Seth, almost certainly *Interahamwe*, who had both spent time in the camps at Goma; cousins Clement, Odette and Xaviera, all poor peasants. Also Antoinette, Beatrice, Emmanuel, Suzanne, Francoise, Agnes and Juvenal.

What did they dream of at night? He found himself staring imprudently at every face he saw. That man of forty or so, a typically flattened Hutu nose, what had he done? Had he hacked someone's child to death? That woman wearing the green-and-yellow *pagne*, a graceful young woman, had she taken up a hoe and bludgeoned her neighbour, or her neighbour's child? Each face had a story; each face had to be evaluated. Did the faces of their victims and neighbours come back to haunt them? He wondered, but he felt his imagination quail; he was like someone managing to arrive on the doorstep of a house but finding he lacked the strength to knock. He was exhausted by this nameless game he was playing with himself.

"No-one smiled for three months," Alexandre said. "The drunk ones, yes, they smiled. But everyone else, nothing. I never noticed it, how necessary smiles are, until they are gone."

Noel realized he had only seen Alexandre smile twice. Once was when they arrived in a village, and a young woman offered him a plate of cooked goat. "She likes me," Alexandre explained, with a rangy grin — the last thing Noel would have expected to see on such a proud, serious face. The second time was when Alexandre told him about Paris, where he worked as a waiter for a catering firm.

"One year we did a modelling party, during Paris fashion week. It was amazing. Amber Valetta, Naomi Campbell, they were all there. They noticed me. I was one of the only people in the room who was as tall and skinny as they were. They talked to me, it was as if they felt I was of their kind. Can you imagine?" This provoked a spasm of fresh laughter.

They travelled in a light blue Jeep that everyone in Rwanda recognized instantly as an international's car. Alexandre loved that Jeep, but in the end professionalism won out and he persuaded Noel to trade in the status symbol for a dusty Toyota pickup. This way no-one realized what they were up to, at least until Noel stepped out of the truck.

They drove roads lined with people walking in an orderly, industrious fashion, plastic jugs and piles of wood atop their heads. Boys of six or seven, seemingly on their own, chased hoops with sticks or walked goats attached with a rubber tether. The roads looked like wounds, gaping and ragged, although prettily lined by corridors of red-plumed celosia and breeze-block walls draped in yellow mimosa. Alexandre identified flowers like a horticulturist: the purple zebrina and cattleya orchids that studded Kigali lawns of a perfect incipient green, the giant ficus and the prickly pear. Noel told him he ought to promote himself as a horticulturist guide to Rwanda. This elicited another fugitive grin.

"Here everyone knows these flowers, although not the names in English. Look—" Alexandre pointed out the window to a field surrounding a church carpeted with flowers. "There was a massacre here. The flowers bloom twice in a season. I like the word for that: *remontant*. Flesh is a good fertilizer."

The note of awkward satisfaction in Alexandre's voice elicited a sharp look from Noel. It was not the first time he had heard this in a Rwandan's voice, of course: the sharp, tinny ring. In fact, in Noel's experience people who had survived the genocide in Rwanda tended to speak either in gelid, casually stunned tones, as if their tongues had thickened in their mouths, or they spoke with the bite he heard then, in Alexandre's voice.

He remembered these drives with Alexandre more vividly than many of the interviews he conducted. At times it seemed his task was really to drive the country and talk to Alexandre, a vaguely touristic meandering punctuated by work. *Where did you live before? Did the government make you move?* In answering his questions, people would refer to "the time before" and "the time after," omitting direct references to those three months. But he could see it forming smokily in their eyes, like the outline of a ghoul. As long as they did not speak of it directly, the ghoul would not be filled in, as if by a child drawing with crayons, and come to life again.

Alexandre followed suit; he spoke rarely of the genocide, but then, Noel reasoned, he had been in France. But one day he suddenly spoke up.

"When I returned, there were still some killings. I went north to try to find my family. I managed to get a ride with a group from UNAMIR. I felt safe, although we all knew the north was unpredictable. We drove into a village where a group of people were dancing and singing. I remember there was a strange smell. There were two young women there, celebrating with the men. I asked a woman why she killed and she told me, 'I didn't really kill. I just killed children. Or I just finished people off.' They were mostly drunk. There was a strange look in people's eyes. I cannot describe it."

"Fixed?" Noel offered. "Glassy?"

Alexandre gave a tight, brief shake of his head, as if to dislodge a fly. "Yes, but there was something else," he said. "Beneath the glass."

At the time Noel only nodded, as if he understood. But later, going over the conversation with Alexandre, he wondered: *What did he mean? Something else.*

Neurofibulary tanglings. Beta amyloids. Plaque.

Eve drank in the otherworldliness of the words, the planetary menace in them. In elegant, mournful prose, the book unveiled the mysteries of the disease.

This disease is like someone leaving a room, permanently. The victim enters and leaves every day, like a dry crew coming on shift, leaving soaked in confusion.

Her father's step: he was walking up the hill from the shed, and Eve quickly hid the book. She could hear the conversation coming before it arrived.

You're going to ruin your eyes reading in that light.

Then put some more lights in this place. It's like a dungeon in here.

She recognized the desperateness of her situation: she was silently rehearsing arguments with her father, before they actually happened. Soon she'd be talking to herself. In fact, she already was.

He came in the door and flicked on the light. "It's like a dungeon in here."

She shot up from the chesterfield. "I need to make a phone call." She went to the porch and lunged for the phone.

Hello, you've reached— what day was it? She was losing track of the days of the week. Wednesday. Five o'clock in Toronto. What was she thinking, trying him at home? She redialled, this time work.

A woman's voice answered his direct line.

"I'm looking for Llewellyn."

"He's in the studio. Can I take a message?"

"No. No message."

She could hear the frown in the woman's voice. "Are you sure?" No doubt she thought it was someone calling about a story — some tip-off, some nervous person proffering information.

It was raining, the urgent, insistent rain of a June Atlantic squall. The sound crescendoed, drumming on the roof in a relentless percussion that made it difficult to even hear herself think. She decided to drown it out with the radio, only to find it awash with the static of approaching thunderstorms.

She plucked the book from behind the chesterfield.

Imagine, now, that complex, vulnerable machine, the brain, so ephemeral by design. Memory loss, spatial disorientation, confusion—

Her father rummaging in the porch, an old, familiar sound, nondescript. A man arranging his fishing tackle, throwing out decrepit snowboots. These were the sounds of memory, even more than the synaptic pictures the book told her were the spark and blood of memories, memories that were, on the whole, made to be forgotten. Casting off from the end of the ferry, waiting for him to reel in the inevitable trout. He always caught something. Her hook remained bare, as if the fish could sense that she didn't want to hook them, didn't want them to die. Swatting mosquitoes, stinking of citronella oil. Black silent trees, they formed a cordon around their bodies: inquisitors, censors, sentries. The forest's bleak urgent whisperings. What were they trying to say? Keep your attachment to the land. Don't be just another lump of flesh, shoved into an apartment somewhere, an airplane seat, an elevator. Crusts of jellyfish, sun-baked. Or alive, gelatin flesh in the water, red, stinging. The world is full of such organisms, out to sear you.

The three of them sitting around a beach bonfire. Her father, Eve, the dog-of-the-moment, the dog's hair turning from honey to amber in the light. The moose meat in the freezer, the canned peas that tasted subtly of vinegar. Baths in a steel tub parked in front of the stove when the pipes froze, kettles and kettles of hot water.

Yes, this was memory, and it was alive now as the day she had lived it. But what use was it to her now, or him?

It is night and as usual he carries no flashlight; like his grandmother before him, who walked for hours through the woods accompanied only by a .22 and a flask of rum, he doesn't need light to see in the dark. He carries fire inside him; its pointed, rigid grandeur lights his way. Sometimes he pretends he is a moose, young, thickening in the night. His leggy, uncoordinated gait, saucers for knees. There are a number of young bull moose in the woods around here; he stumbles upon them from time to time, or they stumble upon each other, then crash away.

The alkaline scent of bog. An old harmony in his ears: the scuff of loose gravel, crack of twigs as bobcats and raccoons flee his path. By his age childhood should be a distant land, but lately it has floated back to moor itself just offshore his consciousness. He can see its outline against the sky, an iceberg, an unhinged islet.

He grew up in a house not far away, but on the coast, the open ocean, so different from the cosseted lee of the lakes. The Atlantic: bulleting rain, harassed waves like bucking horses, garlanded by caramel foam. He slept in a bed warmed with a brick steeped in the fire, wrapped in his mother's Gaelic reprimands:

amathan (crazy person), *d'unth a veeach* (shut your mouth), *gomach* (silly, unschooled person). In the winter he lay in bed and blew breath-clouds into the air until he fell asleep.

Now those years were coming back on him, unpacking themselves like long-neglected heirlooms. Lately a switch had been thrown somewhere inside him and suddenly his childhood was fresh and accessible, as if he were about to live it again.

He had very few photographs of his mother, but these days he could see her more clearly than ever, as if she were back here on earth with him. Her thin, slippery hair, honey-blond, which Anita seemed to have inherited, her generous mouth, so unusual in a land of thin-lipped people, their faces at forty already lined like battlefields. His mother had looked like a teenager until the end. *Pixie*, his father had called her with that convulsive mix of tenderness and possession and sex-shame he remembered from men of his father's generation. She was so young when she died. He had already been granted ten years longer in this world.

Where was she now? She had gone away, and she wasn't coming back. Just as his wife was gone. It had happened on a Friday and every Friday, it still hit him. He had to lie down and go to sleep; it was the only way to disperse the black sun that blotted out the bearable cascade of moments that his life had become. He reached for sleep as his only antidote for the incurable sickness of being himself, of being one of the leftovers, the stay-behinds. The sky a map of storms, taciturn nights. Sometimes he stayed up all through them, falling asleep into the curve of morning, no company to dilute his preoccupations.

He stands a half-mile from a similar house to the one he had grown up in. He hides in the hem of darkness thrown by spruce, the house standing white and stark against the night, caught in the moon's pewter gleam.

Kerosene burns hotter than any other flammable. A little in a small space, and before you know it you have four hundred degrees Fahrenheit. When he was four years old he had knocked a lamp over and nearly burnt down the house. His mother had beaten him until she broke his rib. She took him to the doctor the next day, of course, guilty. *Doctor, I think he fell on a hoe in the fields. He was out playing rough. You know boys.*

At the time he thought his world had collapsed; the person he trusted most on earth had turned into a terrifying force. Later he realized how frightened she had been, to come home from the garden and find the curtain in flames, his older brother — who was supposed to be watching over him — standing helplessly watching it burn, and the neighbour's child who she looked after from time to time asleep upstairs.

She never beat him again, but she did patrol that scalding righteous terrain of mothers. No, his wasn't one of those terrible backwoods stories he had sometimes heard his grandparents talking about, in the days before social workers and telephones. Children locked up in sheds, daughters used for sexual relief, starving children on deepwoods farms no-one even knew existed. These people appeared on the earth, were ground into stone, and then disappeared.

The white house is an abandoned holiday home. The windows have the mute, pleading look of the left-behind. They said, *Don't leave me here.* Oh, but they did leave. The children sold the houses via Internet real estate sites and stayed in Manitoba, Ohio, Ontario. The summer people shut the door and never came back; look at them in their air-conditioned SUVs, on highways heading into the bulk of the continent, leaving dishes unwashed in the sink, caged birds to die of thirst.

It is Christmas Eve. Snow had fallen earlier in the night, and then the temperature dropped. Sharp winds swipe across the land.

"We're just going down to the gas station to get some cigarettes."

Her mother's voice is sharp and explicit through the floor in
the old house, the white one across the lake that now belongs to
a couple of retired teachers.

Eve is eight years old. She is lying on the floor in the hall
upstairs, peering down through the register, a hole cut in the ceiling to allow heat from the kitchen stove to rise to the second
floor. The register has a grille that can be slid open or closed.
When it is open, she can see and hear quite well.

Downstairs a party is in progress. Fifty, a hundred, people
entering and leaving, stamping feet, shaking the astringent fume
of sub-zero cold from their clothes. For a long time, before her
mother's statement, this is all she hears: doors opening and closing: the kitchen, ribbons of sound, "Christmas Ceilidh" on
CJCB, someone tuning up a fiddle, a tapestry of shouts and
laughs.

"Are you sure?" There is a shimmer of uncertainty in her
father's voice.

Her mother is already dressed for outside: she wears her
patchwork sheepskin coat, Anita's mittens, suede winter boots,
black seal fur earmuffs. She turns, looks around. She seems to
stay there for a fraction of a second longer than necessary. There
is another man next to her. Who is he? His voice is familiar, but
Eve can only see the top of his head. He has a small skull, the
skin seems pulled tight across it, and vivid black hair, like the
pelt of some vital animal.

Three heads: her father, her mother's, a neat part on her skull;
the dark-haired man. She has seen him around, from time to
time, since she was very small.

No-one moves, or says anything. Then she watches her father
watch them go.

CHAPTER 8

"Do you know what this is?"

Noel dropped a charcoal-coloured object in her hands. It had the traumatized look of substances formed by extremes of temperature or pressure.

"Petrified wood. Maybe basalt lava."

"That's what I thought. But it can't be."

"Why not?"

"Because I found it on the beach."

"It's from the ferry," her father said, from behind them. "It's a peg that held the wooden decks together."

Noel sat opposite her father on the benches against the table — her father had never got round to buying chairs — their backs bent into conversation, a bottle of moody scotch between them.

"Did you hear they're going to tow the boat away at the end of the summer?" her father said.

"You're kidding." She found it impossible to imagine Clam Harbour without the boat.

"I'll be glad to see the back of it."

"Why?"

"Because it reminds me of Jimmy." He turned to Noel. "My uncle was the captain of that ferry for twenty years," he explained. "He never got over it when they shut it down."

"Did you take the ferry much?" Noel asked.

"Sure I did. I used to even go across to do my shopping at the Seal Island store. It was cheaper and faster than going into Indian Bay."

This gave her father an entrée into a languid, meandering treatise she had heard before, related in subtly different versions:

about legendary blizzards and winters when you could walk from Seal Island point to Indian Bay across the ice, winds that killed grown men, scattering them across the ice like matchsticks, a time when there were no rescue services, no highway patrols, when people had risked their lives just for a bit of company, following a spruce-bough-marked path across fickle ice just to sit in a neighbour's kitchen, then getting halfway back across the ice and finding it unstable… "What to do?" her father interjected, encouraged by Noel's eyes, which were wide with the stark simplicity of pioneer dilemma. "Do I go back, and let my animals freeze or die of thirst, or do I keep going and risk death with each step?" Her father spoke of grown men crying from the cold, how the marine tears refused to freeze on their faces despite the wind-chill temperature of minus fifty-five. Her father always finished his stories of past hardships this way — with grown men crying from frustration, or pain.

Noel obliged with intelligent questions. *When did the lakes stop freezing? Why were island farmers using horse and plough well into the Seventies? What happened when people were lost on the ice — did you go out looking for them, or was it too dangerous to try to recover the body?*

Eve stood against the stove, her back against its cold surface. Noel's curiosity seemed genuine, although with a certain intellectual tinge. She had the impression he would find some use, in the future, for the knowledge her father was imparting.

Her father stood up. "I'm just played out. I'm going to have a little lie down on the chesterfield, if you don't mind." He shucked off his boots and fell asleep instantly, two arms and a leg flung over the side of the sofa. Almost immediately his snores rumbled around the living room.

Noel laughed. "Your father can really snore. Do you want to come over to… to the house." He smiled. "I can't call it *my* house."

"I know. I still think of it as John Rory and Eileen's, even though they've been dead ten years."

They closed the door behind them and stepped into a ripe velvet darkness. The razored shapes of spruce trees were silkscreened black against an indigo sky.

"I've got a bottle of wine open." Noel grimaced. "It seems I've always got a bottle of wine open these days."

"I never think of Americans as big drinkers."

"Well, there's two hundred and sixty million of us. I'm sure a few of us can keep pace."

"I suppose I shouldn't generalize."

"Oh no, go on. Generalizing's fun."

For the first time she heard the sharp corrective note in his voice, the mean bite of sarcasm. She looked at the ground for the rest of their walk; she even thought, for a second, she would cry off, find an excuse to say she had to get back to the cabin. You have to be more robust, she instructed herself. This is a sharp-minded man who won't tolerate generalizations. You're up to this. Stand up to him.

As soon as they entered the house she felt more at ease. She surveyed the kitchen, mentally airbrushing in details of how it had been in John Rory and Eileen's day, tacking up the gas station calendars, the ladybug-shaped oven mitt, the stuffed owl that had looked on hawkishly from its perch above the door.

It was a bereft kitchen. The wounded silence of houses left empty for too many years seemed to become an actual frequency, an expectant hum. Empty bedrooms, their beds unlain-in for years, the plain furniture, ribbed curtains, worn floorboards. John Rory and Eileen's house had the evacuated eroticism of the museums she had visited on school trips as a child — former houses of eminent judges and premiers, Haliburton House, Uniacke House — with their canopied beds, the mattresses straw, sheer curtains swinging in the breeze. Children had been conceived in these beds, these rooms where busloads full of bored teenagers now shuffled.

"You're right," she said. "This house seems to expect something of you."

"I know. I wish I knew what it wants."

The kitchen table was carpeted with photographs. They seemed to have been ordered into piles and sequences, like the unfinished games of solitaire her father sometimes left on the table. Noel casually flipped a notebook closed, but not before she caught a glimpse of pages covered in spindly handwriting.

"I was just thinking how good it is to know your neighbours," Noel said. "It's something we've lost in a lot of places."

"Here you know your neighbours whether you like it or not."

He poured them each a glass of wine and they sat in the briefest silence, long enough for her to rehearse appropriate questions. *How is your girlfriend? What do you do? Who are those people in the photographs?* She struggled to arrive at a question with the requisite combination of reserve and curiosity.

He twirled the stem of his wineglass between his fingers. They shot each other quick smiles, mutual apologies for silence.

"I've been meaning to ask you, he began, what is your family's story?"

"Their story?"

"Their origins. How they came to be here."

"Oh. That. We don't really know. My ancestors weren't the sort of people to keep genealogical records."

"What kind of people is that?"

"Illiterate people. Poor people." She could hear the defensiveness in her voice and modified her tone. Some had been evicted from their land in the Clearances; I don't think they wanted to come here at all. It took people a couple of generations to realize they really were here, forever.

"That sounds familiar."

"Does it?"

He nodded. "I've worked with internally displaced people. Often they're ashamed of having been compelled to leave, as if it were their fault."

"It's true, they did seem to feel ashamed of something, the older generation, my father's uncles. But it was unspoken, I could never figure out what it was, exactly." She thought of the sleek dark animal she had seen in the eyes of her relatives, like a scavenger disappearing around a corner. That is what it had been: shame.

Noel shifted in his chair and laughed, but it was an uneasy, sharp sound. "I'm not a light conversationalist at the best of times. I think I've spent too much time on my own, the past couple of weeks. I thought it wasn't affecting me, but it is." He shot her an apologetic smile.

"I once spent a week completely on my own in the middle of nowhere. At the time I thought I was fine, but later I realized I'd come close to losing it."

"Where was that?"

"Colombia."

He looked surprised. "You've been to Colombia?"

"I travel a lot for work."

"What do you do?"

"I work for a jeweller. A bespoke jeweller. Well, she's a kind of jeweller to the stars."

"What do you do for her?"

"*Did*. I had to quit in order to come back here." As she said it she realized it hadn't quite sunk in: she would not be going back to Caroline's studio in the rambling Annex house that she inherited from her parents and used as a live/work space, where she lived with her painter husband, two children and assorted genial dogs. "I'm a designer, I sourced stones for her," she elaborated. "Booked advertising, fashion shoots, kept her personal diary. In return I learned to make my own work."

"But you haven't gone into business for yourself?"

She shook her head. "I'm not sure I want to."

"You must miss it. There's nothing like that here."

She was startled by his empathy; it was the first time since she had come back that anyone had asked about her work. Her eyes very nearly welled up with tears. Yes, she missed it. She even missed the stylists who came to visit Caroline's studio, groomed girls talking of their intricate regimes: exfoliation, lipids, biohydration. These girls knew the location of the secret Prada outlet on the outskirts of Florence; they called from cellphones in breathless voices in between trips to Mexico or Thailand where they were "prospecting for ideas"; seemingly delicate, they possessed the hard mineral allure of women who knew how to unearth good apartments in Manhattan, who insisted upon chain-smoking even though they weren't actually addicted.

Eve went on. "I've got absolutely no background in design, but Caroline trusted me for some reason."

"I can imagine why someone would trust you."

She looked up sharply. There it was again, the gaze: he was looking at her warmly, appreciatively. But behind this wall of pleasantness she caught it, that dark flash that came and went in less than a second.

"That's why I was in Colombia," she explained. "Some of the best emeralds in the world are brokered through Bogotá."

For two weeks she follows Caroline around Bogotá, poolside appointments in the city's two five-star hotels, air-conditioned suites, the *Esmeraldas*, the uniformly female emerald-brokers. No-one is quite sure why the business is dominated by women, but there they are almost without exception, young and attractive, controlling the not entirely risk-free business of brokering jewels. She needs emeralds because Caroline's next season collection will be entirely green: mossy Tahitian pearls, jade, emeralds. Her reward for trawling Bogotá for two weeks is a break in a house belonging to the cousin of some Colombian friend of Caroline's. Caroline herself will go back to a Toronto winter.

The house clings to a heavily forested hillside overlooking the Caribbean. There she sits on a rickety porch watching anvil-shaped clouds troop across catapulting skies, wading through days that are half sunshine and half rain. The sun is poured vertically from on high and falls on her head, nearly knocking her out. The tropical night is so viscous she is sure it is made from solid matter.

She had asked Caroline to borrow the cabin because she had wanted to be alone, and it works. She feels not merely alone, she is the last person on a contingent earth, abandoned to stare out at the world from a tilting angle.

On the third day she decides to drive into the nearby beach town, if only to verify that some Armageddon hasn't taken place and left only her behind, a solitary survivor, like a beach crab.

She drives through banana *fincas*, the sea a long blue scar on the far side of palm groves and banana trees. She parks on the single dirt street of the village. It is a tourist place where Colombians and a few backpacking foreigners take beach holidays. Dusty palms arrange themselves around squares. The white paint on the park's benches has soured to the colour of gasoline. As she arrives the local evangelical church has just let out and musicians carrying ancient amplifiers and electric guitars hover around the church door. Shy little girls, each wearing a dress of increasingly hyperbolic colour — lemon, cerise, ruby — scatter like confetti at her approach.

She turns a corner and follows the wispy sound of a broom moving across a bare floor. She sees a small man, tanned and dressed only in shorts, waving the broom across the ground.

They speak first in Spanish, just long enough to establish that neither of them are natives. Still holding onto his broom, he introduces himself. *I'm Hash.* He holds out his hand.

She takes it in her own. It is small but strong.

Hanif, actually, but people call me Hash. Not because I do it. He smiles.

Where are you from?

Surinam, originally. My mother was Dutch and my father Indian, as in East Indian. But I live in New York for half the year. My friend owns the restaurant. I come down to work the winters.

He wears long brown hair piled at the back of his head, where it is fastened with a woman's tortoiseshell clip. He has an ageless, delicate face with two brown eyes sitting wide-sprung within its small bones. He is genderless, pretty as a deer.

As they talk she becomes aware of a desultorily current of desire coming off her, wafting and floury, like the fume of noodles from the restaurant behind them.

What are you doing this evening? he asks.

Nothing much. I'm staying in someone's cabina about five miles from here.

He nods, still holding his broomstick like a sentry guarding entry to a joyous city. *Why don't you come back for dinner about seven?* He says this with such easy friendship that she simply agrees.

She goes back out into the town, a collection of muddy sand-and-gravel streets scarred by potholes, the wooden houses on stilts as protection against chiggers and sandflies.

It is four o'clock; one hour to go until a fifteen-minute twilight, then darkness like a heavy velvet curtain dropped by the gods. What had at noon seemed a sharp yellow or a lime green has now faded to pale sorbet hues. She feels melancholy creeping into her bones. She jumps into her rental car and drives back to the cabin. She won't go into Hash's restaurant for dinner. She will stay in the cabin and cook for herself the only food she has: two eggs, some rice, some tinned black beans that she will fry in two careful drops of Tabasco sauce.

That night in the restaurant there are few other customers so Hash sits down beside her.

I didn't think I'd see you again.

Why not?

Just a feeling I had. I'm glad I was wrong. He smiles, but not in an ingratiating way. He is simply happy for company, she thinks. This is what happens in places like this. People will make do with anyone.

So how do you like it here?

It's a relief to get out of New York for the winter. Although I miss it. The nightlife, especially.

From the table she watches as two blond women stagger from what looks to be the local bad-boy watering hole. They are followed by a little girl, also blond, dressed only in a pair of shorts worn over a diaper and little red rubber boots.

Hash catches her looking at them. *Germans. They've been here all winter. Something terrible happens to people who stay here long-term. They just let go.*

Let go?

Of life. They have a fantasy of living in a beachside cabin and running a local café, but eventually they realize there's absolutely nothing for them to do. Except drink, of course. You can always drink. I see them at eight-thirty in the morning with beers in their hands. Without routines they just end up drunks, drug addicts, crazy people.

Who knows? Maybe it would happen to me too.

He gives her an intensely lovely look, poised between rebuke and generosity. *I don't think so.*

Is this going to happen? she wonders. *Is this really me? Flaccid encounters on the peripheries of the world, significance gathering around their edges before dispersing, like smoke.*

She takes him home to her cabin that night. There is nothing wrong with him, she tells herself — he is friendly, smart, balanced — but even so, she is aware that what she most needed was company, rather than his company. She has never taken such a decision before, but she wants to feel another body on hers, to be reminded of her actual dimensions. Four days alone in the cabin have made her feel she has expanded, boundaryless, to fill the whole world.

I didn't come looking for this, you know, she tells him, after it is over.

That's okay. She understands too late that it hasn't occurred to him to judge her. He probably falls into these kinds of situations all winter long, she tells herself. This is not the kind of place where your every action has to be dissected and understood.

Hash goes back to his restaurant and she refrains from going back into town. She feels a subtle form of guilt that she has acted without real desire or urgency; it seems an insult, both to him and to her.

The remaining evenings in the cabin she drinks three beers alone, in quick succession. The evening reveals a blood landscape: the mountains turn carmine and the sea viridian. She swims through a watery solitude, not at all unpleasant, hours spent watching pale lizards dart in and out of cracks in the walls.

She heard Noel's voice travelling toward her from a long way away, thin and strained, as if it were being forced through a tunnel.

"What's the matter?"

"Pardon?"

"I think I lost you there."

"I don't know," she said. "I haven't thought of it in so long, what happened there, and tonight it's here, suddenly. Out of the blue."

He nodded. "Memory is like that. It ambushes you."

He was a peculiar American, she decided. She had always thought Americans essentially naïve, even seemingly worldly, well-travelled ones — the earnest product of a toddler culture which insisted on personal safety at any cost, on having everything its way. She could identify this as a well-rehearsed stereotype but clung to it. Even if she had to admit that Noel had a real ruefulness to him, that he carried a weight.

"Why did you spend a week on your own?" he asked.

"I wanted to be alone for a few days, to think things through. I don't even know what it was I wanted to think about." She shook her head. "As far as I can tell, realization is clandestine. It happens without you being aware of it."

She took a gulp of wine, tried to drown her sense of having revealed herself with it.

"*Clandestine.*" He smiled, a sad, private smile.

Her eyes drifted to the photographs on the table. They looked as if they had been hastily shoved into a pile. She could just make out a chessboard of dark and light faces against hills the colour of bruises.

"Where is this?"

"Rwanda."

Questions immediately presented themselves: *Were you there during the genocide? Did you know what was going to happen?*

"So, you were telling me about why you came here, to the cabin."

She was about to protest his shifting the conversation back to her life, but then reminded herself about a promise she had recently made — a bargain really — forged through her struggles with Lew: that she would permit people to divulge the exact amount of information they cared to reveal.

"You must think it a strange place to live. It *is* strange," she laughed. "It's like going back in time. My father doesn't notice how out of context it is. No TV, barely any electricity, never mind email. Sometimes I don't think he's even in this century."

"Do you have brothers and sisters?"

"My sister Anita. She lives in Glace Bay."

"Oh yes, you mentioned her to me that day you found the horse. You went to visit her."

"Yes." She avoided his probing gaze. She was never sure what people would see in her eyes when she spoke about Anita. "She's older," she said. "We're not close. In fact, we're not on the same wavelength at all."

"That can happen in families."

"But not in yours."

Noel flinched slightly and then recovered himself. "It's true," he said, laughing. "I'm that enemy of the therapeutic industry. I have two prosperous, emotionally balanced parents who brought me up in a loving and stable environment."

"And what do they think of you, your parents?"

His eyes narrowed into an intense, transparent stare that seemed to reach inside her, then pass right through her, then carried on to an unknown destination faraway.

"You know, that's the best question I've had in such a long time. I'm not sure I know. I just wish..." he paused. "I wish they would reveal more of themselves. Sometimes they behave more like role models than individuals. They are still Mom and Dad, still trying to protect us. It drives me crazy."

"Protect you from what?"

"You name it: adultery, hypocrisy, Republicanism — which are of course synonymous." He laughed, then abruptly gathered himself, sat up in his chair with a crack. "Then again who am I to judge my parents? I'm just one of those arrogant, ungrateful kids who when they reach thirty feel they can see their parents' mistakes without the handicap of having made them yet themselves." He crossed his legs, and then uncrossed them. Finally he sat squarely in his chair, his arms folded unhappily across his chest.

"Actually, I think my family romanticizes itself. There's too much love. I find it claustrophobic. Like we're being peddled a lie. But I'm not sure who's selling it, or for what purpose." He turned turbulent eyes on her. A dark cascade tumbled through them.

"I wish my family had an emotional life." She meant it as a joke, however weak, a strained attempt to lighten the tone. But the acute, brooding look in his eye only condensed, until it was a hard, solid substance.

"Every family does," he countered.

"I'm not so sure. In my family we've always seemed to subsist on silence and a reluctant kind of tolerance. I call it the emotional subsistence diet."

This elicited a reluctant, respectful smile. Why was she insisting on *bon mots*? Faced with the struggle taking place inside Noel's eyes, she felt insubstantial, even a traitor.

"You seem to get on all right with your father."

"We're strangers trying to be familiar. That's why we end up trading shouts so quickly. It's like bad theatre. Something has to happen to break the tension of having to be friendly and at ease with someone you don't know at all."

"Maybe you could just admit that you're strangers."

"But there's a defeat in that for both of us. We lived virtually alone together in that cabin for ten years, and we were like two solitudes. We still are. How can that happen?"

She was betraying her father, her sister — her only family in the world — to a seasonal neighbour who would think, *How sad. I'm so glad I live a double-car-garage life, far from the emotional privations of this place.* But the exhilaration was too powerful. It had been years, possibly forever, since she had been able to talk to anyone like this, so that she opened her mouth and it emerged, effortlessly: the *truth*.

"Where is your mother?"

"She's dead."

He dipped his head, very slightly. "What was she like?"

"What do you mean?"

"Was she like you?"

"I don't…," she paused, squaring herself up to this bare question. No-one had asked it of her, ever. Not even her husband. Yet it had a familiar, disused feel: like the kitchen, it pleaded *what's taken you so long?*

The sound of a distant but unmistakable crash came from the direction of the cabin.

"Christ." She stood. "My father."

As she fled down the drive Noel called to her, "Rachel's arriving Sunday."

She turned and saw an expression, surprise or consternation, flash across his face. She recognized it immediately: *Why am I telling her this?*

She waved and called, "Okay." It was all she could think to say.

She found her father standing in a pool of broken glass, plucking shards off the floor with his bare hands. A drop of blood fell to the floor.

"Jesus thing just slipped out of my hands."

"Stop picking up that glass." She took him by the wrists, bloodying her own fingers. "I said *stop it*."

"All right, all right." He jerked his hands out of her grip. "It's just a bit of glass, for Christ's sake."

If she couldn't leave her father alone for two hours, how was she going to keep up her job, or go into town, without rushing back expecting to find the cabin in flames, or that he'd poured boiling water on himself?

Later, when she had applied Band-Aids and he had gone off to bed, she ran her mind over the time she had spent with Noel as if searching for a hidden pattern. They had talked elliptically, as if they were each drawing circles around the other, like that toy she had had as a child with coloured pens and a compasslike contraption that drew endlessly intersecting spirals.

She had been there for only two hours, but in Noel's company time streamed past, had moved as it should, for once. She was so accustomed to feeling trapped in its folds, or that time was carrying on outside her, spiriting experience and memory out of her reach.

She found herself imagining his face in all its possible expressions: Noel in an airport departure lounge, a transitional, boarding-pass face. Even then he would be handsome, she would notice him from across the corridor, where she sat in another glassed-in cubicle on her way to another destination. Might that face turn authoritarian, punishing? Would he use his good looks as a cover for severity? Was he that kind of man who thought women should be tripped up, if at all possible, that they were a code that needed cracking?

No. She would not wonder. With one hand she mentally quashes her interest. She is getting better at these tactics, although they haven't come naturally to her: how to erect emotional boundaries, staking out the territory of what you feel and will not feel. She believed one of the few issues on which people divided neatly into camps was that the world was full of people who on the one hand are prepared to fall hopelessly, pointlessly in love, and those who are not.

She busies herself clearing up, doing the dishes, replacing the candles she has let burn down to the wick — anything to get away from the gnawing rebuke that had sprung up in her mind. She has told Noel about her father, practically asked for his help; she has confessed her failure to get along with her sister. She is someone who gives everything away with the exhausted zeal of the courier who has galloped miles to deliver his message. *Here, I've been holding this all night. Please take it off my hands.*

Meanwhile Noel had revealed, only vaguely, the nature of his work. He said nothing about his girlfriend, and she hadn't found the largesse within her to ask. She envied his circumspection. She couldn't help feeling that at her age there is something undignified about reaching out to strangers, that now, in her thirties, she should have enough personal power that others would simply be drawn to her. Noel has this quality, and she suspects that he is younger than she is.

She resignedly consigns Noel to that category of man she admires but who is unlikely to return the favour. There will always be something wrong with men's admiration of her, some very slight thing will be displeasingly out of kilter. She has had to deal with this less since being married, of course, but she remembers it well enough, subtle rejections that only revealed themselves as such in retrospect, the men who have a broken-wing complex, always searching out delicate, emotionally fragile women to protect, whose interest in her was neutralized by their discovery of her mental toughness, of her backwoods capableness.

Then there are men who like dark horses, unpredictable women, fighters, their dismay when they finally arrived at Eve's soft, sweet emotional core. Then those boyish, gorgeous men who can only flirt and rebuke, tilting between them awkwardly;

their looks have always protected them from having to make an effort toward understanding. Then there are the men who want female sympathy and who invariably choose wives who are teachers or nurses, some nice wifely occupation — not doormat women by any means, but who are fundamentally caring, for whom being mothers is so important that they will allow themselves to be used as cover while their husbands pursue their real emotional lives elsewhere. All these categories of men have always dismissed Eve easily or with difficulty, eventually and after a painful *learning curve* — as one of them termed it — because she evidently did not fit. She does not fit, she is becoming to understand, any category of woman.

She couldn't yet identify Noel's place in her taxonomy of men. She does harbour an untidy, guilty suspicion that Noel might be one of those jackdaw people who gather golden eggs from the lives of others, who take a voyeuristic and ever so slightly avaricious intrigue in the colourful lives of margin-dwellers or bohemia like herself. She already senses his slightly anthropological interest in people who haven't followed the rules, while remaining fundamentally conventional himself. This is a combination she has encountered before, too. These men were usually academics, professors of sociology, or politics; their subtle flaw was to appear as if they understood emotion, to really put on a good show in this department, but really they were mysteriously unable to make the transition from mental to emotional understanding.

Although, really, what is she doing, indulging in these self-protective categories, this corrosive brand of suspicion, these dismaying mental postures and their world-weary, heartless messages? She knows all too well how excessive knowingness can rob life of spontaneity and paradox and risk. And when these things were gone, what is left? Safety, and a certain depleted satisfaction at not having been fooled, or of having revealed your needs.

No, she doesn't want to agonize over Noel, or anything for that matter. Enough agony would come in the shape of whatever was the matter with her father. She has arrived at the point in life where she no longer welcomes challenges, struggles, setbacks. She needs an amnesty from emotional storms, from identity crises and professional dilemmas, even from memory. She wants only to be quiet, balanced for a while on this edge of a racing ocean, safe in this harbour of elsewhere.

CHAPTER 9

Rachel was asleep the moment her head hit the headrest. Noel wanted to wake her forty-five minutes later when they began the climb over the mountain so that she could admire the view of St. Ann's Bay and the Englishtown ferry, but then he reminded himself that she would have plenty of opportunities over the next two months to take in the landscape.

Noel stole a look at her sleeping face. They had been separated many times over the past five years, often for much longer than the two-and-a-half weeks that had passed since Rachel had seen him off in their driveway. No matter how long they were separated, every time he re-encountered Rachel he found he had forgotten some detail or other of her face: the eyebrows so thin and arched, even slightly artificial, although the truth was she never had to pluck them, her fine, judgemental nose, inherited from her Romanian mother, her thin but mobile lips. Rachel was one of those lucky people who had been allocated a face perfectly suited to her character: intelligent, calm, methodical. Still, it perturbed him, how every time he saw her after an absence it was like chancing upon an acquaintance.

She wore a moss-coloured linen shirt she had bought from a high-end women's clothing catalogue, and salmon-coloured linen trousers whose wide legs couldn't disguise her slimness. Her nails were neatly lacquered with peach-coloured semitransparent polish. On her feet she wore those thin-soled, supple loafers that were marketed for some reason or other as women's driving shoes. They made Noel think of druids or djinns — powerful spirits whose talent it was to walk softly.

There was something so womanly about Rachel, and this was part of her appeal for him. He thought himself an imaginative person, but had to confess he was mystified by what it would be like, to be a woman. Surely everything would feel different: food would taste more pungent perhaps, sleep would taunt him — all the women he had known had been light sleepers, and he suspected this of being a cunning biological trick to train them for the years of broken sleep that lay ahead as mothers. Certainly, television-show choice was distinct, and other mysterious miniatures of life like perfume, eyeliner, tights. Rachel was his partner and his friend, but she was also an envoy from the inscrutable world of femaleness, and he assumed that the trill of fear and wonderment he felt for the details of her existence was a crucial part of what had kept men and women together for millennia, bolted to each other by subtle, interlocking fascinations.

Rachel awoke with a start when they pulled in the driveway.

"Sorry I dropped off. You know flying always exhausts me." She grabbed her camel-coloured purse — nubuck, Noel thought it was called, and stepped delicately out of the car. She shivered. "It's cold."

"It's much cooler up here."

"Thank God. The heat in the city is unbearable."

"Did you bring sweaters?"

Rachel yawned and stretched, revealing a map of creases in her shirt and trousers. "Yeah, I brought that white cable-knit one. You know, the one that makes me look like I'm an L.L. Bean catalogue model." She paused to sniff the air. "Hey, great air." She waited for him to open the door.

"It's open."

"You mean you didn't lock it?"

"There's no need."

"Noel, anyone could drive up here while you're away and steal your laptop."

"No they couldn't. The neighbours would see them."

"What would they do, rush out of their houses and blockade the road as the thief tries a getaway?"

He smiled. "You'll see."

He gave her a tour of the house. She said nothing to the hard-lipped figures in the photographs in the upstairs hall. "I love this cream colour," she said. "Don't you think we should paint the floorboards at home?"

"When we have floorboards."

"I know. It's the first thing I'll do when I get back."

He saved his surprise for the last. He went to fetch the rod and hook and shook down the folding stairs leading to the attic.

"What's this?"

"You have to come up and see."

"I don't want to get dust on my pants."

"I've cleaned it, it'll be okay. Come on up."

They stood in the attic where he and Eve had shaken out the sheets. The image presented itself to him whole, in that gustlike manner of things not thought about since the original moment. He recounted Eve's story of Malcolm and how he watched the curtains fluttering in the breeze.

"Why did you have to tell me that?" she said.

"Why not?"

"Now I'll think about some huge man with cerebral palsy or whatever lying next to me when I'm working. I'll be spooked out."

"I thought you'd want to know about the history of the house."

Rachel was idly running her fingertip along the windowsill. Noel only just stopped himself from saying, *I dusted everything.*

They descended the stairs and he folded them away. Back in the kitchen he felt pleased. She liked the house.

Rachel followed him into the kitchen. "You know, this house really is a bit creepy."

"Why do you say that?"

"Maybe I haven't spent enough time in old farmhouses. You've been okay here, on your own, haven't you?"

"There's nothing that goes bump in the night, anyway." He said this in the voice he habitually used to reassure Rachel, hard and rational. Any hope or wonderment he felt about the house had left it.

"But have you been happy here?"

Noel knew this question was camouflage for another, more problematic one: *Have you been happy here without me?*

"I would have rather had you here with me, but apart from that it's been okay." He was going to say something about Eve and her father, about having had company if he wanted it, but a vague doubt stopped him.

Rachel looked at him closely, as she always did when he offered the most diplomatic explanation possible. *I can see why you've ended up in your line of work,* she'd said once, after some similar evasion. It was the only acidic thing he could remember her saying. Sarcasm didn't suit her, and she knew it and employed it lightly or not at all.

"Here, I saved something for you." She fished a piece of paper from the nubuck purse. Rachel was always picking out bits of texts and quotes for him to read. She saved them in a file on her computer called Quotable Quotes.

He took the piece of paper from her and laid it on the table. "How about some coffee?"

"Read it now."

He picked it up. "'Love,' said Picasso, 'must be proved by facts and not by reasons. What one does is what counts, and not what one had the intention of doing.'" He gave her back the piece of paper. "That's good."

"So what have you been doing here all alone?"

"Just what I told you on the phone. Reading, staring at the horizon. Going for walks. It took a while to figure out how everything in the house worked. I wanted everything to be ready for you."

Rachel touched her hand to her temple and winced.

"What's the matter?"

"Just a headache. I've never had to read so much in my life as in the past two weeks. I think I need to get glasses. I'm convinced I'll have to retake at least one exam. Whose idea was it to become a lawyer again?"

He smiled. This was a routine of theirs. "Yours, I believe."

"Oh yes, my bright idea. My head is so stuffed full of this case and that case sometimes I think I'm going to lose it. All so that my parents can die happy."

"They'll probably still complain about your GPA."

She didn't laugh, or respond. He wondered if he had hit too close to the bone. Rachel's parents were high-achieving émigrés who, rather typically, possessed a peculiar mixture of intellectual toughness and utter vulnerability in the face of anything that even faintly smacked of failure. Rachel, their only child, hadn't taken the route they had planned for her quickly enough for their liking, choosing to enter law school at the advanced age of twenty-five after working for a number of charities. It was at a fundraising event for one of these charities where she and Noel had met.

She stood at the window. "So this is Clam Harbour. I pictured it as bigger. You know, like a little town."

"You'll like Indian Bay. There's a yacht club and some good restaurants."

She nodded absently. "I know, you told me on the phone there was nothing here. Maybe it's the name; it sounds quaint, but it looks so… so basic."

"Do you want some wine? I bought some Cabernet Sauvignon. It's from Ontario. I had no idea they made wine in Canada. You'd think—"

She shook her head sharply. "No alcohol for me. Period. Have you got any mineral water?"

He felt a stab of apprehension at her teetotal resolve. Rachel had never been a big drinker, but it was unusual for her to refuse a glass of wine. She had told him once, or rather she had let slip, that she felt intuitively she would have problems conceiving, and if she ever decided to get pregnant she would give up drinking a few months in advance.

"No, but there's water from the tap." When he saw her frown he said, "The house has its own spring. It's safe."

"I'll just have orange juice, thanks."

As he opened the fridge door and extracted the carton of Tropicana he wondered what this was all about: the Picasso quote, her slightly distanced quality.

She started to walk back and forth across the kitchen. "I can't calm down these days. Look at me, I'm pacing. Seriously Noel, the last couple of weeks have been murder for me. I feel like I'm on speed. Maybe I should have actually taken speed. Except I can obviously manufacture my own. I'm sure some people in my class do it."

"You'll calm down here. Don't worry."

Even as he said it he wondered if exams were the reason for her restlessness. He had been a pacer only a few times in his life. Each time it had been on account of that feeling of having been injected with amphetamines, the sudden inability to concentrate or hold a conversation, his voice sheared with impatience, losing weight by the day. Rachel had seen him return from working overseas in this state at least twice. She had assumed it was stress, the adrenalin of negotiating roadblocks and weeks spent talking nonchalantly about body parts, the hyperactive shock of being exposed to decay and frayed memories of murder.

"So what happened to the step?"

"What about it?"

"The front step. I nearly put my foot in that hole."

"Oh, it broke."

"Noel, you should be more careful."

"It wasn't me."

"Who was it, then?"

"The neighbour."

"The old man you said lived next door?"

Something prevented him from correcting her. "He offered to fix it. Or his daughter will."

"I can't believe it. We pay nine hundred dollars a week and the step breaks before I even get here."

"Can you try not to concentrate on how much everything costs? Just enjoy it."

She touched her forehead again and winced. "So have you been being neighbourly?"

"Not very. His daughter lives in Toronto. Her dad's a real character. He fishes eels. He's—"

"Sorry, Noel. I've got to lie down."

"Sure. I'll wake you for dinner."

"Okay. I'm not that hungry though."

Rachel hovered on the threshold of the kitchen. "Thanks," she said and then disappeared.

With Rachel gone the kitchen resumed its formal, expectant silence. *That's that, then,* it seemed to say. He could almost feel it folding its charms away like the ladder stairs to the attic. He opened the bottle of wine and sat down at the table. He addressed the house, although in a whisper. *What's your problem? I thought you wanted me to fill this place.*

He had never seen Rachel in this state before: agitated, hungry. Not that Rachel was placid, or unresponsive, only that she was generally untroubled by leakage between categories, whereas he only saw frontiers patrolled by uncertainties. He loved the cool logic of her mind. He relied upon the law, as a concept, for his work, just as he would come to rely upon Rachel, as a concept also, in his life — as a wife, eventually as a mother, as someone he would go on whale-watching trips or hiking in the Alps when they were sixty and the kids were in college.

They had decided to get married the following spring. They had reached the decision in a kind of silent symbiosis; they hadn't even needed to voice it. This must be the meaning of *tacit,* he thought, delighted at all the implicit decisions and understandings they would yet have together. *It's time,* they had both said — or rather, didn't say — *five years together without being married is enough. I don't want to make it six.* What did you call these conversations that never took place, he wondered, for he suspected the understandings built on them were at least as durable as those raked over in speech.

But in the year since that silent conversation a surprising doubt had formed on the horizon of his mind. What did it matter? Five years, six, too long, too short? He had never lived his life to an emotional timetable. Then again, there was no reason not to go along with Rachel's practical calculations: married at thirty, thirty-one. Pregnant with first child at thirty-three, after the career had been established enough to resume one's position on the ladder after childbirth. Second child thirty-five, max. Then fertility plummets and the dilemmas and threats it heralded: third child? IVF? miscarriage?

One thing he knew for certain: he was looking forward to the exchange of goods and services involved in any successful marriage. Once committed to each other there would be no divorce in their lives, no reconsidering, requestioning. Creeping suburban unhappiness — now there was a possibility, if he was going to stick to the promise he had made to himself, to stop going out into the world only to have the world slap him in the face.

The soothing blackcurrant of the wine washed down his throat. He was relieved the nights on his own would be over, now that Rachel was here. No-one would ever know what he thought about during those nights, nor hear the symphony of scattershot understandings he composed to himself, about the irretrievability of thought, even to the thinker, of forsaken intimacies, faces seen by candlelight, the shape of departing emotions, why did he take responsibility for everything when it exhausts him almost to the point of self-erasure, a line he had read in a novel and that stuck with him: *In the moment before giving, I am loved,* his proclivity to pour himself out on foreign ground, not to accept reality as it is presented to him, not to give in.

* * *

Chez Lando was the expat haunt. The original bar had been destroyed in the genocide when its owner, Landouald, his Canadian wife and their two teenaged children were murdered on the first day of the massacre. Now it had been rebuilt and was run by Lando's sister, a stately, grave woman with a scarred face from an aborted machete attack. He didn't know how she'd survived the genocide: false identity card, perhaps, or maybe she had managed to get out through foreign friends. In any case here she was every night, tending bar or chatting with junior diplomatic staff and NGO workers.

Chez Lando's clientele consisted of ministers in Paul Kagame's government, both junior and senior, consultants with USAID, UNDP, program managers at Save the Children, first and second secretaries in the Norwegian, Belgian, British embassies — in other words, a virtually identical clientele to those who drank and gossiped at Chez Lando before April 1994. Except then, of course, Paul Kagame had been an RPF commander in the Ugandan hinterland and not prime minister; the Norwegians had run only a tiny consulate, and Save the Children's emergency aid program hadn't existed.

Beer and irony flourished in these evenings, as did instant friendships with intelligent, multilingual people who worked for the Red Cross, UNAMIR, Christian Aid — well-brought-up individuals like Noel, hungry to apply their expensive educations to the task of understanding how things went wrong in the world. Most were European; Noel listened to their conversations about internships in Strasbourg, Erasmus stays at Salamanca, a *stage* in the ministry of external affairs, conciliation committees and parliamentary committees, feeling himself for the first time to be on the wrong side of a surprisingly deep cultural divide.

Together they stumbled over numbers, told stories about ossuaries where the bones were stacked like supermarket shelves: tibia on one side, femurs on the other, clavicles hanging from the ceiling. Their conversation was of that ilk he suspected could not exist outside the international sector: sprightly displays of knowledge of extreme places, high-risk anecdotes, trading tips they imagined might one day save their lives in a tricky situation: which border guards were most drunk, most sex-starved and volatile, which could be bribed, which backroads were still littered with RPF mines.

She was UNDP. He knew some of her colleagues, they had been in the country the same amount of time, but somehow he had managed to avoid meeting her until that night. For a while she was only a presence across from him on the other end of the table: a heart-shaped face and candid almond eyes, a thin, aquiline nose. Eventually the composition of the group shifted and they ended up next to each other.

Rachida spoke four languages well, *and another two badly,* she said shyly and declined to reveal which ones they might be, as if this were a real failure. Her father was an Algerian diplomat and her mother was French. She had grown up in Paris and in Zurich, which she hated. *Imagine a live museum of the super-rich,* she grimaced.

She had worked in Togo and in South Africa. She also mentioned Malaysia where her father was currently posted, Corsica where they sometimes took holidays, and Madrid where she had studied Spanish. He found it hard to keep track of her family, her casual cosmopolitanism disoriented him, made him feel provincial. They started out on their careers and aspirations, but soon their conversation took on an urgent, exploratory tone. She had a younger brother who died when she was twelve, she told him. Her mother fell apart.

"I missed him, of course, but I couldn't understand why my mother would not recover. I was a little cold, maybe, as a child."

"How is your mother now?"

"She is sedated, or on antidepressants, or in therapy. In a way the tragedy of my brother has given shape to her life. My father has mistresses, of course."

He nodded at this last comment, unsure of what to make of

it. Rachida's eyes were slippery; they made him think of the word in French: *glisse*. It signalled, not dishonesty, but the evasiveness sadness sometimes breeds. She would be tough, too, he imagined, despite her heart-shaped face and her delicate mouth. Certainly she was disarmingly frank. It was there from the beginning, the resonance he experienced with her, as if she were literally tugging on his heartstrings, if such things as heartstrings really existed. They talked for two hours until the rest of the table finally noticed they weren't participating.

At one point she had turned to him and said, "You are not one of those Americans obsessed with placing pieces of the jigsaw together, are you?"

"What do you mean?"

She paused, swallowed. Perhaps she felt she had been too reckless. Then he saw her take a decision to forge ahead.

"I find some Americans don't engage with the heart of people, with culture. They don't want to get closer."

"Closer to what?"

"To the truth, the heart of the matter. I think of America as a culture of observing, then interfering. This has taken you to a position of power, but it has distanced you from other peoples' existences."

He raised his eyebrows. He found he had nothing to say to this challenge, or perhaps he had everything to say, and couldn't decide where to begin his riposte. He was not used then — this would come later — to being taken to task for what he saw as the accident of being American. He was not yet used to having to answer for his country's misdemeanours.

On the other hand, Rachida might be right. His choice as a career had been to acquire a hard knowledge that supposedly bestowed understanding, and, by association, security. Could it be that he hadn't given himself the chance to embrace the differences between himself and others, in the countries he worked in, because to do so would be to embrace uncertainty?

He turned to her, his eyes brimming with possible answers.

He wanted to say so many things: to rebuke her for being too presumptuous, too falsely secure in her Europeanness, to say, do you really think your creaking continent is the moral guardian of historical truth, just because you've been the scene of two wars in one century? You are too refined and too enervated, but actually just as ready to sap the resources of the rest of the world as ruthlessly as the United States. You come from a spent, indulgent continent, the cultural equivalent of those chain-smoking middle-aged male philosophers on French TV programs about books and current affairs, paid to pontificate randomly on subjects they actually know nothing about.

He should have said all this, should have been angry, but the look in her eyes was impossible to fault. She was smiling into his discomfort, although warmly. He saw compassion. He saw that she had wanted to finger his soul, rough it up a little if necessary, but delicately, if only to see the effect.

It was closing time at Chez Lando. In the confusion of leaving he couldn't get to her, couldn't ask, how long are you here for? Where are you living? As he watched her get into the Jeep with the rest, he thought, there goes another narrow escape.

He turned around to see Alexandre, smiling and waving a small piece of paper.

"I got her phone number for you."

"I don't want it." Alexandre knew he had a girlfriend.

"Yes you do."

A fragment of conversation he heard once between his father and a friend of his, another academic, inserted itself into the moment. He must have been only ten, or eleven. They were speaking in low, urgent voices he had never heard before. *Do what you have to do, but just don't bring it home.* He understood now that what they had been talking about was an affair. With a student, a colleague. *Don't bring it home.* Even at the time he knew this snippet of conversation overheard and not understood belonged to a slippery category of evasions. The real life and the unreal one: the home life and the other life. Did his father and his colleague really think it possible to not let such an event enter their real life, or the one they were privileging as real? Noel had never had sex with a woman and felt nothing, never said to himself: I can walk away from this. This doesn't touch me. I won't bring it home.

I think my family romanticizes itself.

Why had he divulged that to Eve? He felt shocked as soon as he said it, and he was sure she knew it. It was the shock of truth, of course, and of having arrived at an understanding long desired but never until this moment realized. He had made similar treacherous confessions to Rachida, but then they were in Rwanda and trading confidences as a way to neutralize the disarray around them, the kind of chaos that built itself out of nowhere, coalesced, and then swirled away before you properly realized what you were dealing with.

And he could have said so much more. He could have spoken about the internal famine spawned by his well-meaning, well-mannered upbringing. How his family just wanted them to be happy, he and his two sisters, but they also wanted that happiness to emerge uncalled-for and perhaps unfought-for, and to continue unfettered, forever. Any sign of doubt or questioning was erased efficiently from the landscape by their judicious, caring hearts. He sometimes felt it would have been better to have a drifter father and a factory piecework mother, kids screaming, welfare, neglect caused by exhaustion — anything but this smothering blanket of comfort he had been bequeathed, emotionally, by his family.

He could have revealed to Eve how he ascribed to the idea that in every family there is a sacrificial lamb, someone who is slaughtered so that the rest can prosper. No-one in his family would ever admit to this of course, they would be horrified. On the surface of things it would seem unlikely that Noel would play this role, being the boy, the youngest and — in the family lore at least — the smartest of them all. But his family feared him, although subtly, and he knew it. Somehow, with his steely commitment to human rights and his paradoxical waywardness, he undermined everything his family embraced. He had escaped being the sacrifice only by luck and through his family's imperfect understanding of vulnerability. Noel knew he would never be able to share his sacrificial lamb theory with Rachel, who would call it "dark" and "paranoid."

He had an older sister who worked in the financial services industry — he was still hazy on what she actually did: securities, futures, maybe she took care of Third World dictator portfolios in Credit Suisse, who knew? It wasn't like Noel not to be curious, not to know the details. But in her case, he really didn't care. He did know she worked fourteen-hour days at a large investment house. She had a plan for her life and intended to live it out in Stalinist five-year instalments: apartment in Gramercy Park, second house somewhere in the country, private schools for the kids, eventually early retirement, perhaps in the Caribbean. His parents were upset, of course, that she showed little interest in politics, social welfare, nuclear proliferation, but they were too cowed by her ability to make money to say so.

Noel loved her, of course. But he couldn't say he knew her well. Perhaps, he reasoned, there wasn't much to know. She had their mother's sweet temper; seemingly, she was the even-handed one who ironed out the silly gutless squabbles that passed for arguments in his family. She always sent Christmas and birthday presents and professed loyalty to the family in loving emails that detailed her tribulations at work but that omitted any references to her husband or her private life. In some deep, nearly unacknowledged chamber of himself Noel thought of her as a quiet predator, secretly delighted at how she earned more at thirty-four than the incomes of both her parents, her brother and her sister put together.

His younger sister seemed poised to perpetuate the happy if dishevelled marriage of their parents. She was bright, with a good degree from Brown. Ostensibly toiling for a prestigious current affairs magazine in Boston, really it was a cover for looking for a husband. He didn't judge her for this, only noticed how readily both his sisters seemed to accept what was given to them by their parents, to play the roles that were so subtly expected of them.

That left Noel. He had deftly avoided the issue of what his family might want from him by adopting the double strategy of appearing to be academically gifted — although really his success was owed to a sustained effort of will rather than any innate brilliance — and by spending as little time at home as possible. The day after he finished high school he moved out, to the protestations of his parents, taking a shared apartment for the summer with friends before starting at Yale in the fall.

He never told his parents or his sisters about his depression, although it had been so difficult to conceal. He had the impression they were poised for his failure and the subsequent sacrifice, remedial love at the ready like a thick comforter clasped in their arms. *You were too young. You shouldn't even have been there. It wasn't your fault.*

He caught sight of his reflection in the window. He was not a man for looking at his own image, but in the times he couldn't avoid it, what did he see? A face he knew from a young age women thought handsome, although flawed. A boyish face, a sneaky grin, a confident but not complacent manner.

Inside that face is a voice that speaks a language of destruction. It is his own voice, if he really has to take responsibility for it, and its language is of drained swimming pools, their tiles smeared with blood, television sets being carted off by gangs of young men in white pickup trucks, roads peppered with landmines, kidnap victims kept chained to trees in the jungle — the language of a wrecked paradise. It was a mystery to him, even now, how it could thrive inside him.

She passed them on the highway near the Little Bras d'Or turnoff, Noel and his girlfriend, returning from the airport. Or at least she thought it was them: a silver car with New York licence plates, a woman in the passenger seat, her face obscured by her forearm thrown across her head to ward off the sun.

Her father's sister lived in a lime green bungalow in Sydney Mines, on a hill overlooking the Atlantic. Eve drove into the driveway and parked. She sat in the car a moment, even though she knew her aunt would have heard her arrival. She would be waiting for her knock behind the front door.

She had never known her aunt well, although Maureen spent a lot of time in their kitchen when they still lived in the white house across the lake. Then, Maureen had been a star attraction among the women relatives who she had eavesdropped on through the register, drinking in the bickering, inconsequential quality of their conversation. Maureen wore her hair in an auburn beehive right to the tail end of the Seventies, loud dresses, her lipsticked mouth a red slash. When she laughed you could see the purple of her throat, her pink-sheared teeth. *She has zing,* her father was given to saying, with the blind affection of the younger brother. Eve had thought her at once gaudy and perishable.

I know who my people are had been one of Maureen's refrains. *I know my place in the world.* Maureen had been the keeper of a complicated grid, a foldout, foldaway construction where everyone was pegged according to their Place. She was given to speaking at length about being content with your lot; the people who weren't were frustrated and deluded, the people who were humble and God-fearing. Eve supposed every family needed a Maureen to provide moral ballast and an air of seething restriction. The Maureens of this world gave you something to fight tooth and nail against, and that was a good thing.

She squared herself up to the moment and got out of the car. At the door she knocked once, then, with far less conviction, twice. The door opened.

Eve had to adjust her gaze downward; she had been expecting to look up to her aunt, as she had done as a child. But the woman in front of her was small; literally she had shrunk and contracted, like one of those dolls whose face was made of apple. Her mouth was puckered and yellowed from a lifetime of chain-smoking, and childishly small.

"Took my storm windows off too early this year," her aunt said by way of a greeting.

You haven't set eyes on me in fifteen years and this is what you say? At the same time it was familiar: people on the island dealt with the long absences of family by behaving as if they'd seen them only yesterday.

"Now what would you like to drink? A nice cup of tea, dear?" Maureen ushered her into a spic-and-span kitchen. New toaster, new microwave, new kettle — all fresh out of the box.

"You've got some new appliances."

"Got them after Malcolm died, dear. On the insurance."

Maureen's husband had died five years before. Her four boys had all left the island; Eve hadn't seen them since she was eighteen or nineteen years old.

"How's Stanley?" Stanley had been the closest to her age.

"Good, dear, good. He's working on the ferry. He's got a lovely wife and two sons. Don't know what it is about my family and boys. No-one ever comes out with a girl; it's the same with Donald and Malcie's wives. It's a wonder I'm here myself." A fluted laugh followed, which Eve also failed to connect with the Maureen she had known.

"So how's my brother? Poor soul, Alistair. All alone in that cabin. For the love of God, it pains my heart to think about it."

"He's not as far gone as I feared."

"Oh no?" Her aunt frowned.

"He forgets things, but it doesn't seem like he's…" Eve paused. She had yet to develop the requisite breezy, casual vocabulary for dealing with serious degenerative illnesses.

"But he's not himself," her aunt said. "That's the way I see him. He's a bit *volatile.*"

Clacks of teacups, the ticking clock. Something is wrong with the tick, but what?

"So they've rented John R's place have they, those sisters? Spruced it up? Who took it for the summer?"

"Americans."

"Are they friendly people?"

"They're…" Eve used the plural, although so far, of course, she had only met Noel, "fine."

A cloud settled over her aunt's face. "He's got no friends."

"What about Lauchie? And Malcolm?"

"Malcolm's dead two years now, dear. Lauchie he fell out with, over a catch of gaspereaux."

"Why?"

"I don't know the details. But they went out fishing one day friends and came back sworn enemies."

"But Lauchie's been his friend for forty years."

"I know, dear. I know."

She heard the slow, unstable ticking of the clock. Eve looked up and saw that the hands had frozen at 11:15 a.m. It was near-ly two o'clock. She was about to point this out to her aunt when she spoke.

"Has he shown you the shed?"

"What shed?"

"The one where he keeps his fishing tackle. All that stuff."

"No, why?"

"There's something in there you should see, dear. It belonged to your mother."

"But…" she faltered, "I don't want to see anything of hers."

Her aunt pursed her lips. "Don't you ever think about her, dear? She was your mother after all." There was more pity than condemnation in her aunt's voice. This made Eve want to rebel, to say terrible things, clanging, disastrous words her aunt would have ringing in her ears until she hit the grave.

She said, "No."

"Well."

Eve rose. Her aunt rose from the chair slowly, folding for-ward and upward, as if undoing a complex piece of origami.

They stood in the darkened hallway. She felt Maureen's hand on her shoulder. They seemed to pivot there, in the hallway by the door, her aunt's birdclaw hand on Eve's shoulder, not moving or saying anything, as if commanded into stillness by some force greater than either of them. Eve had time to take in the Afghan unwrinkled by the limbs of guests, doilies gathering dust, the rattle of the refrigerator, the wind sneaking through the eaves.

"You were always on the outside." Her aunt's voice was too loud and reverberating, as if it had come up from somewhere deep and surfaced into a void. "You're a natural outsider but you put yourself there, too."

She blinked. She thought for a second she might cry. Her aunt opened the door. "You take good care of him now."

Eve walked down the drive. Before putting the key in the car door she turned around to see her aunt waving from behind her picture window. She waved back.

Eve knew instantly the house next door was occupied by two people, even though there were no overt signs. It was a feeling houses emanated; like Noel said, they liked to be filled. She would see less of him now; she could get on with her own time-occupying projects. She had set herself the task of rereading her high school geology textbooks, digging them out of her closet from behind the rack of clothes she had worn in high school — her father hadn't touched them — and which she could not bear to look at. Books were safer somehow, they held fewer humiliations.

Her old books tell her that over thousands of years peat has been compressed, first into lignite, then to coal. The coal was a tenth of the thickness of the original peat. The Maritimes is quilted with seams of this coal: Minto, Joggins, the Foord Seam at Pictou, Boularderie to Sydney Mines. She reads the flinty names of the minerals that lace the province: feldspar, mica, gneiss. For so long the province was waterlogged with ancient mires, with bogs, swamps, fens, marshes. Floodplains and mud-pots were subjected to repeating sequences called cyclotherms, changes in sea level, the nonchalant migration of river systems: cycles of drowning, emergence, recolonization.

She pores over the artists' impressions of the ancient coal ferns, *Calamites, Sigillaria,* born in brackish water and that had fanned out over alluvial plains. Eventually these became the barren forests of the carboniferous age, grassless, flowerless forests of clubmoss trees, mop-headed, towering and anorexic, their draping crimped ferns.

She senses the presence of it sometimes, down by the gypsum ponds, that raucous soupy world: giant ferns, Komodo dragon lizards, fish that masqueraded as stones. She senses them coming, the men who would mine these crushed Amazonian rainforests three hundred thousand years later, their lungs thrashed by the dust of ancient tropical wildfires. She always guarded her tendency toward fancy from others, hiding it in the stiff robes of scientific inquiry, to guard herself from her father, her sister, her aunt's rebukes: *That Eve, she's been dreamy and impractical since Day One. Don't know where she gets it from. My people were doers.* Her aunt professed to be worried for her. How was she going to make it in the world? *Imagination doesn't put supper on the table.*

She loved natural history in part because it brought her closer to the other lives: her own possible lives, the life she would have lived as a fish, a scaled creature, or as another person, the world turned on its head by the simple fact of being inside a different body. Would it even be possible? She dreamed of being furnished with a fresh soul. Even if these other lives were only glimpsed in a rush — akin to cars streaking, or hollow blips of Morse code ringing through empty air; signals picked up, then lost in clouds of static.

CHAPTER 10

She spent the morning cleaning the kitchen. In the end, she decided the entire enterprise was futile unless she took up the filthy linoleum flooring that had been there for twenty-five years, at least. She would lay wood instead.

Her father came in just as she was pulling up a square of linoleum. "I thought you said you'd clean it, not break it."

She paused to wipe her brow. "I have to break it to clean it. You've let this place go to the dogs." She stood up straight. "I thought I'd have a go at the shed."

Her father stiffened. "What's the matter with it?"

"I had a look in yesterday. You haven't so much as dusted that place in ten years."

He flinched, but she saw him decide to let it pass. He hovered in front of her.

"How's that job going, anyway?"

"It's all right."

"Do they treat you good?"

"Not too bad."

"Tips good?"

"They're okay. It should keep us in gas, anyhow."

Jesus. Tips and gas.

"I know this is a step down for you. I mean, you're a qualified person."

"Well, as it turns out there's not much need for jewellers in Cape Breton." She hadn't meant to sound sarcastic so much as resigned.

"Well, I'll be looking in on the beans. They're coming up good."

She breathed a sigh of guilty relief as he left. She put down the strip of linoleum she'd been hauling off the floor and went to the phone.

"He's out of the office," the voice on the other end said.

"Where is he?"

"Vancouver."

"Tell him Eve called. Tell him my life is about gas and tips. I'm working on the welfare checks and thinking maybe I'll change my name to Wileena."

"Pardon?"

"Just tell him. He'll understand." She put the phone down.

She didn't know Lew was planning to go to Vancouver. Maybe it was a last-minute assignment. But they always called each other before they got on a plane, it was a sort of mutual superstition they felt. She felt strange and afraid, that she hadn't known he was travelling, hadn't known where his body was in the world. They were husband and wife; she had always thought that was a reason for being married — once you called yourself husband and wife you would know where each other's bones were.

They had been married for six years. It all began at a dinner party. Llewellyn was only a figure at the other end of the table that night, holding forth, commanding the conversation so that eventually all the guests tilted their chairs toward him, and the dinner had the feel of a captain's table on a listing cruiseliner: conversation, food, candlesticks, cutlery — everything made a judicious decision to head for Llewellyn, as if he were magnetized.

Her body was swayed by this unstable glamour. Her body liked him but her mind had said: *I'm not sure.* She quickly tried to disguise her shock that this charismatic, well-travelled man wanted her. But Llewellyn saw it anyway, and registered it. Llewellyn understood from the very beginning — he had told her so — that in relationships one person was always more powerful than the other, for so many reasons — one person needed the relationship more, they were dazzled and somehow beholden to the other's greater power, which they themselves felt lacking; the person who needed it more would always be beholden to the one who needed it less. Her husband did not question any of this. It seemed to him the natural order of things.

Doubt loped through her, lean and hungry as a wolf. They had an understanding, she reminded herself. She would be away for three months; in that time they would remain faithful to each other. It wasn't much to ask, they both agreed. If they couldn't do it for three months, they had agonized mutually, then how could they call themselves committed, or adults, or responsible?

She reminded herself that they felt similarly about so many things. Like those humid summer days that enveloped Toronto like a shroud: *dispossessed* was Lew's word for it: half enervation, half uncertainty, days when they felt sapped of themselves, when the most expansive thoughts seemed petty, when pleasures acquired a used, picked-over quality. Making love at four in the afternoon in thirty-degree heat, an ineffectual air conditioner clacking in the window, their mutual fear that nothing would ever be fresh or good.

This effect had something to do with geography, the city's flatness, the lake's heavy presence and the way it pressed upon them at night. A concentrated burst of light in the wilderness; giant freshwater seas to the west, glacial lakes turning to boggy taiga to the north and the ragged rim of Hudson Bay. In all her years in Toronto she had never been to Northern Ontario, or at least not beyond cottage country, although she had a sense of the nickel allure of that landscape, the rectangular summer nights.

She heard the gravelly slide of a car in the driveway. Through the window she saw Anita getting out of her car, dressed in a blue V-necked sweater and dark trousers, a pair of Timberland rip-offs on her feet, sunglasses pulled down over her eyes.

The door squeaked and she was in the kitchen. "Pulling up the floor, are ya?"

"Trying to anyway."

"Thank Christ someone's doing something about this dump. It's got to have a better heating system. He's going to get pneumonia." Anita leaned back against the piece of wood that passed for a kitchen counter and folded her arms across her chest. "Where is he?"

"In the garden."

"Have you got him to go to the hospital?"

"They've done the bloodwork. I'm taking him for a scan next week."

"What kind of scan?"

"A brain scan. It's still not easy to get him there. Last time I had to find him on the shore and drag him up the hill."

"Can't blame him. I don't think I'd rush to have my brain scanned. I can just see the technicians looking at the screen and saying, but there's nothing there."

She laughed. It was the first joke she could remember Anita cracking with her since they were kids.

"Your hair looks good." Anita's hair had been lightened tastefully to a hue of acacia honey, rather than the brassy amber that small-town salons usually turned out.

"I just had it done."

Anita shot a look out the window toward the bent figure of their father weeding the garden. "I've been looking up stuff on the Internet. Did you know it attacks the parts of the brain that formed last? The areas that have less myelin. It's strange, don't you think?" Anita frowned. "I mean, no-one in our family ever showed any sign of… of anything like that. Mind you, we never knew them. Grandma died too young and Grandpa had a heart attack. And Ann's family, well, we don't know much about them, do we?" She crossed her arms and then just as quickly uncrossed them. She huffed a sigh. "We're probably supposed to die at fifty like we've been doing for most of humanity. We start living longer and things start going wrong. But too many people are getting it. The way I see it, there must be something environmental about it."

"Whatever's causing it, there's no cure." As Eve said this, the dread seeped back into her veins, her arteries, as if someone had injected her with ink. Just then their father came in the door, scuffing his feet clean on the mat, eyes down, until he saw Anita.

"Well, look who's here. How ya doin?"

As Eve watched them embrace she was overtaken by a disabling lassitude. She had to lean against the table for support.

The door slapped again. An unknown voice called out from behind the screen door. "Hello there. Is it all right if I come in?" Without waiting for an answer a middle-aged woman stepped into the kitchen.

"Can we help you?" Eve said. She hadn't heard a car pull up in the drive.

"I hope so. I'm—" The woman said a name that Eve had seen on signs nailed to trees, on the waterfront, in front of houses. The woman was from the South Shore. She had made a killing selling cottages down there and had extended her business up to the island.

"I thought I'd drop by because I've got a client looking for land in this area. He can pay top dollar. An American."

Eve frowned. "Top dollar?"

"It means a hundred thousand US, dear."

I'm not your Dear. She resented people who came to the island and felt they could use Cape Bretonisms.

"You've got to hand it to them," Eve said. "Those Americans are good at buying things."

"You're kidding," Anita laughed.

"No, dear, I'm not." The woman looked deliberately from Eve to her sister. Her lips were perfectly painted with a high-end long-wear lipstick. Elizabeth Arden, Eve thought, or Lancôme. Certainly not the Mary Kay stuff the Indian Bay drugstore hawked.

"He wants waterfront and there's not much left around here. He also wants a view. Just like this one, in fact. You've got a lovely view here." The woman turned to their father. "Alistair, is that right?" She didn't wait for confirmation. "Do you know how much this place is worth?"

Her father swivelled his eyes around the room; Eve tracked them, taking in what they saw: kerosene lantern, old fishing net in a heap in the corner, fishing rods, tackle, trick wooden chairs that folded underneath you if you sat on them the wrong way.

"If you sold up, Alistair, you could live wherever you wanted."

"My father is happy here," Eve said.

The woman turned a calm glance on her. *What are you doing answering for your father?* Eve returned it with one of her own. *What are you doing vulturing around us?*

The woman, she could see, got the picture immediately. The old man would be malleable but the daughter's a problem. She's going to stand in the way of her father having a retirement fund and one of those nice old people's apartments in Florence or Dominion, where he would have a postcard view of extinct heavy industry.

The woman shifted her appeal to Anita. "You know what it's like, don't you dear? You live here all year-round. You know what an American dollar can buy here. You've got kids, is it Anita? Is that right?"

"Three."

"Three. Well, If this American buys the land the money will be enough to send them all to college."

Eve struggled to keep her voice level. "Who exactly do you think you are, asking how many kids my sister has and promising to pay for their university? You just walked in the door five minutes ago and you're talking about my sister's children's futures. Is this what you call the hard sell? Is this the technique that's made you a couple of million on the South Shore? Because it might work there, but here you're going to have to modify your methods."

The real estate agent gave her a quick once-over, no doubt wondering how she had miscalculated. This was no down-home family, even if the woman standing in front of her was streaked with sweat and linoleum dust.

"I'm just telling you reality."

"I think you put in an extra vowel."

"Come again?" The woman's blue eyes had hardened.

"You're telling us about *realty*. The only reality here is the commission you'd make on the sale."

"Eve, for Christ's' sake," Anita snapped. "Don't be so rude."

"Who's rude here? You've got plenty of people wanting to sell their land. Why come in here and start making promises about money and inheritance? It's just unconscionable."

The woman frowned at the word, which pleased Eve. *If the day came when real estate agents understand the word* unconscionable, Eve thought, *the profession's in trouble.*

"I don't, as it happens, have that many people wanting to sell. At least not that many people with waterfront and a view like your father has. So I have to go looking. Well, that's fine, I can see there's nothing doing here. Sorry for the bother."

As the woman was reaching for her bag Anita spoke. "I think we should ask Dad what he wants to do."

They all turned to face her father. He had stood stock-still, one hand leaning on the stove, his eyes cast down to some indeterminate point during the entire encounter. She watched as he concertina-ed himself, tucking himself away like a folding ladder. She wondered again, *Who are you? An enigma, a space. Do you have no opinion? Can you not speak up? This silent, withdrawn man, surrounded by three possibly too-vital women. Eve didn't know if this indefinable quality was a great strength, an heroic protest vote, or if it made him a grey man.*

"I'll see myself out."

"You're just... just...," Anita stammered. "You just take the cake."

"Whose cake? The cake that woman just offered you? Look, Anita, she's smart. She's been through this thousands of times with other families. She even did her research — she knows your name, she knows Dad's name. She probably knew how many kids you've got, she waited until you were here."

"That's paranoid."

"Is it? That kind of information is easy enough to get around here. She's asked around, the neighbours, maybe even Celyn told her. One daughter in Toronto, doesn't give a shit about anything but champagne and frappuccinos, one daughter in Glace Bay with three kids to educate. Bingo."

Anita's eyes narrowed. "You just think you know...," she foundered. *"Everything."*

"Not everything, no. But this kind of thing...," Eve threw her hand out toward the window, toward the departing agent in this year's model car. "This kind of thing I definitely know about."

"You forget there's things I know, too."

"Like what?"

"Things about you."

Of course. This was another thing she had forgotten about Anita: how, when she was cornered, she would use the heaviest weapon she could lay her hands on.

Eve felt her temperature dropping, felt something drape itself over her mind like a cool white shroud. "And what are you going to do with those things?"

"I'm just saying if Dad here knew."

"If Dad here knew what? Why are we talking about Dad as if he's not in the room with us?"

"I can't. I can't...." He turned away from them. God almighty, was he going to cry?

Eve and Anita both fled the house, nearly breathless. They came to stand on the gravel, their feet in the groove marks of the departing woman's car, circling each other warily.

"You'd do anything to discredit me in Dad's eyes. Don't you realize I don't have any credit anyway?" She threw up her hands. "You're the one he loves, the one he'll listen to, not me. You don't need the upper hand, Anita. You've always had it."

"You think the world owes you something, just because you had it tough," Anita countered. "Well, I've got news for you. Plenty of people have it tough and they don't go around morose about it for the rest of their lives, expecting compensation and disappointed when they don't get it, and then making sure everybody else has to suffer too."

Oh, yes. This was the Anita she remembered. She thought of another email Anita had sent her over the years, in between the messages labelled Common Sense and How Do You Get to Heaven? It was about a great uncle of theirs who married, moved to the States and became a professor of "Social Science," as Anita put it — it was Sociology — and never came back to the island, not even to visit. And now he was dead, ecumenical service at the funeral, plaudits from fellow professors, obituaries in all the papers, pillar of the community — the works, and the island branch of the family hadn't even been informed. Anita finished the email with *C'est dommage, c'est la vie.* Anita didn't even speak French. Eve hadn't known how to reply to this breezy absolution, of Anita's endorsement of this conspiracy between shame and life.

There she is, standing in front of her. Look at Anita growing in stature by the instant, rising above things, superb in her condemnation. Look at her consume the horizon like the gypsum boats that pass through the strait in front of the cabin once a week.

"He needs *money.* He's not like you; he's not going to earn any money, ever again. Look at him, Eve" — she received each use of her name by her sister as a minor blow — "he's barely surviving here. He's cold in the winters, he's lonely. He's not well. We just can't let him rot away here."

"Nobody's *rotting away.*"

"He is. Look at him, he's depressed, he's disoriented. He might have a disease."

"Why don't you come here and take care of him?"

"Because I've got three kids and a husband." Anita ran her

hand through her hair. Eve saw it was shaking, although slightly. "I'm not always sure I want them, but I've got them."

"I can't come back to live here."

"So why did you come back now? You could have just sent money."

"I don't have any money."

"Why not?"

"I spent it all."

"On what?"

It was a good question. On opera in Milan, a two-week luxury tour in the Pantanal in Brazil, a Christian Dior belt, three pairs of Emma Hope shoes from London, good red wine, dinners out, a compulsive book-buying habit she exercised indiscriminately in whatever country she happened to be.

"I just…," she paused. "On living. On life."

She received a look of such clarity from her sister, she nearly forgot to breathe. Her sister had likely scrimped to get the boys new skates every winter. She could have sent some money to Anita, although she also knew her sister would never accept it. But maybe she could have set up an account for the kids, or at least bought them Christmas presents.

She tried to offer Anita the only concession available: she asked her advice.

"What would you do?"

"The same things you're doing, I suppose. Take him to the appointments; see if we can find out what's wrong. One thing I do know, he can't spend another winter in this dump. And if he needs to be put into a home, well, a hundred thousand US will set him up for life. You're not going to come back and live here. I don't need the land, but I could sure as hell use the money. Doesn't that make any sense to you?"

"But this land is all we have."

"It's *his* land. It was never ours. Maybe while… while Ann was here. Now it's just dead land. He can't keep it cleared; the eels aren't coming in the numbers they used to."

"I think it might kill him to sell it."

"I know. I can't picture him in one of those retirement apartments either." Anita gave the cabin an accusing look. "To think of all the sadness attached to this place, and he's stayed here. To think the little he has to show for his life...," Anita swallowed so hard Eve heard it. "And still, he can't part with it."

They stood in silence for a while. Then Anita looked at her watch. "Gotta go. I said I'd pick Kelly up from a friends'."

"How is Kelly?"

Anita stared at her for a second before answering. "She's fine. She wonders who you are."

As she climbs into her truck she feels as if she might pass out. But she can't afford to faint, her shift at Kay's starts in half an hour. Her hand is on the ignition, the gearshift, the gravel crunch. Go. Thank God, she is out of there. Driving down the hill, coming up for air, a deep-sea diver decompressing.

She wonders who you are.

Anita had always known how to go for the jugular. She had always known how to say the most scouring, exposing things. Anita had meant something else, too, of course: it was an old rebuke tied to her threat. *You forget there's things I know. Things about you.*

The first exit to Indian Bay rushes up to meet her. If she could only just keep driving: past exit ten, then exit nine, hugging the rim of Whycocomagh, then over the Causeway, not stopping until she hit oblivion or the 401, whichever comes first. Or she could drive to the airport and leave the truck in the long-term parking lot. He wouldn't say boo; she would get away scot-free. All that would be left would be to wait for the phone call from Maureen or Anita, this year or next, or maybe five years down the line, their voices tight from the effort of withholding condemnation. Then the funeral, the drive to the airport again through the familiar corridor of censorious spruce.

She drives over a furry lump in the middle of the asphalt.

Porcupine. Only seconds before it was waddling furiously across the highway. She thinks of the deer shot in midvault, the silverflash torque of the hooked fish — things killed while moving.

I'm going to get rid of it.
    It's not yours to get rid of.
    Whose is it then?
    God's.
    Which God? The God you dreamt up between my getting pregnant and now?
    He's always been there. He sees everything we do.
    Anita, you never even go to Mass.
    I never had to. Before I had kids.
    I don't want a baby. It's not God's. There is no God. There's only me, and you, and all of us. And we're alone here.
    In retrospect it seemed a remarkable thing to say, at nineteen. But then she was never as old as she was at nineteen, never so resolute.

Anita was twenty-eight, Eve two months short of twenty. Eight years seemed exactly calibrated to keep them apart: they had only briefly been children together, never been teenagers at the same time.

Eve believed what she said, although she understood even then that there were degrees of loneliness and that it would be her, and not Anita, who would map their outer limits. Anita fit in; she was a need-attender, a caregiver who passed seamlessly from girlhood to a rueful woman, jokily intolerant of men, over-aware of life's pitfalls. She gave back to the community.

Eve was exhausted, not so much by the fetus growing insistently, multiplying its cell count exponentially by the hour, as by harassing visions of her future, should she not be able to get an abortion: she would be a waitress at a place much like Kay's Lobster Hut. Or there she is, five years later, banding together with other assembly-line women to mount industrial action to safeguard her job from the Finnish-owned pulp and paper mill. Or living in a shared flat in a city smelling of fish or chemicals, slinking to her job as a secretary at a bank or a university department.

She had gotten the job as veterinarian's assistant for the summer. The vet's permanent assistant was on maternity leave; working for the summer would pay her entire second-year university tuition fees. That was how she had met him: he owned a border collie.

She realized she had almost succeeded in forgetting the whole episode: the unremarkable sex that led to it (her first time, of course), the gall of having to confide in Anita because there was no-one else to turn to, knowing that Anita would throw it back to her one day when she was most vulnerable, when she most needed to forget. She hadn't imagined that day would take nearly fifteen years to arrive, but it had.

She remembers the vomiting, the bloating, the running to the bathroom to pee every fifteen minutes. She wondered how some women managed to be pregnant for months without realizing it. For her it had been apparent she was harbouring another creature right from the moment of conception. Something had stolen inside her and was using her for its own means. She felt an awkward fury, a razored anger on which she cut herself deliberately. In all the years that have passed, she has never even approached the intensity of this feeling.

Where could she go? She knew from ATV news reports that the Morgentaler clinic in Halifax was phalanxed daily by the baying righteous, holding graphic placards of aborted fetuses. She would appear on these nightly news programs, being bundled into or out of a car, and the relatives in living rooms in Clam Harbour, in Sydney Mines would say: *Doesn't that look like Eve, Alistair's girl?* It would be less traumatic, she thought, not to mention more anonymous, to do it in a large city — Montreal or Toronto.

She took the train to Toronto; it was the days when you still could. Her father thought she was going back to university and in fact she was. She had taken books for the trip but found she couldn't read. Instead she stared out the window all the way there, as if keeping vigil on behalf of the child that would never exist, watching as the train wound its way west through dark corridors of spruce, boggy alkaline flatlands, the miles and miles of anonymous lakes nobody had bothered to name.

∼

After the funeral they come to the house like mummers. Dressed in black and white, waiting outside on the doorstep, a silent troupe of relatives, friends, forty-ouncers clinking inside NSLC paper bags, the women holding trays of cut sandwiches and squares.

It is hot inside the house, their old house, the one across the narrow channel in the lakes everyone calls the gut. Hot even though it is mid-January and outside it is minus twenty. Anita opens all the windows. Eve is wearing a hand-me-down sweater that has pilled around the shoulders; Anita wears a backless dress, too revealing. Someone — an aunt, a woman with the moral authority their vanished mother would have wielded (people are already doing this, taking her place, taking on her roles) — tells her this. Instead of changing Anita goes to put on more eyeliner and mascara, but her mouth remains pale.

What's the matter, Eve?

She is in Toronto. Someone is mixing iced drinks. Vermouth. This is all a memory: the cabin, the father, the mother who died, the older sister with three young children living in a clapped-out house in Glace Bay.

She looks around and sees women with surgically cut bangs that cut a swathe across their foreheads. A man wears platinum-wired glasses that look like a miniature airplane. The women have dark shades of lipstick, perfectly applied. They look as if they had drawn themselves in outline first, as children do when learning to colour-in shapes, before filling in the centre.

The apartment is decorated in black and silver; the carpet charcoal grey, the walls steel blue. A bunch of slim, delicate lilies droop languidly from a vase. On the CD player is Nina Simone or Janis Joplin — some gravelly voiced woman singing grief-stricken songs. She hears this kind of music at almost every party: raw, emotive songs sung by women with men's voices.

She is twenty-three and she will never look older than she does now. What is she doing in this city of psychiatrists, publishers, gender studies professors? They treat themselves like porcelain bowls, with their manufactured dramas and emotional emergencies. But this is definitely a better place to be than the mossy cabin, her father's woollen socks draped over the arms of chairs. Someone asks her to fetch more Absolut from the freezer. This is what I aspired to, she reminds herself. The sweater she wears now is too old as well, her makeup may be misjudged, but still.

She talks too much about her past, which no-one particularly cares about but which she yields like a truncheon. She makes the usual assumption of the wounded — that no-one else knows about loneliness and deprivation as she does, because they have been brought up in a city, because they had two parents on the scene. She has yet to learn the essential lesson of adults: don't confide, don't confess. Never.

CHAPTER 11

"Why don't we do the— what's it called? The Sunrise Trail?" Rachel pored over Nova Scotia Tourist Board maps at the kitchen table. "Evangeline Trail, Glooscap Trail, Marconi Trail. It's like they've made one big park out of the whole state."

"Province."

"Whatever. I'd hate to live somewhere so dependent on tourism. I can't imagine what it's like to be here in the winter."

"Rachel, it's July. Let's not think about winter just yet."

Noel turned to stare out the window. During his weeks alone in the house he had fallen into a habit of watching the lake in the morning. He liked to observe the precise, predictable changes of the lake's surface. In the morning they were mirror-calm and in their reflection he could see the porous linen texture of the sky. But around nine in the morning a wind appeared from nowhere, ruffling the water to taffeta. Two herons appeared each morning at precisely 9:40 a.m. and flew low over the lake, their stomachs skimming the surface.

Rachel got up, poured herself more herbal tea (she was off coffee as well, he noticed), sat back down. "I don't know what there is to see out there," she said.

"Hmm?"

She followed Noel with her eyes, tracking him back and forth, like a cursor on a screen. He seemed completely at home in this old farmhouse, even more so than in their own apartment.

"So where do you want to go?" she asked.

"Wherever you want."

She wasn't sure how much patience she would have in the face of this new passivity of his. She had never wanted to assume the role of the animator. Lately this is what Noel had been requiring of her — he had left her to arrange the deposit on the house in which they now sat; it had been Rachel who had bought the right maps and booklets for their vacation. It had been Rachel who urged him to update their camping equipment.

At least that morning she had awakened to find him sleeping next to her. There had been entire months when she had awakened to find him bent over books in his study at 5 a.m., or curled up on the sofa, his glasses askew on his face. *I keep waking up at four-thirty out of nowhere,* he explained at the time. He didn't say, in a panic, although she wondered if that was happening — nocturnal panic attacks, catapulting him out of REM sleep.

At first she thought his reluctance to confide in her was part of his solicitousness. He had always been mindful of the feelings of others. Noel was that kind of person who, if a friend gave him a book as a present, he would make sure it was lying around when the friend came to visit, open to page 100 or so, even if he actually hadn't had a chance to read it. While she admired his consideration of others, Rachel couldn't help thinking that there was also a disingenuous in his solicitousness. If it were her, she would simply say, *I'm sorry I haven't had a chance to read that book you gave me.* It might hurt, but it would be true.

She turned back to the map. "I'd like to go to this place that has the highest tides in the world. The Bay of Fundy."

"It's quite far away, I think."

"How far?"

"I don't know. I'll ask Eve."

"Who's Eve?"

"The neighbour. I mean the neighbour's daughter."

"You didn't say he had a daughter."

"Yes I did."

"How old is she?"

"I don't know. Late twenties, thirty, maybe."

"So what have you been talking about together?"

Christ, she really was giving him the third degree. "Just local history, geology. Where to go and what to do. She's been really helpful."

A smile toyed with the corners of Rachel's mouth. "You've been talking about *geology*?"

"She studied it; the natural history here is really interesting. Geologically, the island resembles the Amazon basin. That's where it was located during the breakup of the continents."

Noel always had to get the facts. Rachel admired this, of course, but there was also an indiscriminate aspect to his voracious appetite for knowledge. He seemed unable to separate what was necessary to know from what wasn't, like whether or not the island they sat on had been part of the Amazon zillions of years ago.

"It's a shame they don't have whitewater rafting here," she said. They had gone whitewater rafting when they were on vacation in Costa Rica the year before and she had gotten hooked on it.

"No, but we can go kayaking."

Noel said this with the requisite enthusiasm, but in fact he didn't like adventure sports and their manufactured thrills. He considered the whole business — whitewater rafting, scuba-diving, parasailing — a consolation prize for a mode of life that presented no real challenges. *We did this trail. We got through in our 4x4.* In fact, just the other day he had come upon a carful of tourists while walking down the abandoned road, an SUV with Maryland licence plates. Four middle-aged people whooped and cheered out the window at him. He ignored them. *So you drove your gas-guzzling car up a mildly challenging abandoned road,* he wanted to say. *Big deal.* Meanwhile, in all this flash and bang of achievement, the moment is lost — he thought this as he walked along the road the morning of the cheering tourists. Unanticipated experience, and the moment... and something else. What was it? Something about the *unbidden*.

This was one of the growing reservoir of thoughts Noel felt unable to share with Rachel. He had assumed that the things he couldn't tell his partner would diminish over the years. They would be part of each other, they would become each other; secrets would be unnecessary. But instead they were multiplying. He took a quick inventory: Rachida, certain gradients of fear and depression, long hours tinged with anxiety waiting in glacial airports, the shock of emerging into a sunlit country corrugated with violence... he heard a tentative scribbling at the outskirts of his mind. Another word was writing itself there: *Eve*. But why? They'd done nothing, only talked. *I know you're not the kind of man to have affairs,* Rachel once said to him. At the time he'd taken it as a compliment, a donation of trust. And it was true, since Rachida — and this was four years ago — he hadn't, unless he counted the Englishwoman he met by chance in the Miami airport and whose name he had never learned. They had spent a night and a day together after their connecting flights were delayed by tornadoes.

Affair. The word was so cheap, it begged to be discarded. But for him these affairs (if that's what they had to be called) contained something so forceful it literally winded him. They were the thrust of life, pure and undiluted, and he found he was in no position to refuse. Maybe this was his weakness, he reflected, his flaw — at thirty-one he considered himself a complex enough character to merit flaws — that he valued raw experience too much and the thrill it gave him, no matter who got hurt. But it was not a cheap thrill, rather a gleaming focus thrown onto an everyday life and its meagre rations of delight. These affairs had led him into an electric sunlit place, taut with possible hungers.

Now, with hindsight, Rachel's comment sounded less like a compliment than a bid for control, and a warning. He could see it coming: marriage, children, the wholesale scrum to get them into good schools, then good colleges. How could he allow himself to participate in such a prescripted play? On the other hand, his parents had done it, as had both sets of his grandparents, one Russian, one Galician, laying down their lives for those of their children in that immigrant Darwinian bargain with eternity: I sacrifice my hopes and desires, you give them to my children. Rachel's parents had done this too. It was one of the many things they had in common.

He was still hungry for experience. There was something vaguely scandalous about feeling so restless in his early thirties, when he should be squaring himself up to the real struggle in life, for long-term love, family, for stability. Still, the very idea of settling for anything caused tiny stabs of panic to erupt all over his body.

"Noel?"

"Hmm?"

"I'm trying to work out where to go and you're not listening to me. I said let's go up the Cabot Trail to start. Then we can think about the Bay of Fundy."

A ribbon of annoyance fluttered across his face. He was too well mannered to let it show for long, but she caught it all the same.

Rachel stared at his figure framed in the window, in the promising blue of a July summer's day. She saw Noel struggling now, at thirty-one, with facts she had mastered at nineteen, twenty. He thought her unaware of the internal scraps he fought so hard to hide from her. She wanted to say to him, and not particularly kindly, Who do you think you are dealing with, here? Who do you think you are fooling?

Then there were more wounding questions, although for Rachel they were relatively impersonal; she would have asked them of her parents, of her future children, as easily as she would have asked them of Noel: Whoever promised that all your hopes would be fulfilled? Whoever suggested that the people you loved would love you back? Why spend years of a short life tracing that most unstable frontier, the one between delight and abandonment? She didn't understand how people like Noel managed to survive experience. Enough of living was precisely about exposing illusions, denying desires, showing you up as vain and ridiculous and completely *wrong* — why go out and court these realizations, any single one of which could finish you off, never mind their stealthy accumulated effect? Rachel preferred to tailor her desires to her horizons. She would never consent to live on that rim of impossibility that Noel so liked to inhabit, that microfibre edge stalked by fear and ecstasy.

"We need to get our camping gear sorted out."

"I did that while I was waiting for you," he said.

Good, she thought. *He really has been waiting for me.*

It was nearly noon. Noel heard the sound of tires on gravel. He looked out the window to see Eve driving down the road at the wheel of her truck. He caught a glimpse of her face, uncharacteristically set and closed: a going-to-hospital face, although she was alone.

He shook his head once, quick, as if to dislodge a thought.

"Come on, I'll show you the local metropolis," he said, borrowing Eve's rueful phrase.

He felt a sudden and obscure urge to tell Rachel about Eve: she lives in Toronto, she works for a jeweller, she's smart and wry. *That's great, Noel,* she would say. *Let's have her over for dinner.* Eve would come with an open mind and Rachel would vivisect her with that flinty ambition of hers, top girl in class, *summa cum laude.*

No, he would have to allow Rachel to meet Eve casually, without any character reference on his part. This would put them on equal footing. They could work out their own dynamic, circle each other, compare experience and conclusions, wrap their competitive instincts in a pelt of friendly mutual affirmation. He had seen women do this so many times. Sometimes he wondered if women loved men only to keep from devouring each other.

A blue-and-white porcelain coffee grinder, bait hooks, punctured cans of Valvoline oil, an expired Ontario driver's licence, a province-shaped key chain sponsored by the Liberal Party (she wondered, could this be a joke?).

As she excavated artefacts from the nether regions of Duncan's body shop, the mystery grew deeper. How had all this junk got here? She pulled out a roll of olive green wallpaper patterned with loud squarish shapes — classic Cape Breton Seventies bathroom décor, so outmoded it might even be back in style. There was even a tattered moosehead lurking underneath a pile of sodden cardboard.

"What are you keeping this for, a rainy day?" She held up a clump of fur on which some small creature had been gnawing.

"That old thing? You can throw it out."

She wiped the sweat from her forehead. This was going to be a bigger job than she thought. She had put on a pair of Duncan's old overalls; she'd had to roll up the hems. On her feet was a pair of battered Tevas. She caught a glimpse of herself in one of the smudged old mirrors Duncan used for peering at the undercarriage of cars. She looked like Lucky in a particularly punishing staging of *Waiting for Godot*.

She looked up to see Duncan coming into the body shop trailing a customer behind him. She realized it was Noel in the same second she saw a woman's profile in the passenger seat of the car parked in the forecourt.

"You're here too," he said.

She backed away into the darkness of the body shop. She didn't want him to see her too clearly. "I'm everywhere."

"I'm just showing Rachel Indian Bay."

"Tell her not to blink or she'll miss it," Duncan said, and then went to release the gas pump.

"Do you want a hand? I could come back when I've dropped Rachel off at the house."

She couldn't help smiling at the thought of Noel dusting off the moosehead. "Thanks, but I've got to get home myself. I'm taking my father to the hospital this afternoon."

"Is he all right?"

"So far. This is just for tests."

"Well, I'd better get going." But Noel didn't move. Instead he cast his eye around the dark recesses of the body shop. "I can't believe you're doing this on your own."

"It's got to be done. He's losing business to the corporate world, you know, the Ultramars down the road."

"The one with the Tim Hortons? That's a popular place."

"Duncan needs to offer something local. I told him he could get homemade ice cream in, or put in a fruit stall. A farmer's market–type place."

"That's really good of you."

She looked down and caught sight of her feet, their dust-blackened nails, the grime caked between her toes. "I've got a soft spot for Duncan. He gave me my first job. Besides, I can think of it as my little stand against globalization."

"Here you go." Duncan handed Noel his credit card.

She watched him walk back to the car. The woman in the passenger seat was looking straight at her. She smiled, but the woman gave no sign of seeing her. It was the way the light fell, she supposed; the garage was in the dark, while the car was bathed in sun.

"That's good, Alistair. Could you turn to the right a bit?"

Technicians. Subtly threatening machines. Supervising doctor. Those translucid gloves the colour of phlegm. Turning his head, these murder fingers on her father's head, just another patient, just another guy who is soon to die. Piece of meat. Not faraway, the rattle of the instrument cart. Knives.

In times of stress, she made lists. As long as whatever frightened her could be separated and labelled, she felt less anxious.

"You going to be okay, Dad? I'm just going out to get some air."

She received a slight pleading gaze in return: *Please don't leave me here.* "That's okay," he said, his head still gripped by the murder-glove fingers.

Out in the corridor, she breathed deep, closed her eyes, and then opened them to find herself facing a wall of diseases.

Leaflets pinned to a bulletin board warned her about
Hepatitis A, Malaria and other Tropical Ailments. She stifled
a laugh. The latter was obviously aimed at the 0.02 percent of
the Cape Breton population who could afford to contract a
tropical disease.

She accepted a scorched and watery coffee from the vending
machine, vaguely nostalgic for the Toronto hospitals with their
own Starbucks and Second Cup franchises. Here the nurses were
neat Bonnie-like women with good haircuts, quick to smile,
laughing and joking by the gift shop. A monosyllabic security
guard, vaguely camp male nurses. Outside, broccoli-shaped trees
shimmered in a windless heat.

When she returned he was sitting in the waiting room. For a
second she didn't recognize him. He could have been any man,
a curiously ageless person wearing a cotton short-sleeved shirt
Anita had given him for his birthday in May, before she arrived,
presentless, and dark jeans, two light streaks running down the
thighs where he had rubbed up against weirs or wood. His knot-
ty knuckles gripped his knees.

"Can you come in now, please? I'm Doctor Schwaor." He
held out his hand.

"Pleased to meet you. Are you from India?" she said, idioti-
cally.

"Mauritius."

She managed not to say, *What in the name of God are you
doing here, then?*

"Could you come through here, Alistair?"

They sat in a room where the lights had been turned off, staring at a lightbox, as in a private film screening. The doctor
flicked a switch and the box lit up to show a miniature cosmos
of red, blue, green. They had made a map of her father's mind
and it was spectacular.

"Why is the brain blue?" she asked.

"Because it is cool, for the most part," the doctor answered.
"The red shows places of activity. Now, normally with problems

like Alistair's we would expect to see a reduction in function here—" he pointed to an area on the periphery of red, fading into orange-yellow.

"But there isn't?"

"It all looks entirely normal. With Alzheimer's, for instance, we would normally see a reduction in the peripheral myenalized areas of the brain. They would go cold, literally. We would see them here as blue and this would represent the neurofibulary tanglings and plaques associated with the disease."

Not for the first time she marvelled at the breezy, clinical tone doctors wielded like a weapon. To them, life was just another mortuary fact. No emotion seeped from the tight capsules of reality they fed their patients. Hope, No Hope. Death, Life. What did it matter? She thought of them as in love with the supreme rationality of being an organism, with the risk involved, and with their knowledge of all this. They towed the same line as the books she had read about the disease, with their shocking message that life wasn't consciousness, after all, the exquisite desires of the body or the will, but amino acids, proteins, chaos theory, stealth.

"We'll run more tests, of course. I'll ask you to see the nurse on your way out."

Her father's face was expressionless. All through the appointment he hadn't said a word, had only cast furtive glances at the lit cosmos of his brain.

The doctor stood. They stood too, her father scraping out his chair noisily on the floor. Her knees, she noticed, were trembling.

"Eve. Could you stay behind, please?"

She watched her father drift out the door. "I'll see you in the wait—" she called after him, but the door shut in the middle of her sentence.

"He hates that," she explained to the doctor. "It makes him feel like a child."

"Have a seat, please."

Jesus. He wants me to have a seat.

The doctor smiled. Was that a guillotine smile? "I wouldn't have had your father in here if I thought he was unwell."

She nodded. That made sense. She would not allow relief to rise within her, at least not yet.

"So how is he doing?"

Isn't that what you're supposed to tell me? "He's all right. He hasn't dropped anything lately. He seems less forgetful." She realized he had been much better of late, at least in the last week. She even caught him humming once, when she burst into the kitchen to fill the mare's waterbucket. The lethargy that he had been dragging around with him had diminished. He was more alert, more involved.

"How long has this been the case?"

If she thought about it, the improvement dated from the previous Saturday, the night Noel had come over. "About a week," she said.

"Well, from what I can see there is no current evidence that your father has a degenerative condition. It doesn't mean he won't have it. He could be in the very early stages of the disease, for example. It has a very unpredictable progression."

"I know. I've done some reading."

"There are a few more investigative avenues I'd like to try. Would you consider being part of a clinical trial?"

"What kind of trial?"

"It involves DNA testing. We are trying to establish genetic links in the population between Alzheimer's and other degenerative diseases."

She bit her lip. "Does that mean I'd know if I were likely to get these things? Because I'm not sure I'd want to know."

"You don't need to know anything you don't want to know."

"What's involved?"

"We would just take a swab of your mouth, and one of your father's, and send them off for testing."

She shrugged. "I can't see why not."

An hour later they pulled into the driveway. She shut off the engine and jumped out of the truck. She had the impression years were falling off her. He doesn't have Alzheimer's. She felt elated, but also addled, as if a small creature was taking little bites out of her.

"Well, I'm just played out," her father said. He really did look drawn. "I'm going to have a nap."

She watched him walk through the door, close it behind him, his slight frame obscured by mesh. She went outside and did something she hadn't done in ten years: she lit a cigarette that she had bummed from one of the male nurses on the way out.

She realized it had taken courage, what he had done today. For her, it had been a task, frightening, yes, but something to get over and done with so she could get on with the rest of her life. But for all her father knew he might be facing the abyss, right now.

She smoked most of the cigarette and then threw it on the ground with one drag left. She had never been a dedicated smoker, but on the occasions she had felt the need to smoke she had always discarded her cigarettes like that: one puff short of finished.

That night the restaurant was packed and she didn't see them come in. They were seated at table ten, her section. She could pass them to Connie, but that would mean Connie would have to walk clear across the room from her section to serve them. It would be too obvious. Be friendly, she chastised herself. Be neighbourly.

She wiped her hands on her apron and tucked her hair behind her ears.

"Hi there." It had been three days since she had seen Noel in the gas station. He looked rested and alert.

"Rachel, this is Eve. Eve's father lives next door. Eve brought us the jam."

"Oh," Rachel said. "Thanks."

For a second, Rachel was a blur. Then she cohered into some-one not so much pretty as formidably symmetrical; a long but slim nose, two brown eyes draped on either side of it, perfectly spaced, a slightly olive complexion. There was something glossy about her, as if she had just been buffed. Actually, she shone.

"How are you enjoying Clam Harbour?"

"Oh, it's fantastic. Noel probably told you, but I need to study, and it's very quiet."

"It certainly is."

Noel swung his eyes up toward her. They arrived like flutter-ing birds, a sinuous, avian sweep. "How's your father?"

"The same. We went to the hospital for tests today."

Rachel looked up from the menu. "What's this?"

"My father..."

"...memory problems," Noel said, simultaneously.

"It's not...," Rachel paused. "Alzheimer's?"

They all flinched at the word.

"We don't know. We hope not. It could be so many things."

Rachel nodded, slowly, her mouth set. "I really I hope it's not anything serious."

"Thanks." A breath escaped her; she realized she had been holding it, possibly for some time. "So. Welcome to Kay's. What can I get you to drink?"

"A beer for me."

"Diet Coke," Rachel said. "I love lobster but I'd like to try something different. Maybe crab. Is it fresh?"

"Everything's fresh here."

Lean fingers tipped with perfect nails handed Eve the menu, transparent peach, two-tone nails, the white scallops of perfect cuticles.

She went to do their drinks. She went through the motions: appetizer, refreshing drinks, main course, ice water, is everything all right here? Would you like some coffee? More coffee?

She didn't use the hi-folks voice she used with other customers with them. She felt as if she were moving under water. She watched them covertly while pretending to concentrate on the neighbouring table's discarded lobster shells. Noel's hands, which he used less than Rachel to illustrate his conversation, were not so much soft as unmarked, unscarred by experience. There was something slightly pampered about him, she decided; he would have been a loved child, he would never have questioned his right to love. Yet somehow this hadn't led to unexamined confidence, to entitlement; somewhere along the line he learned vulnerability. Then there was his cool hesitancy — she could almost hear the sound of it, as if it were a neglected frequency only certain people tuned into. But at the same time his uncertainty was related to a genuinely outgoing attitude, a real curiosity about the world.

Through snatched glances her initial impression of Rachel solidified: an elegant, elliptical face. Something of the brittle delicacy of twigs and sticks, a mouth like kindling. There was a residual Europeanness about her. She took a wild guess that her parents were Central European, perhaps even Italian, although from the north, maybe Trieste, that town on the Croatian border with the melancholy name. She might lack Noel's scattershot curiosity, she judged; she might be very careful with appearances, emotional as well as physical.

She cleared their table. Noel and Rachel sat for longer than usual after the meal, their heads bent together, as if they were afraid of being overheard. When she put their main course down, or took their plates away, they backed away, they sat bolt upright in their chairs, suspending their conversation just as she came into earshot. Through her early years of working in restaurants Eve had observed that there were two species of couples in restaurants: those who didn't give a damn about the waitress overhearing snippets of dialogue, and those who took the MI6 approach, bolting back in their chairs as soon as she came near.

Peggy rushed up to her. Another busload just pulled in.

A bus full of tourists from Vermont spilled through the door.

There had been a steady river of them since the beginning of summer. She really didn't understand why people from Vermont would come to Nova Scotia — didn't they already have enough spruce and freshwater lakes of their own?

She dragged tables together by herself with maximum scrape and bang. Connie was busy with several demanding family units in her section. She wanted to tell the Vermont people to go home, Rachel and Noel too. Everyone should just piss off. At some point as she was banging tables back and forth they left. She picked up the bill and the change tray off the table to find, nestling underneath, a hideously large tip.

The next morning he was on the step.

Noel looked down at the ground. He started to speak, and then hesitated. "I wanted to apologize for yesterday. I think I put you on the spot."

She shrunk back. She was still angry about the tip. She wanted to slip it under their door and then ignore them for the rest of the summer. She didn't know whether to be impressed that he would be aware of her discomfort, or so deeply embarrassed she would never be able to speak to him again.

"Rachel really wanted to eat out."

"I'm used to waiting on people I know," she lied.

"It wasn't the way I wanted you to meet."

She nodded. She barely restrained herself from saying thank you.

"And I also realize that...," he floundered. "Rachel insisted on leaving a big tip."

"Did she?"

"And I guess... I realized later that it could seem... insulting. Then again, not to leave one is also an insult, so..." he shook his head, looked away from her.

"Don't worry about it. We don't take it personally," she lied again.

He made a few twitchy movements of his hands, as if discarding possible responses. He was so ungainly and transparent in his discomfort she couldn't help herself.

"I was just making Dad some tea. I'm going to take it down to him in the Thermos. Do you want to come?"

Noel cast a quick glance in the direction of the house. "Thanks, but I should be getting back."

But he stayed, hovering on the step. To fill the silence she asked, "So, how is Rachel liking it here?"

"I'm not sure she's noticed her surroundings yet." He flashed her the rueful smile. "She's under a lot of stress."

"But she's finished her exams?"

"Technically, except she'll have to retake a couple. I don't envy her. I don't think I'd be able to absorb that amount of information."

"Have you been getting out to see the island?"

"So far we've been up to Ingonish. We're going to do the whole trail next week, go camping."

"That'll be fantastic."

He nodded. "It's so beautiful."

They both seemed to become aware, and in the same moment, that their conversation had shifted into pleasantries, even banalities, and that Rachel's presence had something to do with this transformation. Only a few days earlier it seemed they could talk about anything.

"I'd better be getting back," he said, again. "How's your father?"

"Much the same."

"Well. Take care."

"Take care."

She went to the window over the kitchen sink. She watched him walk down the drive in his pleasant, straightforward gait. She began to wash the teapot. The skin on her hands was drying and cracking, she noticed, the cells becoming more distinct.

Her hands were changing far faster than her face. Someday she might wake up to find they looked like the appendages of another species.

Suddenly she couldn't move; she stood as if paralyzed, the teapot half-washed in the sink, the cold faucet running over her aging hands.

She tried to perceive the nature of the rush of feeling passing through her, to break it up into its component parts: resentment, embarrassment, eagerness to please, anger. She knew this elaborate play between ambivalence and desire from other times in her life; they were so wound around one another that they are nearly identical, twins masquerading as strangers.

As Noel disappeared from view around the corner of their drive, the cascade of feeling pooled at her feet. It had run through her, it was out. She felt drained of something essential. How insane it was, she thought, the acres of life that had to be waded through, just to inhabit one true moment.

She checked to see her father was asleep, and then took the keys, got in the truck and eased it out of the driveway in neutral, leaving the headlights off until she was well out of sight of the cabin.

The night streams by. If she were in Toronto she would be walking along Queen Street to get spring water at two in the morning, cut flowers wilting in buckets outside corner grocery stores. Lew would be cycling from the CBC studios, the hollow roar of the Queen Street streetcar alongside him, spewing teal sparks. Here there is nowhere for her to go, no bars she would dare walk into alone; the nearest cinema is in Sydney and it is on a non-stop diet of summer blockbusters. There is a sort of theatre, of dinner-theatre ilk. *Discover our Heritage. Ciad Mille Failte.*

So she drives. She did this as a teenager. Nights she couldn't sleep, she would get in her father's truck-of-the-moment while he slept in his bed. Even if it is a waste of gas, she can't afford it, she drives to give herself the feeling that she is going somewhere, that there is somewhere to go.

She drives past the Ultramar, Tim Hortons, the wide empty bay at Nyanza. Lobster for Sale Here, strawberry U-Picks, Farmers' Market roadside fruit and vegetable stands, the Ceilidh barn, then the Reserve, bungalows with gaping wounds where the tarpaper exposes gashes of insulation, wrecked cars, unpredictable dogs that bark as she passes. Vi's truck stop, the oyster and salmon farms that net the bay. Googoo's craft tepee, where her father once bought her beaded necklaces and feathered headdresses.

Past Whycocomagh she turns around. On the way back she stops in at Duncan's gas station, parks the truck and sits listening to some country music station broadcast from PEI and which is caught in an early 1980s time warp, Roseanne Cash, Anne Murray, Kenny Rogers, Willie Nelson, her face lit by the submarine light of the dashboard.

It is safer to remember at night. Years which melted so effortlessly away are congealing again until the version of herself she had been when she had last driven up and down the highway to Indian Bay emerged: the high school misfit who preferred the company of men old enough to be her father, the trials of school-bus friendships, homework, the eternal dilemma of what to do at lunch while cliques undulated in the cafeteria, walking through the forest by the lake alone and returning just in time for English or History.

Mona. Her best friend in Grade Ten and Eleven. The excitement of their trips to the mall in Sydney to see movies, eat rubbery popcorn. One night they stuffed themselves into an automatic photo booth and took three strips of pictures of them pulling idiotic faces. Their classmates hadn't known where to locate them: they were neither Stoners, Jocks, nor Brains. She and Mona called themselves the Unclassifieds. Swathed in the cameraderie of the nomenclatureless they went to the hockey rink, then the Dairy Queen, dipping the ends of fries in livid ketchup. Mona kept getting perms that wouldn't take. *The Impermanence of Permanents*, their running joke.

They were the first girls in the school to transfer their allegiance from lip gloss to proper lipsticks. Other girls thought them too smart, above their station. *Who do you think you are?*

They were there still, she surmised, Mona and Eve, trapped in some pallid parallel dimension, sitting by the window in the Dairy Queen. Men driving by in their pickups see two teenaged girls in an otherwise empty restaurant, parkas flung across their chair backs, hair scraped into ponytails. *Boy, would I like some of that.*

What had happened to Mona? It really was amazing, how people lost touch.

CHAPTER 12

She opened the door to find a teenager in a RCMP uniform on the step.

"Morning. Is that your truck parked in the driveway?"

She squinted into the early-morning sun. It couldn't have been later than eight o'clock.

"You've got licence plate..." The teenager consulted a notepad before rattling off her licence plate number.

"Yes, why?"

"A truck matching the description of yours was spotted the night before near the scene of a fire."

"What kind of fire?"

"I can't tell you the details, but it's being investigated as a suspicious fire."

"There's been suspicious fires, as you call them, up and down this coast for the last twenty years," she countered. "Do you mean you've finally come round to investigating them?"

"Do you have any witnesses?"

"Witnesses for what?"

"To say you were here last night?"

"You think I was out burning houses?"

"No offence, but you never know."

She stared at him. He looked vaguely familiar. She might have known an older brother or sister, at school. She resisted the urge to ask his name.

"We have a witness who said they saw a truck like yours, same make, same colour, everything, being driven around up there."

"A *witness*? What time?"

"Two-thirty a.m."

"I was in bed asleep."

"You don't think anyone could have driven off with your truck without you knowing?"

"There's only one set of keys, and I've got them. I don't let my father drive. His memory...," she started, and then reconsidered. "His reflexes aren't so good these days."

"Where do you keep your keys?"

"Under my pillow." She waited for him to laugh. Instead he wrote it down. "Wait, don't write that down. That was a joke. I keep my keys in the kitchen. Don't you think I'd notice if someone was making off with my truck in the middle of the night? It's always parked right where I left it. There's always the same amount of gas in the tank as when I went to sleep."

"Do you mind if we go outside and take a look?"

She laughed. "I've been waiting for years for the police to find this guy who's been burning people's houses and barns, and you, when you finally do something about it, you show up here."

He gave her a penetrating look. He didn't seem to see the joke.

"How many trucks are there like this one?" she pressed on. "There must be hundreds on the island alone."

"In fact there are only twenty. It's not a common make."

"And where are the other nineteen?"

"We're working our way through them. So in your opinion there was no way anyone could have been driving your truck?"

She shook her head. "I don't see how it's possible."

She hadn't slept well the night before. In fact, if she thought about it, she had been waking up just before dawn every night for a week now. She had gone outside to smell that sweet, predawn air. It was still dark. The truck was in the driveway — but did she look, or did she just assume it was there?

"How can you catch him?"

"Not much chance unless we catch him red-handed, or at least get someone to get the licence plate. Can I have a look in the back of the truck?"

"Go ahead."

She watched as he peered into the empty flatbed and the driver's seat. He shut the door and dusted his hands. "Great view you folks have got up here."

She watched him walk to his squad car. She was almost in the front door when her father stepped out of the bushes. She nearly jumped out of her skin.

"Christ. Don't lurk like that."

"What did he want?"

"A truck the same as ours was spotted last night around where that house was burned down. He came to check it out."

"What'd he want to know?"

"He thinks I've been burning down houses in my spare time. As if I had time for arson."

She spent the rest of the day attacking the shed. In what her father referred to as his "office," she peeled away browning scraps of paper tacked to the wall bearing numbers of automated weather forecasts. Oyster shells gathered dust on the windowsill; faded business cards from hardware stores and sallow letters from second-hand car dealers fluttered on a cork bulletin board stiff with age.

In the back of the shed she found single oars missing their pairs, gasoline cans, and a hefty ancient scale of the kind with weights that have to be balanced in the middle. She peeled away an epidermis of rotting cardboard and discovered their old Eldis wringer-washer. She hadn't seen it since she was a child, and had assumed it went to the dump long ago. In the tub was a nest of empty Old Port cigar packets. Whose could these be? Her father had never smoked.

At the back of the shed was a locked cupboard. She was about to ask her father for the key, but she had only to touch the rusty token lock and it fell away. She opened the cupboard doors and one promptly fell off the hinge. She shone the flashlight's beam into the cupboard. A stack of vinyl record albums rested on the bottom shelf. She picked one out: Sibelius's *Concerto for*

Violin in C Minor. She couldn't recall her father ever listening to classical music.

Above the albums was a single shelf of books. They were mostly *Reader's Digests*, damp paperbacks, and a few mildew-spotted leatherbound books. She dusted the spines, coating her fingers with a thick black substance — the dust of decades, she guessed, rather than years. The titles of the books revealed themselves one by one. She was surprised to see Rilke's *Sonnets to Orpheus*; next to it a copy of *L'étranger*, in French. At the end of the shelf lay *The Alexandria Quartet*, a few thick books by someone named Leon Uris, and Doris Lessing's *The Golden Notebook*. She pulled one of the books out and opened it although the pages were nearly stuck together. In the flyleaf of *Sonnets to Orpheus* she read an inscription in faded blue ink: *for Ann.*

She put the book back and rummaged. In the farthest corner of the cupboard was an old ledger book like those once used for accounts, bound in leather pitted with mildew. Underneath it a long brown envelope of the kind used for legal letters poked out, gouged and charred, as if someone had tried to set fire to it. As she opened it bits of paper flaked away in her hands.

Inside the envelope were a dozen mildewed photographs. Gently she pried them apart. Their old Econoline van leapt out at her. She'd completely forgotten about the van they'd owned for a year or two before her father drove it off an embankment in a snowstorm. It was still there, probably, rusting in the culvert. Then a photograph of herself, or a version of her, dressed in a pink-and-white knitted poncho. She must have been eight or nine; the photograph might have been taken in the autumn after her mother died. Then a stack of much smaller snapshots, a group of ten or twelve, all glued together.

She pried them apart. They were all of her father. In them he sat alone, in the cabin by the look of it. He stared into the camera with a bare, reproachful expression. There was a violent, uncanny dimension to his face; like a fish that finds itself landed on a trawler deck, it was a single convulsing muscle of shock. He looked so young — he wouldn't have been more than thirty-nine when her mother died, she reminded herself. She studied these barren auto-portraits. Had he held the camera up to a mirror, or used a timer?

In the next photograph her mother stood in the driveway to their old house, her boots muddy, her hair in disarray, a restless cigarette gripped between her third and fourth fingers. She had always smoked like that, holding her cigarette tight, like an eagle with a squirrel it had plucked from a tree.

The picture provoked an odd jolt deep inside her, in her bowels. It had been years since she had seen a photograph of her mother. They were few in any case, and the ones that did exist, her father kept tucked away. She had never asked her father to see them because she had known instinctively that he would consider it a weakness, even a betrayal.

As she was inserting the pictures back into the envelope a rustle came from the doorway. She turned around to see Noel standing there.

"I wanted to have a word with your father, if that's okay with you."

Why was he asking her permission? "Go on in."

"Thanks."

She placed the photographs and the ledgerbook in a plastic bag. She would sneak them into the cabin later.

She found her father and Noel seated at the kitchen table, one of her father's nautical maps of the North Atlantic spread between them. "Fishing's been on the go here for five hundred years, maybe more," her father was saying. "You wouldn't believe the tonnage of cod they pulled out of the ocean. Even in the late Eighties."

"So what happened?" Noel asked.

"The fish just crashed, ten years ago now. Nobody knows why. Some blame it on the environmentalists stopping the seal hunt."

"What was that?"

"They used to cull the seals. Seals eat a lot of fish. The environmentalists didn't like that."

"How did they kill them?"

"Oh, it was nasty, to be sure. They used to go out on the ice floes where the pups were. They'd wear a mask, see...," her father's hands flew to the back of his head, "with the face of a seal on the front, so the pups wouldn't take fright. Then they'd club them to death. Them environmentalists who stopped it, because all they'd ever seen was something in a store. They weren't brought up seeing things killed the way we were, they couldn't take it. They eat bacon every morning, all right, but they don't know where it comes from."

"So now the seals are eating all the fish?"

"Myself, I think the seals aren't the whole story. I think it's the Spaniards and the Japanese with their draggers. They drag the ocean floor, and they take whatever they find there. All the plants, all the phytoplankton and zooplankton. Like clear-cutting a forest." Her father's hand drew a flat plain in the air. "There'll never be a fishery, ever again. And in Newfoundland, phew...," he whistled, "five hundred years of fishing dead in twenty. Those men still wake up in the morning thinking they're going fishing, and then they realize they're not. Out there on the open ocean, you can get killed out there like that...," he snapped his fingers. "They took the real risks, the offshore men, they're the real thing. You take me, I just put myself in the way of whatever's coming. I don't have to go out there and put my life on the line." He stood up with a crack. "Well, I'm off down the shore."

When her father had left, she turned to Noel. "Don't worry, he always does that. He's talking, and then suddenly he's off somewhere."

He nodded. "I'll try not to take it personally." He bent down and reached for something. "I brought this back, thanks for lending it to me." He held out a book. *Fish of the Atlantic.*

"I really enjoyed it. I learned all sorts of things I wish I never knew."

"Like what?"

"About conger eels. Or the Butterfish. That's my favourite. It's covered in mucous. Who made up those names anyway? Tompot Blenny. Five-Bearded Rockling. John Dory. Gudgeon. Tub Gurnard. Apparently the Tub Gurnard actually walks on the seabed. It also grunts. In fact the name comes from the French *grogner*, to grunt." He smiled widely, ingenuously, and she thought again how in some men a mere smile returned them to boyhood.

"Why do you want to know all this?"

"All what?"

"About the island, about my father's life?"

"You sound suspicious."

"I'm just... not used to people taking an interest."

"You think I have an ulterior motive."

"Do you?"

"Not that I'm aware of."

An awkward silence came and went, like the tide.

"So what do you write about in that notebook of yours?"

"I don't know." He had caught her off guard. "Moments, observations. Things I remember. What my father told me about eels, what I remember about our life together, those years after my mother left. I realize I'm old enough now to be nostalgic for a lost way of life." She stopped. She hadn't meant to follow the contours of the truth quite so closely.

Noel got up. "You know, I've never seen your room."

"There's a reason for that. It's a mess."

"I'd like to," he insisted.

"All right."

Noel sat on the lower bunk and looked around her spartan room.

"As you can see I was the only kid at camp who found the lodgings more comfortable than home."

His eyes snagged on *Horse and Train*. "It's a bit sinister, don't you think?"

"It's inevitable, but not sinister."

"Why do you have the Periodic Table on your wall?"

"Oh, that. I had to learn it by heart for chemistry in high school and I never got around to taking it down."

"I was wondering if I could borrow it."

"Sure. I'll take it down at some point and bring it over."

Noel stayed seated on the bed. She was sure he was about to ask her something, or do something. She looked at him expectantly. What was it about his face? It seemed to hold the key to all faces, those mobile, fluid masks we wear and which are — whether we like it or not — our ambassadors in the world. Noel's was a Bergman film face, quite dramatic and sublime, shifting effortlessly between anger, sorrow, delirium, and also a frank, bare quality. It had a shadow of the tropics — a lassitude but also muddy rigour that was best expressed in that judicious gaze of his, which attempted to mask a wince of susceptibility.

He raised his hand toward hers, as if he were about to touch her. But he stopped just short of her body. He let his hand fall.

The telephone rang and she went to answer it. It was Anita; as she was talking, Noel let himself out the door.

The following Saturday she went to a dinner party at Celyn's, a typically varied gathering with Bob in from Boston for the weekend accompanied by a client he'd flown up in his plane, and a couple of teachers from Indian Bay Eve had met once or twice before. Celyn had invited Noel and Rachel as well, Bob informed her as soon as she was through the kitchen door.

Celyn had put a Rankin Family tape on the stereo. Eve spoke to the teacher couple, who were originally from Ontario. "We went down to the festival in Judique last weekend," they said. "Next we're going up to Big Pond. You don't go to the concerts? You don't know what you're missing."

Noel and Rachel arrived. Rachel was dressed in slim jeans

and a cream top. Eve had learned the hard way that she could-
n't wear cream, it made her look like a parsnip, but Rachel
looked casual and regal. Out of the corner of her eye she
watched Rachel go through the motions of arrival, proffering a
bottle of wine, comments on the elegance of the kitchen, issu-
ing a keen request to be taken on a tour of the house. Rachel
was a rose quartz woman, Eve decided, delicate but flinty, with
a vitreous streak.

Noel stood in the kitchen at Rachel's side. For a moment she
felt inexplicably exposed, even defenceless. *This is your home,*
she reminded herself. She had grown up here, while people like
Rachel and Noel were the equivalent of a gust of wind passing
through.

Dinner was roast chicken in woody pungent tarragon from
Celyn's garden. First they would have grilled asparagus, also
from the garden, to be followed by strawberries from Celyn's
patch.

Celyn commanded them to sit wherever. "You'll all switch
places between courses in any case," Celyn announced, "so
you'll get to talk to your favourite person eventually."

From the other side of the table she caught the sound of
Rachel's laugh and it was easier, more mellifluous, than she had
imagined it would be.

With a scraping of chairs, everyone was seated. She was the
first to plunk herself down in a chair in a flurry of indifference.
She really didn't care if she ended up sitting next to avuncular
Bob, or Rachel, or Bob's client, a red-haired man she thought
might be named Charles. It really didn't matter.

She looked up to find Noel across from her and Rachel on her
right. She met his eyes in the briefest of glances between the candle and the flowers.

She turned to address Rachel. "I understand you've just finished exams."

Another xylophone laugh. "It's more like they've finished
me."

"When do you get the results?"

"In a couple of weeks."

"Do you think you passed?"

"I might have to re-sit one of my weaker subjects. If I did, I'd re-sit as quickly as possible. There's a summer exam session in mid-September."

"You can't just take the course again next year?"

"I could, but I'm too old," Rachel sighed. "I'm running out of time." Her eyes had turned hard and resigned, the hue of onyx Eve had bought for Caroline's autumn collection only a few months ago. Caroline would set it in milky white enamel.

Rachel leaned in toward Eve and spoke in a low voice, "I didn't realize Clam Harbour was going to be this small."

"You don't get much smaller."

"The idea was for Noel and I to be on our own for a while. We don't see each other that much these days, between his job and law school. We felt we were leading separate lives and we had to do something about it, before we found ourselves *really* leading separate lives." She smiled ruefully.

Eve was surprised by Rachel's openness. She suspected Rachel's trust was not easily earned, and she wondered what she had done to deserve it.

"It's the same with my husband," Eve said, savouring her use of the secret weapon word.

"You're married?"

Eve basked in a balmy moment of having bested this woman, who had certainly thought her too unconventional, too marginal, to be married.

"What does your husband do?"

"He's a researcher — well, assistant producer now — on a national news program. It's like working for CBS or NBC," she said. *Except it's not,* she could hear Lew's voice correcting her. *They make real money and get to cover real news.*

"Will he come to see you at some point?"

"I'm not sure. He can barely get two days off in a row, let

alone a week. He might come in August for a few days, when things slow down, newswise."

Rachel directed a quick, thin smile to the other side of the table. Although Noel was talking with Charles, he seemed to be keeping one eye trained in their direction. She saw him pick up Rachel's smile and return it to its bearer. Rachel straightened and moved back, elongating her already elegant frame, her back curving tautly, like the flexed tension of an archer.

"People call us back-to-the-landers but we didn't see ourselves that way," Celyn was saying to the table at large. "Sure, we didn't agree with Vietnam. But that was about it. We didn't have this idea of being self-sufficient and growing our own organic children. I mean, vegetables," Celyn corrected herself. "Now there's a Freudian slip." Everyone laughed, although Eve suspected Celyn's substitution was deliberate. It occurred to Eve that she might have done it to impress Noel. She had caught a glimpse of them talking intently across the table.

"We're too rich to be back-to-the-landers," Bob said.

"I don't think that's true," Celyn countered. "We came up here looking for a simpler life, the good life."

"And what's that, for you, the good life?" Noel asked.

Celyn turned to Noel to address his question. Eve caught something both wistful and indulgent in Celyn's expression. Eve shot Rachel a quick sideways glance to see if she had noticed Celyn's look, but Rachel was looking out the window at the wild seagrass Celyn had planted around the house. It waved languorously in the night wind, barley-hued against an indigo sky.

"We wanted a place where there was a community and culture, somewhere that offered a sense of belonging," Celyn answered. "This was the Seventies, remember. It seemed easier then, to say, that's the life I want. There were fewer options, and the good ones stood out. What was Boston or New York in the Seventies? Burnt-out cars, winos everywhere. Nixon, Vietnam. We just didn't want to live in our own country anymore. We wanted to be somewhere we could still see our families, have our kids go to school there if they wanted to, but have them grow up in a place where people actually talked to each other." Celyn turned to Eve, "I know it was different for you. You grew up here. You had no choice."

She nodded, grateful for Celyn's acknowledgement that she was in a different position from everyone else around the table.

Celyn turned back to Noel. "The good life is a personal choice, obviously. Everyone must have a different idea of what it is."

"I'm not sure. The good life used to be a concept everyone shared, outside of personal morality." Noel sat straighter in his chair now, his shoulders square, his voice judicious and allowing. "The idea of a common good created a bond for centuries. Now it's become another victim to personalized morality." He looked only at Celyn as he spoke, although Eve had the impression his words were destined for someone else.

All through his speech Eve felt a dangerous glow spreading through her, which she quickly categorized as respect. She was reminded of what she had liked and admired in Noel, almost instantly: that he didn't seem to be interested in influencing people, in charming them, bringing them round to his way of thinking. She had sat beside her husband at so many tables and watched him go to work — this was how she put it to herself — on people. And invariably they were charmed, invariably they did in fact come round to Llewellyn's way of thinking.

But neither was Noel obtuse, she thought, take-me-or-leave-me, blind to his faults. He didn't seem to have any particular agenda, other than the truth.

She startled at the sound of Rachel's voice beside her.

"What do you mean, Noel?" In Rachel's voice was a strange mixture of indulgence and sharp query.

"I mean our preferences are now our only ethics. I mean the 'it just feels right' brigade. That's how we make decisions and choices now, 'it just feels right for me.' We don't ask ourselves any questions about collective responsibility."

"'We'? Surely you're not including yourself with the hordes? Rachel's voice swaddled an ironic bite in a thin blanket of teasing."

"Of course, I do it too. I operate on instincts and desires. But I also try to be aware that that's all I have at my disposal, that I'm no longer able to identify the common good."

Noel would have said much more had he been more confident of the company. But he couldn't count on Rachel to be his ally in these exchanges. Later, when they were alone and he didn't have to risk exposure by her responses, he would explain to her his suspicion that people like Celyn needed to flee the real world, to opt out of its responsibilities and that there was a cowardice in this reluctance to face it down in all its ugly, mortal glamour. He met these people everywhere, people who had left Boston or Philadelphia to move to an island in the Queen Charlotte Sound, say, where they put in solar panels and their own spring and quietly stocked their pantry for some imagined future apocalypse. Like them, Celyn could afford to opt out because her husband went to slave in the canyons of Mammon every week. In fact, he imagined that most of the Americans who had moved up here had had some cushion of family money behind them. Certainly they didn't seem to fetch up in the fish-processing plants where locals toiled.

He caught Rachel's eye. There it was, the subtle warning look, just as he'd expected. He knew she would try to deflect the conversation if he began to express any of these spiked thoughts, thoughts that she considered had ruined a good many otherwise enjoyable dinner parties. He heard the inevitable conversations in the car later, sitting in the driveway in the void space between ignition and heating or air-conditioning, her rigid profile beside him in the passenger seat.

Not everyone wants to hear your sociological theories, Noel. Don't you realize you're dismantling people's existences when you could be sharing them?

I don't want to condone people's fantasies. I don't care if they don't like me. Have you heard of sincerity?

Sure. The kind of sincerity that makes sure you're never invited to peoples' houses for dinner again. I'm really familiar with that kind of sincerity.

Before dessert, Celyn had them shift again. This time Eve ended up with Charles on her right and Noel next to her, on the end of the table. Almost immediately Charles began to talk about his marriage, or rather, his recent divorce.

"We got married too young, that's all; we just ran our course together." Charles said this breezily, almost happily. It made Eve think of a horserace, two racehorses straining side by side, until finally one fell behind.

"We want to spend our vacation together with the kids," he said, after he recovered himself. "We want to bring them up as normally as we can. We're on good terms. I don't understand how people who live together for years can just stop speaking to each other from one day to the next, just because one of them has moved on."

She had the impression Charles had been storing up explanations in his mind; they all floated together in a buoyant balloon. She had an impulse to burst it.

"Because it hurts too much," she said.

Real anger flared in Charles's eyes, although for the briefest of seconds. He had not just been hurt, she saw, but wounded to the quick. He knew so much more about hurt than she did, and here she was stumbling around in this landscape of rigid truths, without having earned her passage.

From then on their talk was all thrusts of confidence, easy, cheery laughter. But even as they held a light-hearted discussion of the zombification of CNN newsreaders ("Why do they have that rabbit-trapped-in-headlights look? Are they *trained* to blink slowly?") she could see something — a film, a counterpoint? — running behind Charles's eyes, like a film, a counterpoint score.

"We saw you down by the ferry yesterday." Noel addressed

her from where he sat on the corner of the table. She registered that the I had become a *we*. It looked like you were writing.

"I was."

"What were you writing?"

"Just notes about what's... happening. Or not happening, more like it."

Noel looked instantly intrigued. That was another thing she liked about him: the speed of his reactions, the fact he never hid them.

"I always wanted to..." she paused to see if anyone else was listening, "to write a book."

"You mean a novel?"

"I don't know." *There*, she thought, *I've told him something. He knows what no-one knows — not even Lew.*

"I'm sure you can do it, if you put your mind to it."

"Do you really think it's that simple?"

His expression changed and she caught a flicker of annoyance. She could imagine him thinking: of course not, nothing is that simple, but what's wrong with believing in yourself?

But you've had it so easy, she countered silently. *You don't even know, and I can never tell you, of the things I've had to do just to get to a position where I could compete, where I had a chance against all you middle-class kids with two parents and a college trust fund. I'm not talking here about the kind of fighting spirit that gets you a good GPA and an internship with a think-tank.*

But this would sound bitter, of course, and defensive. So she said nothing. The fight would be endless, she realized; first against silence, then against speech.

She ended up talking to Charles for the rest of the evening. It had a certain reassuring symmetry, to be sat next to a pleasant, intelligent man at the table with Noel and Rachel. From time to time, Noel glanced at her with a puzzled expression, as if something were out of order.

As for Charles, he listened intently, certainly, but behind this diorama of engagement she caught a faint whiff of endeavour; he was making an effort to understand her conversation, her patterns of thought, scurrying after her words. That was the problem: he was *trying*. Noel, on the other hand, listened and spoke easily, with a porous, effortless intensity. Charles could never do that, and this was what she missed.

He sits alone with his books and magazines and his pack of cards, as he has done for years of nights. He'd been invited to dinner up at the neighbours', of course. Them schoolteachers, community types, back-to-the-landers. Americans, or no, it was Ontario. They had a buck or two. It's all right for them, they can afford to go back to the land. Everyone else wants to get the hell off it.

Then Celyn, who he would never say a word against but who in all of fifteen years hadn't asked him how he was doing, just been bright and breezy in that way people with money have, expecting everything to go the same way for others as it did for them. Why would he do a stupid thing like that, go to dinner with these people and their eager talk and sit there like a lump himself.

So he reads, accompanied by the loud metronome tick of the old clock. This has become his only pleasure in the last few years, along with his solitaire games. Alongside the faded *Reader's Digest*s and *National Geographic*s from 1979 are his reference books. *Der Aal,* the Danish tome on the life cycle of the eel — he couldn't read a word of it, being in Danish, but the line drawings were superb — and his other books: *Dictionary of Weather, Fish of the Atlantic.*

He opens the latter to a creased, well-thumbed nautical map of the Atlantic Ocean. In the middle of it is an indigo blotch, the Sargasso Sea. *Sargasso.* He loves the hiss of this word, its lonely slide. He had read that the word came from *Sargaço,* Portuguese for seaweed. There, thick mats of weed were buoyed by sponges of mustard-coloured polyps. No-one knew why; the seaweed itself was not found anywhere other than in this spiralling patch two thousand miles long and a thousand miles wide. The weed circulated in a counter-clockwise direction, herded by currents.

He imagines seeing it from a plane or a satellite, a matted glaucous patch of weed in that lonely stretch of ocean between the Azores and the West Indies. The Sargasso is home to the Bermuda Triangle, the doldrums, and the horse latitudes, so-called because horses driven insane by thirst were pushed over-board by sailors eager to conserve drinking water. Other ships came upon their bloated corpses and would know that trouble had arrived.

The eels he kills have been farther than he has ever been in his life. Brazil, Lisbon, the Eastern Antilles, the Azores, the desert coast of Africa. Like them he is interested in the rim places of the world; he would never venture far into the interior. Away from the smell of the ocean he becomes disoriented and claustrophobic.

He has been off the island only a few times in his life: the first to visit cousins in Boston: a hot, cruel, impatient city. When he tried to buy things in a store he spoke so slowly that they'd be serving the guy behind him before he even finished talking. Then to Halifax a couple of times, a nice enough city, but he didn't know anyone there. Without family, that web of uncles and cousins, how did you orient yourself? Once, walking down Barrington Street, he'd had what he knew now from reading the newspaper was called a panic attack. Heart racing, blood rush-ing around his body, as if looking for a way out. Bubbles of air forming in his lungs. He'd had to sit down, right there on the sidewalk. People walking by him had taken him for a tramp; a couple of people even gave him money and he was in such a state he forgot to refuse it.

If he couldn't walk down a street in Halifax without falling apart, then what hope did he have of keeping himself together in the places he read about in his magazines: Mauritania, Santander, Cabo São Vicente, Belém? What hope did he have of seeing a jaguar, the cobalt shadows of the rainforest, white river dolphins, the Sargasso Sea?

At times he catches glimpses of another version of himself, living in a modest bungalow in some small Ohio town after a lifetime of working on the ships that ply the Great Lakes, or an inhabitant of the tidy Crescents, Closes, or Avenues of Kitchener, Ontario, of Chilliwack, B.C. Would he ever have survived such an exile? Other men could, sure: tougher men, perhaps. He has stayed where he belonged, only to find that he is deserting himself, although in increments, following the eels and the cod into some unmapped oblivion.

He is surprised at how much he likes talking to the American. It has been so long since he has had an audience. But he had the impression Noel was genuinely interested in what he had to say. He told Noel how people still say, "If the fish come back." As if they've gone somewhere else. The fish were never coming back, he said. They were simply gone.

He told Noel about the eels, how Aristotle studied them first and noted they were *anhydrous*, meaning they could live in both salt and freshwater, and that, unlike all other fish, eels migrated from the sea to rivers and back again instead of the other way round. No-one could locate their sexual organs, so Aristotle concluded they had none. They were not produced from sexual intercourse at all, he wrote, but were spontaneously generated from mud. Three hundred and fifty years later Pliny the elder thought that eels reproduced by rubbing their bodies against rocks.

Then there was Sigmund Freud, he told a delighted Noel. Yes, he was involved with eels too. He was a medical student at the University of Vienna, from which he received a grant to search for eel testicles. How eels reproduced was one of the burning research issues of the day. His laboratory was in Trieste, at the time on the margins of the Austro-Hungarian Empire.

Imagine that, he told Noel: a young Sigmund Freud in his outpost laboratory, unaware of who he was yet to become, dissecting eels, sawing through their supernaturally tough skin, rooting around in their innards. There he discovered ribbons of ruched tissue, like frilled curtains, but he failed to conclude that these were the reproductive organs he was seeking, and it was left to another scientist to confirm his suspicions. Futile weeks on the Adriatic, the grey-blue sea and its stubborn, opaque creatures.

He told Noel how when eels reach the mid-Atlantic bight, just before the Sargasso, they vanish. In the Sargasso there are no adult eels among the mats of seaweed and flotillas of jellyfish, only young eels, those same thumbnail scraps, drifting on the ocean currents. He told him how an adult that is ready to spawn had never been found in nature, nor have eels been observed mating, and they refuse to reproduce in captivity. How they perpetuate their species is a mystery.

Her mother kneels beside the Eldis wringer-washer, her back to the door. She wouldn't know Eve was there.

I'm scared.

A sweater lies flattened between the two rollers, its arms flung uselessly into the tub.

I want to hold your hand.

Her mother's thick, blasted wails remind her of the 45 record of whales' songs her father plays for her. They had come inside a copy of *National Geographic*.

I just want to love you.

Her mother's face is in her hands. She is breathing heavily, sobbing the words.

She realizes it in a flash, a child's canny instinct. More and more these days she thinks of him, the man with black hair. At seven years old she can feel the appeal of his authority, his tenderness. When he visits she is careful not to bash into him, careful not to step on his toes. Although once she did and he scooped her up into his arms and hung her upside down until she squealed with delight.

Her mother sinks down to the floor until she is resting on her haunches. Her lethargy, her submission, are frightening to behold. She wants to comfort her mother but she knows that if she makes her presence known her mother will snap to attention like a dragoon, will wrest that sweater from the wringer. She will shout at Eve, maybe even shove her away.

These scenes, buried for so long, are cohering now, collecting themselves from remnants of memory into haphazard squalls. She has been mistaken: memory is not a jigsaw puzzle but a fume, a network of smoke.

Look at her, so youthful at thirty-two that she might be the creature time forgot. Everyone comments on this, how it is almost eerie, her mother's girlishness, how she has stayed thin and small with a wild nest of auburn hair.

That morning by the washer, as for so many mornings white and long with snow, she is waiting for the return of her beloved, as if awaiting the return of her husband from wars strange and taxing.

But she is not waiting for her husband. Her husband is here, down by the river.

The ledgerbook is not for accounting. Her mother writes in a cramped, desperate hand. It has been so long since she has seen a word written by her mother. She thinks she may have old birthday cards saved somewhere. Happy 5th, my Eve.

My Eve.

She is twenty-five, he is eleven years older. He is the son of her grandmother's sister, born late, when his mother was already in her early forties. He comes back to the island twice a year with his wife and their young family. They arrive in June after school lets out and stay until Labour Day, then show up again in

December, for Christmas and New Year's. He has lived off the island since he was twenty-one, first in Montreal, then in New York State. *But he hasn't forgotten his people,* she hears her mother say. He earns enough money to come home twice a year and see his extended family.

He has dropped in to meet her mother for the first time, because they are cousins. He sits at the table with her husband, Alistair, drinking a cup of tea. When she comes into the room he bolts to his feet, unsmiling, and proffers his hand.

"Nice to meet you."

"Nice to meet you. I see Alistair's made you some tea."

"He has." He puts his hands to his sides, smiles — a slightly awkward and interior smile, as if he has been moved by some private thought. He sits down again in a relieved manner.

The three of them sit and talk. He is their senior and from time to time he makes them feel the distance, little anecdotes of tricky mining jobs, his months working in the tropics, his hard-won place in the world. He is not deferential but neither does he condescend. He is animated and responsive, but then he will pitch headfirst into a brooding silence, his eyes turn fixed and troubled, then snap out of it with an instant smile. He has large eyes the colour of light rum, a prominent nose, drastic cheek-bones, a generous mouth — an emphatic, moody face. Her mother watches him speak, gesticulate, smile and laugh, sees a dextrous, intelligent, experienced person. She thinks: *Oh good, an interesting distant relative. Maybe I can learn something about the world from this man.*

She dismisses her perception that he is the most handsome man she has ever seen, or ever expected to see, and that he made her heart lurch the first second she saw him. No man has ever done this. But it does not feel exciting, and this is why she banishes it so thoroughly. Already it hurts.

She sees him two weeks later, and then at unsteady intervals through the summer. Much to her dismay they are hostile to each other, sometimes genuinely unkind. She doesn't know how this has happened; she has only tried to be pleasant. The surprise at the enmity between them, this creature sprung up, fully formed but unbidden, is present in both their eyes.

Other people notice, of course, and ascribe it to some half-forgotten family drama, some old resentment between her grandmother and her grandmother's sister, his mother. Still, their succulent unease violates the decorum of the community — feuds and resentments are few, people get along really quite well, women trade recipes and child-care tips, and men help each other find work when they can.

A field party at night on a neighbour's farm, one of the last, left over from the days when haying was done by hand.

It is the apogee of summer, late July 1967. The party is lit by the headlights of cars and trucks because the summer has been dry, too dry to light the usual bonfire. Fireflies amble through the night, blinking like the lights of the transatlantic flights that will in a few years' time streak through the island's nocturnal skies.

They stand in separate groups; he with his wife and her family, she with cousins from Middle River. He stands legs apart, feet flung out at near right angles, leaning back slightly, his arms crossed over his chest — a master-of-all-he-surveys posture. She is conscious of his watchful, cutting gaze. That summer she has taken up smoking again for the first time since Anita was born. She doesn't know why, only that she is nervous, even anxious, and smoking seems to calm her.

She can't find her matches. Does anyone have a light? No, why doesn't she use the lighter in the truck? But she'd have to turn the engine over and she's hot already; she rises to rummage for matches in the glove compartment of the truck. Halfway back to her group she stops to light up, but a wind harries the flame. Even if she cups her hand, it refuses to ignite.

"Do you want me to light that for you, Ann?"

He is reclining in the grass now, supported by his elbows, his thin legs thrown out in front of him, crossed at the ankles. Instead of invitation or friendly helpfulness, his voice is nailed closed with challenge.

She is in awe of him — she doesn't think she has ever been in awe of anyone in her life. But she is also amazed by the strange nervous calm he inspires in her. Like a diffuse tenderness, although threaded with something much darker, and urgent.

She hesitates, then bends down and gives the cigarette and the matches to him. He levers himself into a sitting position, inserts the cigarette into his mouth. He cups his hands around it; his fingers are delicate, slender but not overly long, with neatly trimmed, clean nails. He lights the cigarette effortlessly.

"Thanks." She takes the lit cigarette and matches from his hands, careful not to touch his fingers.

She dismisses him as a flirt, and not a gracious one; in fact, that kind of man who sets out to undo women for sport. But no, in the next conversation he is gallant and yielding.

She is twenty-five, she has hardly been off the island and she is as yet unschooled in these contradictions. Her family and friends are coherent characters; they may become amusing or maudlin when drunk, of course; they have their peculiarities, but emotionally they are fairly consistent.

But him — she doesn't know what to make of him, nor of the strange intimacy that has sprung up between them. She spends the best part of that year, the long absences in between his visits, puzzling him out.

They are at a beach picnic, the same one that will be captured in one of the few photographs her father will save. As usual they keep a cordial but defiant distance. She is talking to one group, he to another. She goes to fetch a bottle of pop from a cooler that is holding down a corner of her beach blanket. To do this she has to walk past him. This she does successfully, although she has to hold her breath because every perimeter of him — his ears, his skull, his shoulder — shimmers with a kind of threat. She feels herself list dangerously toward him, a ship with a hole in its hull.

On the way back, he stops her.

She turns, very slowly, to face him. They don't speak, but they look at each other. The drastic slopes of his face, the mournful expression in his eyes, rueful eyebrows that tip down at the outer edges. Something in the angle and expression of his face suggests he will deliver another of his rebukes, his tart challenges.

But his voice is pleasant. "Ann." To detain her he touches her, very lightly, on the shoulder. "Could I get a drink of that?"

"Sure. Let me get you a cup."

"Thanks." He takes a draught and hands the bottle back to her. "We're having a cookout on the beach next week, we wondered if you'd like to come. You and Alistair."

Oh, she thinks, frowning. *You're being friendly.*

"Sure." She smiles.

"Good."

"Good. See you then." She walks away from him, back to her group. Anyone watching from behind would see that her step is a bit unsteady, but they would ascribe it to the fact that she is walking on bare feet in the sand, and everyone knows how sand can shift underfoot.

At the cookout they attempt a conversation about nothing — the weather or the way the lake moves at night. As they talk he doesn't look at her, as usual, but keeps his gaze trained on the lake. His eyes are dark and liquid. Firelight shadows the hollows in his face. He was sick the previous winter, he tells her, when she remarks on his thinness. Some tropical ailment picked up while overseeing the opening of a new mine in Gabon. *Gabon* — she absorbs the name of this unknown country, and resolves to look it up in the *National Geographic Atlas* Alistair bought on mail order last year.

Listening to him speak about Africa, the pills he has to take in order not to get malaria, the heat — which he tolerates well, he says, for someone from their latitude — she has a vertiginous, streaking feeling, as if she has just been pitched from a great height.

They have been speaking for twenty minutes, it is the best conversation they have had so far. The fire burns low now. She basks in its bronze glow, watches it settle in the hollows of his cheeks, in the clefts of his eyes.

He tears his eyes away from the lake and they settle upon her like a cloud. What she sees is tenderness and also desire threaded with a thrilling searching quality. She gives him back a look of fear and delight and defiance.

His wife calls his name from the other side of the fire. Something about needing more marshmallows. She swivels away, her step unsteady. She feels drunk or as if someone has just hit her over the head with a large object.

She goes to where Anita is sitting sleepily on the edge of a log and gathers her in her arms, buries her face in her neck. He comes after her with a purposeful step, smiling, an alder stick topped by a marshmallow in his hand, moving into the hem of darkness beyond the fire's halo.

She takes her face away from her daughter's neck.

Anita says, her voice drowsy, "Mommy, why are you crying?"

He has been about to give her the alder, to touch her on the shoulder, but he hears Anita's question and pivots away.

His face seems to be coming from inside her. It has always been there. Now it has erupted from her bones, her skin, to take its place in the world. Her mother thinks, straightaway, of a word she has never before used in her life: *fate*. Then another word, hard on its heels, like a chaperone: *joke*.

He has latched on to her. This is what her women relatives say in the kitchen, the women Eve will overhear, unbeknownst to her mother, through the register in the ceiling.

Latched on. She allows a deep and undulating happiness to wash through her insides.

But don't you forget. Men cleave to their wives.

This time her mother has to resort to the dictionary. She looks it up: cleave. It has two meanings: one is *to divide, to rent in two.* The other is *to stick fast. To adhere.*

Night paws at the window. It is 4 a.m. She hasn't been able to sleep through the night in months. Each night she is catapulted awake by a ripe current of love and dread and desire. She keeps herself warm by sitting in front of the coal stove, a housecoat and two blankets around her shoulders, writing in her ledger-book.

What kind of heart do you have? This is the only question to ask, the only question whose answer is worth knowing. She wonders and wonders. He seems so severe, so in command, he might be genuinely cold. Can a heart really be so sullen, so rebuking? She has never encountered this species of intimacy before, flowering out of a burst of hostility, bog flowers blooming in rusty ditchwater. She is genuinely spooked by the ill-defined hungers he has sparked in her. They are ravishingly strange. They are ignited by the smallest things. It is an old code, poised to reveal itself in everything he does: his alert agile stance, the vein that throbs on his forehead. As if, in each of his cells, his smallest gestures, she is already there.

And what kind of mind does he have? Stiff, to a degree, and categorical. He thinks: this is my wife, this is my daughter, this is my colleague; I will behave toward them thus. As if reading from a script. Then a renegade presence — a dark horse, some-one like her — comes on the scene. He can't quite react. She thinks she can hear the sound of pages being shuffled. He is looking for the part she will play in his life, for his next line.

Her feet are encased in thick woollen socks; splayed in front of her, shoved into the bottom oven compartment. Even the angle at which her feet are positioned make her think of him: it is an unconscious mimicking of his wind-up toy posture, the way he seems to march, feet turned out, toward any pretty woman on his radar.

She is contemplating the rift valley between men and women: if he were hers, she can't imagine looking any further. But if she were his, she doesn't kid herself that he wouldn't always look around him. He is burdened by his beauty; he needs to hove it abroad in the world, needs to see its effect. She has never liked womanizers, if that's what he is; then again she has never liked uxorious men either.

The clock in the shape of a butterfly ticks loudly. Anita will be up in just two hours. God, she's so tired. If she could sleep, she would.

CHAPTER 13

An unannounced early July heat wave made them grateful for the air-conditioned car. They drove, weaving through scenery they considered barren but beautiful, on increasingly narrow roads, stepping gingerly out of the car from time to time, on the wind-whipped Cape Smokey lookout, Noel drawing Rachel's attention to the Point Aconi power plant shining like an obelisk in a sea of trees, watching as the white bone of the Newfoundland ferry scissored its way though a tourmaline ocean to St. John's.

They stopped at gas stations and bought unfamiliar brands of chocolate bars and potato chips — Crispy Creme and Humpty Dumpty — delighted that Canada was, after all, a different country, Noel picking up an eight-pack of beer by the HANDLE/POIGNÉE and laughing with Rachel at how Canada was a country in the grip of a strange compulsion to repeat everything, even the most obvious details, in French. They drove through folded hills, reading the names painted on faded mailboxes — Chiasson, Gallant, Matheson. The poetic rusticity of the place-names delighted them: Militia Point, South Gut, Framboise Cove, Goose Harbour, Moose Bay.

They tried camping only once in the National Park, but they forgot the mosquito repellent and had to abandon the idea after the second day. They decamped to a country inn the tourist guide recommended, a secluded spot near trout-laden rivers in the interior of the island. Rachel liked this place best. There was a log fire in the main house, nightly ceilidhs, and a long tree-draped drive that reminded her of Kentucky stud farms.

They stopped on Inverness Beach. It was a clear day. A translucent light seemed to etch the already pungent contrasts of the landscape in graphite and silver. Prince Edward Island appeared as a mauve bruise on the horizon. The beach was lined with spruce so black it looked purple.

Rachel sat under a giant beach parasol she had brought with her, while Noel lay in the full sun. He had always tolerated the sun well; even in the tropics he rarely burned. He turned over to lie on his back and regarded the safe-to-swim flag fluttering in a delicate breeze, the manic trot of sandpipers scurrying in the wake of the waves.

Something in the arrangement — Rachel next to him, sitting in a pool of shadow, a book propped up on her knees — brought to life an older tableau. He must have been four or five, those summers his family went to the beaches of Rhode Island or Massachusetts. He was the youngest, and the only boy. His mother seemed to have had some kind of prolonged anxiety attack after his birth. His father told him about it once, although obliquely. She became convinced that she wasn't able to care for him and his sisters properly, that she was a bad mother.

As for his two sisters, he watched them swimming, carrying air mattresses in and out of rolling waves. They disappeared into their barrels for a second before popping up, covered in seafoam. If he tried to join his sisters his mother fetched him back from the sea, dangling him in stiff arms. Later he would consider his mother made the same mistake so many women did — undervaluing their daughters while overrespecting their sons. In any case, he would never be attracted to women who fussed or tried to take care of him, or who were too declarative about their emotions. He wanted women who were tough, spiky if necessary, who kept themselves more than a little remote.

"What are you reading?" he asked Rachel.

She turned the cover to face him. *Comparative Tax Law.*

"I don't know how you can sit on a beautiful beach and read that."

"I don't either." Rachel put the book face down in the sand and drew her knees up to her chest, clasped her thin arms around them. She looked vaguely French, just then, in her black one-piece suit, outsize sunglasses that were some designer make or other covering her eyes, her face a mesh weave of shadows thrown by a straw hat.

"Do you want to swim?"

"It looks cold."

"It's much warmer than the Atlantic."

She frowned. "Isn't this the Atlantic?"

"Yes, but it's the Northumberland Strait. See that shadow on the horizon? That's Prince Edward Island."

"Really? Let's go there."

"We can. Although from what Eve says we'll have to fight our way through busloads of Japanese tourists on Anne of Green Gables tours."

"That's where those books are set? I loved those books. Now I really want to go."

It had been the right thing to do after all, Rachel thought amidst her surge of enthusiasm, coming all the way here to this place where they knew no-one. The alternative had been to spend the summer with her best friend from college who lived beside a lake in Minnesota, or to rent a farmhouse in the south of France. Her agenda was slightly different than Noel's, of course, and she hadn't really shared it with him. At times she felt the knife of guilt as it glided lazily through her, glancing her innards, taking casual, arbitrary decisions not to rupture anything. Like Noel, she needed a blank slate to consider her next move. Their next move.

Rachel considered herself a decisive person. Her goal was to not be one of those women who let life be decided for them. She would wrest the initiative from biology; women's lives had been decided for them by biology or circumstance for so long, she considered, they might possess an almost genetic predisposition to let events overtake their will. So she made decisions, even wrong ones, because it seemed less dangerous than taking none at all. At the moment she was standing on the threshold of becoming a fully qualified lawyer. Although — and this was another thing she had neglected to share with Noel, or anyone — secretly she felt alienated from the law. She didn't want to be a human technician. She needed to find the humane element in law that her professors kept so cunningly hidden.

On the other hand, if she decided to, she could become a full-time mother for a while. There was a part of her that wanted, although guiltily, to be just that: another woman in an Anne Klein turtleneck, manhandling an SUV full of kids — her own and other peoples'. At Christmas she would have a Victorian-themed tree decorated with her own handmade ornaments, she would make skilful pancakes for breakfast, she would handwrite a hundred thank-you cards after the baby's christening. And why shouldn't it be like this?

"Come on," Noel said. "Let's go in."

"Are you sure?" She was so warm. She had just applied sunscreen.

"Let's do it now, or we never will."

They ran into the waves together holding hands and swam around, buffeted by gentle riptides. At one point Noel felt himself being carried out to sea, although not particularly fast, and he did what he had learned to do in countries where riptides were of a more lethal variety, swimming back in parallel to the shore rather than straight. Eventually he extricated himself from the pull.

They flung themselves down on the beach, breathing hard. After a while Rachel said, "She's got interesting looks." Her voice was muffled by the towel.

He considered his response. He could say, pardon? Or, who? But they both knew who she was talking about.

He made his voice lazy. "I hadn't really noticed. Do you think?"

"I've never seen green eyes that dark before. Like spinach."

"Her father's a real character. He told me some great stories one night."

"What about?"

"Survival, mainly. Ice fishing and hunting in years when the game was lean. I loved the way he said that 'years when the game was lean.' I love the way people around here speak with a kind of unself-conscious poetry."

"What else did he tell you?"

"That he fishes eels for a living, but he hasn't always done. He's had a variety of jobs — he called himself a jack of all trades. He said people around here have to be versatile because you never know when some industry or other is going to close down. His uncle was in the coal mines but they were shut, then his cousin — I think, or maybe another uncle — worked in the steel mill, but that went bust. Others used to fish for cod inshore, but the cod stocks have crashed. His brother was the captain of the ferry for twenty years."

"God, that boat is such an eyesore. They should get rid of it." Rachel yawned. "We should ask them over for dinner. It's the polite thing to do."

He murmured his assent and closed his eyes. A few minutes later he turned over to see that she had fallen asleep. He stood and arranged the parasol so that its shadow covered her feet. He lay back on the sand, looking into the wispy herringbone clouds scattered across the sky, the clay-red beach flanked by a forested promontory, the mauve hem of Prince Edward Island.

He tried to sleep, but couldn't. He thought about why he liked the island so much, why he felt so eerily at home. Perhaps because the violent places he had been to required so much apathy, a certain numbness to see them through, meanwhile his real life, where he lived, was spent in well-fed nations gorging themselves on their neuroses. He wanted off this carousel, a whole world tilting between neurosis and apathy. Cape Breton was one of the few places he had ever been that didn't seem infected with this schizophrenic dynamic.

Like spinach. It was true, Eve had eyes so dark it was unclear, until you looked at them closely, what colour they were. He had seen them turn indigo in some lights, or even black, as when they had sat talking in the cabin by candlelight after her father had fallen asleep.

Before he could stop himself, he began to imagine Eve's life as a teenager in Clam Harbour, building a picture from the fragments she had let slip. Her addiction to the bookmobile, studying geology, getting on the schoolbus every day to go into Indian Bay, the house they left behind across the lake. He pictured winter mornings helping her father to break the ice in the water butts, darning holes in his socks, and the night, that viscous black square he had stared at on his evenings alone in the house, the night pawing at the windows like an animal trying to get inside.

And him in his parallel dimension, his parents rambling, casually prosperous house in a town on the banks of the Hudson, his teenaged years spent in an obstacle course of planned activities: soccer practice, debating, model UN, a school exchange with Guadalajara, Mexico, a senior-year school trip to Greece, filling in college application forms.

It fascinated him, how stealthy change could be. He wouldn't be able to identify the precise moment in which he had left that teenaged boy behind and had started the long journey to becoming the Noel he was now. Nor could he say when he would move on from his present incarnation. Now, he imagined himself to be caught in a peculiar age, between the remnants of innocence and the slow dream of hope, which was linked to the possibility of a genuine love. But nor had he yet reached the age of having to consciously imagine happiness, while actually caught up in a reverberating pain. He knew this was coming, although he did not know how soon. Time was gold and shadows, a dark cascade of moments that made up the present, then the past. And the future, depending on how you looked at it, it could be a freight train coming down the track, or a conference to be organized, people — some of whom had yet to exist — mustered into place.

Seagulls wheeled overhead, just above the breakers. A thin film of wispy clouds coated the sky. For a minute it was completely silent, as if the world was holding its breath — no children's voices shearing the air, no dogs barking. Only the sigh and gather of waves breaking. This was how time should be, he told himself: that he ought to be able to pause it like a video, or at the very least slow it down long enough to savour the taste of contentment. Why was it that this pause could never be sustained for more than a few moments? Just like a video, after a while the picture began to wobble, and then disintegrate into static.

Rain turned the roads to mud. Rivulets of angry red water washed away all traction. After their fourth attempt to extricate the truck from the ditch into which they had slipped helplessly, tires spinning, they stopped to wait it out in a deserted house.

The house was little more than a concrete block, a pre-genocide home, Alexandre observed, a now-tattered roof of palm where a corrugated tin one used to be. Someone had carted off the roof after the killing was done.

They watched the rain cascade in silence, both keeping an eye on the inevitable wasps' nest in the corner of the ceiling. There seemed to be a lot of wasps in Rwanda. Then Noel made some comment — he can't even remember exactly what now — something bland and observational about the village they had just been to and where as usual he was interviewing people who had been displaced, first by the genocide, then by the government's resettlement program.

Alexandre turned to him and it was there instantly, the anger, as if a switch had been thrown inside him.

"You're just here for the information. *Neutrality*," he nearly spit the word.

He flinched. "Alexandre?" he said, uncertainty trilling his voice. "What's wrong?"

"I watched them riding out in their trucks every day to assess the damage. Trying not to see the people still hiding in the bushes. Coming upon groups of men with hoes and machetes in places where there are no fields. They had guns. Do you understand? They had guns but not once did they use them."

Noel was confused. Alexandre hadn't been in the country during the genocide. He must have been referring to UNAMIR 2, the UN force sent in after the genocide, not the original force that had been hamstrung by their peacekeeping mandate.

"They couldn't kill, you know that. It wasn't in their mandate," Noel replied. "If they had they would have been killed themselves, they would have been disowned by the UN."

A small vein on the side of Alexandre's smooth temple had appeared and was throbbing dangerously. "*Mandate*. That is the single most cowardly word in the English language. It makes me sorry I ever learned it. If they had killed a single *interahamwe* it would have saved hundreds who were going to die in the next twenty minutes."

"No, Alexandre. Another one would have come to kill those people, within minutes. You know that."

Noel turned away. He found it impossible to look at Alexandre's face, contorted by anger, like a puppet version of the taut, intelligent one he had grown used to. He almost welcomed Alexandre's wrath, even if it disoriented him to have it blow his way. So far he had the impression Rwanda was labouring under a forced anger amnesty. It was the way people talked about the atrocities that had been visited upon them, their glassy, slightly wondrous tone, as if to say, isn't it amazing? Who would think? A little anger was what was needed, Noel thought, although he didn't particularly want to be its target.

"If the UN had shot those *interahamwe*, they would have all been pulled out of here so fast they wouldn't even have known what was happening," Noel expanded. "Soldiers would have been killed in retaliation. Another *interahamwe* squad would have come to replace them. Those people would have died anyway. It was too big; it was beyond the scope of a few peacekeepers."

In one sense, Noel knew what he was saying was true. But another, simultaneous and powerful voice within him said: Listen to yourself. Can you believe what you're saying? You are condoning bureaucratic inertia in the face of murder. Perhaps Alexandre's attack had shocked him into shoddy reasoning.

Alexandre gave him a transparent, ambiguous look. "I am so sick of soldiers. Their shaven heads, their Brut cologne, some of them say they fear God but then they kill."

"Which soldiers?"

"Any soldiers."

Noel stared out at the downpour. For the first time since he had come to Rwanda these sudden showers depressed him.

"Why did you come back here?"

"It was my country. Sometimes I don't like it, in fact I hate it. I wish I came from anywhere else in the world. But then you only have one country, unless you try and live somewhere for twenty years and forget the person you were in your own place. And I asked myself, will I feel worse, sitting in France, knowing what is happening to my country, or will I feel worse being there. I think that is what you call negative reasoning: we do what we will least regret, rather than what we really want to do." Alexandre gave the curtain of rain a severe look. "So I chose to come back. Some people have told me, you chose death over life. But as you see, I am still alive."

The meaning of his comment was immediately clear to Noel: Alexandre was saying that there were gradients of aliveness, that something of Alexandre's asceticism predated the trauma of Rwanda, that he had been knitting himself together from diverse components for years — his rigid posture, his slightly clinical curiosity, his frequent disdain for those clever, jaded individuals for whom he worked, the "international community." Those quasar-burst smiles of his were renegade envoys from another Alexandre, the impulsive, reckless young boy perhaps, or the refugee huddling for warmth in the tiny apartment on the out-skirts of Paris. These miraculous smiles betrayed the presence of a delicate, unpredictable element. Although what this might be, Noel couldn't say.

The rain abated; they left the cement house, both of them casting a valedictory eye toward the wasps' nest — another of the casual, even lazy threats Rwanda threw up averted — and carried on their way.

They drive back from the beach late that night, Noel at the wheel. The day on the beach has bleached them of energy; he can barely keep his eyes open. As they near Clam Harbour a tractor-trailer comes barrelling up behind him. It balloons in his rearview mirror just as he has to slow to make the hidden turnoff into Clam Harbour. He applies the brakes once, then twice, to try to shake it off.

In the same instant he sees the silhouette of a creature standing on the gravel shoulder. At first he takes it to be two incredibly tall hitchhikers. He is gaining on the silhouette rapidly. The hitch-hikers look nervous, poised to leap in front of him. In another second he sees that the rangy adolescents are in fact a young moose, helpfully standing right underneath the MOOSE CROSSING sign.

He hesitates. The truck is on his tail. He can make the turning early and swing into the other lane, but there are lights in the distance and he already knows traffic travels at least a hundred and ten kilometres an hour on this stretch of the Trans-Canada. He might not have enough time to make the U-turn and hit the shoulder before the next car comes.

The lights of the truck grow from saucer size to floodlights. Then, it seems, they are in the car with them.

"Noel..." Rachel's hand grasps his forearm.

He brakes and cuts into the shoulder at sixty miles an hour, gravel flying, stopping just short of the moose. For one serrated second he thinks he will hit the animal; in the next second he is convinced it will leap out from in front of him and straight into the oncoming truck.

But the moose stands there, statuesque and transfixed. Once the truck has passed as if on a spring the moose hurls itself onto the highway, galloping across the four lanes and missing an oncoming car by a couple of feet. They watch it scramble up the opposite bank, its knees buckling, pitching forward. It rights itself and charges into the forest.

"Christ," Rachel breathes. "I thought we were going to die."

They sit in the car in silence for a few minutes, their faces lit only by the green light of the dashboard, headlights slicing the night in front of them into two neat strips.

He is driving, too; he is the two headlights poised at the Clam Harbour turnoff, waiting to swing onto the Trans-Canada.

He sees the moose, the car braked and hushed with near-disaster on the shoulder; he sees the tractor-trailer juggernaut pass by. He knows immediately what has happened, although he doesn't recognize the car, he doesn't know it is the young neighbour couple. It's nearly happened to him a few times. Like the night he hit a deer and rolled into the bank, flipping over twice. Him with no seatbelt on and he was fine. A bit bruised, maybe, where his stomach hit the steering wheel, but fine. He had crawled out the window and walked the three miles home.

There were other near-accidents. He'd had to go back to the cabin and calm himself down, a little whisky, a little rum. His wife, Anita, Eve — they were all gone. Only the dog looking at him, the moist alarm in his eyes. There was no-one to tell about these near-misses, no-one to marvel at the miracle of his escape.

She went to shore to look for her father, but he wasn't to be found on the beach, or at the weirs. On her way back up the hill she took a path that brought her out of the woods just below John Rory's. There, on the edge of the woods, in a spot of damp ferns, she caught a fragment of Noel's voice, plain as day despite her distance from the house. She remembered this odd amplification of the acoustics between the two houses as a child: if she stood downwind, just in that spot, she could hear what was being said through the open kitchen window. She had eavesdropped on John Rory and Eileen this way as a child, although they had never said anything, just: *It's a large day today. Yes, it's a fine day.*

Water sucked at her ankles, seeped into her shoes. She'd forgotten the eavesdropping spot was so marshy.

She heard a bang, followed by a clink. Glasses or dishes being put away. Then Rachel's voice.

It's just a bit creepy. It's the dead-end feel of the place.

Look, the old road goes all the way along the mountain. It comes out on the highway.

I know, but still.

What are you worried about? That I'm at a dead end? That we're a dead end?

Don't be so paranoid. It's not about us, it's about the place.

There was a familiarity in the brutality of Rachel's tone, and in Noel's brittle, wounded response. She recognized it from conversations she and Llewellyn had; the tone of two people who really cared for each other, who had been together long enough to have tested their love. They have reached that impasse in love when the passion stage is definitely over, although something else, something arguably more satisfying, has taken its place. But it is no longer possible to romanticize each other. It should be a relief, to mature into a kind of love that did not inhabit the outskirts of delusion.

She couldn't bear to hear any more. Bulrushes rasped in her wake. On her way out she stepped in a deep pocket of mud and felt its cold slime sink into her shoes.

Her father wasn't in the cabin, the shed or the garden. She went down to the ferry and untied the canoe. Paddling along the shore, she had to resist the urge to cry out his name. She couldn't be sure what her voice would sound like so she concentrated on paddling, the dip and pool of the oar in a liquid echo chamber.

Overhead, seagulls tormented each other, picking on some outcast member, and then dispersing. She paddled close to the shore in the shallows along the shore. It was littered with shattered glacial rock, bleached plastic bottles, Baxter's Milk cartons, bits of twine and anonymous gristle, the sun-dried body of a dead seagull. Also empty mussel shells, starfish, a dead squid ransacked within minutes of its beaching by crows. She turned a corner and saw an eagle perched above her on a low branch, massive and eerily human, like a person who has donned an eagle costume. She saw it swivel a ruthless eye in her direction.

Where was he? Rounding a corner wide of the shore to avoid an outcrop of rocks, she caught sight of a red rag fluttering in the wind. In another second she realized it was her father's red work shirt hanging on a branch.

The air in her lungs thickened until she felt she was breathing porridge. By the time she saw him, she could barely get air. He was standing on the tip of a small sand bar, next to what looked like a wood sculpture.

He turned at the sound. He was wearing only his undershirt and blue work trousers. As soon as he saw her he snagged his shirt off the branch and began to button it.

"What are you doing here?"

She slid the canoe onto the sand. "I was just going to ask you the same question. How did you get here?"

He folded his arms over this chest, cupping his hands in his armpits. "I walked."

"But there's no path."

"I don't need a path."

A rivulet of blood snaked down his torso. "What happened to your hands? Look, they're all cut up."

He extracted them from his armpits and looked at them with disinterest. "Just thorns."

"What's this?" He had arranged pieces of wood in a pile, one tall pole rising from the middle. On this he had fixed serpentined pieces of driftwood. The overall effect was of a stick-deer with antlers.

"Oh, just fooling around. I started putting together some wood for a bonfire and got carried away."

"Come on, I'll take you back in the canoe."

He didn't resist. She hadn't taken an extra paddle, so he sat in the bow while she paddled from the stern. He ran his bloody hands in the water to dry the wounds. She watched as his blood swirled into threads, and then sank beneath the surface.

"I'm played out," he said, when they returned to the cabin. He closed the door behind him.

The thick silence of a summer afternoon closed in on her. The only sound was the drone of bees hovering above honeysuckle. Just as she was contemplating tactics to dispel the heaviness she felt, she heard footsteps on gravel. She opened the door to find Noel there, looking off in the direction of the horse. He turned, smile at the ready, but it vanished at the sight of her face.

"What's the matter?"

She put her finger to her lips and led them outside, into the garden. "I couldn't find him all morning. Eventually I found him on the shore about a mile from here. He'd walked there, ripped his hands to shreds on thorn bushes."

"What was he doing there?"

"Building a sculpture!" She threw up her hands. "He said it was a bonfire, but he was making this... giant deer, is what it looked like, out of driftwood. What do you make of that?"

Noel shook his head. "I really don't know." An acute uncertainty flickered on his face. "I think we were nearly killed last night."

"How?"

"A moose nearly ran out in front of us. There was this truck on my tail. If I'd had to turn, or if it had jumped in front of me...," he gave her a bare look. She could see the fear in his eyes, still, dark and bundled, like blackberries.

"I don't think I can even talk about it."

"It didn't happen, that's the important thing."

He seemed to accept this strategy with relief. "I came to ask if you'd like to have dinner with us tomorrow night."

"I might have to bring my father. I need to keep an eye on him."

"Of course, you're both invited."

They stood in silence for a few seconds. He seemed poised between leaving and staying. He looked over his shoulder toward the house. As a gesture, it was ever so slightly hounded. Was Rachel counting the minutes he was away? Would she interrogate him: *So what did you talk about?*

"I should be getting back."

"Of course you should."

He looked at her, an indistinct hurt poised in his eye.

She wanted to say, I'm sorry. That was bad manners. I'm so tired. I feel like I'm running a protection racket here, protecting you, my father, my sister, your girlfriend even. Who's going to protect me?

She watched him walk up the driveway, her hand shading her eyes, until he disappeared around the corner.

He hears them talking outside, his daughter and the neighbour. He can't quite make out what they are saying, but the sheared note of panic in Eve's voice tells him their conversation is about him.

He is grateful for Eve's concern, but it has come too late. She was always in such a rush: hurry here, hurry there. As if she were living a constant emergency. In a rush to grow up, to get out of here. As a child she had leaned out of speeding cars, trying to gulp the air; no oxygen, wisps of breath and speed. It was as if she couldn't quite believe that she wasn't going to die tomorrow.

She will never know about those years of nights, nights alone with his dissident memories, nights that prowl like lions on the outskirts of a town ringed by oil refineries. Flares of flame, the seared sky. Nights when he dismantled what he thought had been a colossal intimacy, piece by piece. The gradual, drawn-out shattering of a dream. Nights of sedge, dry grass stunted by the wind. The wind itself becomes slices of understanding. They cut right though him, as if it is he and not the wind that is made of air.

Kay's has few customers that evening. A breeze wafts through the window but it gives no relief. The evening is too hot to eat indoors; everyone is having barbecues in backyards or on the lakeshore. When she steps outside, Eve catches the meaty fume of charcoal.

"I mean, if it happens, fine," Peggy is saying. The three of them sit on the back doorstep, leaning over the verandah railing. "If it doesn't, I'm not going to think it's a tragedy."

They are talking about love. Eve envies them, Peggy, Connie. They are twenty, twenty-one, but they still have the brazen languor of teenagers.

"When did you fall in love for real, Eve?" Peggy asks.

"It's never for real. You think it is for a while, and then you revise your opinion."

The girls groaned in unison. "Eve, don't be so cynical."

"That's not cynicism, it's jadedness."

"How's your neighbour? The American guy. You know, the good-looking one."

"With the equally good-looking girlfriend."

"They're nice."

The girls give her a disappointed look. A humid sheath of heat drapes itself over her. A sailboat in the bay pulses a flash of metal light — the evening sun glinting off its fibreglass hull. She closes her eyes against it and when she opens them the lake is changing colour. Gold becomes silver, silver to malachite, then tourmaline, amethyst.

When did you fall in love for real? Was there really a single moment when you fell in or out of love; an identifiable piece of time, or was it only an accretion of minute, almost unnoticed things?

She is in a bar with Llewellyn in Toronto. Thin women in black, she's one of them. Other men, large blonds, they look like brothers. Mouths open, tongues visible, saliva sloshing as they laugh. What do you want to drink? She has a beer. It's slightly too loud to talk so she and Lew watch the crowd. He scans the crowd, his eyes flitting back and forth across the bodies. His head bobs slightly in time to the music.

Yes, this is it. This is the first moment in which she does not love him.

CHAPTER 14

She could smell the chalky tang before they even reached the step. Noel opened the door. Behind him a giant aluminum pot, spanking-new, belched steam.

"Just in time. We're in a Woody Allen film here. The one where he and Diane Keaton chase lobsters around the kitchen."

"Annie Hall."

"That's it. Rachel bought the lobsters and she forgot to say cooked." He craned his head over his shoulder. "*Cooked*, that's the word, isn't it? As in, when the lobsters are red, not black."

"Okay, Noel, I get the message." Rachel's voice came from somewhere just outside the kitchen. "I know nothing about lobster."

Rachel came to greet them. She was wearing a pair of red gingham-checked trousers cut just above the ankle and a dangerously white shirt. Behind her Eve saw tentacles twitching in the kitchen sink. "That's two that have gotten away," she said. "I don't know when they crawled out. One's behind the fridge."

"Like in the film," Noel grinned.

Within seconds her father was crossing the room with a lobster pincered between his thumb and index finger. Rachel looked at the lobster in her father's hands unhappily. "I don't think I can bear to put them in the pot."

"That's all right, dear." Her father plopped the lobster on top of the others in the sink. "I'll do the killing."

After he had despatched the lobsters to the boiling water, her father went to scout out the house. "Take a look around," Noel had said, in a voice of the easy largesse of the host, even though they all knew that her father belonged more in this house than any of them ever would.

"Noel tells me your father fishes eels." Rachel spoke when he was out of the room.

"For part of the year."

"I hope the money he makes is worth it."

Eve considered possible responses to this. "It used to be, but the eel population is declining everywhere, even in Europe. It's only the Japanese who keep the whole business going. Anyway, we won't have to worry about it much longer. This is my father's last season. He told me he's quitting."

"But how will he make a living?"

"He doesn't know yet."

Through her exchange with Rachel, Noel stared at her intently, almost rudely. She felt the pleasing sensation of being observed and, in the same moment, a pungent, almost physical desire for access to his mind. Eve had rarely been so hungry for the approbation of another human being, so ravenous to know his thoughts. She feared this appetite showed on her face, her body. Her father returned from his exploration of the house. Not much changed here, he announced.

"I'd put a bib over that shirt if I were you," Eve advised Rachel, pointing to her shirt. "You don't know how badly lobster juice stains."

Her father all but smacked his lips at the spread on the table: coleslaw, white bread, butter, melted butter, white wine and in the centre, a plate of livid crustaceans. She became aware that Noel and Rachel were waiting to see how she and her father tackled the lobsters. Eve loaded the breadboard and took them to the sink, first putting on the old pullover she had brought for the walk back to the cabin. She twisted the tails off, drained the bodies of juice, uncorked the claws from the bodies, smashing them open with the bread knife and the hammer. She returned them to the table, duly shattered.

"You sure know how to dismember a lobster." The way Noel said it, it didn't sound entirely like a compliment. She met his eyes for several seconds too long, daring him to look away, which he did.

"Did you ever fish for lobster?" Rachel asked her father.

"Never. I never had the licence."

"If I lived here I'd keep ducks," Noel said. "Did you ever have ducks, Alistair?"

"I did, sure. For a year I tried to keep them, chickens and ducks both. The ducks were a sight to behold; blue tips on their wings and everything. By the Jesus, they were beautiful." Her father's face took on an awestruck expression. "But they used to watch me, the wildcats. They'd wait until I went down to the weirs or into town, and they'd pounce. It didn't help if I locked the ducks in the shed, they'd find a way in."

Eve caught Rachel's grimace. On that lean, clear face, even a grimace had a certain delicacy.

"That's right," her father nodded in recognition of Rachel's disgust. "It was an awful terrible way to die."

"What did you do?"

"Went back out and got myself some more ducks. This must have happened three times in all, came home to find the bobcats killed them. And you know, that last time I snapped. I just couldn't get over it. I got in the truck, found a stretch of road where there was nobody and tore up and down it. I was trying to get up the courage to drive into the water, I was so mad. But I couldn't. Half an hour later I was back home, sweeping up the feathers. I left a few good skid marks on the road, though."

They all laughed.

"Do you still have much family here?" Rachel asked.

"Not much," her father answered. "A sister. Two brothers out west. I had an eldest sister who died, but that was a long time ago."

Eve had never heard of an older sister, but she didn't want to say so in front of Noel and Rachel.

"She must have died young then."

Her father paused to wipe a rivulet of melted butter from his chin. "She did, yes. She was the eldest so she had to take care of the rest of us. That was always the way, then — girls knew how to be mothers by the time they were twelve. But she'd been born with a hole in her heart. I remember you could hear her heart beating when her mouth was open. Every breath she took was a raspy sound, as if the breath were being sieved out of her."

"No," Rachel said.

"True as I'm sitting here, you could hear it. When she was eighteen they took her to Halifax to have open heart surgery."

"What happened?" Rachel asked.

"She died on the operating table. She just wasn't strong enough. Everyone knew that, of course, but my father was ready to try anything."

Rachel shook her head again, a slow, mournful sashay that brought to life the slim architecture of her neck, the muscles and sinews. "That's just so sad."

Her father looked alert, even surprised, as if Rachel had just uttered a profound truth. He pushed his chair back. "Time for me to hit the sack."

"Don't you want dessert?"

"No, dear, thank you. I'm usually in bed right now. You all carry on without me."

When he was almost out the door Eve called, "'Night, Dad." He looked back in faint surprise, as if he had forgotten she was there.

"Don't take his abrupt departure personally," she said, to both Rachel and Noel. "He always does that."

"Your father's had a tough life," Rachel observed.

"He has. But then everybody did, then."

"It doesn't seem that way now."

"No, it's changed a lot. There's a lot more happening than when I lived here."

"Like what?" Rachel asked.

"Dinner theatre, museums, ceilidhs. I guess it's called cultural regeneration."

Noel was watching her carefully again.

"I've thought about buying some land here."

Rachel looked at him in obvious surprise.

"It's something I've been thinking about," he explained.

Eve witnessed a struggle taking place in Rachel, not to start a full-blown argument at the dinner table. She realized that for some reason until this point she hadn't thought of Noel and Rachel as a couple, hadn't considered them really together. But now she looked across the table and saw how much Noel and Rachel were a single entity. They shared a certain golden quality she noticed in the sailing couples who parked their boats in front of Kay's: the pale freckles lining Noel's forehead had darkened. Rachel's hair, which had been a dark brown when she had first seen her in the restaurant, was now streaked with gold. Framed in her dusky face, her eyes lightened to a liqueur hue, yellow-amber, like the cognac diamonds Eve had sourced for Caroline's collection the previous year.

"So your husband still can't come to visit?"

She shook her head ruefully. "He has to work."

"How did you meet?"

"A dinner party. A one-night stand that's lasted for five years. No, six." Eve laughed, as if to say I can't even remember how long I've been married for, but Rachel's face remained serious.

"I think we were fated to meet." Rachel was speaking to Eve, but her eyes were on Noel.

"Why's that?"

"Because I can't imagine being with anyone else. I can't imagine how it would have worked out differently. I believe in fate." Rachel swung her eyes back to Eve. "Don't you?"

"I believe in chance, yes. Or accident. But not in fate."

Rachel frowned. "Why not?"

"I'm not sure fate exists, at least as we want it to. I think there are things that happen, or we allow to happen, and any other arrangement of things is possible. It's about what comes to the surface. I used to think of it like dragnetting. You scoop the bottom of possibility and net what you net. Only you lose a lot on the way to the surface." She paused. "I think fate is only what you can bear." As soon as she said this she was aware how negative it sounded. How resigned, devoid of hope.

She looked up, poised to change the subject, to find Noel's eyes upon her. From somewhere deep within them she caught a brief glimpse of that light, like the sun striking malachite. In another second a veil was drawn away and it stood bare on the stage: recognition, empathy, even approval.

Rachel was asking her another question. "Where did you go to college?"

"*Rachel.*"

"What?" She turned to Noel, laughing. "It's a harmless question. Okay, what did you study?"

"Science. Geology, mainly."

"Why did you choose that?" Rachel's question was warm, alluring, not at all testing.

"Because I had always loved the story of the earth, how it came into being," she said. It seemed so certain and yet such an accident at the same time.

"So it was accident, not fate?" Noel's voice was neutral, but his eyes smiled.

"I believe so. And because I loved the names of rocks. They seemed to hold a mystery that needed to be unlocked. But I found out the hard way that I'm not a scientist. I just don't have the rigour. I suppose I should have studied literature or philosophy but I was afraid of the world. I thought if I had some hard knowledge, something that was useful to the world, I would be safe."

Just as she expected, Noel called her on this. "Safe?"

"Safe as in getting a job. Getting some certainties. An intellectual centre of gravity." She permitted herself another laugh at her own expense. "I thought that if I knew how the earth worked, how the ground we stand on was formed, then I would be able to count on that in any situation, no matter how disorienting life became."

"But you've got a job that you like." There was a note of anxiety in Noel's voice. He was pushing her toward happy resolutions.

She indulged him. "Yes, I do."

Rachel nodded, and Eve knew she had passed some kind of test, although narrowly.

"So what kind of work do you do?" The test was not completed, not yet.

"I work with a jewellery designer. I source stones for her. I help her with designs and customers — sometimes I design myself."

Rachel threw Noel a look of censure. "Why didn't you tell me that's what Eve did?" She swivelled her gaze back to Eve. There was a new intensity in it. "What kind of jewellery does she make?"

"It's kind of outlandish, but also restrained. That shouldn't be possible, but somehow Caroline pulls it off."

"Have you got any pictures?"

"I've got one of her catalogues in the cabin. Do you want me to get it?" Of course Rachel did, so she jogged next door to retrieve the catalogue, pausing long enough to hear deep, scooped breaths coming from her father's bedroom.

Back at the table Eve opened the page onto her favourite work, a series of long silver stalks — earrings, brooches — bounded on both ends by beads of amber.

"Caroline did this for Armani a couple of years ago."

"It's so *refined*." In Rachel's voice she heard a note of real respect, even awe.

"Caroline refuses to do those heavy encrusted designs. Only a certain tasteless segment of the super-rich want that. Although there are some good things done in that tradition — Boucheron, Van Cleef and Arpels, Graff."

"I love those names," Noel said. "They're so voracious. They sound like monsters about to eat you alive."

They paused to admire another piece, a necklace of cascading white, gold and cognac diamonds. She showed them more — the kunzite, aquamarine, chalcedony, tourmaline, moonstone.

"We should get going with the rings, Noel." Rachel turned to Eve. "We're getting married next spring."

"Congratulations."

"But I think Caroline might be a bit expensive for us."

"Not necessarily. She does discounts for friends. I could ask her."

"Do you really think so?"

Watching Rachel's face ripen with expectation she felt a complex pleasure, striated with thin veins of pain, in being able to offer something to this woman who had everything, including something she might very much want for herself. She remembered a line from a novel she was reading, which she had underlined: *In the moment before giving, I am loved.*

"I'd better be going." She rose. "I've got a double shift tomorrow." Strictly speaking, she didn't need to go. But a dark cloud had powered in from the horizon and parked itself over her heart.

Noel accompanied her to the door.

"Thanks for dinner. My father really enjoyed it."

"But did you?"

"Of course." She smiled. "Congratulations again on the wedding."

She knew he would recognize this for what it was: a rebuke, although an obscure one. She watched as uncertainty and hurt unfolded in his eyes, and it was one of the most beautiful things she had ever seen: tentative, lavish, sullen, like the opening of tropical flowers that bloom only at night.

Rachel returned from her small-town salon experience feeling enervated. The heat inside the beauty parlour was intense. In the fifteen minutes it took the dowdy girl to give her a trim she thought she would fall asleep.

She drifted into the kitchen, suddenly swamped by a wave of malaise. What could she busy herself with in this house, this place, Clam Harbour, which seemed to almost be willing the world to stasis? She had cleaned, she had cooked, she had studied, although desultorily. It was too hot to read — how could Noel concentrate with this heat? She would have loved to go for a swim, but she didn't like the lake's rocky bottom and the long tentacles of eelgrass, not to mention the spectre of actual eels.

She remembered the attic; she had been meaning for a week to go up and dust it. She had never got round to studying there, even though Noel had set it up as her study room. She found the pole and latch and managed to pull down the stairs by herself. The attic was hot, but not oppressively so. She opened the windows to a flurry of dust.

Noel was right, the view was lovely; from the attic she could see past the point of Seal Island to where the strait opened into the wide palm of the lakes. Yellow goldenrod hemmed the midnight blue of the water; it was as if the elements of the land were conspiring to be as charming as possible in the brief season that was available to them.

Out of the corner of her eye she caught sight of Eve, kneeling in the garden below the cabin. She hadn't realized the cabin was visible from the house; she thought the birches that stood between them would have obscured the view.

Rachel recalled the first time she had seen Eve in that garage where she seemed to help out sometimes. She had taken one look at the place and said, "Noel, you're going to buy gas here?" "Why not?" he'd replied. "It just looks so scruffy. Won't it be cheaper out on the highway?" "I like to patronize small businesses," he'd said. She'd answered, "*Patronize* is the word," and they had both laughed.

Rachel watched as Eve bent and straightened over a black patch of fresh-turned soil. Eve deferred to her, she thought, although very slightly. She tried not to expect this, nor take it as her due. Eve was married, so it could hardly be the nearly unconscious credence single women give their married (or about-to-be-married) contemporaries, so Rachel assumed it was her spectacular education that prompted Eve's yielding. Even the toughest-minded people, she knew, the pure individualists, were cowed by the glamour of academic achievement. She was grateful now for the parents who pushed her, who had scrimped and saved to the point where they almost had no lives of their own. It was unhealthy, yes. But their sacrifice had been part of what had admitted her to Yale, and to Noel.

She's got interesting looks.

I hadn't really noticed.

Their conversation on the beach again, popping up like an ugly puppet. It was a lie, or at least an evasion. Of course he noticed Eve's eyes — Noel was alive to detail, he never failed to reflect on a person's physical presence and the ways it mirrored their personality.

She recalled Eve's assessment of her jeweller employer: *Caroline is one of those people who have the courage to be genuinely grandiose.* This was just the kind of thing Noel liked: a quick, psychologically plausible survey of a character, told with a bite of humour or paradox. Eve's comment had elicited that mauve spark from the depths of Noel's seemingly black eyes, the rare reflex that was his way of expressing admiration. He hadn't wanted Rachel to see it, of course, but she knew just the same. The fact that so few people felt admired by Noel was down to the speed with which this current passed from his eyes and into the world. Most people simply missed it.

On the other hand, she wasn't really bothered; men with PhDs from Yale don't fall in love with waitresses, she thought, unless of course you're in a movie. Noel's instinct was to involve himself in people's problems and to try to solve them, but this was a purely professional response. Nor was he one of those men with a wounded-bird complex, picking up fragile and damaged women to rehabilitate.

Although Eve was hardly fragile, Rachel corrected herself. She had the spiky energy, that almost defensive toughness small people often have. Nor had Eve presented herself to them in the role most available to her, the talented woman going to waste in the boondocks, consumed by rage and frustration, using both hungrily as fuel by which to feel more alive. For this Rachel respected her, even as she pitied Eve for that element in her life — some constellation of hurts, some dreadful taskmaster — that required her to defend herself so thoroughly.

Her father appeared beside Eve in the vegetable patch. He looked a bit of a mess, with that grey-brown hair of his. What amazing accident had kept her from being born here, Rachel reflected, from having this haphazard figure for a father? Or from being born in Colombia, in Rwanda, any of those countries whose random hells Noel documented? She knew the answer: raw luck, of course, although neither had she quite won the lottery with her father and his exile-bred melancholy, her Soviet-trained chemist mother who became enraged when the elements of life did not cohere quite as neatly as molecular structures. Her parents were in their early forties when she was born, and she remained an only child, a product of the Communist work ethic and, she imagined, unrestricted access to abortion. At least they'd had the good sense to emigrate to the United States instead of Brazil or Argentina — their second choices, they had confessed to her, if they had failed to get US visas.

They had settled in a prosperous town where Rachel had access to preschool nurseries, cavernous sports facilities, Saturday painting classes, ballet, accelerated science courses. Eve might have ridden the same carousel of capacity-enhancing activities (as the teachers had called them at Rachel's school) had she shared Rachel's background. Of course, Eve's education hadn't been a disaster. She had studied natural sciences and literature. Rachel wondered idly what her GPA was.

"Hey, I found you," Noel's head poking through the hole in the floor. "What's up?"

"Just admiring the view." She moved away from the window lest Noel came to stand beside her and catch her spying on Eve.

"Why don't we have lunch in Indian Bay?"

"I've already been to town today."

"Well, we can go again."

"There's nothing to do in that town."

"I thought that's why we're here, to do nothing for a while."

She shook her head. "It's too far away."

"Too far away from what?"

She bit her lower lip. She was going to have to be clear about this. "Noel, I think three weeks in this place is all I can take."

The expression on his face was just as she expected: not disappointed, rather confused.

"But it's so beautiful," he said.

"It's pretty," she agreed. "But it's too quiet for me."

"I thought you wanted to get away."

"I did. Maybe I overestimated the time I would need out of the city. It's just…," she tried to quell the twitching of her hands by folding her arms, "we've already exhausted the possibilities here."

"What do you mean, possibilities?"

"We've had dinner at Celyn's. We've had Eve over to dinner. We've gone into town half a dozen times. We've gone sailing, we've done the National Park. We've had picnics on the beach, we've been to Fortress Louisbourg."

"You're restless."

She laughed, and it came out sharp, even to her ear. "Who would have thought it? Restlessness is usually your department."

Without a word Noel turned away and walked back down the stairs.

She felt winded. It was so unlike him, to turn away like that. It was worse than if they'd had a fight. Which of course they'd never had — not in that sense, a *fight*.

Would she really do this to him, cut their vacation short, drag him away from a place he obviously loved, back to the thirty-five-degree heat of New York? She felt it sidle up and rub itself against her, a small sleek animal: her fear that something would happen, something that would not be part of the program she had devised. That was Noel's opinion of her, she knew: a programmed, deliberate person. Once at a dinner party he had said, *Rachel expects life to come with a Satisfaction Guaranteed warranty.* At least she knew what the Good Life was, even if her own sense of dinner-party etiquette required her to restrain herself from arguing it out among half-strangers. The good life was precisely that which she never had: brothers, sisters, a convivial family, a rich life of the mind and of the world, giving back to the community, hosting departmental barbecues, doing *pro bono* work for the local halfway house. She wanted all this for herself; she didn't see the need to sneer at it.

Only a year ago she had dedicated herself fully to law school. Now she felt compelled to hurl herself at life, to get off the fence, start to mould it into a shape she wanted to inhabit. She had legally been an adult for twelve years now, but for the first time in her life she felt *capable.* Would Noel ever understand that the deliberate way she attacked life was only a method to shield herself against her own uncertainty, to give form to her rampant hopes? She wondered if she could find a way to explain all this to him, before it was too late.

Anita volunteered to take their father to the hospital. Eve was only too glad to escape the hepatitis leaflets and the blue waiting room, so she stayed behind, alone, in Anita's house. Anita's boys were out swimming on the Mira River, and Kelly was at a friend's.

With each minute that passed she felt stranded in a house with no books and a television that blared baseball and soap operas. She wandered around the kitchen, poking aimlessly into cupboards and cataloguing what she found there: Barbour's pure black pepper, a bottle of Co-op raspberry jam, King Cole loose tea, Kraft peanut butter, Lantic sugar. She was relieved when, after two hours of this desultory spying, her father and Anita walked in the door.

"CAT scan, ECG, cholesterol levels, blood pressure, blood, they're all normal." Anita dropped her purse on the table with a crack.

"That's good news," she said.

"The only thing they found was a slightly underactive thyroid." Anita threw her hands up. "Nothing to worry about, were the good doctor's words." She frowned. "I forgot how much I hated hospitals. I haven't been near one since David was born."

Anita took the kettle off the stove and poured them both cups of herbal tea. "I'm off caffeine," she explained. "My nerves are bad enough as it is. You missed the best part. They tried to give him that basic Alzheimer's test they do, what's it called?"

"The MMSE. Mini Mental State Examination."

"Well, he walked out — stormed out is more like it — in the middle. He was just so cheesed off at the questions. You know, like, what year are we in and what's your address?" Anita smiled. "He said, 'I'm not that far gone, you want to deprive a man of his dignity?'"

"He hasn't done anything strange for a while. But he doesn't sleep at night. I think he goes for walks."

"Goes for walks where?"

"Who knows? He wouldn't tell me if I asked him. He's preoccupied. He's much more temperamental than he used to be. I think he's steeling himself for this being his last season."

"Well, it's a relief, I guess," Anita said briskly. "For it not to be… what we feared. Maybe he's just going through a life change." She was staring at her cup of tea, her hands worrying themselves over a sugar spoon.

"What's the matter?"

"Oh, just about that. How you think you're living with one person and the next day they're someone else."

"What's going on?"

Anita sat back in her chair, sighed, but kept fiddling with her spoon. "Kelly, that's what's going on. She's the first of my kids to turn into an adult and I'm not sure I can take it." She took a breath. "She's just so... composed. Butter wouldn't melt in that one's mouth. But I know what she's up to. Drinking and God knows what else."

"Drinking at fifteen?"

"Eve, where have you been?"

"I never did."

"Well, you weren't exactly representative. You spent more time in the bookmobile than anywhere you might have actually had fun."

"I did have fun in the bookmobile."

Anita threw up her hands. "I rest my case."

"Where does she go drinking?"

"Out at Table Head, when the weather's good. They sit in-between those old concrete blocks, you know, where the transmitters were."

"The old Marconi station?"

"That's the one. And you know what, a few feet away is a thirty-foot drop. No fence, of course. And she goes out driving with friends who've had their licence for two minutes. I try to tell her to use her senses, to not drink and drive. But she's at that stage where she doesn't even want to see me. In fact, the sight of me seems to make her sick. She'd listen to anyone before she listened to me."

Eve watched her sister in the kitchen, pouring glasses of pop, taking hot dog buns out of the bag, wiping the counter, cutting the plastic off the tip of a pitcher of milk. She moved deftly, with a restless energy at once familiar and seemingly new to her sister's being. Eve realized that was the shock, when she first saw Anita. Not only how thin she looked, how young, but also how like their mother had looked, when she had died.

Before they left, Anita shoved an envelope into her hands.

Poised in her eyes was a shy, concerned look Eve had never seen before.

"What's this?"

"Wait until you get home before you open it. Call me if you need to."

She took it without comment. Only later, when she was driving them home, did the expression on Anita's face strike her, the fear she saw in her sister's normally composed features, as well as her unprecedented offering of comfort. *Call me if you need to.*

She turns around to find her father with a pie in his hand.

"Can you drop this next door? I wanted to say thanks for supper the other night."

"You made that?"

"Last night, when you were at work."

"I don't remember you being much of a baker."

"I wasn't. It's something I learned to do after you left."

She stubs out her cigarette. Two cigarettes a night have multiplied seamlessly into five, six. She goes outside the cabin and smokes beside the mare, stroking her absently, trying to synchronize their breathing, but the mare breathes so much more slowly than she does.

"There's a book I wanted to loan Noel anyway."

She retrieves the book from the smokehouse and sets off to the house, pie in hand. But the car isn't in their driveway; almost certainly no-one is at home.

She knocks on the door anyway. It opens. She looks up to find Noel on the threshold. "Where's your car?"

"Rachel went into town." His eyes and his voice are unhappy.

She thrusts the book and the pie at him. "My father made this to say thanks for the dinner. Oh, and this is the book I thought you might like."

He cradles the pie in his right hand. With his left he turns the book to see its title. *A Natural History of the Maritimes.* He lifts it to his nose. It smells of tobacco.

She is mortified. She briefly considers saying, *that book's been in the smokehouse for years.*

"I'm smoking for the first time my life. I don't know why." She backs away from him to perch on the step. She studies his face, looking for censure, but it is expressionless.

He sets the pie on the counter behind him. He has not asked her in. She remembers their exchange on the step after dinner, her rebuke, the nocturnal flowers in his eyes.

When he turns back toward her he is holding a peeled orange in his hands. "This is the best remedy for tobacco smells." He opens the orange, scattering spray over the page. He raises the book to her nose. "See, it smells of oranges now."

He hands her half the orange. They are careful not to touch each other's fingers.

"Thanks," she says, and backs down the doorstep.

She walks back to the cabin, the phrase ringing peculiarly in her ears, not like an echo, but as if someone, somewhere, were chanting it, low and soft: *It smells of oranges now.*

This is the vacation version of his dysfunctional work desk: an empty bag of Doritos, the free movie voucher inside it, an Iberia baggage tag, a forty-eight-cent Canadian stamp showing what he discovered were sea anemones but looked more like burst galaxies, a five-dollar bill (he loved the colours of Canadian money, blue, purple, pink — like candy) and rocks and bits of sea glass he has scavenged on the beach.

I don't know how you can work in these conditions, Noel. His colleagues' reprobations have trailed him all the way from Manhattan. In the office no-one doubted which Noel's was: the computer studded with fluorescent Post-it notes (despite being expressly forbidden by the IT department) marked with cryptic messages: AUC — research; Madeleine, UNHCR. If his career change went to plan, he would have to address the desk chaos, although in his new role as absent-minded professor he would get away with a certain amount of disarray.

This would be his last year in his job at Global Witness; he had already accepted a post at a small liberal arts college, one he hoped would turn into tenure track, teaching anthropology and human rights. That was why he and Rachel had just bought a house upstate. He had not told his colleagues yet, but he would, as soon as he was back in New York.

He wants, suddenly and pungently, the moment of departure. He wants to leave Rachel behind with an incline of his head, shut her out of his peripheral vision. He wants to walk through the departure gate and arrive somewhere — anywhere — new and stark, and start work. The guilt is choking, a slippery animal that has forced its way down his throat.

There's something about you that's very every-man-for-himself. Rachida had said this. It was one of the most apt and wounding things anyone had ever said to him, emotional and clinical at once in that way the French could be. He didn't say this, of course; Rachida would have instantly recognized it for the cheap cultural stereotyping it was, not at all becoming to someone of his subtlety. That was another thing the French were good at: complimenting and rebuking you in the same sentence.

A disturbing hunger had struck him, looking at Rachel in the attic, a vision in her camisole though which the curve of her breasts were visible, the dust leaping from the filaments of her hair as a shaft of sun slipped over her. His sleek, beautiful girlfriend, standing in the room where Eve had told him about the handicapped son passing his final days, watching the sheer curtain drift in the breeze. Something was badly out of place: either the man-boy's condition, his sadness, the tidy devotion of his mother, caring for him day after day, until he died at twenty-eight. Or Eve, the sheet ribboning out from her hands, dust guttering in streaks of sunlight. His sudden realization: I don't know why, but I could love you. It seemed obscene, impossible that we could look at someone we barely knew, had in fact only laid eyes on for the first time in his life ten or fifteen minutes before, and think: *I could love you.* But this is exactly what had happened.

And Rachel, that creature so obviously not destined for dusty attics of old farmhouses on the tilting shores of Cape Breton Island — was he really that ruthless, was he really thinking of jettisoning her merely because she was part of his past, because of the things she knew about him, things that no-one else ever would? The fearful, midnight phone calls home from other time zones, the antidepressants, the neurological scans, the therapy.

He wanted so badly to be admired again, to be taken at face value, to be new to someone, and thrilling. Rachel still loved him, he was certain of it. But he was equally sure that a grain of pity had crept into her estimation and he knew too well how even a particle of pity could kill love. She had been part of those days of his, days marred by inertia, by defeat and error. He had failed to be strong for her, to perform for the world. He had neglected the first thing he had learned about being a man: don't let them see that you are weak. And if you are weak, for Christ's sake, don't let them see where.

Rachel had been stalwart, but he knew he was running out of time. Possibly this ultimatum about leaving Cape Breton was part of a larger plan. She was testing his love by saying: give up the rest of your vacation for me. I've done the same for you, several times. She would give him six months more, he calculated, to *work things out.* He could see the conversation coming, like a freight train travelling toward him from a long way away. *Look, I want to start a family. Are you up to this? Because if you're not, I'm going to have to find someone who is.*

And that would be it. Six years of cascading love, of negotiations and compromise and understandings would be flooded by a single conversation. She had told him once, *there are so many things I want to do in life and so little time.* And if he did not, or could not, give her what she wanted? Rachel would leave him and find someone who would. He would understand. He couldn't expect her to wait around forever. He was adult enough to know that needs were stronger than love. Needs won every time.

In another second he dispatched the thought as absurd. Of course they would go on together. They have bought a house; they will get married next year. Very soon after that they will have their first child. Not for the first time he asked himself, do we make decisions or do decisions make us? He feels the presence of something much bigger than him in his life. He can almost feel its workings; it was like a hand steering him in a certain direction. *This is how it should be,* that hand suggested, with its light but insistent touch.

Although this would leave a certain question unanswered, of what he would do with the secrets populating him, making him more than just himself. He was multiplying into more Noels than he ever wanted to be: the Noel that loves Rachel, the Noel that wants to throw it all away, the Noel that loved Rachida and even that Englishwoman whose name he had never learned in Miami airport, the Noel that held nocturnal, confessional conversations with Eve. Did Rachel know about these doppelgangers? What she would do about them when she did?

The truth is, Rachida still whispers to him, ignores him, stares at him with those candid almond eyes as she did before they had slept together — a hungry, unblinking, frightened stare. They knew each other for only three weeks, she had no part of him now, not in his days nor his nights, but at times Rachida is more part of his life than Rachel is. This is his worst treachery; more than anything else he is responsible for, it convinces him that life is little more than a series of half-committed crimes.

July turned seamlessly into August. The accumulated heat ripened the earth, released a metallic fume of warming strata of cadmium, magnesium. Strawberries extinguished themselves and are replaced by blueberries, then the pale green buds of what would, in a month's time, be blackberries. Bees fly erratically,

drunk on honeysuckle. In the rivers the eels are thickening, growing darker.

In the afternoon the buzz of crickets is so loud Eve thinks she
will need to shout to make herself heard. She goes for walks on
the abandoned road, tracks and droppings of lynx, pine marten,
white-tailed deer, rabbit and beaver; the animals are drowsy,
drunk on light the consistency of acacia honey. Even the nervous
opportunists, the bobcats, muskrat, raccoon, the otter — they
are all quelled and oiled with heat, they don't even bother to run
away when they hear her coming.

She walks through the mossy primeval woods, thinking of the
island's vanished earlier inhabitants: the Devonian shark
Doliodus, the huge millipede *Arthropleura*, with its armoured
back like an armadillo, the mastodon, the woodland caribou
Rangifer, the spear-nosed narwhal *Monodon*.

It hasn't rained in three weeks. Every time she turns on the
radio it spews out another forest fire warning. Don't throw
matches on the ground, even if you think you've snuffed them
out. Don't light camp fires. Concerned, authoritative men's voices use words like *tinderbox* and *kindling*. *That's right Gordon*,
says a park ranger on the local CBC call-in show. *The island's a
tinderbox. She could go up in smoke.*

A dance, not long after the summer field party. It is August; he
will be going home in less than two weeks.

The party is in the community centre, a former grocers
spruced up, painted red and white. It stands like a beacon on an
exposed hill above the ferry.

Inside it is so hot and smoky, she can barely see who's who.
Alistair is outside somewhere, drinking beer with his friends, sitting on the open tailgate of someone's pickup.

It's a younger crowd than usual, and a sound system is belting out music she knows is now called disco. Most of the older generation don't know what to do to this noise; they hang back on the fringes in the hope that someone will put the reels and the step-dance music back on.

She joins the teenagers on the dance floor. She is an energetic dancer, although her style is a bit Woodstock. She hasn't had enough information to update it. She flails around; her long hair catches him in the face as he approaches her.

He grins, she grins back. She thinks he has come to dance with her. He puts his mouth to her ear.

"You try too hard."

His voice is unmistakably corrective: tender, intimate, hovering on the edge of dismissal. In another context she might call it fatherly. It is the most complex thing a man has ever said to her. It makes her sit up and realize that he is an older man, she is a younger woman, this brute fact is at the heart of their interactions and there is no further point in trying to banish it.

"No, I don't think I do try too hard. I think I just like to dance."

She is surprised not to hear defensiveness or anger in her voice. The anger will come later.

She watches him walk back to the periphery of older people who can't dance to this newfangled stuff. She goes back to dancing.

The brash and tender feelings he provokes threaten to swamp her. It is so close to what she felt when Anita was first born — primal, bruising feelings, not far from anger, terrifying in their intensity. She hates him; she resents his dismissal of her. Still, when she is near him her body hums with delight, she all but has to remind herself to breathe.

Swimming at the beach the previous summer. A gang of them, all parents, go running in together for solidarity. It is late June and the sea is still so cold. The kids stay in the sea for an hour until they are hauled out, half-blue. The adults running out covered in goose pimples, flinging themselves on the mercifully hot blanket, warmed by the sun.

He sits up straight, his arms gripping his legs, smoking. She takes note of the surprising delicacy of his wrists, his ankles. They look too slim to support his body, these narrow isthmuses, just as the fetlocks of a horse seem far too fragile a platform for their bulk. He is still so thin, more than halfway into his forties.

He holds himself erect, alert. Compared to him other men look accepting, resigned, fatally relaxed. Just watching him do simple things — wrap a towel around his shoulders, lean over to say something in a friend's ear, his smile — witnessing the seriousness he brings to these gestures, his natural, not displeasing reserve, makes her heart sing so loudly she is sure everyone can hear its chorus.

It is summer again; she can't believe a year has passed. They are at another field party, identical to the one last year when he offered — no, she corrects herself, *threatened* to light her cigarette.

The headlights fail to completely illuminate them. They stand in the perimeter of light, half in darkness. Some random event has pushed them into proximity, but they don't speak. She is so relieved when her aunt comes up to her.

"Ann, dear, you're still the prettiest girl." Her aunt takes a tendril of her hair in her hand, twists it around her finger in an affectionate gesture.

"Thanks," she says, even though she is wondering about the *still*.

"Pretty?" He holds his head high and rigid, his face angled away from her, staring into the night. She doesn't like what she hears in his voice: a fastidiousness, a denial of delight, a lie.

"You don't think I'm pretty?" Her voice is not defensive or inviting or wounded, but matter of fact. It is the voice she would use to ask her own father if he thought she was pretty.

He looks at her, slowly, turning away from the night and the field, the scythe of headlights. His lips move, but no words come. The wince in his eye tells her how strict he is, how difficult to impress, never mind seduce, yet how susceptible, strict *because* he is susceptible. He is censorious, even rude in the face of his own yearnings, and she has no doubt he would be cruel to her if she challenged him. She wants to say, it's not fair what you do, putting the burden of your disdain on me. I've done nothing to deserve it. But at the same time she is beginning to think he is also a good man, an honest man, and there are others he needs to protect from his weakness — a regular weakness, for youth and beauty.

What is the point, she wonders, of having a mind, an intellect, if it is to be undone — picked apart, really — by a face? She finds his face so moving; she has never seen a face that even approaches its complexity. It is like a natural landscape, a mountain harried by wind and shadows. Looking at his face is a spiritual experience. She can feel the horizons of her mind being pulled apart, peeled back. His eyes cause her to question the whole nature of eyes, how they might be blank or full, sweet or broken. His eyes seem to contain all these possibilities at once. In some harsh lights or when he is passing judgement they turn brittle, flecked with experience. In the night they are a dark tide that laps against her edges.

"Well," he says.

"Well," she says.

They swivel away from each other, look desperately into the crowd for someone to save them from the pain of further conversation, to save them from each other.

His wife is American and pretty. With her she is friendly, as befits the wife of a cousin. They trade recipes for pies.

She sees him at these intervals, from the last week June to Labour Day, then at Christmas. He and his wife stay with his parents, who live ten miles down the road.

She never thought that love could move so slowly. In films and novels, the lovers get together within hours, a week, a month. But two years after they first meet, the man across the table from her is still beautiful, and still married. She is only twenty-seven but she is growing up fast. She realizes that he is that sort of man who will always be married, far before she or anyone else ever meets him, and that because she is not his wife she will only be some woman or other who will always want him.

It is the 1970s and supposedly an era of free love, but among her people, on this island, divorce is rare. In extreme circumstances couples might separate, but even this causes an almighty ruckus in the community. She has witnessed these unfortunate ruptures second-hand, through the gossip of her mother and her aunts and friends, gorging themselves on pity and condemnation, tut-tutting like sated birds of prey.

Their eyes brush. The look he gives her in that sliver of time is openly desirous, but warm, and fringed with pride. She can't fault it. She gives him a frank, slightly startled look in return. She doesn't pay lip service to the common view of flirting: that it is playful, an expression of innocent desire, a laugh. She flirts only when she means it. Her flirting is deadly serious.

Emanating from him is a thin current of loss, she can't imagine of what. A defined, narrow sorrow. Also a grandeur, combined with a natural restraint. But he has everything — what can he be lacking?

She hides her attraction and her vulnerability behind bravado and wit. They say cavalier, in-control things to each other studded with small clearings of exposure. Sitting across from him at the table she finds herself thinking — really daring to think — *No matter who you go home to at night, you're mine.* She interrogates herself: Mine as what? As the dead of my family are mine. My unborn children.

She knows straightaway that this love will make her life — with her husband, her daughter, once willingly tolerated, even loved — into an instant desert.

She spends months in a blasted place, hoarding her secret. The love comes and goes like a recurring illness. Some days she thinks: thank God, I don't care about him, I can get on with my life. But the next day she is swamped by desire. The fact that they see each other infrequently, with these long-drawn silences in between, keeps their love alive well past the normal lifespan for such combustible emotions. She is quite sure she has never felt this before: a longing and desire that is like being gnawed by a swarm of small-mouthed animals. Their little red-and-purple tongues. Their sharp, cunning teeth.

The Fireman's Ball in Little Bras d'Or. He sits on the other side of the room, at a long table with his extended family. She sits with Alistair, his sister and Anita, who is methodically spooning chocolate ice cream into her mouth. Couples sashay around the room to a reel; in a moment the band will stop and they'll put on some newfangled music that hardly anyone will dance to.

She shoots glances across the room. Every time she looks at him, he is laughing. Instead of feeling resentful that they are not nearer to each other, that he is enjoying himself with other people, she feels calm, at peace. Simply being in the same room with him is enough.

Later Alistair is talking with his friend Donald; Anita is running around with the other kids outside. She sits alone at the table making a carnation from coloured Kleenex she has fished out of her handbag. The table is scattered with crumbs of cake, acid yellow icing, a forest of smudged wineglasses, cloudy pools of white wine in their hulls.

He glides up to her. "We got separated."

She stares at him. Does he know that she thinks this sometimes? That they have been separated, cruelly, by fate.

He pulls out a chair and sits down at the end of the table, leaning into it, his torso tipping toward her. Her body starts to hum a tune, known only to itself. *I've waited and waited to be with you.* The way he sits down next to her, shy and assertive at once, she is sure he is about to take her hand in his own.

He smiles. "Not talking tonight?"

She doesn't feel like being teased. Does he think her a child? She shakes her head.

"Not dancing?"

She tries and fails to stifle a smile. She throws open the palms of her hands on the table. "As you can see."

"Want to dance with me?"

"I don't think we'd better."

He purses his lips, drops his gaze to the cake-crumb table. When he raises his eyes to hers, there is a needle of genuine regret.

"I guess not. But we can sit here and talk."

She smiles, instantly and profoundly happy, like a child.

This is the best time ever. They sit together trading clever observations about the décor, the band, the get-ups people have on. These moments are compensation for all the hours of arid doubt, the frightening sunsets, the cold spring rain. A diffuse excitement disperses itself inside her. She feels a momentous tenderness; she wants to hold his hand, to stroke his earlobe. Her hand drifts toward his fingers but has to settle for grabbing hold of a salt and pepper shaker. The mystery and the thrill of his being circle her, settle somewhere inside her, a living coil. She is sleepily alert, like a child trying to stay up beyond its bedtime. She can feel its nearness, love. They are only one step away from it.

They sit together alone at the table, talking or not talking, happy in each, as the evening slips away.

But most of the time she is a lonely acrobat, vaulting through nights that rebuff her. She can barely sleep; in fact she hasn't slept through the night for six months now, she fears she will go off her rocker.

Time becomes imaginary. Occasions like the Fireman's Ball,

the dances and the weddings where they see each other become only half-real, like a film or a novel. It couldn't have been her sitting there, her fingers an inch from his among the disintegrated cake, the paper streamers. She learns that there are actually several kinds of time, running alongside each other: there is the time inside her and time as the rest of the world lives it. She hones her patience until it becomes a living thing, a squirming creature inside her fed on a paltry diet of persistence. She loves her husband as best she can, but really he is part of that waking dream her life has become, a place of not-him, a means through which to cultivate this delicate relationship with time and which even she understands is ultimately a kind of extravagance.

She does the housework, listens to strathspeys and reels on the CJCB radio station, she weeds the garden, she dreams of the things she may study one day when she has time to go to college, she dreams of the places he has been to and which one day she might see. This is a good training for death, she thinks, in one of those black-mood moments that plague her. Dead, she will have to be very patient.

Well, dear, his father was the same, and his grandfather before him. All of them sharp-minded men with a sharp tongue to match.

Love makes her crafty. She has taken to discreet conversational sorties to find out as much as she can about him, quizzing relatives, using the guise of her shock at his rudeness to ask questions.

You've got to be careful of a man with a tongue like that, someone else says. What they mean is, *Don't fall in love.*

But an honest man, you've got to admit. Nobody's fool. A strong man, too.

These women are always talking about strong and weak men. Her mother wonders, are women so divisible? Why are women never spoken of in these terms?

His family has been in mining for generations, she learns

from these intelligence-gathering missions. He went first to Montreal to work for a Canadian mining firm, and then was poached for a rival American firm. From a young age he made it his purpose to see the world, her relatives tell her.

She reflects on all this information. She can see he is a serious man, built for shouldering responsibility, like many men he found so much pleasure — an unexpected pleasure, a deep shaft of contentment — in simply providing, in sending money home for his wife and children, who he often does not see for three or four months running. His work and travels have made him a more self-sufficient and introspective person than he would otherwise have been.

Her mother takes the measure of what is being denied to her. Not only his love, his company, but also his experience. Men get to go out into the world, acquire complexity through hardship, deceit, endurance. Women rely upon their innate character, their goodness untrammelled by disappointment, their charm. She herself might have been a more complex person; she might have been *him*, if her sphere of experience had been wider.

I want a bigger life, her mother writes. *I want to live as he has lived, see the world as he sees it. I want to be him.*

They are in the pantry at a neighbour's house; a party roars in the kitchen. It is three days after Christmas. Although it is two o'clock in the morning the children are still up, dancing and clapping. An impromptu duo, a fiddle and electric guitar, is playing in the kitchen. Forty or fifty people are dancing, and they have both been despatched, separately, to fetch more bottles of Coke and 7-Up from the pantry.

They rarely have the chance to be alone and so they seize the moment. So far they have only kissed. She loves the taste of his mouth. Actually, it is tasteless. It never seems to retain the flavour of tobacco or rum. This tastelessness is part of what pleases her so much about him. He is odourless too, although smelling his skin makes her brain stand bolt upright.

His tongue prowls her mouth. He scouts her palate, her molars. It is like having a wild animal inside her.

Her own husband she hasn't kissed like this, ever. In fact they have not kissed in years, although they are affectionate, in other ways.

For a long time she denies her desire to make love to him. This generosity — insane, unprecedented, childish — is at the heart of her love for him: she doesn't want to be made love to herself so much as to lay her hands on him, there and there and there. She wants to make simple gestures that are not obviously carnal, although the instinct behind them is perhaps more violently sexual than sex itself. To hold his hand, to run her index finger on the cool, white insides of his arm, to finger the mole on his wrist, to take his earlobe in her mouth and lick it, to brush her lips through his hair.

She hadn't been prepared for the sweetness. Lust, yes, that bog diamond, sharp and muddy. But not this frenzy of tenderness.

Her husband no longer makes love to her. She does not complain or try to provoke him; his response makes sense, it is the only just one, given that she is thinking about making love to another man. She takes on a disused feel. If she were an object, she would be coated in a film of dust.

She has always thought herself an honest person. But if she were honest, she would say to him, I love you. It is killing me to see you with anyone else. I feel as though I am the living dead, or the dead living.

She would go to his wife, say: I am in love with your husband. I can't imagine the world without him in it. When he is out of my sight, the world goes dark. She would go to Alistair, whom she respects more than anyone else in the world, including the object of her affections, and tell him. But she is terrified by the fact that what she feels for her husband, the father of her daughter, cannot compete with what she feels for her married second cousin. It does not even come close.

She says nothing. She is not an honest person after all. But then, she wonders, might honesty not be a force for good, but for destruction? This whole experience — if you could call it that — is causing her to think about things she has never considered before. She is learning, although she never wanted to be schooled by pain, to be an habitué of ambiguity, one of those people fingered by fate, whose special destiny it is to almost grasp the meaning of their own tragedy.

Eve wonders, who is this man? Her mother's observations and judgement provide some clues, but they are the writings of someone besotted and not to be entirely trusted. Should she give him the benefit of the doubt? Should she think him not a villain, a willing adulterer, a cruel man?

Like many men she suspects he has a disconcerting ability to turn his emotions off and on: hot water tap, cold water tap; two separate streams he has learned not to mix. Among his other weaknesses, besides the sharp tongue, are a self-involvedness that stymies curiosity about others, and the insensitivity of the habitual flirt. With her mother he finds himself in a situation he never called for. Despite his offhand, almost reflexive flirting, he possibly has never seriously thought of anyone other than his wife. That he will never leave his wife and children is another reason why her mother would love him: his constancy, his principles. He is a man of internal laws and rules that are not necessarily about happiness or satisfactions, and some of which he will never divulge.

At times, reading her mother's entries, Eve can picture him perfectly, like a figure leaping from dark wings onto a glaring stage. Indeed there is something of the theatrical — a slight, not displeasing artificiality — about him. Look at the abrupt, deliberate way he moves, the way he takes charge. He can barely sit still; he changes posture every few minutes, throwing his legs out in front, gathering them back up, propping his elbows on his knees and cupping his chin in his palm. He frequently looks troubled; his gaze turns sullen. This is another reason why women flock to him: he is that dark-haired handsome man, good fun and quick to laugh, but there are depths as well, it seems; he is a raw landscape of quarries and sudden rift valleys and danger signs posted next to steaming volcanic lakes. He has lived in exotic realms, has been so many different people: farm boy, hockey player, university student, industrial worker. He worked in the oil fields of Texas, did a stint as a supervisor in a copper mine in Peru. He combines masculine prowess with a questioning sensibility, a curiosity and desire for knowledge. Although the choices that underpin his life — wife, family, stability — are quite conventional.

He has classic qualities women look for: an honest, caring man. Someone who will be loyal, who will provide, who will be self-sacrificing if need be. He will be professionally status-seeking, competitive, ruthless even at times, the sexy man who will say no to sex with other women who in turn flirt with him with a forlorn grace, understanding that nothing more is on offer.

In return he will expect his wife's love, her tolerance, her goodness. She will need to be an essentially sweet, loving person. Other women will occasionally refer to her as "long-suffering" but will envy her bitterly because they themselves are married to whining, inflexible men, full of hurts and impositions, and it is she who has his lips, his tongue, his sex.

Eve's mother is intelligent and wants to avoid the fate of those envious women, nor does she want to covet another woman's husband. She tries to accommodate herself to the love that has sprung up inside her, a hunger string plucked every day by an invisible hand. She tries to treat it as she would an unwanted pregnancy: learn to conquer the anxiety and the fear, and then learn to tolerate it, to love it enough to let it go, to realize it has its own destiny in the world.

She never thought she would want such a man, someone more than ten years older, a man who looked like no-one else she has ever seen. A mournful, sharp face, but also liquid, slipping effortlessly from delight to disapproval. Black hair still so dark halfway into his forties, his champagne eyes, the hot pearl sting of his lips.

CHAPTER 15

Palladium, Molybdenum, Rhenium.

It is a ripe summer's night. Rachel is out there, somewhere, trying to expend her restlessness by pacing underneath the stars.

Their argument brewed up out of nowhere an hour earlier. Noel hated this aspect of relationships most, these internal earthquakes — how the ground could shift underneath you, without any warning.

They had been talking meanderingly and innocently of relationships — other people's relationships. Arturo and Sue, for example, their best friends; and other couples they knew. Noel remarked how they were all so steadfastly couple-y, even in their early thirties. They held each other's hands at dinner; they kissed each other in the lineup for movies. There was a determined element to these displays of affection, he thought, an enforced bonding. They allowed no sign of turmoil or indecision. Their friends seemed to have settled into a pleasant, secure happiness that Noel couldn't help but think of as premature. They talked about how all of their friends were trying for a baby — Noel registering that a new phrase had entered his lexicon, one which five years earlier he could not even have voiced. *Trying for a baby.*

"What frightens me is how as we become older relationships are more about outcomes than love," Noel said. "Sometimes I think we want *things* from each other more than we want each other."

"There's no such thing as unconditional love." Rachel's voice was suddenly tight and thin. "When you're a child, yes, but you're not a child. We are adults and we want things from each other, we *need* things from each other."

"Why are you telling me this?" What Noel had meant to say was, *What makes you think you can instruct me in the proper codes of feeling?*

"Because... Because I don't know what you want. Because I can't reach you."

"Because I acknowledge the essential ruthlessness at the heart of people." God, was that his voice? It sounded tangled, reedy.

"You're the one who's ruthless. You don't see that, but it's true." Rachel's eyes were hard. With that she got up and walked out of the kitchen.

"Where are you going?" he yelled.

Her voice trailed behind the slam of a door. "Nowhere. I'm nowhere, you're nowhere. We're *nowhere.*"

That was how he ended up in the room he set up as his study, staring at the Periodic Table, thinking. *I'm right. There is no love, only wants and needs. Whether you fit in with those wants and needs determines whether you are loved. Love is just a romantic fallacy, a terrible duping story.* Rachel is really telling him that his feelings don't count. He can go along with this and have her company, have her love, her loyalty, for as long as he lives. Or he can — this is how she would see it — stamp his foot like an angry child, say: That's not good enough. And be alone. Or at least, not be with her.

At least he'd had the presence of mind to form some sort of riposte before she had stormed out.

"You know, you speak to me as if I were a child. As if I didn't understand anything about commitment and compromise. What makes you think you can do that?"

"I don't see any evidence of it."

"And who gave you the right to deliver these moral truths? Is it because you're a woman and you want things? You want children. Is that why you think you can instruct me in the proper ways of feeling?"

Rachel was staring at him as if she had never seen him before.

"That's what you think, right?" he pressed.

She shook her head, heavily and with regret. I know I never thought I'd be having this conversation with my fiancé.

"That's just it, Rachel, I'm not your *fiancé*. I'm me, I'm Noel. You want the form of it all: you want a fiancé, a wedding, children, happily ever after. The form doesn't guarantee the content."

"You're wrong. I know how to compromise. I can do that, for the person I really love."

"Who is that person you really love? Because it isn't me. It's an idea you have — no, it's an ideal. You thought it was me, and now you're learning I might not be your storybook prince. And it's true — I'm not. I can't be that to you. It's not real."

"It is."

"You just want control; you want me to do your bidding and you're trying to shame me into it."

"I can compromise. It's you who can't. You want everything to be passion, forever. It doesn't work like that. You take the person you feel most passionate about, throw in cohabitation, hairs in the bathtub, shit streaks on the toilet, and in a couple of years I bet you wouldn't feel so passionate."

"Rachel," his voice was low, and level with shock, "that's crass."

"But true. Unfortunately."

"I know more about compromise than you can imagine." As he said this Noel felt heavy and old, as if he had been too long in the world already and had outstayed his welcome.

He didn't want to think of Rachel at all, and she knew this on instinct. He wanted to think about the past, about Eve, the island, the Periodic Table of Elements — anything but Rachel and their exalted future together.

That was when Rachel left, banging the door behind her. Noel felt strangely unperturbed; in fact, her departure imbued him with a mischievous contentment. He propped his legs up on the desk and allowed his mind to wander.

Eve had taken a risk in showing her anger with him the night she had come to dinner. She was angry he was getting married.

The pleasure this provoked in him was delicious and clandestine. At the time he had made a quick inventory of his choices: ignore it, as if he had never perceived the power of her emotion or her vulnerability; reward the fact that she had the guts to express it, or humiliate her. He understood how a fine, even invisible, line divided love from humiliation, so fine you really might not be able to distinguish between the two.

Boron: a transition metal. Yes, she had bared herself to him. He found vulnerability moving, sexually addictive. *Promethium: a lanthanide.* When Zeus stole fire from man it was Prometheus who recovered it by trickery and returned it to earth. As punishment Zeus chained him to a rock, where an eagle fed on his liver. Like poor Sisyphus and his boulder, although no metal was named after him. What was it with the Greeks and their bitter stones, he wondered, their never-ending apexes, their readiness to be vanquished by impossible challenges? *Polonium, Strontium, Caesium, Sodium.* The sodium light in his room at the Mille Collines, angling through the window from the streetlight outside and carving the room into ochre squares. The carpet — always a misjudgement, in African cities, to use carpet, even with air-conditioning — that smelled of other people's sweat, other people's fear.

"Should I drop you at Madame Fidèlés?"

Alexandre usually stayed at a guesthouse, "Madam Faithfuls," run by a terrifying teetotal woman from Burundi.

They were on the outskirts of Kigali, returning to the capital after their trip to the South. Alexandre looked out the passenger window. "I don't want to go there."

"But you've been staying there for years."

"The last time I was there I met someone I know. I don't want to see him again."

Noel decided not to press for details. "Where else can you stay?"

"Nowhere."

"Do you want to stay at the hotel?"

Happiness lit on Alexandre's face, like the arrival of a rare bird. "But isn't it too expensive?"

"It's outrageously expensive, but don't worry about it."

He put Alexandre's room on his credit card. He would have the room next to his. "There's an adjoining door," he said. "In case you get lonely." It was a joke, but he saw Alexandre's face lurch into an expression Noel had never before witnessed, a kind of stricken euphoria, a shimmering, transparent fear. As soon as Noel saw it, he dismissed it. Over the coming years he would learn this was a habit of his: he had the ability to recognize the truth of an expression or a situation, to be almost supernaturally sensitive to it, but he would discard this in favour of his second more rational and explicable impulse.

Alexandre retired to his room. Noel drew the curtains against the night. There was something reassuring about having Alexandre in the room next to his. He had never worked in such close contact with anyone before; he normally didn't need a translator, as he usually worked places where French or Spanish were spoken, but in Rwanda most peasants' French was poor, and there was no way he could have done his job without a Kinyarwandan translator.

They had spent a solid month together now, talking about everything apart from personal matters — football versus cricket, world affairs, the current political intrigue in Rwanda, the habits of the wild gorillas of neighbouring Uganda, the pests that preyed upon the avocado plant, Alexandre's incessant questions about the US electoral system, the vapidity of the Oscars ceremony (which Alexandre had watched for the first time in his life in Paris), and did Noel think the civil war in the Balkans was similar to Rwanda's, and what had gone so badly wrong in Somalia?

Noel found that he could answer most of Alexandre's questions. In those weeks he felt the pleasing sensation of knowing more than he thought he did, of being admired — for his knowledge, his education, for being American. It had cast a warm glow in the place where the disappointment at not having seen Rachida again lived.

He was asleep, and then he was awake. The dogless night howled its silence. A figure, an apparition, really, sat on the bed. He jolted upright.

"Who's there?"

A flash of white teeth in the darkness. "I couldn't sleep."

It was Alexandre. "Christ. You scared the shit out of me. What are you doing here?"

From the end of the bed came the sound of ever so slightly laboured breathing. "I want to sleep with you."

For a second, he thought Alexandre meant that he didn't want to sleep alone. Then the meaning hit him in a strange rush, in the lungs first. It sieved the air from them, he could barely breathe. Of course, how could he have missed it? The admiring glances. The women who liked his gentleness. His own complicity. *I'll get you a room.*

"Alexandre, I... I can't. It's not you; it's not that I wouldn't like to... I'm flattered. But I can't. Believe me, I've tried before, and it's just not in me. As soon as he said it," he was relieved. At least he had spoken the truth.

"I know you want that Swiss girl. I know you don't want me. But I had to try. Can you explain that to me? Why I had to try?"

Before he could answer, Alexandre stood up so sharply Noel heard a bone crack. He disappeared through the adjoining door. In the morning he was gone.

She launched the boat from the concrete slipway under the NO EXIT sign. Rachel and Noel sat in the bow, swaddled in lifejackets. Eve had promised to take them out in the motorboat. Rachel wanted to see the coves and the old cemetery on Gypsum Point, and to make the trip across the lakes to Seal Island.

"The lake's choppy," she warned them. "You'll get sprayed."

The sky was clear, threaded with thin herringbone clouds. Seal Island appeared as a dark charcoal line where its back met the horizon, as if it had been etched into it. Rachel sat wearing her Jackie Kennedy sunglasses, peering through binoculars, trying to locate eagles, Noel next to her. From the back — Eve's perspective — he appeared tanned and erect, like an obelisk.

They arrived in the cove and cut the motor. A strange airlessness engulfed them and an echo poured in, as if they were at the bottom of a deep chamber.

"Who are they?" Rachel asked, pointing out the four tombstones slumped at various angles on the beach.

"Gillises."

"How did they get here? Did they live here?"

"Nobody knows much about them," Eve replied. "But they couldn't have lived out here. There are gypsum sinkholes all over the place. They must have brought the bodies out in a boat to be buried."

"Just like in Venice," Noel said. "Rowing the dead in gondolas out to Santa Croce. I wonder if they exiled them out here, if they didn't want them in the cemetery."

Rachel looked away, spruce trees tilting in the sepia mirror of her sunglasses. "There's an echo here. It's eerie."

Eve started up the motor.

At Beinn Breagh Point she steered the boat into the lee and cut the motor. They bobbed in silence for a few minutes, admiring the view of the mansion house where Bell had invented his version of the telephone. The house had been painted dark brown for as long as Eve could remember. It was a wide-girthed mansion, squat but not inelegant, with a glassed-in vestibule and a semicircular verandah that looked out on a commanding view of the lakes. Eve had never liked the house much, although she couldn't say why.

Noel's voice came to the back of a breeze. "Any news yet on your father?"

"Tests came back negative for everything." She remembered she still hadn't looked at the envelope Anita had given her.

"That's good news."

She convinced herself she had been correct in her observation that Noel's concern had a clinical tang. He seemed to cast an intense, interested gaze on people; he appeared so engaged, so involved. But really she suspected he was using others to solve an ambitious puzzle he had set himself.

"Can we go over to Seal Island?" Rachel asked.

Eve took a quick measure of the waves in the strait. "This boat is only good for crossing the lake on really calm days."

"We can go slowly, surely."

"All right, but you have to hold on." She demonstrated to Rachel and Noel how to grip the bench beneath them or the gunwales if the boat became unsteady.

She yanked the motor into life. The water boiled to yellow on either side of the boat, the dark blotch of a jellyfish was shredded by the blades.

When they puttered into the concrete slip of the wharf on the other side, Rachel was the first to get out.

"Let's go for a walk."

Noel cast Eve an apologetic glance. Rachel was inviting him, but not her.

"You two go. I'll wait here."

"Are you sure?"

"Of course. Take your time."

Rachel was already up the bank and walking up the road, so that Noel had to jog to catch up with her.

Eve installed herself on a piece of driftwood and looked across the lake. The cabin was clearly visible, perched on the side of the mountain, also John Rory's house and the crippled barn next door. Celyn and Bob's house stood out like a brightly painted beacon. Apart from these individual islands of habitation, the mountain was covered in a matted tangle of black forest.

She didn't know how long she sat there before she heard footsteps approaching from behind.

"There's a lot more life on this side of the lake," Rachel said. "Why is that?"

Eve turned around. "Better farming land. The cottagers like it because it gets the evening sun."

They climbed into the boat and she pushed them out again.

On the way back the mid-afternoon wind was at its peak. She had to concentrate on the angle and speed at which they met the largest of the waves. Somewhere near the middle of the lake the splatting against the hull of the boat became more violent, and she decided to cut the motor almost entirely. Then immediately she changed her mind and kept it running.

She had seen the wave, of course, and meant to meet it straight on, smack, that was the only way, to cut it in two. But the wave met the boat on the side and for one wild second it seemed they might capsize.

"Hold on," she yelled.

The flimsy aluminum hull seemed about to flip, then in another second it steadied itself. But by then Rachel was no longer in the boat.

"What in the name of God happened?"

She chucked the lifejacket into the porch. "She fell out of the boat."

"Who?"

"Who do you think I'm talking about, the Queen of Sheba? His girlfriend, Rachel."

"What were you doing out in that boat on a day like today?" her father all but barked. "Look at the wind."

"I saw the wind, thanks. They wanted me to take them across the lake. I hit a wave the wrong way coming back. I told them the water was choppy, to hang on."

"Is she going to be all right?"

"She's fine. She got wet, that's all."

"I don't think you should be taking strangers out in that boat. It was never very stable. It's just tin, remember."

She started to form an answer, a complaint, a riposte, but she found to her horror that she was about to cry.

"I'm going to take a hot bath," she managed to say, and fled.

As soon as she realized what had happened, she cut the motor. That was her only real fear: running Rachel over with the outboard motor. Otherwise, she would be all right. She wore a lifejacket, she could swim, the water was warm, there were no treacherous currents.

Noel pulled Rachel out of the water while Eve sat on the opposite gunwale for ballast. But Noel couldn't pull Rachel into the boat by himself. Shock had sapped the strength from her arms and they slipped like noodles from his grasp. Eve hauled the outboard motor into the boat and manoeuvred it into the side of the boat to ballast them and then kneeled beside Noel. They pulled her in, one on each arm. Rachel kicked and flailed at the water. When Rachel was safely in the boat Eve had to perform the delicate operation of getting the motor back in the stern without capsizing them all.

"I'm fine, I'm fine," Rachel kept saying. When they reached the jetty Rachel stepped out of the boat with a quick martinet stride.

When she had reached a certain distance, she turned around. "You could be sued, you know."

Eve looked up, a wet tie rope in her hand.

"If you take people out on the water, you should know what you're doing."

"I've been taking boats out on this lake since I was eight years old. If you want to sue someone, go sue that freak wave."

"You have responsibilities. It's the law."

"I'm not the hired help, Rachel. And I know lawyers don't believe this, but there's such a thing as an accident."

Rachel walked away. Noel hesitated for a moment, and then followed her.

Later, sitting in the cabin with her hair drying in a towel, an uncharacteristic whisky in her hands, she has a flash of Rachel's fashionable, thin-soled sneakers disappearing over the gunwale.

It had all happened so slowly, her perception of the wave, no more than a vague disturbance on the surface of the water at first. Then the lug-headed, deformed wave, far bigger than the others. The roar of the motor, a tear in the afternoon's skin. A tumbling figure, ragged and inept, like a doll. Rachel hadn't been holding on with both hands. The surprise as the sole of her sneaker tipped over the edge. The little togs on its sole, like bubble wrap.

Wet, Rachel had looked even thinner, sharper. She was a whippet: unbreakable, emphatic. Even the way the water dripped from her hair suggested knives. Eve had once aspired to be this kind of woman; someone with edges, a person on whom, if you were not careful, you could cut yourself.

Rachel was an on-top person, Eve decided. She had never contemplated failure but this was less about arrogance than a simple survival tactic — she knew she would never survive failure, or in fact much ambiguity at all, so she sensibly avoided it.

This is why Eve felt such intense satisfaction when Rachel was tossed out of the boat: normally it was she who was jettisoned overboard. For once in her life she managed to hold her ground.

They made one last trip, to Prince Edward Island, sunning themselves on red clay beaches, marvelling at the expanse of potato fields, their patchwork quilt thrown over the undulating hills of the island, how the grass in PEI was of a strange incipient green, as in garden furniture catalogues. Against the red of the soil the island took on the aspect of naïf painting, all vivid surfaces, but with little depth. Noel failed to mention how the colour scheme — the cadmium red of the earth, the unnatural green — reminded him of Rwanda.

Rachel was thrilled to find that the sea was warmer than in Cape Breton, and they both came to the conclusion that, if they ever took another vacation in this part of the world, it would be in PEI. Sure, it lacked Cape Breton's rugged beauty, but there was a fascinating softness to it, with its clay soil, shifting sand bars, dunes, and the tepid, shallow ocean.

In those three days Noel watched Rachel pick her way gingerly around the growing realization that she had damaged something important to both of them. He received her elusive, guilty smiles without comment. In the same moment that he deplored her behaviour — so *American*, threatening to sue when instant satisfaction was not forthcoming — he couldn't help but think, *I admire her more than ever now. She will never let me down.*

He watched her now, dressed in her expensive linens, sashaying through the Anne of Green Gables museum, a strangely wistful look on her face, occupied (as he well knew) with equating this down-home museum with her own clinical upbringing, and yet he could not suppress a faint distaste. It was a source of constant surprise to him, that you could hold two entirely contradictory thoughts about someone and believe them equally, without splitting in two.

They arrived back in Clam Harbour late at night, Rachel asleep beside him. Approaching the turnoff he looked for the young moose, half wanting to see him, but he didn't appear.

He woke Rachel by nudging her gently on her shoulder and they stumbled, exhausted, into the kitchen. Rachel had forgotten her cellphone, left it on the kitchen table. She picked it up to find six missed calls and two messages.

Eve was sunbathing in the lee of the wharf, her eyes shut, when a shadow crossed her face. She started and sat up.

"Your father told me I'd find you here."

Seeing Noel now, after five days' absence, was like staring full into the sun. She had to cover her eyes.

"I'm not going to even attempt to apologize for Rachel."

"That's surprising, because you seem to do a lot of apologizing for her."

He dipped his chin slightly. "I'm really sorry it happened at all."

The slapping of the waves against the ferry, the distant caw of a crow.

"Do you mind if I join you?"

"I'd rather be alone."

He nodded crisply.

She closed her eyes and lay back down on the ground, listening to the sound of the grass swishing as he walked away.

An internal symphony blares to life each morning, four-thirty or five o'clock, catapulting him out of sleep. It is a glass orchestra, percussive and insistent.

Noel rises and tries to silence the sound with the dawn air. He knows Eve is similarly afflicted. Twice he has seen her meandering around the cabin at the same hour, heading down the road or to the shore. He doesn't approach her, in part because he needs to preserve the illusion of aloneness, that his dilemmas are unique. Also, he feels wary of her, even frightened, after their conversation at the ferry.

The wind is sudden and bright, like cymbals. Anxious melodies — pentatonic, Eastern-sounding — wind their way through him, drawing patterns he tries to retrace during the course of the day, after he has climbed back into bed next to Rachel, after he has regained sleep until seven-thirty or eight o'clock. These dissonances tell him that his internal censor is back on the job. This is what wakes him so rudely, ready-packaged punishments installed in his mind.

You are intellectually avid but emotionally languid, his censor tells him. *You are not at home.* And this is true: not in his family, not in his country. He has rebuked himself enough for this failing, shoving himself out in the world among the diasporas, the terrorized, the displaced, thinking that maybe, somewhere among this tribe of lost souls, he will find home. *You insist upon being in command, you think pragmatism will save you from the messiness of life.* He can't find the switch that will turn off this voice just as he can't extinguish desire, he hasn't learned the trick of indifference, and probably he never will.

Stop going out into the world in search of your own annihilation, his censor instructs. *Call off your search for the person who will throw your image of yourself back at you. Who will be that savage mirror.*

There had always been fires. He remembers his father carrying his sister-in-law out of the blaze on his back. She wore only her nightgown and housecoat. It was minus-thirty-five degrees that night and his father carried her the two miles to their house through a blizzard.

His uncle's farmhouse burned down in the middle of winter. In the morning there was nothing left but the bathtub. He lagged behind as his father staggered through the snow, his brother trailing a hastily packed sled with the few fragments they salvaged from the house. He stayed there and watched things gathering and dissolving, trapped in the surface fission of fire. He knew the content of his aunt's house well: thin plywood wardrobes, a Formica table, the nylon housecoat left in the kitchen that he watches melt like a sliver of plastic. The ironing board, legs soldered together. The hideous ceramic owl, its lacquer popping before it exploded.

He stood for half an hour watching the house burn, accompanied by his father's dog, even though the blizzard was raging. The dog glanced at him apprehensively: *let's go.*

He remembers another fire, at an adjacent farm. The farmer was old and infirm; one of the smudge pots he used as a lantern at night had ignited some hay, and within minutes the barn was in flames. His father dousing himself with cold water, even though it was March and still below zero, and running into the barn to beat the horses out of their stalls. He remembers his father emerging behind the galloping horses, his face and bare arms streaked with carbon and manure. Horses are afraid of fire, his father explained afterward, standing at the washbasin in the old house, but their fear of abandoning home is stronger. Home is their refuge, he said, even if home is burning.

Noel stood at the door.

"I want you to tell me about diamonds."

"Why?"

"I'm getting married. I need to know." He raised his eyes to hers and they were miserable.

Suddenly she was afraid: for him, for Rachel, for herself, all of them. She wanted to say: Don't be unhappy. Don't squander love.

"I can't really tell you where to buy them. Go to Tiffany's, I guess."

"No, it's not that. I want to know how they are made."

Graphite and diamond are the same substance, in molecular terms, she told him. They are not dissimilar from coal; like coal, diamonds occur in the metamorphic rocks found in Cape Breton and all over the Canadian Shield.

Diamonds come from magmas more than three hundred miles below the earth's crust, deep in the mantle. They occur in old, continental areas — Siberia, Southern Africa, Canada — in ancient shields called cratons. They are punched up through fractures in the continental crust called pipes. The pressure and temperature that catapults them turns them transparent, or semitransparent. She tells him the word *diamond* is derived from the Greek *adamas*, meaning invincible. Relative density 3.50 to 3.52. Cleavage eminent among octahedral faces. Fracture conchoidal. Tenacity brittle. Lustre brilliantly adamantine. Diamond is harder than any other substance on earth.

She learned all this on the job, she tells Noel, although she has only very occasionally sourced diamonds for Caroline. Eve doesn't really like them, as stones. They are too easily admired, too complacent in their beauty, because they know they are made to persist. Noel expresses his admiration that she should know so much about them anyway, without having had to consult a book. It's true, diamonds have hardly passed through her fingers, she tells him, but she is one of those people who makes it her business to know the properties of things she may never touch.

∾

"What's that, Mumma?"

Her mother swivels around. She stands framed in an odd chrome light against the water. She clutches a shawl or blanket around her shoulders.

"Eve. What in the name of God are you doing here?"

"Couldn't sleep, Mumma."

"You walked, my darling." Her mother shakes her head. "Without a flashlight, I suppose."

"Yes," she says, stubbornly.

"Eve, what are you doing walking through the woods alone at night?"

"You do it. Daddy does it. Anita does it."

"That's the point, my girl. You're too young."

She points to the soaked telephone books on the beach. "What's that?"

"Those were a whale's teeth. It's called baleen."

"What happened to the rest of him?"

"He sank to the bottom. Or he was eaten."

She imagined the whale, toothless, plummeting to the ocean floor, settling on the edge of a submerged mountain. Would all deaths be as lonely?

A mint sky gives way to the pale pink of lupines. She holds her hands in front of her face, fingers splayed against the amber light until they glow like candlesticks against the black canvas of the water. Her mother's hair catches the dawn light too. She likes to take her mother's hair in her mouth and suck until she had made a spittle-coated arrow.

She is too young to ask her mother, what are you doing on the shore at dawn, although she knows. She heard them the evening before.

You can't give me any better than this cabin, is that right? Is that right? This is where I'm going to spend the rest of my life?

His voice, growing louder, *I don't know what you want. Tell me what it is you want.*

Eight years old, eavesdropping, guilty but galvanized. In her head a little tuneless song crescendoing: *now, now, now.*

The sun mounts the island's back and it is like the delayed appearance of long-expected foreign envoy, not so much celestial as prehistoric. It rushes toward them, the sun, a golden sword. Then it is through them, carving them into separate dimensions: here, now, then, what was, what will be.

She is thirty-two and in Venice, a trip tacked onto the end of Milan fashion week. The shiftless, radiant armada of fashion people. Glassy desiccated palaces, the strange jade of the lagoon.

The headlong summer is already weary in June; it is forty-five degrees and the sun enters her head like an axe. She walks the narrow streets near the Campo Santa Margherita, sweat soaking her linen dress. All the streets are dead ends, they tip into the Grand Canal.

Lapidary water, dark and forbidding. After midnight along the canals near the Accademia she sees rats the size of foxes. She takes the Vaporetto to Lido; it is a weekday and the beach is empty and scrappy, littered with white plastic bottles thrown overboard from Adriatic trawlers.

She watches wan dawns; in summer in Italy she stays up all night, always, she doesn't know why. There is something forsaken in the night. She finds it easier if she simply stays awake. She is being gnawed by some strange craving, also an old vigilance. But there is nothing to watch for. Perhaps she wants to be witness to the wind, if such things have witnesses.

CHAPTER 16

When she arrived back from work at Kay's, Anita was sitting alone at the kitchen plank.

"Where is he?"

"Oh," he tore off out of here.

"He's not supposed to drive."

"Well, there's nothing wrong with him, is there?" Anita threw up her hands. "I can hardly stop him."

"Did he say where he was going?"

"No, he just slammed the door. He said he didn't mind staying with us from time to time but a whole winter in our house would just kill him and he might as well do the job himself and get it over with."

"He's going to run out of money before the winter's over. I can try sending him money from Toronto but he'll never accept it."

"He's so lonely, he doesn't even realize it," Anita said. "He goes for walks for hours by himself. Just like you used to, when you were a teenager. That's exactly what you did. Spent hours sitting on the ferry, collecting stones and sea glass, arranging driftwood."

"I did that because I wanted out of here."

"Exactly," Anita said, with her there-that's-done-and-dusted voice. "I really think that if we leave him here on his own this winter he will just die."

She sat down beside her sister. They sat for a while in silence, looking out the window.

"For years, I blamed her. I even thought, what a harlot."

Eve flinched at the word. She could have asked, who? But she knew who.

"I took his side," Anita said.

"What do you mean, his *side?*"

"There's always a side to take, don't you think? I never thought that much of him myself," Anita said. "He was that kind of man who wants everything for himself, but he wants it to come to him. He wouldn't stick his precious neck out for it."

Who was she talking about? Was there a *kind* of man who did such things?

"He just wanted to see himself admired by a young pretty woman," Anita went on. "She loved him like crazy and he said, oh, sorry, but I'm married. Some people provoke affection so they can trample on it. They know they're locked into something long-term and there's no way out so they keep themselves amused by playing with you. Most people seem to think this is all in a day's work of being married, but I think it's mean." Anita sounded so bitter Eve wondered if she had experienced any of this herself.

"But he was a beautiful man," Anita conceded. "I always thought how hard it would be to be married to a man like that; every woman would fall in love with him."

"Did you?"

"Of course. He was the first man I fell in love with." Anita gave a laugh, but there was a hard, grinding quality to it. "Imagine that — the first man you love is your mother's lover. Except you don't understand that's what he is, of course."

"How could you be in love if you didn't think much of him?"

"Because that's the way it is, most of the time." Her voice had that flinty tone Eve associated with un-absorbable hurt. Something must have gone very wrong for Anita, at some point. She knew she would never be able to ask what.

"I cried when they died," Anita said. "Everyone thought I was crying for Mumma, but it was for him too. Even now I catch myself wanting to see him again. I still look for him."

"Where?"

"On the highway, in the mall. On TV. Everywhere." A breeze

through the window lifted Anita's hair, exposing dark roots near her temple. "Sometimes I think everything I'm doing — everything I've done — is a reaction against what happened with Ann. What she did to us." Anita tipped her head back, tilted her eyes to the ceiling. "Anyway. Look at me. I'm all right." She started to laugh. When she brought her head down again, her eyes had watered, their rims flushed red.

"I don't know his name. She only ever writes his initial."

"You found those books?"

Eve nodded. "And her diary. It's disguised to look like a ledgerbook."

"I was going to tell you about that."

"Why didn't you?"

"I was waiting for the right moment."

"Why are you thinking about this now?" Eve asked.

"Because it destroyed him." Anita swivelled her eyes around the cabin, as if looking for evidence of this. "Although he's still here." Anita's mouth was set. Her sister might have been disappointed, Eve considered. She might have thought all these years that the wrong man had survived.

They perch on driftwood logs, ringing the fire.

"That's how you know it's mid-August," Bob says. "All of a sudden you get a cool night."

Noel is deep in conversation with Bob; Eve talks to Celyn's friend, who is visiting for the weekend, a potter with galleries in Boston and New York.

"I do replicas of artefacts dug from Egyptian tombs," the potter is saying. As in Tutenkamoun. She pronounces the name correctly, the emphasis on *moun*. They talk about the potter's work; she doesn't ask what Eve does. They eat wieners, roast marshmallows. "Just like when we were kids," Celyn says. Her tinkling laugh like jewels scattered across a hardwood floor.

Celyn no longer looks at Noel. On the other side of the fire Bob is singing the praises of Rachel aloud. Noel must have told them she hasn't come to the bonfire because she has a headache. "Very educated," Bob is saying, "very smart. One of those women who don't take any shit." Everyone nods approvingly in Noel's direction, although Eve wonders, what does it mean, exactly, not to take any shit?

Bob yawns. "Time to hit the sack." Bob is a morning person, up at five, off to work on his sailboat most mornings by six. Celyn and the potter stand up, thwacking their hands on their thighs. "Look after the fire, will you. Make sure it burns down. We've had some rain but you never know. Things are still dry."

Tendrils of looks, trailing behind them up the hill to the road. Celyn, Bob, their friend walking in trio, heads leaning in together at a judicious distance, like diplomats.

She gives him her best wry smile. "That'll be the rumour mill starting up. If you listen closely you can hear the grind."

He laughs. In the middle of the bonfire the wood burns the dark purple of dog's gums. Smells of woodsmoke, citronella, a vague fume of almond. She has a wholly unfamiliar sense, ripe and immediate, that everything is cohering, a camera pulled into focus. The sounds, smells are all familiar, even prearranged; she has walked onto a theatre to perform a play she knows by heart.

"Why didn't your father come down?"

"He's got better things to do, I guess."

The fire pops and spews burning twigs at their feet. She takes out a cigarette. "You won't sue me if I smoke?"

He gives her a curious look, half hurt, half accepting.

"Rachel really regrets her behaviour, how she spoke to you."

"She could tell me that herself."

"It was such a misjudgement," he elaborates.

"Why didn't you say so at the time?"

"When?"

When you were getting out of the boat and following her up the hill without so much as a glance of apology or commiseration.

"I needed to let her cool off."

"And then did you tell her?"

"What?"

"That you thought it a misjudgement?"

Noel gives her the first truly sullen look she has received from him then, the look of all men who have been caught at being less honourable than they thought themselves to be. But there is something else, too: a rigid, dark glint behind the morose exterior. Might he be a ruthless person, both intellectually and emotionally? She didn't even try to kid herself that this ruthless streak would absolve her of her love for him, if indeed that was what she felt. What part of her needed ruthlessness?

They stare into the firelight, following the curve of night, the exact point where the flames disperse into darkness. The wood is burnt into convex arches; all at once it collapses into a pile of embers.

He reaches over and takes a strand of her hair, winds it round his index fingers. "Your hair looks golden in this light."

She stares at his fingers, just below her jawbone. They are finely made, like thin candlesticks.

"I could melt you down."

"Maybe you'd only find dross."

He laughs, withdraws his hand.

She switches on the flashlight and leads their way home.

At the top of the drive to John Rory's they both shift from one foot to the other. She lowers the flashlight; the light falls in a neat buttery pool between their feet.

"'Night then."

"'Night then."

Harassed voices buzzed in the background.

"What are you working on?"

"Oh, another mother with an eight year old with cancer seeks incredibly expensive treatment in Arizona." In Lew's voice is his characteristic mixture of tension and nonchalance. "What's the matter?"

"Nothing."

"That was an impatient sigh I heard. I know an impatient sigh when I hear one. Or could it be exasperation, disgust, indifference?"

Lew had interviewed hundreds of people over the phone. He was quick to pick up anything from voice.

She tried to rally. "I'm just tired. This nickel-and-dime lifestyle is wearing me out."

"Yeah, you told me. Go back to the Maritimes, and poof! your life is about gas and tips. Did I tell you we're thinking of doing a feature on that? We're coming to get you and make you a national example of the thin layer that separates the urban middle classes from the destitute periphery."

"This is serious."

"I know. But at least it's not Alzheimer's."

"As far as they know."

"Then you can get out," he said. "Just come home."

Home. Could that really be home? Toronto, Lew. She was already forgetting what her apartment looked like. Was the ficus tree by the window or by the door? What kind of bed did she own?

"It's not that easy."

"Listen, we're only twenty minutes to airtime. I'll call you after the show."

She waited for his call that night, but by midnight and he still hadn't called she went to bed.

The weirs are full; the exodus has begun, tumbling downriver to accumulate in the estuaries, the mud and brackish water. Here they will wait for the transformation. They will turn silver, their eyes will widen and turn saucer-shaped and blue, so that they can see in the lightless ocean.

They have gorged for years and they will never eat again. Just before they begin their journey their digestive systems will seize up. Their blood chemistry is mutating too, in order to support the shift from the ten or twelve pounds of pressure per inch of a freshwater river to the more than a ton of pressure per inch in the sea.

Where do you go? Although he knew the truth, in a fashion. They dive into depths, to a place cold and dark with unimaginable pressure. The Sargasso is the deepest part of the Atlantic. The continental shelves of North America and Europe plummet there to an ocean valley some four thousand feet beneath the surface.

He read that when Europe and North America were still joined by land, at the time of the great continent Gondwanaland, this valley was where eels were born, lived and died. It was threaded with freshwater rivers, cascading from mountains now long under the sea. Even as tectonic plates drifted apart, eels continued to mate in this rift valley. It sunk and sunk, through the long corridors of time, but they still hatched in the ancient valley, and went in search of the river homes that had once bordered it. Even as the distances became so much farther, as they had to undertake thousands-mile journeys, their origins and end remained in that submerged place.

What could be the point of this blind fidelity to a sunken home? That they should persist with this valley as their home, so remote and inhospitable, that they should believe there could be no other.

"You'll be missing them, I suppose."

Duncan inserted the hose into her tank. She couldn't quite hear him over the racket of the gas pump.

"Who?"

"Your neighbours."

"What about them?"

"Don't you know?" He removed the gas nozzle from the tank. It dripped the ripe stench of gasoline. "They left."

"What do you mean, left?"

"They drove out of here this morning, luggage in the car. I asked him if they were on their way home early, and the feller said yes."

She drove back at seventy miles an hour. She parked the truck at a reckless angle in their driveway and leapt out. The door was locked. Standing on tiptoe she cupped her hands and peered into the kitchen window. She could only make out the surface of the table, which was clean. No photographs were spread across it, no coffee maker or jam jars sat there like witnesses waiting to be interrogated. She could find no note, not on their door, nor at the cabin.

That afternoon it started to rain, the first in weeks. She watched it run down the windows in fat rivulets that reminded her of a pair of earrings Caroline once designed in the shape of two tiny pewter worms.

At night she woke from a dream in which she had been dealing tarot cards out to demons. She was trying to keep them in line, to convince them not to unleash their wrath upon an innocent world. But the world is never *innocent*, the dream-demon informed her, bossily. She went back to sleep and fell immediately into another series of lurid dreams. In one, it had all been a mistake, she never finished high school. She was exposed as a fraud. She had to forfeit her job and her Toronto apartment and go back to Clam Harbour and take Grade Twelve again. In another she was in a fire, there were horses; they were galloping away, flint flying from their hooves. She could hear the sizzle of wood, see the flames in the dark pool of their eyes.

At 2:20 a.m. she levered herself out of bed and went to the living room. If she listened to music she might be able to sweep the dreams from her mind.

She sat in the rocking chair, headphones on, lit only by the pale light of the amplifier, listening to the songs she loved as a teenager, some of them for the first time in nearly twenty years: *Fire and Rain, The Last Time I Saw Richard, Like a Hurricane*. Her father's record collection never made it beyond the 1970s: James Taylor, Carol King, Carly Simon, Joni Mitchell, Neil Young.

I am just the dreamer and you are just the dream. She ripped off the headphones, Neil Young's voice still reverberating in her ears, and sat tense in the darkness, suddenly gripped by the certainty that someone was in the cabin, or trying to get in. Had her father awoken? It came to her gradually, as if from very faraway, the sound of knocking at the door.

CHAPTER 17

She stared at him, trying to decide whether he was real or a dream.

"I heard you left."

"Rachel left, I didn't. Can I come in?"

She stood aside to let him pass and closed the door softly. "We have to be quiet — my father." She motioned to the bedroom.

"But I saw him driving down the road."

"When?"

"Just half an hour ago."

She went to the door and peered outside. The truck was gone. With the headphones on she wouldn't have heard anything. Or he could have driven away before, when she had been sunk in her punishing dreams. What was he doing driving around at night?

"Have you got anything to eat?"

"You want to eat at three in the morning?"

"Not if it's too much trouble."

"I'll see what I've got." She lit a candle and put it on the kitchen table. Of course! This was another dream. She must have fallen asleep listening to music. Any second now she would wake and be forced to confront the fact that Noel wasn't really there.

"Rachel failed her tax law exam," dream-Noel said. "She wants to re-sit it in two weeks' time. Her books are at home, so she left. I'll follow her in two weeks. That's what we agreed."

Two weeks. No time at all. A few hours ago, two weeks of his presence would have been a luxurious miracle. Now that Noel was here, in front of her, it sounded like deprivation.

"I've only got pasta and tomato sauce. I could sauté some mushrooms and onions. It's all I've got in the house. I've got hamburger but it's in the freezer."

"That's okay." Noel remained standing, his back hard against the wall. He seemed restless. She had the feeling that if she didn't say the right thing he might leave.

"What's the matter?"

"I don't know. I'm thinking about things I haven't thought of in years."

"What kind of things?"

"It's four years since I was in Rwanda and I'm thinking about it more now than I ever did. I thought time was supposed to take you further away from the past, not closer to it."

"Maybe you haven't given yourself time to consider it until now."

"That's possible." A note of scepticism hovered in his voice. "I thought it was just another experience to put behind me. But then out of nowhere I started thinking about it again, and I can't stop. I haven't been able to talk to Rachel about it." Noel sat down at the table, his face framed by the two long candles she had placed at either end.

So now you're here talking to me. Within her delight at discovering that he hadn't after all left, there was a sliver of suspicion, even anger. Noel might be one of the many men who felt that the first sign of intimacy with a woman gave him the green light to unburden himself of all his uncertainties.

"It was just so... so *eerie*," he went on. "You go to this place where two-thirds of the population had tried to kill the remaining third, and almost succeeded. And there they are, a few years later, living side by side. I met so many survivors and their stories really came down to 'I don't know why I survived.' There was a kind of wonder in their voices. They grinned like little kids, just to still be alive. Like they couldn't believe their luck. Like it was a joke."

She wondered at this new Noel she was witnessing, nervy, dissatisfied.

"Some people really get underneath your skin," he said.

"Like who?"

"Anyone, even random people. People you see once in your life and never again. We spend most of our time forgetting people, even our parents."

He thought about them, of course, but he didn't ruminate on their existence. But those people he had met during the course of his work in Rwanda, in Colombia, were lodged in his memory hard and fast, like jewels.

"I've been unfaithful to Rachel," he said. "I don't want to do it again."

She stopped stirring the pasta. She had the impression he had blurted this out, without fully meaning to.

"Do you think Rachel's been faithful to you?"

He flinched. "That's not the point. I have to stand by my own intentions, and leave Rachel to do the same. How can I tell her when I'm not sure I'd be able to forgive her the same thing? Have you had... affairs? While you've been with Llewellyn?"

"Only once. My first and last one-night stand."

"And that's it?"

"That's it. I'm a failure at infidelity."

"There's nothing wrong with that."

"It's not as bad as being a dilettante."

"You're not a dilettante."

"Oh no? What have I done? I've worked in restaurants, I became a jeweller. I work in *fashion*." She sees him start at the bite in her voice. What she meant is, I deal in surfaces, in proxies.

"And at the margins, too," she went on. "I didn't even have the conviction to be a full-blown slave to beauty and form."

"What did you want to do then?"

"I suppose I wanted to be a scientist. But I didn't have the commitment — or maybe I didn't have the patience."

She had tried, of course. She had laboured in laboratories and gone out on field trips. She had tried working with a research scientist at the University of Toronto. She was an assistant — a glorified secretary, really — on an underwater volcanology project. They studied vents, black smokers; they hauled these buttresses of ash to the surface and laid them out on the decks of ships. Her fault was to be too ornamental, too dazzled by form. She hated the outdoor life as well — shorts, muddy knees, sunburn. It was too much like her upbringing in the cabin.

No, she hasn't tried hard enough. Noel has a commitment to issues beyond his own experience. He puts himself on the line for strangers. For what, or who, has she ever put herself on the line? For her jeweller employer, for the stones, those substances she loves, yes, and for beauty, but it is ornamental and transient. This is not the first time she has realized this; the original realization came to her in the cabin on the coast of Colombia; she had parried it, and then evaded it altogether.

"I admire what you do," she said. And in that simple statement lay the trouble: she wanted to be admired for what she did in the world.

"Everyone thinks it's heroic, but I don't even know who we're benefiting, really. Sometimes I think it's a delusion, this business about finding out the truth. The truth happens in the moment and then it's unrecoverable. It may even not matter."

"But don't you think the truth will set you free?"

"I must have done, at one point."

A rosy glow had appeared behind Seal Island. They went to stand in front of the living-room window. A waxy, uncertain light spread itself across the horizon.

"Talking with you I always feel relieved," she said. "I feel lighter."

Although her words were only an approximation of what she meant. What she meant was that speaking with him released a painful echo inside her. She was speaking to him but she was also talking to a version of him that seemed to always have been inside her. It was like excavating a memory from the time before she knew him, before she even knew that she was.

"I know. I feel it too."

Noel stretched out on the chesterfield and fell asleep instantly. She lay down on her bunkbed, but sleep did not come easily. Finally, as she was drifting off, she thought she heard an engine turned off, the door opening, the jangle of keys. When she woke it was after noon and she remembered it as a dream.

There are only two weeks of dependable summer left. Time seems to be accelerating, as in time-lapse photography; flowers grow in an instant, the sun and wind rush over fields. Everything she does and that happens to her takes on a breathless quality. She can barely register one moment before another has begun.

They are driving to Ingonish — sandbanks, estuaries, dunes sliding into giant reeds topped by thick brown cigars. Then through the National Park gate, the brown beaver National Park insignia, uniformed guard in his little hut, a parking lot full of far-flung licence plates. This all happens as if it has been pre-imagined, as if she is remembering her past and present and future, all at once.

They arrive and are changing into swimsuits, change rooms, stick-man and stick-woman-with-skirt. Concrete rough beneath her feet. Her swimsuit, a checked bikini bought on sale in the kids' section of Benetton. In a country of increasingly giant people she can do that, buy children's clothes, albeit in the larger sizes. She keeps her shoes on to negotiate the piles of rocks, smoothed and flattened, that scallop the beach. Beyond two spurs of land the open sea is just visible, thrashing and foaming. The Keltic Lodge ribbons the promontory.

Outside the change huts, self-conscious in her teenager's bikini. That is what she had been the last time she came to Ingonish with any frequency: a teenager, not yet morphed into a woman. Her lumpen Speedo one-piece, blue with red maple leafs, a special edition to commemorate the Commonwealth Games in Calgary that year. Tourist girls already womanly in bikinis; they are "advanced," as their sex education teacher puts it. Better nutrition and access to fashion magazines have bloated them immanently into women. The lifeguards and their mahogany skin, windburn, they tip their heads imperceptibly beneath white baseball caps as the bikinis strut past. She lays her head on the hot sand, consoling herself because none of the lifeguards look at her: little girl in nationalistic costume. Maybe we'll have to save her later, plucking distressed maple leafs from seafoam.

Even if she didn't own a bikini, she could still fall in love. There would be one person for her, maybe only one. Even then she knew her task would be to find this person, to put herself in the way of serendipity or jeopardy, to be discerning, judicious. To recognize him when he arrived.

They dangle their toes in the rush of water. He jumps back. "It's freezing."

"It's the Atlantic. You've been hanging out in the Northumberland Strait too long."

A man calls out them from the water. *C'mon in. It's refreshing.*

This, she knows, is polite code for "it's friggin' cold." She has lost the knack for responding to these friendly sorties by strangers. She has acquired, without really meaning to, a certain citified *froideur*. She gives the man a tight smile back.

They stand there, half in the water, half out. The smell: pine, hot asphalt, the sea. Overhead the sky is a cloudless soldered blue, like enamel.

They drove the last twenty kilometres with the gas gauge on empty. Eve kept one leery eye on the needle.

"You'd think after all these years I'd remember there's only one gas station between the Trans-Canada and Ingonish." Any minute they expected to be on the shoulder, thumbing a lift to Duncan's. She was relieved when they pulled into the forecourt with the gauge hard on empty. It was eight o'clock and nearly dark. Duncan emerged from the perpetual dusk of the body shop.

"Never go round the trail with less than half a tank," he commanded, before fetching them cold beers. They sat on milk crates on the edge of the asphalt, away from the woody fume of gas and oil. She surveyed their work: together she and Duncan had painted the pitted brown brick white with navy blue trim. He'd bought flower baskets and hung them on either side of the office. Wooden bays of vegetables and an ice-cream freezer lined the body shop's walls.

"She's going good," Duncan said. "I've got newspapers in now and everything. Even the *Globe and Mail*. That comes trucked in from Halifax." He raised a beer in her direction. "You should have seen her when she worked here. Even when she was a teenager she was always trying to improve things."

"No, you did it yourself."

The slinky sound of beers sliding down dusty throats. Noel's face beside her was a blue shadow soaked in night.

She stood up. "I'd better be getting back to Dad."

She drove into John Rory's driveway to let Noel out, but they ended up sitting in the truck for half an hour in his driveway, talking, doors open, windows down.

He moved to get out. At the last possible second, when his legs were already on the running board, he turned around.

It was near noon when she awoke into an oily vat of heat. Even with only a sheet over her she was sweating. A record summer, the radio programs proclaimed. *Global warming finally hits Cape Breton.*

The cabin had a vacated feeling that was not recent; wherever he was, her father had left some time ago. Still half-asleep, she put on a pair of shorts and a T-shirt and stumbled down to the shore. She picked her way along the shore to the ferry and found their canoe gone. She stumbled back, cursing, her feet slipping on wet rocks and jamming against driftwood.

She took binoculars and a five-litre bottle of plastic water and jumped in the truck. She drove down the abandoned road, gravel spewing behind, radio antenna snagging in the lower branches of overgrown alder and birch. Three miles below the cabin she slowed and stopped where the electricity pylons flung their wires across the water to Seal Island. She hoisted herself into the flatbed of the truck and stood surveying the shoreline with her binoculars.

Her father appeared, walking down the road, dressed in his blue woodsman's pants and a white undershirt. Sweat dripped from his forehead.

"What in the name of God are you doing here?"

"I should be asking you the same question."

"I went for a walk."

"You go for *a walk*—." Her voice trilled with censure. "How long have you been out?"

"A couple of hours."

"You go for a walk on a scorching day without any water?"

"I know where to find water if I need it."

"Are you trying to kill yourself?"

He didn't answer straightaway. Finally he gave a sullen, "No."

"That's all you're going to say?"

He raised his chin in defiance. "I went for a walk, I wanted to think."

"Think about what?"

"None of your business, that's what. All those times you went for walks for hours when you were in school, when you came back did I ever ask you what you were thinking about?"

"No. But I wish you had."

He looked away.

They drove back in silence, apart from the pat-pat of birch leaves slapping against the windshield and the swish of her father's hand sweeping hair from a damp forehead. He stared out the window; when she stole a look at him she saw a thin, slightly mischievous smile on his lips, like that of a truant child being carted back to school. Could he know she didn't come home last night, and that this disappearing act was his way of expressing disapproval? He didn't sleep through most nights, she reminded herself. Of course he knew.

In the instant of seeing Noel again, door held open, standing on the doorstep in his usual baggy canvas shorts and a white T-shirt, the night before cohered like a puzzle of fragments snapping into place.

His mouth, just as she thought it would be: tentative, searching, capable of understanding. Also a longing in the crevices of his gums, in the smooth languor of his tongue. Some men's mouths were hard, purpose-built for thrust; they produced kisses by numbers, one-two-three. But now this kiss, moulting out of memory, growing insistent, turning itself over and over. It must have lasted — how long? You lose track of the sequence of things, she thought, in such situations. Her memory could only fast-forward to the shock of him against her, lush and rigid, almost repelling her. He bit at her neck, pressed the small of her back into the wall.

They pulled each other, bashing into corners and steps, up to the sepia portrait hall. They leaned hard against a thin-lipped pioneer woman, she felt the frame on the back of her head.

"Let's move." These were the first words he had spoken in ten minutes and it was vaguely scandalous to hear there were still words between them. The way they kissed she thought all words had been extinguished, forever.

He dragged her, or she him, into the empty bedroom — not the room where he and Rachel had slept. A coating of dust flew up as they hit the bed and they both fell into fits of sneezing.

She remembers what happened after in fragments. His body too, which her memory dismembers, almost anatomically. His feet are delicate and amiable. Their nails are not yellowed; the heel of his foot is smooth. They lack the smug look so many people's feet have. He has thin ankles, and she likes the way his wrist bone moves — such delicacy in these isthmuses of the body. His pupils grow huge in the night until his eyes are black; his mouth turns down ever so slightly at the corners, an imperial, unforgiving mouth. Her memory snags on these frontiers of the body, these jumping-off points: eyelashes, fingertips, ends of noses.

Now he is framed in the door. She stands half a foot below him, on the top step she nailed together herself. For the first time since they have met they do not break into instant smiles at the sight of each other.

"I brought some beer." She held up two fast-melting bottles she had put in the deep freeze half an hour earlier.

"So I see. Come on in."

So I see. Was that a rebuke? At the same time as doubt colonizes her, she is aware of basking in the moment. He is here in front of her. It dispels her vague belief that the night before was nothing but a fever dream.

He sweated lightly but she didn't mind his sweat. In fact he was odourless, beautifully so. She caught a trickle of it coursing down his round, smooth shoulders, down the spine and into the hollow of his lower back, where her tongue waited to catch it.

He hesitates, if slightly, before taking a bottle from her outstretched hand. What's wrong? He is moving astringently. Look at the way he puts the bottle on the table with a little clap! Look how he frets to find an opener! But then he turns to her and smiles, and it is like the first time saw him.

"Can't find the bottle opener." There is a trill of nervousness in his voice.

She has to sit down. She finds it painful to look at him. She marvels at how exposed she feels, the shock of recognition, the tinny echo speaking with him sets off in her head, the lights and the electric impulses.

They tip the bottles up in the air, sucking at them, but keep their eyes fixed on each other.

She puts down her bottle. "It seems we've murdered conversation."

He doesn't smile. In fact he looks stricken. He takes her by the hand, no, by the wrist. His fingers firmly, almost painfully gripping her wrist bone. Wordlessly, he leads her upstairs. The half-finished bottles of Alexander Keith's Pale Ale sweat on the table, until they stand in two neat pools of water.

"You're spending an awful lot of time next door."

She had her answer prepared. "He's bored. His girlfriend had to leave."

"People will talk."

"People?" Her percussive, slightly hysterical laugh, like tinfoil torn suddenly from a roll. "Who? You, me, the wind? There's no-one here anymore, Dad."

At the confusion in his eyes she feels the exhilaration of cruelty. *Your people are all gone, dead or moved away. No-one cares what you do here; no-one cares what I do. The bonfires and haying and community chowder challenges are gone.*

"What I meant is that things have moved on from your day, Dad. Women and men can be friends now. It's allowed."

In a second he drew himself up, rigid. His face was contorted with the effort of containing something uncontainable. "You're still the same. You only think of yourself, your pleasure and your dramas. You still treat me like an idiot, and I'm telling you, you're more wrong than you know."

The screen door slapped shut behind him.

The second time was less stop-and-start, less bathed in fear. The sense of mortal combat was still there, although they were not battling each other but themselves.

Just before orgasm he opened his eyes and stared straight into hers. There was something different about the look she received: his eyes reverted to chippy obsidian. Their expression was spent, challenging, dismissive. It could have been the choking alarm of climax, the nearly instant aftershock of pleasure, or it could be lust. Was that what lust looked like? She realized she didn't know. There was another possibility, which she registered and then dismissed: anger.

"I think your father is depressed."

They sat in the kitchen drinking glasses of lemonade with ice, their feet propped on the legs of a kitchen chair between them.

"Of course he's depressed."

"As in clinically depressed," Noel elaborated. "That's why he's absent-minded. He *is* absent. He's actually not here."

"Where is he, then?"

He was silent for a minute before answering. "I don't know." A hesitant expression, nearly a frown, passed over his face.

"What's the matter?"

"It's just an uneasy feeling I have. There's something else."

They were distracted by desire and she never had the chance to ask, what do you mean? *Something else.*

August wraps itself around her like a cloak. Hidden inside its folds is pleasure like a blow, a wallop. This pleasure must have been sleeping inside her all these years because it has sprung up, fully conversant with the language of clandestine desire. She is a patient being operated on under a reverse anaesthetic. She is waking up, rapidly, to find herself soaked in life. The moments when she does not see him are like individual departure lounges at four in the morning, garish with waiting, with the promise of departure after a long delay. She sits them out, suspended between gusts of emotion.

How empty it seems now, her brazen confidence of only three months before. She saw herself as if in a film, arriving at the airport with her Gucci sunglasses balanced on her head, international flotsam-style, ready to be lowered whenever the tarnished landscape of Tim Hortons and car dealerships and abandoned coal miners' houses became too much for her.

Noel has deprived her of these gestures; he has given her something less certain but more true. Of course, this is the twisted genius of transformations: something is lost, as well as gained. There is a price to be paid for the world looking different from one day to the next.

Now the change is drawing itself, guided by an invisible hand. It is as if she is learning to remember. She is thirty-four, the age her mother was when her mother disappeared into the night on Christmas Eve, and only now does she feel it cohering inside her, this orphan story. Stories require resolution, but this one is a truncated tale, watchful and judgemental as an abandoned child. It is her story, and her mother's, and so many other peoples', but it hasn't had a long enough life in the world and it is angry.

Her father was wrong about the loop, she realized, all those years ago on the beach. We are not caught in a loop, on a repeating tape, but in a spiral.

∽

Ten inches of snow today. Water butts frozen solid. An inch of frost on the windowpane. Heather dropped by, she's still trying to give up smoking. Chewing that gum substitute they give you. Went to town to buy a snowsuit for Anita, they only had purple in stock. She'll probably refuse to wear it: "wrong colour" and so on. Was I ever like that? Picky, ornery. More snow expected tonight.

She passes these cold cathedrals of days in tasks. She sits up late at night with the headphones on, listening to country and western, thinking about the time they danced together last, in the summer. She feeds herself on scraps of memories from the summer and by Christmas they are frayed with use.

They hold each other close, in a full-body embrace. These are the moments she will store in her memory like fabulous chests. When she is lonely or distressed she opens them, strokes them as you would expensive silk. No-one seems to take much notice of their dancing, including his wife and Alistair. She is amazed at how unobservant people are. But they have more steadfast hearts, she rebukes herself; they are good people and can't imagine the kind of treachery her heart is capable of.

Although her sister Catherine, who is eleven years younger than her, notices. She frowns and says, to no-one in particular, *But they don't even like each other.*

Some memories stick in her throat: the way he clasps his wife around the waist, delicately, when they are all dancing in a kitchen party. Watching his children running around on the grass, he laughs at them and rolls his eyes — exactly as she would have a man laugh, droll but kind. His mineral eyes, sometimes dark, other times they gleam with light, eyes stacked with roses. The sleekness of him; wet from swimming he looks like an otter, his dark hair plastered to a small skull. How light he is on his feet, he almost seems to float, or glide, the opals of his fingertips, the sullen expression which so quickly transforms itself into wreathes of vulnerable smiles. The angle at which he tilts his head to listen to someone as they speak, mouth-to-ear, at a loud party, his eyes roving the room to return to the speaker full of laughter. The quick, furtive way he smokes roll-up cigarettes. He is restless; he can hardly sit still for thirty seconds. He puts his hands underneath his legs and jiggles his ankles, like a boy.

Even within these tarnished moments, thin with knowledge that he will never be hers, she thinks there would be no other way to do these things, there is no other man she will ever want. In some occult way they are kindred spirits. She likes this phrase, the intimacy and camaraderie it promises. Then she realizes it is built on the word *kin*, which is what they are: family, second cousins. Although removed by distance and time.

Once, after they have made love, she gets a nosebleed.

"Henry had one only last week," he says. She is felled by an image of him attending to his son with these same hands that grip her waist, that explore her insides.

"Here...," he brushes her hair from her face.

He is not much given to tender gestures. This is one of the things that attract her to him, sexually. But now his touch on the back of her head is light. She reaches up and takes his hand in hers. They are caught in a strange posture: her with her head tilted back, pincering her nose. With one hand he holds the back of her head. She grips his hand tightly. They are enveloped in a shimmering parcel. It is not carnal, or not entirely, but a natural sympathy, an effortless understanding. It makes them both realize how hard they have been trying, with other people in their lives.

She has taken to going to the regional library and furtively extracting books with titles like *The Psychic Path* and *Fire from the Mountain*. This is her attempt to get to the bottom of the fascinating mystery that has overtaken her life. The books talk about reincarnation, how souls are given form in bodies again and again, and how souls who might have known each other in previous lives find each other again in this life. We might travel in soul groups, the books say, something akin to contemporaries, although in the departure lounge where souls wait for reincarnation there is no time, no past, no present, no future.

She hides these books in the shed, and steals in to read them, paragraph by paragraph, when she can grab a moment. Should she tell him about these theories? The only time she tries she says, "I just like being next to you. I don't need to even say anything. To be with you feels like home. It's like the world comes into alignment. I didn't realize how lonely I was, before."

"I know," he says. "It just feels right."

But his voice is bitter, the shutters on his face drawn tight. He recognizes the connection, he knows they are linked, but he doesn't like it. He has made commitments elsewhere. But there is another reason — he might not want to be known, in that way. He needs only a small amount of understanding from the people around him. He possesses a self-sufficiency that is unavailable to her. This shimmering, effortless understanding is not manna to him as it is to her. He can likely live without it. Later, she will think, men are forests of rigidities. They cannot accept love, or only under certain circumstances, ones that are exactly to their liking.

He makes her ask answerless questions: *Who are my parents? Why don't I know them, as people? Why have they kept themselves remote from me? Who is this man I am married to, with whom I share my days? Where have I come from? Who have I been before?* With him she feels accompanied, at home in the world at last. But his absence provokes long droughts of doubt and anger. Bankrupt days, inhabited by the ghost of his saturnine presence, her stealing snippets of books about souls. She thrives on him; her love is an alert succubus. She is trapped in an iron cage, migrating back and forth, thinking, I am your blood, your nerves your thin wrist swishing as you write. I so need to be near you. I want to die.

She sleepwalks through winter, a dove in its eyrie, hooded, pulsating, stunned with sleep. Her life is a tangled forest of rules and flux, bound to the night, missing lost dramas. She is caught in the rampant grip of a planetary fear, of this satire of adoration. She has so much time to contemplate it — the value and the lack of him, her turquoise husband of another life.

Eve closes the ledgerbook, shoves it back on its dusty shelf inbetween her mother's mildewed paperbacks. She'll be late for her shift at Kay's.

Ten minutes later she is driving down the Clam Harbour road when she remembers the day he came to the house and she was playing in the field, obscured by long grass. She stood stock-still and watched him get out of the car. He looked like he had just done a long drive: his shirt sticking to his back with sweat, crumpled jeans, a road-weary face. He might have driven all the way from New York, dropped his wife off at her parents' house and headed straight for theirs on some premise or other — to pick something up at the store, get a full tank of gas. From her hiding place in the hayfield she watches as his gaunt face springs into a smile at once reckless and kind. He looks at her mother and says, *Now you're a sight for sore eyes.*

In their last year living in the white house across the water she drives by the spot every day, in a schoolbus, her father's car, her uncle's truck. She plays a game with herself: if she doesn't speak, or think, or breathe, her mother will not scramble up from the bank and flag them down. So each time she drives by the spot she stops speaking mid-sentence, looks away and holds her breath, until she is past.

CHAPTER 18

They passed Curry's Funeral Home — HAVE A SAFE SUMMER said the sign outside St. Michael Junior High — then the fire station, the YMCA enterprise centre, a boarded-up carwash. She drove too fast, nearly running over the nonchalant crows who barely deigned to move out of their way.

What was she going to do with him in her sister's house? As it turned out she didn't have to worry about Noel amusing himself. He played baseball in the backyard with David; he watched TV with Lloyd. He didn't even blink at the velour-painting-and-sports-trophy décor.

Kelly drifted into the kitchen. "So is he your boyfriend now?"

"No."

Eve saw an opaque thought flash deep in her niece's eyes: *Maybe I have a chance.* She didn't know whether to be frightened or nostalgic for this stage in life, for the primal vanity of teenaged girls. It was like having a cheetah in the house, padding softly from room to room, looking for a baby dik-dik to devour.

"Why'd you bring him here then?"

"He wants to go to the Marconi Museum."

"It's a beautiful day, come on and sit outside." Anita took her by the hand. It was the first time Anita had taken her by the hand since they were children. She followed her into the backyard where four white wooden chairs faced the sun.

"These are the chairs from the old house. I'd forgotten about them."

"Dad gave them to Maureen when we left Seal Island. I took them off her last year."

They sat in silence, drinking the sun. She opened and closed her eyes, slipping between the dark weave of her eyelids, the pale sharpness of the light, razored tops of pine trees, ragged crows sallying back and forth.

"You know, he once said to me, 'I was a zombie in my marriage.'" Anita was looking at her, their father's incredulity mirrored in her eyes. "'I was no good at being married,' he said. 'It just sapped my will. I didn't know anymore what it was I wanted. No wonder she left me.' And I said, 'She never left you. She died.' And he said, 'She left me the first moment she set eyes on him.'"

"When did he tell you that?"

"Oh, years and years ago. He blamed himself, you see. But I think the fault lies somewhere else entirely, if you ask me."

A silence, in which the only thing Eve heard was her sister's breath. Then another breath, given shape in words, which winded her.

"He told me the only thing that would bring you back was him stretched out in a coffin."

Eve let this gust of wind pass through her. She turned to look at her sister, but Anita's eyes were closed.

"I never belonged here. You did."

"You went out of your way not to belong."

"I didn't mean it to turn out this way," she said.

"Of course you didn't. No-one does."

She had been expecting this: one of Anita's choice rebukes, poised halfway between the oblique and the direct. Inside it was a vast chest of truth. Yes, she was easily bored, she was judgemental, she thought herself better than the people who raised her, or not exactly better than them, personally, but deserving of better than the surroundings she had been granted at birth. She listed her other faults in a silent inventory: she was easily misled by other people; she thought people could be coaxed into being something better than they were. She has an angry impulse to grab the attention of people who are unavailable to her, who are impossible, who are on their own track, away from her, until they die. She could not accept that she had to run along this track, that it was all decided, long ago and by an entity she had no knowledge of but which other people called *fate*.

Eve sat, her eyes closed, beaten by the sun. There were elaborate defences she could have mounted against her sister's comment, of course, and thought to do so. But when she opened her eyes, she found Anita had fallen asleep.

Marconi and his staff stand stiffly posed for the camera in front of a shed. It is December 1902. Behind them are four giant wooden towers connected by a net of wires. Beyond them is a low, frozen horizon.

In less than twenty years' time the station will be made obsolete by Marconi's own discovery of the long radio wave. The Marconi Company will close the Table Head facility and move everything to Montreal. The buildings will remain stocked with giant Hertz valves and VHF transmitters until the War, when they are melted down for armaments.

Other photos show Marconi as a young boy in his attic room in Reggio Emilia surrounded by coils of copper wire. There he often caused explosions that brought his father running with reprimands. Later, half the world away in Glace Bay, Cape Breton, he is dressed in a leather jacket and high, well-made boots. Behind him icicles as tall as a man hang off transmission wires. A dog sits at the men's feet. Eve always feels haunted by dogs in old photographs. The people have irrevocably gone — this is clear from the outmoded moustaches and felt boots — but the dogs always look the same.

They drift through the tiny museum looking at these sepia promontories, a web of copper wires strung between massive towers. The transmitting station is dangerously close to the cliffs, whose sandy stone erodes an inch each year. In glass cases are letters written in a sloping Victorian hand between Marconi and Alexander Graham Bell. Their correspondence is about spark transmitters, valves, batteries, Marconi recounting his excitement at his original discovery, that radio waves travelled twice as far by night as by day. Sound is a longitudinal wave, the exhibit plaques declare. It is comprised of compressions, of fluctuations in pressure. A sound wave is denser than air. The human ear is capable of detecting sound waves within a wide range of frequencies, from 20 hertz to 20,000 hertz. But sound waves are almost ponderously slow, only 750 miles an hour. Light travels 900,000 times faster than sound.

She remembers a story of her father's, about an American scientist's theory of how eels found their way to the faraway rivers. The scientist was convinced the land itself emitted delicate microwaves, far too sensitive for any equipment yet invented.

The eels oriented themselves by the magnetic pull of the land, and then used geological radio waves like a grid, constructing their own longitude. There was a whole GPS system, the scientist believed, programmed into their cretaceous brains.

It is four o'clock and Eve and Noel are the only visitors in the museum.

"Everybody goes to the miner's museum in town," the young man on duty tells them when they ask.

They wander outside to stand near the cliffs at Table Head. Rocks straggle into the sea like stepping stones, as if they were attempting a footbridge to Europe. Bonsai scrub and wind-stunted evergreens cling to the cliffside — broccoli lichens, the dull mauve of hawthorn flowers. Below, the roar of the sea, the pale tourmaline of waves split open by rocks.

They do not hold hands, or brush against each other. But even without touching she detects a subtle hum coming from him, a low, reassuring frequency. She listens to it, hoping to decipher the message.

The road back to Clam Harbour was studded with the unmistakable signs of the approaching autumn: billboards announcing corn boils; Back to School Value proclaimed the sign outside the Staples store at the Mayflower Mall. In front- and backyards men in overalls could be seen refitting smoke sheds, stripping the hulls of Cape Islanders named *Heart's Desire* and *Sybil.*

They decided to go for a quick swim at Grove's Point Beach. On a Thursday afternoon the beach was nearly empty apart from a damp man still in his bathing suit, standing by his truck and talking loudly into his cellphone. *You'd never believe it, b'y, the way they were carrying on, cryin' and yellin' and goin' on.*

They swam in the bath-warm late August water, and then found a spot to dry off on the grass at the reedy end of the beach. They lay on their backs, blinking into a flaming sun. This sometimes happened in late August, she explained, island sunsets took on the brick-red hue of ceramic.

"I love this time of year," he said. "All the anticipation of what's to come," he went on. "How the world starts up again in September; these last weeks of August always feel like a waiting room. But at the same time you're savouring it. You know, trying to catch the moment."

She turned her face away. She felt something rise in her chest, a heavy, wet surge.

I was like a zombie in my marriage. She thought of her marriage, Llewellyn's whims; she followed him where he wanted to eat, as she would follow him wherever it was he wanted to make his career. She would end up in Los Angeles, in Vancouver, in Atlanta — would it really matter where? — shopping for them at warehouse-style supermarkets, bullied by the squalid wealth of the place.

They lay there in silence, then, their eyes full of sky.

"I used to do this as a kid," she said, after a while. "Lie on my back in the grass and watch the clouds forming and splitting apart. All the clouds looked like Scotland. They still do."

Noel's voice was thick with drowsiness. "I'm so glad you're here."

She knew what he meant. "I'm glad you're here too," she said.

They walked into the cabin laughing at something Noel had said, to find a man who was not her father seated at the table with his back to them. There was something very familiar about this man, but she couldn't place him.

He turned around. Her husband. She had forgotten all about him.

"You never told me you lived in paradise," he said.

"I never realized I did. Where's my father?"

"He made me a cup of tea and then skedaddled."

The shock of her husband, the reality of him, hit her. She put out her hand and gripped the counter to steady herself.

"How did you get here?"

"I took a cab from the airport."

"You took a cab from Sydney?"

"Well, another thing you neglected to tell me is that it's five thousand miles between one place and the next here. I suppose I should have rented a car." He sighed. "I'm sorry to turn up like this, but you don't have a message machine and Susannah suddenly found it within her reduced producer's heart to let me have the long weekend, so here I am."

She became conscious of Noel standing beside her.

"Lew, this is Noel. Noel, this is Llewellyn. Noel and his girl-friend have rented the place next door for the summer."

"I'd better be getting back home. Thanks. Good to meet you." Noel nodded to Lew. "I'll... I'll see you around."

The suddenly stiff expression on Noel's face sparked a con-striction in her lungs, so that for a second she thought she might not be able to breathe. She watched him leave, feeling like a sink in which the plug had just been pulled. She tried to gather herself.

"So, how long are you staying?"

"Just until Tuesday. So, who's he?"

"He's the neighbour." She sat down opposite him and tried to look resigned. "I've been playing local tour guide to him and his girlfriend."

"Where's his girlfriend now?"

Should she tell him she wasn't here? He was bound to talk to Noel at some point. She calculated the time in front of them — today was Thursday, Llewellyn was here until Tuesday. Five of the eight days she and Noel had left together.

"She has to stay in and study. She's a lawyer, or she will be soon. Noel works for Global Witness, the human rights organization. They're very well educated, very nice people."

Lew nodded. She saw him discard the possibility of jealousy, and felt both relieved and stupidly, immensely, guilty.

"I'm really sorry to drop in on you unannounced."

"Don't apologize. It's great to see you."

Before, she would have reached across the table, taken his hand in hers. But a vanished ocean had welled up and wedged itself between them. She stayed in her chair.

For months Llewellyn had receded to become a concept, an idea. She stared at him: blond hair, green eyes placed wide apart, they have a watery amphibian quality. A delicate face, neither masculine nor feminine. A certain meanness in the sleek Celtic quality of it: his Welsh name came from a token grandfather from Cardiff, otherwise his parents' families were both Irish aristocrats, which of course meant ultimately they were English. She has never liked blond men, or green eyes. Everything was too close to the surface. She can only get excited about men whose physiology suggests hidden strata.

"It's great, but I don't even get a welcome kiss?"

She felt herself rise, move toward him, take his face in her hands. Felt her lips meet his.

"What's the matter?"

"What's the matter? You just show up here," she flung her arms around the cabin, "a place I was never sure I wanted you to see, without telling me, and you're unhappy about something, and you won't tell me what it is."

"I just didn't expect to find you with some guy."

"He's not *some guy*. He's the neighbour. He's practically married."

Lew put his head in his hands. He squeezed his hair so that it spilled through his fingers, rough and dishevelled. "Eve, you haven't even called me in weeks."

"I have. I've left two messages for you with a mystery woman who picks up your phone at work and doesn't convey them to you."

"You've what?"

"I've called you twice at work, two weeks ago and this week. They were amusing messages too, you would have liked them."

"Why didn't you call me at home?"

"I did. You're never there and my message machine was full with someone else's messages. For you, I'm assuming, otherwise you would have passed them on to me."

Confusion came over his face in knifelike strokes, as if someone were buttering his face with it. "When did you leave those messages?"

"You don't believe me? Is that who answered the phone when I called, Susannah? Is that who didn't give you the messages?"

She sat back hard against the window. She felt her back connect with it, felt it bend in its frame. "That's why you're here," she said. "You're here because you're having an affair with Susannah with an 'h' and you're trying to break it off, so you've come to see me to remind yourself of who you really love. That's why you're so upset to see me with Noel. You expected me to be pining away for you. That's the image of me you've been holding in your mind to convince yourself of something — whether to stay with me or whether to leave."

"That's really impressive." Lew's mouth chewed back and forth. "Your *insight*." The bite of resentment in his voice. "I did sleep with her."

"How many times?"

"More than once but not enough to get used to it. And it's

over, and I feel terrible. I wanted to see you. I missed you. I've done something I very much regret and I've been very stupid and you don't deserve it and most of all I wanted to see you. I'm sorry."

She put her head in her hands. She realized she had always known, on some submerged level, that she and her husband would have this conversation one day, traded in any or all combinations of those words: *Regret. Undeserved. Stupid. Sorry.*

Herons skittered their takeoffs and landings on the lake. They sat on the edge of the ferry, shoulders nearly touching. Eve heard a breathy spew and sure enough, a humpback whale broke the surface half a mile away, near the middle of the lake. They watched as its maw surfaced, delicately, saw the glint of baleen, a lapidary back lustrous with spray. They heard its distant breathy sigh.

"It really is a whale."

"You've seen one before."

"I have, but in those Zodiacs, you know, when you go out deliberately to see them. I've never had one just appear like that."

"You don't see them in the lakes much anymore."

"Clam Harbour isn't like I imagined it," Llewellyn said. "I think I saw it as a foggy version of that film set out west somewhere, you know, two lesbians in dresses and cowboy suits when they're working at the casino. What's it called?"

"*Desert Hearts.*"

"That's right. With Helen Shaver. Whatever happened to her?"

"I don't know. She's probably doing commercials somewhere. Why the lesbians?"

"Oh," he smiled. "Flight of fancy."

"Well, it's not like that at all."

"Nope. No slot machines, no cowboy boots. No lesbians. At least that's what they want us to believe."

All this was so Lew: games of chance, passé films, forgotten actresses, chrome and shadows. He had never spent much time in Canada as a child, and at times she thought he still saw it much as foreigners did: comfortable, modern cities surrounded by a wilderness periphery stocked with outlandish characters. He had never really considered the Maritimes, except as the backdrop to a regional news story.

"Bras d'Or. Arm of gold," he translated.

She told him about how the French explorers who named it — Boularderie and Nicolas Denys — had likely stood on the mountain behind the cabin, just as worn and stunted four hundred years before as it was now, and watched the lakes at sunset shift from gold to pewter to the glitter green of malachite, then, as evening deepened, titanium. But gold was what they saw and wanted, as explorers were wont to do, so gold they had named it.

"I wish you'd brought me here before."

"I never thought you'd think much of it."

"Well, you're wrong." He sighed. "You know, in the office the other day we were all so bored. It's August, not much going on. The British call it the silly season. So we started trading dystopian futures. We weren't particularly inventive: designer babies, universal private health care, random surveillance, genetic hierarchies, you know, like in *Gattaca*. And we thought, shit, they're all here. They're not futures anymore." He lapsed into silence for a moment. "You could escape from the future in a place like this. The past seems so real here. It's like going back a century."

"I don't know. It's got all the problems of modernity," she argued.

"Like what?"

"Drug addiction, alcohol abuse, weird utopian schemes to create employment."

"Like what?"

"They wanted to create a technology park — that's what they

called it, I think — in Sydney, a kind of East Coast Silicon Valley. Then there was a film studio. I don't know what happened, they failed to attract the right kind of investment."

They watched a sailboat slice through the water on its way to Indian Bay. Llewellyn turned to her and gave her the most serious of looks — although seriousness, in his eyes, was a transitory, rushed presence, a figure alighting from a train and then immediately disappearing into a cab.

"Why are you married to me?"

"What do you mean?"

"Just that," he said. "Why do you want to be married to me? Is it me or is it the marriage you want?"

"I've never wanted something that...," she paused, "that impersonal."

"I'll tell you what I think. I think you like the convenience of being married. It anchors you to the world. It seems to offer a slave for the hole at the centre of your life. I think you use it as cover, actually as camouflage, for your real pursuits."

"You're the one who's having the affair."

She said it neatly. For the first time in her life, she savoured the cut of words. They would slice efficiently through his argument, which was as true of her as it was of him, she supposed. She was only just beginning to wonder how she might live without her camouflage, how she will survive the exposure.

His voice was a murmur. He might have been speaking to himself. "I just wanted to have a crush on someone, not for that crush to have a mind, a heart, a soul."

"That's hardly fair on the crush."

His hands flurried up. "What's fair? Can you tell me? What in this life is fair? God, I sound like my father." His face twisted into a grimace.

He surfaced again, the spectre of his father. Llewellyn's virtuous, *realpolitik* father, schooled in a mathematical approach to realities of the world: I give you this, you give me that in return; things in proportion, nothing given away or squandered, the humiliation of generosity avoided — a horse-trading outlook he learned in his profession and that he had chosen also to apply emotionally to his family.

Eve realized with a shock that she could no longer imagine being with her husband, romantically. She could not imagine laying a hand on him in desire. She nearly said to herself: *I think of him like a brother.* But this would have been imprecise; husband, lover, brother, father: she was not sure the boundaries between these categories and the feelings they elicited were really so distinct. What she felt for Lew was neither filial nor disinterested, but it had been drained of desire and fantasy, of that alchemical element that lit the heart and mind with a pale fire.

But she also suspected that this mild repulsion might fade, with time and proximity and opportunity, and that this might be why marriages could be so durable. She could imagine them turning to each other in bed again eventually to make love, simply because they were both committed by feelings other than desire to be in the same place. There was something scandalous about this of course, but she could imagine that it would be overridden by a mysterious sense of possession — it was there in the ringing, processional sound of the word: *marriage.* And also time; the sheer weight of time spent together, how difficult it is — how truly terrible things have to be between you — to untangle the embroidery of time.

"You know what really hurts?" Llewellyn said. "I can't quite take myself seriously. Even my upsets — my agonies, actually — I have to make a joke out of." His words were hectic with pain. "And I'm so tired of myself, my nomadic mind. I can't concentrate on anything long enough to feel. To really *feel.*"

She studied him as he spoke. There was something unfinished about him, as if he had not established the boundaries between what he would and he wouldn't do. He had the feel of a wanderer, all easy-come, easy-go, someone who had lived an essentially indolent life and who found he liked it, but understood that it was not considered proper to admit this.

Yes, it had taken years for Llewellyn to properly come into focus for her, like a photograph developing slowly — so slowly, the original image had been erased. Nothing she could have done would have prepared her for the shock of the realization, years into their marriage, that Llewellyn did not feel very deeply. Everything about him suggested he did. But she had dug through his conflicting layers of crassness and sophistication, his vulnerability and swagger, his lovely and sometimes devastating wit, and arrived at the depths of his feeling only to find them vacated, just a second before, by emotion.

"Maybe it's for the best this has happened."

He looked at her with suspicion, even disgust. "How dare you say that? You know, I've spent years with you with my heart in my throat. Worried about what you will say at parties, at dinners. I'm always the dilettante for you, while you inflict your hard upbringing on everyone. I don't think I've gone to a single dinner party with you when I haven't felt disconnected from you. One word in the too lighthearted direction, and you would abandon me."

Those dinner parties obediently filtered back, evenings when someone or other would remark how great the neighbourhood was, what kind of Indonesian high-altitude blend they had discovered at the St. Lawrence Market or about where they yearned to travel — there was always talk at these gatherings about *yearning* to travel, usually to places like Mozambique or Vietnam. Lew fell easily into these discourses about neighbourhoods, travel, food, objects of desire. She said little, allowing him to steal the show, as he often did with his endless supply of amusing multinational anecdotes stored up from having lived in six different countries by the time he was eighteen, thinking — and simultaneously guilty at the thought — *Llewellyn is one of those people who want to make jokes so badly, to be wicked and witty, that they will sacrifice their friends as material.*

Lew was staring at the lake. "What really kills me is that we haven't built anything together. We don't have children, you travel all the time, I work at night. We hardly see one another."

"I know."

Water slapped at the hull of the old ferry.

"So, what's Susannah like?"

Lew dipped his head, nearly imperceptibly. "She's a nice Rosedale Girl. I know, I know," he said, pandering to Eve's sensibility far more than to his own, "it sounds like a recipe for disaster. But she's nice. She's smart."

Yes, Eve was sure she was nice, sure she was smart. There were so many women like this on the planet, pleasant, intelligent individuals. She met them all the time.

"We always knew we were so different," she said. "That's why we liked each other." This was, she realized, a protest as well as an acknowledgement.

Anyone observing them in that moment would see two figures perched on the edge of the ferry, their backs bent. Perhaps they were fishing, or contemplating the lakebed. They would not look like two people trying to figure out whether or not to divorce.

Would they really forego all the petty intimacies they had built in their marriage? Her rolling her eyes at him walking around the apartment with a thermometer in his mouth all weekend, even though he only had a cold. Lew scoffing at her seemingly redundant collection of delicate sandals. The scandal of his inability to ever clean the bathroom properly, to have an opinion on which costly print should be hung above the mantelpiece and other tiny delinquencies which, framed in the possibility of their loss, seemed suddenly tender and precious.

"What are we going to do?" he said.

"I don't know."

He had betrayed her and had confessed. She felt unable to do the same because, unlike her husband, she was in love, or thought herself to be.

In that lonely moment, observed only by herons and a departing humpback whale, she felt an acute sympathy for this man who sat beside her; it rippled through her like an electric current. She didn't know if this signalled the beginning of real love, or its end.

During the four days of his stay she patrols the house next door for signs of desertion, surveying it with binoculars to check that the car is still there, that the lights are still on. Once, when Lew is in the shower, she runs up to the door and knocks. Noel comes to the door, a tattered back issue of *Harper's* in his hand.

"Promise me you won't leave without telling me." As she speaks, the breath is being sieved from her. "I'm terrified you'll drive out of here and I'll never hear from you again. I don't have your phone number; I don't even have your email."

He gives her a hard, inscrutable stare.

"I have to go." She runs back to the cabin.

They are beneath contempt, these betrayals, they demonstrate what a ruthless mechanism her heart is. She tries to feel ashamed that her husband is here in the cabin with her, trying to enact a reconciliation, and she can only see Noel's car heading down the driveway, forever. But shame will not come; perhaps it is of the order of feelings that only come unbidden.

That night she finds a piece of paper tucked in the door frame. She plucks at it and it falls to the ground. His handwriting, a street address, an email address that looked suddenly like a mathematical formula.

She lurches out into the night and jogs down the road.

The light is on. He comes to the door and they repeat their routine of staring at each other wordlessly.

"I thought you'd left."

"I won't leave."

"Then why did you give me this then?"

"You wanted my address and email, you've got it."

"You're punishing me."

Still he doesn't speak.

"I'm not sleeping with him. I couldn't possibly. It would be unnatural. It would be a bad dream. I wonder if you could say the same if Rachel were here?"

"You'd better be getting back."

She recognizes the cruel bite in his voice and the hurt that spawns it. She marvels at how the body can throb in sympathy for someone even as they hurt you, at how easy forgiveness is, like a sluice of cool water on a hot scalp, when you are in love.

She turns around and melts back into the moonless night.

Saturday. She makes cups of tea for Lew and herself; they sit across from each other with the weekend paper's entrails scattered on the table. The social section proffers AA meetings, card games at community centres, ceilidhs. She stares at the date. *Saturday* — the day of Saturn, that stern planet of responsibility and thoroughness, its taskmaster gasses. On Tuesday he will leave. Three days later, Noel will be gone. Can she detain time? Could it perhaps be persuaded to expand? All she needs is more time, to properly understand.

Llewellyn reads the *Globe and Mail* aloud to her — this is a habit of his, as if she were blind and needed to be read to. Really it is an excuse for him to insert his own comments in the News.

"Is there some international agreement that at the end of every summer we review the ways in which our civilization could disappear? Let's see. There's a piece about the giant methane bubble under the ocean, then the Facts and Arguments is going on about the Maya calendar stopping in 2012 — that can't be good news — the volcano on the side of the Canary Islands that's ready to slide into the sea, unleashing a lethal tsunami, never mind the meteor strikes. That's quite apart from the man-made disasters we're storing up." He pauses. "This is the kind of place I think I could forget about the methane bubble."

She smiles, a thin, reluctant smile. "I think the tsunami would get us."

She lights a candle in honour of Saturday night, and tries not to miss having somewhere else to go, next door, dinner parties with friends to diffuse the thick incomprehension that has knitted itself between them, soundless as felt. They smile at each other, careful approximations of concern, before pitching headlong into sprawling silences. Greasy striations appear on the surface of the lake. Two mallard ducks swim silently across them, and then disappear into the mist.

At night Lew lies asleep in the bunkbed above her. He has brought memories of her life — her old life, it already seems *old* — with him. They sit beside her bed like unpacked bags, memories of the years she has spent in that underwater realm: beauty, delight, the transient lustre, like shoals of fish glimpsed in gleaming depths. The jewels she has helped fashion, their ripening shadows, their ardent praise, the endurance they promise. So hard and pure, these strange-looking fruits of consolation.

She is looking for the emotion that has eluded her in life in the form of objects. She might have known this all along, intellectually. But it can take so long for the knowledge of the heart to catch up with that of the mind. It might never even happen.

She realizes that her dilemma is more basic than she thought: whether to remember, or to forget.

∾

They steal away to meet at night at the ferry. The kids have been put to bed. His wife reads magazines at night; Alistair is always in bed by ten.

The ferry dock is empty; the boat is moored overnight across the lake in Clam Harbour. Shreds of jellyfish shimmer, caught by moonlight. From the distance an observer would see only two orange dots, the burning embers of cigarettes, and think them fireflies blinking on and off.

"Do you think about me?"

"When you're there, yes."

"And when I'm not here?"

He shakes his head once, twice.

"Why not?"

"I don't know. I just don't."

She tries to absorb the shock of this. She knows he is telling the truth. He is disciplined. He has a tart, even savage, heart.

Her voice is defiant when she says, "I think of you all the time." This is also true. This is also honesty.

He has no reply. He wants to tell her how much he loves sitting next to her. She is so quiet, like sitting next to a pond. She reminds him of the girlfriends he had when he was five, six years old. Even then he had admirers. They were small girls with big eyes, completely lost. They would jump out of the bushes and try to scare him.

She wants to know more about him; he so rarely divulges his thoughts, his uncertainties. But she can't bear prying and she doesn't want to beg for his love. For his part, he refuses to pull that old trick of men who take advantage of the love of women who are not their wives, admitting mistresses and lovers into their hearts and minds, although not into their lives. He will not parade his dissatisfactions to create an intimacy they will both know to be a consolation prize for the real love he cannot offer.

They sit listening to the slap of the water, the rustle of burning tobacco. This is the strangest thing: even the silence, even his rejection, feels right. This must be the meaning of it, *feeling right*, because mere proximity to him — to sit side by side, not touching, not speaking even, staring into the dark lake — feels more like home than anywhere she has ever known.

How lucky for him, Eve thinks. To have a lover who does not have to be made love to constantly. To have a lover who consents to be fed on scraps.

And for her mother how sad, that love for her should be this savage season, alternating cycles of hunger and balm.

There is another possibility her mother writes about in the ledgerbook.

She knows she is inexperienced in the darker side of human behaviour, she has been too protected. He might be playing with her, using her as a mirror for his fading beauty. Or merely doing what any long-married person does: flexing their muscles, keeping romance alive by flirting, in passing crushes. These people are only stimulating themselves.

But too quickly her admiration of him intervenes. She thinks of the situations he has faced in his work. Drunk local men who want to pick a fight with a salaried white stranger who is robbing them of their copper, their cadmium. A tricky foreman, volatile roadside checkpoints, buzzing in Cessnas over vertiginous rainforests, volcanoes and mountains that seem to be reaching up to claim him. Rain dripping from his nose, his gouged fingers, stopping under an awning to light a cigarette as rain cascades from its edges.

He has honed his courage in places where fear and trust operate equally and this is visible in his physical decisiveness, how he does even small things — light a cigarette, open a door — in a way both certain and uncaring. He will yawn openly at a party as another man holds court with an interminable story, let his beacon gaze probe the room, piercing objects of his interest. He is not a people pleaser, this man. His existence is unthinking; he is guided by impulses, feelings, he responds to external rather than internal pressures. She likes him for this, for the fact that for him there is only a thin membrane between world and self, that his existence owes its strongest impulses precisely to the fact that it does not know itself.

In her longing she is naked and impoverished. She longs not just for his volatile wit, for how she has to steel herself against what he might say next, but for the dark grey hairs on his chest, his caramel eyes and the strict look in them and how it blossoms suddenly into desire, but also for the idea of him. This seems unique, that she can know him, put her hands on him, but he still exists in the abstract. He is a lean, heroic wind blowing through her mind.

Covetous. An old word, it carries a fume of zeal she associates with the Old Testament. A word she had never expected to take into her life. But that's what she is: she covets someone else's husband. She still can't believe he belongs to someone else, that he is not hers. She tries, but her mind staggers on the bleak fact of it.

Is this honest? An interrogation to him, to herself. To stay and stay and stay, to fight your deepest impulse, to grapple with instinct. *I have given Alistair my word.*

Her mother writes this in a slanted, desperate hand. The ink is smudged. She imagines her mother's fevered writing at night by the light of the kerosene lamp, at the very table she sits at now.

I stood up in front of all those people and said I loved him.

"Do you think?" someone is saying, in the kitchen of the white house across the lake. Eve is, as usual, eavesdropping through the ceiling. They still haven't reckoned on the register, how the voices of her aunts and her sister and her cousins travel upstairs, perfectly audible.

"Well, it makes sense, doesn't it?"

"It wasn't as if they never saw each other, couldn't be together. They saw each other twice a year."

"Maybe it wasn't enough."

"They had children, homes. They had everything to live for."

"Except each other."

"Come again?"

"They didn't have each other."

"You mark my words. Never underestimate how jealous people can be of another person's happiness."

"What does that mean?"

"Just what it means."

"You could see it clear as day; it was plastered across their faces."

"What?"

"That they had their fingers up each other's you-know-whats."

"Jesus, have you no shame."

And so the ribald aunts vied with the lone sensitive soul who said it was love. The kitchen relatives were the first inkling Eve had that humanity might really separate into two neat emotional camps: the flinty realist and the sensitive romantic. At twelve years old she already knew which she would be.

She puts the journal down and reaches for the photographs she found in the disintegrating manila envelope. Her father has destroyed most photographs of her mother. She has always known this, ever since she was a teenager and went looking for the albums. *I burnt them,* her father said. She was shocked, scandalized, but more afraid of the look on her father's face. She never asked again.

She is surprised to find that in these few surviving photographs her mother and this man are both in the frame. Group photos taken on stony beaches, picnics on drives around Cabot Trail, harried visits to Fortress Louisbourg with the kids running amok. Her mother and her lover are always on the opposite sides of the picture, as if willing themselves apart. Her eye is hungry for their faces. She can't believe these few images, with their buttery Kodachrome colours, are all she has to feed herself upon.

He squints into the sun, the lines of forty-eight or -nine years in the world etching his face. His eyes, whose expression teeters between lavish and taciturn, his mouth sloping down at the corners, his eyebrows dipping at the outer edges, giving his face the cast of a disappointed Inca. Not at all a Scottish face. Light and shadow play on its planes and hollows, its moody patchwork like a wind ruffling a field of oats.

She is discovering this all slowly and in retrospect, like an old image cohering out of darkness. Just as she is meeting her mother, a stranger, but someone with whom she is intimately connected. Eve doesn't think for a second that knowing her mother will hand her a magic key to unlocking herself. No, she is interested in her mother in the way she might be fascinated by an intriguing stranger who she later learns is a close relation, but the connection has been broken.

She is intrigued to learn that that her mother isn't very wifely in that acquiescent way, although she is kind. Yes, she is a tender person, underneath her bravado. And funny; look at the sandwich her mother proffers to the camera, pointing, which she has prepared in the middle of the night for the drive, her face a parody of Fifties' housewife commercials. Her silly, reckless smiles.

CHAPTER 19

The journey to Zaire was a blur, as was anything he did in those months without Alexandre. Without his company, his beacon-like observation, his calmness, travelling became a chore.

Noel drove into Goma. Now he can only remember his most general impression, which was that Goma had been preparing all its life to be the location for a science fiction blockbuster which called for a Town at the End of the World. Perched on the northern shore of Lake Kivu, Goma was ringed by conical volcanoes of a kind Noel would later learn (after looking them up in the *Atlas*, as was his wont) were called Strontian — which meant, essentially, ready to blow at any moment. The ground was corrugated lava, black and hardened. A cholera epidemic at Goma the previous year had lasted four weeks and killed thirty thousand people. As if on cue the Nyaragongo volcano had stuttered to life at that precise moment, so that the dying multitudes and the surviving million refugees camped out on the sharp, glassy shale could add pyroclastic flows to their worries.

By the time Noel arrived, the camps were all but dismantled; they had been emptied of their apocalyptic humanity but for a few stragglers who hadn't yet been allocated a new life. His task was to interview those local officials who had presided over this scene.

He thought he would feel relief to be out of Rwanda, even if Zaire scored little better on the chaos index. He should have been impressed by the landscape: the searing authority of the volcano, the lake that turned the colour of good Merlot at dusk, a rosé sky. But he missed Alexandre, his astringent laughter, the severe consonants of his World Service English. Once he got back to Kigali he vowed he would track him down. In the end, it was Alexandre who called him.

"How did you know I was back?"

Alexandre laughed. "Haven't you figured it out yet? There are no secrets in Rwanda."

Good, Noel thought. *We can still be friends.* "Let's go to Lando's."

"No," he could hear agitation in Alexandre's voice. "I need to go somewhere we can talk. Where no-one will see us."

"Are you sure such a place exists in a country where there are no secrets?" As soon as it was out of his mouth Noel regretted it. What was once a gentle intellectual sparring now sounded like flirtation.

He picked Alexandre up on a street corner. At first he couldn't see him, but then a face approached the car, dissolving out of night. Noel had the impression Alexandre had been standing there for a minute or two, watching him, savouring his face, which would have been just visible in the green dashboard light.

Alexandre got in and he drove until he signalled for Noel to stop. They sat in the truck on a dark side street in silence, Noel waiting for whatever was coming. He couldn't guess what it would be: another declaration of love, a confession, regret.

"I was here."

Alexandre kept his face turned away from Noel, so that only his profile was visible.

"Here when?"

"In April 1994. I wasn't in France. I came back in January."

He waited to hear more.

"The sky above, the land below your feet," Alexandre said, looking up into the sky through the windshield. "The moon in the sky, just like always. And you. The moon looks friendly, but it is not your friend. It can't help you."

Noel registered that Alexandre had drifted into the present tense.

"That was the strangest thing," Alexandre said, a whiff of the childlike wonder of survivors in his voice. "I was still alive, but

I felt already dead, as if I had disconnected myself from my body. It must be our way of preparing ourselves for death."

He nodded again. Noel had heard this many times, although he never expected to be hearing it from Alexandre.

"Why did you lie to me?"

"Lie?"

"Why did you tell me you weren't here?"

"Because I didn't want it to be true. I wanted something else to be true." Still Alexandre didn't look at him. "We thought someone would come to rescue us." A scouring laugh.

He felt compelled to respond with the instant analysis of the situation at the time and that both he and Alexandre could quote thoughtlessly, like a litany: Kofi Annan. Hands tied. State Department, the Clinton Administration, the Belgians. Madeleine Albright. What happened in Somalia.

"Some people on my hill they... they knew about me."

"Knew what about you?"

Alexandre gave him a disappointed look. "What you know about me, now. They were neighbours. Or they used to be, that was how I thought of them: *neighbours.*" He swallowed the word.

"They told me how I was going to die, what they were going to do with me. We will treat you like a woman, they said. I said, fine. Kill me. Get whatever pleasure you will get out of it. And they—" he turned sharply to face Noel for the first time. "These are my neighbours, for my whole life, remember — they said, no, no, Alexandre. It's not that simple. I said, what could be simpler? I felt calm, utterly calm. Like ice. I thought: I can take anything you throw at me." He laughed. "'Can you kill?' they asked me. I said, no, I cannot kill. 'Would you not kill us, if the situation were reversed, if we were standing here defenceless and you had a gun?' No, I said, I would not. I said, I am tiring of this interrogation. Go ahead, make good your threats.

"And Joseph, he was my age, I sat next to him in school. He said, 'If you will help us kill, then we will not harm you. But if you refuse, we will keep you tied to a stake like one of those women — he pointed to the village compound, where we knew they had taken women prisoner — and rape you at least thirty times a day. If you survive, you will never be able to take a shit again in your life.' I remember that, because that's exactly what I had to do, in that moment." One of his quasar smiles flashed across Alexandre's face and was gone immediately, leaving a trail of black burn. "They said, if you kill with us, we will be blood brothers. We will not harm you. We may even hide you, so that when this is all over you will be set free. I said, do you think this will ever be over? Yes, they said, when the last Tutsi is dead. I said, I am a Tutsi. It won't be over until you kill me. They had no answer for that one."

Alexandre turned away to look out the passenger window. "When I was in France, I thought I had forgotten this place. How I wanted to forget! I came back because it was like a black magnet, pulling on me. I knew what was coming, I knew it in my bones. I wanted to put myself through it. That is the only possible explanation. I could easily have stayed in France." He gave Noel a bare look. "I needed to leave. I thought it was the best thing to do, to come back, to confront. But I cannot even breathe here."

"You could go back to France."

"I was an illegal immigrant in France. I probably wouldn't even make it through immigration. They would deport me. I'm not like you. I can't fly around the world. Where have you ever been stopped and asked to explain yourself, with your American passport?"

Alexandre had always been censorious, demanding, but never bitter. For the first time Noel tasted its balsam tang in his voice. He wasn't merely bitter about Noel's mobility, his nationality, his being part of the global ether of prosperous humanity who thought experience was there to serve them. No, it went deeper. Had anyone ever held him with real tenderness? Had any man had enough generosity to do that? Had any man yearned for Alexandre?

He saw how easily he could solve Alexandre's life without much effort. He could take him to the States, enrol him in a university program, sponsor him for a Green Card, or call on colleagues and contacts in France, see him through the immigration process, use his First World name.

And how much more he could do if he loved him, or at least wanted him.

They sat in silence for a while. Then Alexandre said, "Aren't you going to ask me?"

"Ask you what?"

"What I did? What my choice was?"

"If you want, I can ask. But I already know the answer."

Alexandre gave him a stern look that then transformed itself, within a single blossom second, into the most simple and genuine smile Noel had ever received. "That is why I like you so much," he said.

With that Alexandre opened the door, got out and walked into the night.

Later Noel sat in his hotel room, staring into the mirror. Normally he avoided his own reflection. He wanted to be reminded as little as possible how he looked to others, exactly what sort of performing doppelganger this was alive and at work in the world. You didn't deserve that, he told the doppelganger. You with your searing honesty, which is your professional trademark. His rangy smile, his delight. What did you do to deserve that? He wanted to tell you, and you didn't let him. Or no, perhaps, he addressed the mirror spectre, you did the right thing. You freed him from having to tell you the story of how he sullied himself. How he bargained for his life.

Noel drew the curtains of his hotel room across the dark Kigali night, lit only by a few weak sodium street lights. It was almost impossible, he thought, to separate what was right from what was wrong. He had made a career of this task, and still he didn't know how.

Two days after his meeting with Alexandre he had to give evidence at the International Criminal Tribunal in Arusha. When he returned to Kigali a week later, he heard about Alexandre.

He had gone back to his hill in the north, against the advice of everyone who knew his case. They knew he had been in France as a refugee, and that he worked for foreigners, so they had made it look like a car accident. The brothers of two of the women he had helped the *interahamwe* kill ran him into a barbed-wire fence. Then, for good measure, they ploughed his body into a concrete hut.

"He was a Tutsi who had killed other Tutsis," Odile, another translator, told Noel. "Of course, they knew about his... character."

"What do you mean, *character*?"

Odile shied away from his question, dropping her eyes. In Rwanda direct confrontations were frowned upon. She probably thought him rude.

"What about his niece and nephew? What will happen to them?"

Odile shrugged. "There are so many orphans in this country."

He tried to imagine Alexandre's broken body, ribbons of flesh dragged along barbed wire from the assassin's bumper. Lean forearms sticking out of his beige twill shirt, which he wore rolled up. His dignified, even austere stance. Prominent neck muscles, all the sinews and veins on display, but smudged, a little deranged in Noel's memory, as in a Francis Bacon painting.

He sees them sheltering from another sudden shower in a concrete block house which they assumed was empty and finding an entire family huddling in the corners; Alexandre went to speak to them, he offered them the only money he had in his pocket so that the father could buy a new hoe. He sees Alexandre ordering a round of beer at Chez Lando, insisting on keeping up with the largesse of the internationals, despite his meagre wages. He sees Alexandre that night in the hotel: triangles of light filtering through the curtains, moonlight geometry on the floor. *Alexandre, I can't.* His crisp movements, acute, so restless, how they suggested risk and revelation, these lean ambassadors of what the mind — Alexandre's consciousness — had experienced. Killing changes you, chemically, Alexandre had once said. It changes you all over, not just in your mind, but your body too. The body of a killer has different blood from the body of an innocent man. At the time Noel hadn't questioned this, or how resolute and also how frightened Alexandre sounded as he said it. He merely thought it was an opinion gleaned from observation, from conversation with others who had done such things. How lonely, even disappointed he had felt when Alexandre had stood up from the edge of the bed with a crack and left the room. He knew he didn't want to sleep with him, but that he had felt a desire beyond sex, a desire that lived in the simple pleasure of another human being's proximity.

"I know how these people feel," Alexandre said once, when they visited an area where Hutus who had taken part in the massacres had returned from the camps at Goma and were settling into the abandoned houses of dead Tutsis. Their new neighbours in some cases were their former victims, the ones who had survived. Noel remembers it as a particularly tense, sad place in that country of sorrows, the men's eyes scuttling away as soon as he came near — the women who wouldn't even look at him.

"They feel as if they are the dead ones," Alexandre said. "They think someone is trying to trick them into thinking they are alive, but they know they are dead." He said this while surveying the fields of plastic, almost hallucinatory green, with that hard stare of his. "They believe this is all a dream."

She lay awake listening to the ragged, snatched breathing coming from the top bunk. From time to time Llewellyn emitted bursts of voice and grunts sounded. It had taken courage for Lew to come and confess to her, she realized; she could so easily have sent him away. She wondered if Lew understood, on an instinctual level, that it was her own guilt about Noel that forbade her from taking the moral high ground.

She edged herself out of the bed and across the floor, which duly emitted gnashing squeaks. She pulled open the front door with a single wail from the door hinge. In her bare feet she padded down the road.

The night was moonless and she had the thrilling sensation of moving through dark matter — she couldn't tell where her body ended and the night began. She closed her eyes and tried to walk in a straight line, floating through the night like an apparition.

She let herself in the kitchen door, which she knew would be unlocked. Feeling her way up the stairs she followed the sound of his breathing. He was sleeping on his stomach in the big bedroom, his shoulders a dark yoke across the sheets. He looked glossy, his skin tanned to wood the colour of blood: rosewood, padouk, mahogany.

She edged herself onto the bed. He opened his mouth. She heard the tack of saliva of tongue against palate, but he did not wake. She ran her fingers, very lightly, through his hair. It had the texture her fingers remember: much thicker than her own, slightly wiry but smooth, as if coated with lacquer.

In the morning Noel will remember that he dreamt Alexandre had come back from the adjoining room at Mille Collines. He had sat on his bed and run his fingers through his hair.

He had told Rachel we would stay ten days more. In those days he has performed small treacheries he had always thought beneath contempt, dodging her cellphone calls with claims of disappearing signals, skulking over to the cabin at three in the morning to wake Eve with pebbles thrown against her window, sitting on the ferry at midnight with her, feeding each other blackberries they had picked in the dark, their fingers stained with the night juice of the fruit, their open-mouthed laughs, the sudden amnesty from the world that physical happiness, and the newness of someone, brings.

Now Eve's boyfriend — *husband*, he corrects himself, although for some reason he doesn't believe in their marriage, doesn't see this man as capable of being her husband — shows up and Eve's instinct is correct: he does want to drive right out of here, leave stealthily, cowardly, in the middle of the night.

He attempts to take an inventory of reality: Eve has a life in Toronto, he has one, or had one until recently, in New York. But he doesn't want his life! He wants to go away. He will move to Paris. He will find another Rachida there, or he will go after the real Rachida, get work in Geneva, wrest her from her boyfriend and family; it will require him to resuscitate his rusty French, but what the hell.

Or he will go to Mexico and disappear.

No, he won't do any of this. He will stop pitting one department of himself against the other. He will cease needing to see himself in turmoil in order to feel alive.

He flips angrily through the magazine article he has been trying to read for days, "Postmodernity and the Disappearance of the Intellectual." He tries to read, but all the words— *atavistic, frippery, moral famine* — are tiny, insidious whips. Duly lacerated, he drops the magazine and falls asleep.

The sounds of August envelop the land like a cloak: the crickets' electric buzz piercingly loud like a hundred malfunctioning electrical wires, the industrious crises of the small red squirrels as they sense the sun tipping toward autumn.

The light seems to speed toward them from a long way away at a listing angle. At times Seal Island looks distant, other times she swears she could throw a stone and hit it. Sound congeals over the lake in the evening, forming an echo chamber; a dog barking on the other side is heard as if it were next door. The water glitters into night, an unstable aluminum hue.

Corpses of porcupines that have been driven out of the forest by drought litter the road, and flying beetles the size of hummingbirds drop in mid-flight. The evenings are plagued by a ghost rain that falls from a seemingly cloudless sky. She looks up the phenomenon in her father's *Dictionary of Weather. Serein: A fine rain falling from a cloudless sky after sunset.*

Lew will leave the following day. Noel will be gone soon. There should be a richness in this, having two men she loves, or thinks she loves, beside her. She should exult. But she has never felt so exposed. She has never been so conscious of time as both her maker and her adversary. She remembers overhearing someone counselling to her father once, not long after her mother died: time is like water, they said. The more you try to hold onto it, the more it slips away.

The airport is miniature, like a maquette of the real thing, studded with papery plastic plants, vinyl benches, the thin worm of a single luggage belt.

She stands beside Lew as he checks in. Ticket, plastic plant, the lean, marbled air of airports. She feels giddy, as if there isn't enough oxygen.

He turns to her. "Well, out of the frying pan and into the fire."

"What do you mean?"

"Back to the world of middle-class professionals." He tried a smile, but it twisted into a scythe on his lips.

"That's your world."

"Yours, too, or it was until recently." He sighed. "Do you know what I hate? These intelligent people, these journalists and academics and dip people like my parents. They always have to have some gripe or other with you. To your face they're kind and appreciative, but they've always got some put-down hidden behind their backs, like a club."

She nods. What can she say? She says, "Yes, that's how it is. These people are grudging in their esteem. They make a point of it."

Lew gave her another twisted smile. "I know I'm not as experienced in the world."

"As experienced as whom?"

"I always felt you wanted someone hard. There's a part of you that wants to be instructed; you need to be with someone you think is better than you, more noble. It's like you want to break yourself open on someone else. I don't understand that instinct."

She shakes her head.

"I know you think I'm...," a rueful smile, "*amusing*. You think, loving Llewellyn is like loving a little boy."

"I don't."

"Oh, come on. At least give me credit for seeing what's in front of my eyes. We've lost respect for each other. And I'm not sure we'll get it back."

Even as she prepares her denial, she senses the truth of what he said, and also the injustice of her feelings, the ruthlessness of all feelings. She sees the vacant anguish on his face and she wants to tell him she loves him. For your lightness, she would say, which, despite what you think, is not the same, is lack of seriousness, or frivolity. The way you go around the apartment interrogating the marigolds and tulips I buy in Spanish: *Quienes son? De donde vienan?* Because you gave me a way out of myself, my self-imposed horizons, because you give me succour for the industrialized loneliness of the city where we live, because you tolerate my unhealthy interest in people's motives, my wilful decision to see their flaws. And, realizing that all these reasons were about herself, she added, mentally, because you are honest, because you don't indulge yourself in contrived dilemmas. Although the latter was not strictly true.

The ghost conversation would end with Lew instructing her: but love has to be more than an exit door, more than an escape.

An announcement crashes through the empty corridors. His flight. Around them, passengers gather themselves and move with purpose. Eve feels she is being shorn of something with each step she takes. She is coming to understand the archaeological spirit of pain: how it strips hungrily through layers of defence, self-respect, the deflections afforded by humour, to arrive at a deep, hollow level. The inhabitant of that chamber is like the last survivor of a major catastrophe, wiry and tenacious: love.

"See you in a couple of weeks." He turns and walks through the security gate.

And it is here, already, unfolding with the luscious vitality of a late-blooming rose, the doppelganger of the autumn she would spend with her husband, if only this summer had not happened: spiralling leaves, the long burnished autumn of the mid-continent, Saturdays at the St. Lawrence Market trying cheeses — Manchego, Cornish Yarg — buying complicated coffee, seasoned catfish, purple-sprouting broccoli. She will think about randomness, and how we try to convince ourselves there is a design. She wants to be Noel's wife; she wants to have a child with him. She could never have foreseen this terrible ambush, which she understands is in part biological. She should be able to take her desire and graft it onto the man who is available, the man she is married to and who is at this moment walking through glass partitions into a departure lounge. But she will not be able to; she knows this well enough to not even try. She will wonder whether her inability to compromise on love is temperamental, or some useless zealot principle, or both. Lew's parents will go to Mexico for the winter, Zihuatanejo, the golden age of diplomats roaming the world on a thick pension. Her father meanwhile scraping rabbit pelts in the cabin, stitching them together to make a new blanket. And Noel — where? A small town by a river or a lake, trees a mineral riot of ochre, amber, carmine. His lissom students, *caffe lattes*, departmental lunches. On the weekends he and Rachel will go hiking in the mountains. To think she might not have known of his existence. Even if she cannot touch it, see it, his life will be a counterpoint, a harmony, a ghost score to her own.

She watches as Llewellyn's boarding pass is ripped, then he is out the door and walking to the plane, a stiff back, a dishevelled shirt, a bag hanging from his arm. She waits behind the glass partition, willing him to turn around and wave, as he has always done. He disappears into the fuselage without even a glance in her direction.

After tomorrow, it will all be over. This dusty ringmaster role he has had to play for years, whipping himself into performance. Get out of bed. Fish. Make his solitary supper or, increasingly, not eat at all.

Time feels different now. He feels as if he is skimming very fast across a surface. That ghost tribe of dead people, his family, suddenly they are here: his grandmother, his mother and father, his sister Eileen. They are all present in his life in a way they haven't been since he was a child. This seems to be another signal.

And what to do with them — his daughter, her husband, the neighbour who has become her boyfriend, all of them still trapped on that gruesome carousel of need and desire. They all want so badly to be someone in the world, to the world, they want to justify themselves.

Look at him with his mug of tea, sharpened knives, the buttery slices they make in the rubber hide of an eel, campfires, walks, the delicacy of the summer, short-blooming, opportunistic flowers, the long periods of containment called winter. He had lied, or been lied to, by whom he did not know, by all of this, possibly — the summer, the land, the cuts on his fingers from muskrat bites, from the slippage of a knife. It was clear now.

Tomorrow. For the first time in years he heard promise in the word. Tomorrow he will have three things to fear: witnesses; getting it wrong, somehow, some detail. And himself.

She arrived back from the airport to a ringing phone. Her father was nowhere to be seen. She picked it up. It was the RCMP, calling about the horse. Part of her had forgotten that the horse was not hers. As it turned out the mare belonged to a McGillvary in Tarbert whose barn burned down in May. She must have survived for a month on her own on the mountain, the officer told her. The McGillvary man is fine with them keeping her for the moment. He has a new barn to build, after all.

She went outside to tell the mare. "You've been identified," she said. A flicker surfaced from the depth of the mare's eyes, a signal that looked so beguilingly like understanding.

That evening the sky was dark. An electrical storm was on the way. Around nine o'clock towering unstable clouds appeared overhead. Noel and Eve went to sit by the shore and watch the storm's processional arrival. They were nearing the ferry when the air was suddenly split in two. A tree blew apart not more than a hundred yards away, spewing silver shards of light, like a box of sewing needles thrown across space. The hairs on the back of Eve's neck stood bolt upright.

"That was *close.*"

Another lightning bolt; this time it seemed to come from inside them. The trees were shouting, the grass whined.

She dragged him away from the lightning strike. The only secure cover was the ferry, with its disintegrating rubber bumpers. They clambered onto the boat, Eve first. She reached her hand out to help Noel over the crevasse of black water.

Noel hesitated, and then leapt over the gap.

She looked down to the shattered deck, beneath it a dark knit of rafters caked with seagull guano. Beyond that was the hull. If either of them fell down there they would at least break a leg.

She tried the door to what had been the bridge. It gave way. She pulled her flashlight out of her pocket and shone it on what was once the captain's table. A laminated nautical map of the channel was splayed across it, faded but quite intact. Two old pencils riddled with wormwood holes nestled in a felt of dust. Her uncle's fingers would have been the last to grip them.

"It's just as they left it."

They heard another crack, followed by a soft patter which quickly built to a roar. Rain, real rain — the first in six weeks.

Then he was against her, his mouth on hers. At the touch of his lips a rough current coursed through her. They fell on top of a pile of old netting in the corner of the captain's cabin, Noel on top of her. It serrated her back. The only sound was the bass drum of rain.

What was happening? *Making love* was too tame, too congratulatory. Sex; it really was a dark contract, the reptilian part of her brain coming alive with a spark, sucked back aeons into the core of herself. Before humans were human. When there were only minerals, sulphur, catalysts. Whatever it was they were doing, it escaped the normal precincts of desire. She felt herself being towed to a panic-strewn, isolated place.

They stayed there for a while, the netting cutting into their backs, listening to the rain. It had the sound of time passing, to a minus time countdown, like at Cape Canaveral before rockets and shuttles are launched.

Noel's face was lit from the side by a single ray of light that fell dustily through the smudged cabin window. Even now, when she knows him this way, his face has a curious effect on her. It is both balm and dazzle. He is the first man who has made her feel excited and calm at once.

A face weighs too heavily on the soul, she thought, lying beside him on the heap of netting. A face is everything.

The light was still on when they returned to the cabin. It was unlike her father to be up so late.

"Looks like we got some rain," her father observed, when they were barely in the door.

"We needed it."

"I'm going to cook you supper tomorrow night, down on the shore. Both of you."

She glanced at Noel. "All right."

Her father went to bed. They sat up for the rest of the night, sitting at the kitchen table lit by a kerosene lamp.

What Noel told her that night made Eve, apart from Rachida, the only person to know the full story about what had happened.

Rachida returned to Geneva a month before he was due to leave Rwanda. He tried calling her from Kigali once on a line thick with the chatter of satellites, but her boyfriend picked up the phone.

He was due a break, which he took as a week on the beach at Mombasa, his first rest after three solid months of work. This was in June 1997. It was supposed to be his recuperation, and for a while it was. At first he was relieved not to be required to talk to anyone, to coax them to reveal information. This was the worst aspect of his job: that conversation became work.

He breathed in the hot salt air of the coast. The water was an uncanny colour, pale green striated with darker strands, like jade. Fey palm trees leaned languidly over the sands. Slim fishing boats, their graceful outriggings like shoulders, rode the breakers.

He came upon a young girl wearing her Sunday best, a little pink dress. She sat splay-legged on the beach, scooping fistfuls of sand between the V of her legs.

He said hello and received a reluctant hello back.

"What are you doing?"

"Looking at the sand. There's all these black bits. Look."

He bent down. "That's burnt wood. Someone's made a fire. Where's your mother?"

The girl inclined her head nearly imperceptibly, back toward the beach. "At church."

"Why are you out here by yourself?"

"Because I was bored. I fell asleep. They sent me out. They said, if you're going to sleep in church you can wait outside." She yawned.

He was still squatting beside her, just about to rise and move on, when a man, no a boy, a teenage boy, approached him, anger swirling in his eyes.

"Hey. What are you doing with my sister?"

He stood up.

"I said what are you doing with my sister?"

He looked at the little girl's position, her legs flung wide in a V, and saw the possibilities.

"She was sitting by the beach by herself. I was just asking where her mother was. I wanted to make sure she was okay."

The boy was trembling. "She's fine. Leave her alone."

He backed away down the beach, the waves biting at his ankles. When he was sure the young man was not going to attack him he turned his back toward them and walked away. For an hour or so he walked, trying to admire the bucking skies, the crushed silk of the Indian Ocean, and then he went back to his hotel and drank six beers in quick succession.

It was supposed to have been a week's break but after only four days in Mombasa he wanted to leave. He didn't want to return to Kigali, nor did he especially want to go back to New York. For the first time in his life there was nowhere he wanted to be.

Noel paused the story there. He gave her a searching look, which Eve returned to him across the table. She did not understand the plea in Noel's gaze, but she did catch a sliding, occulting look, as if Noel were tucking something inside an envelope, out of sight.

Noel had stopped because he had to create a gap, as much for himself as for Eve; into it he dropped a memory of what had happened next, and which he would never tell anyone, including himself. It would be one of those secrets shared between parts of himself, the Noel he knew and liked and the Noel he faintly despised, forever.

From Kigali he flew to Brussels, then to Geneva. He felt an instant distaste for the city. It reminded him of Bonn in the days when it was the capital of West Germany, or of the trim upstate towns he had grown up in: not a twig out of place, the neighbours having an orderliness competition with their antiseptic patios, calculated bougainvillea draping over balconies at just the right angle. He did not find Rachida at home, but he found her father. The scene that ensued he does not want to recount to Eve, or to himself. When he thinks of it he pulls down a steel shutter in his mind.

For a week he wandered around Europe. In Paris he got drunk on his own, which he hardly ever did, and stumbled back to his gargoyle-festooned hotel. He took the Eurostar to London, and had a mild panic attack as it passed under the Channel. The faint chalky smell in the air, the clammy walls, the strange hollow sound as it passed through, which he attributed to wind dynamics but which sounded like the prolonged groan of a gigantic, mortally wounded animal. Then surfacing into the hedgerows of England, the last gasp of a sunset on the horizon.

In those weeks he felt sure he was going to have a breakdown and for the first time he properly understood the term in its dual meaning. Break. Down. He was riven, fractured in two. Where the break occurred a terrible oozing pain leaked out, staining his every thought. He was sinking, although slowly. He was on his way down — to where, he did not know. With each motion — buying a ticket, picking up his backpack — he was assailed by knives. He tried to escape into sleep but all his dreams were cruel allegories. He was in a schoolroom of the subconscious; his dreams screeched his failings at him, taunting him. He felt certain that he was having his face rubbed in his fate.

From London he returned to his New York office. That January he asked to be transferred to the Americas team. He'd never been to Colombia but he spoke Spanish so they sent him anyway, accompanied by two much-more experienced researchers who hardly — and rightly — gave him the time of day. Annerys and Jaime were Latin American (although neither was Colombian) and had given most of their careers to the country. To him they seemed fascinated, even dazzled, by the violence, by its sheer prevalence and its illogic, the ghoulish octopus forms it took: kidnap for larceny, kidnap for politics, mass murder, torture and mutilation to terrorize the civilian population, displacement, assassination.

He couldn't match Jaime and Annerys's nervy commitment. He might have once been like them, powered by a zeal to be near and to unravel Byzantine daily horrors, but something in Rwanda had siphoned that out of him.

In Colombia he had the distinct impression he was being manipulated on all sides, instead of the usual one or two — deftly played by the NGOs, the police, public prosecutors, even in some cases the victims themselves — a crochet of agendas endlessly knitting itself until he lost track of the pattern.

They were camped out pseudonymously in a nondescript Bogotá hotel; their presence, if known, usually sparked death threats from the paramilitaries, who understandably hated the reports they wrote. Ringed by glittering mountains, Bogotá was not unlike Kigali, he decided, that ugly-beautiful species of city best viewed from a tall building or an airplane rising above the valley, or even the spiralling perspective of God — if he had believed in him — who could look down on and see his most moving and depraved handiwork, all in one convenient drive-thru location.

He felt dizzy. He had to sit down on the bed, or he was sure he would pass out. It couldn't be altitude sickness; he had been in the country a week already. The next day he fainted in the street. As he slid into unconsciousness he was vaguely aware of three or four people stepping over him, before a middle-aged woman with bright blond highlights and pink nail polish stooped to help him up.

He didn't mention it to Annerys or Jaime. He battled against a particularly congealing form of fatigue, like being swathed in gelatin. Thinking back, he can identify the instant it began: they were interviewing a prominent lawyer who had taken on *habeas corpus* cases for the families of kidnap victims. Afterward Annerys gave a punishing but largely correct dissection of the lawyer's motives: "one of those pure types, who believe in the logic of the law above the logic of politics." Her point was that politics really ran the show: blood feud, legitimacy, negotiation, mutual aims, ideological hatred.

He could only agree with her — everything he had seen suggested she was right — but really Noel believed that all failings were personal, even those that looked indubitably political. He was aware that this was not a very sophisticated political philosophy, so he declined to share it with his colleagues. As soon as he had thought this — reminded himself, really — about the boundaries and the silences he must observe (like a member of a cult, he thought) while walking down the broken sidewalks of a clanging Bogotá street, he nearly fell down, then and there. His limbs were too heavy to carry on. He was so tired of politics, of trying to figure out the cause and effect of things. He was tired of professional middle-class people and their serious-mindedness, tired of being bested by people like Annerys, high-achieving, second-generation Latino-immigrant, very likely more intelligent than him, Brown-educated as she was. He suspected people like Annerys were more delighted with their ability to cope in such rapacious environments than interested in making an actual difference to anyone's life. There would always be a fresh supply of people like Annerys. The world needs new blood to feed its emergencies.

He was not afraid in Colombia; over the years in his work he has cultivated a particular relationship with fear. He tried to accommodate it, rather than banish it. If you did, he knew, fear just came skulking back, meaner with exile. Rather he felt heavy and deluded; he was accruing mass and boundaries at an alarming rate until he felt like a Japanese garden, divided into clean geometries, decorative stones, miniature waterfalls, gnarled trees.

He still saw them, sometimes: dead people piling all around him, dumb with tragedy.

On a winter evening after the Colombia trip he was riding the subway home from the office. A businessman in the seat beside him careened precipitously into his shoulder, fast asleep. Noel let him stay there, drool staining his shoulder. At the next stop the businessman shook himself awake and bolted away from him. He was sorry to lose the man's dead weight against his body.

At home Rachel was waiting for him with his favourite take-out, Singapore noodles with chili and coriander, but he went straight to bed. He lay alone in the darkness, amazed as a new world unfolded itself in front of his eyes.

He found he was stranded on a hot plain punctured by tors of rock. Black birds swung on the thermals that percolated from them, flying in haphazard circles, like kites abandoned by a child's hand. The grass buzzed with the threatening voices of insects; here and there it parted with the wakes of long, thick forms of impossibly large snakes, like outsize anacondas. Strange animals he'd never seen before, like giant squirrels, grazed on thin grass. The sun was a black stone in the sky.

It was the beginning of his depression and it was hallucinatory, shape-shifting and indefinable, a dream that refuses to end itself upon waking. In the centre sat one fact like a paperweight preventing the individual sheaves of his mind from scattering in the wind. It was the sum of what he learned about life in Rwanda, Goma, Colombia: that when life took on the quality of a hyper-real nightmare, the only way to deal with it was to absorb the nightmare, to make it yours. Through the nightmare he could participate in Alexandre's waking moments, his dreams, his life and his death. He would never have called an experience as damaging as depression positive, but — and he never explained this to Rachel, to the bevy of caring professionals forced upon him — neither was it entirely bleak.

* * *

"Sometimes I feel I'm living my life for him, that he's living through me."

"Why do you feel so connected to him?"

"That's it," Noel said. "We connected. Alexandre and I were friends; he was the first real friend I've had on my field trips. It was like we'd known each other before. There was an instant familiarity. Maybe it's that simple: we were friends, and I feel I let him down."

As he said it, Eve wondered, and not for the first time, if Noel had chosen his work as a kind of expiation for some deeper sin he felt himself to have committed. If somehow he knew he would be a *genocidaire*, given the right circumstances; he knew he would be that conscript in the FARC, charged with watching over people whose lives they had stolen for a vague political purpose.

"You know what all this makes me want to do?" he said. "It makes me want to have children. I want to create some new, urgent life."

She allowed herself, for a moment, to imagine their lives together: the bright antiseptic hospital where she would give birth, the expensive obstetrician, the subsidized university kindergarten. She can feel the texture of their lives together so clearly it seems to already be inside her. But in a week or two she will not know where his bones lie. She will not be able to phone him at home and say, *How are you? I think I love you. Let me be your family, let me be your children, your father, your sisters. Let me be you.* Why then can she also feel the thrilling forever with him, or at least its shadow?

"I hate to think of you going to waste in a place like this."

The word sliced through her deftly, almost casually.

"*Waste?*"

"No," Noel retracted. "Not like that." But it was too late.

"You think this place is waste?"

"I meant that you would be wasted here."

She felt a very slight nausea erupt in her stomach. "Don't pity me."

"I wasn't. I don't." Noel stared at her. "I... I think you're a fascinating person."

A well of deep dismay opened in some hidden and unnameable place inside her.

She did so want to be thought a fascinating person, a strange jewel. She had hoped to be loved, for that. But Noel does not want to have a fascinating woman next to him for the rest of his life. He is an essentially conventional man, and he might quickly find his fascination sliding into incomprehension, then disgust.

He is staring at her intently, waiting for her reaction.

She wants to move away from him right away, to surgically excise him from her heart. But she can't react quickly enough. The heart is a ponderous mechanism. It can't accommodate the loss of love in an instant, so it soldiers on loving until, through some process still utterly mysterious, the love is gone.

That night fiery dreams take her faraway, beyond her paltry boundaries. Dreams are our rehearsal for being dead, she finds herself thinking, even while trapped in her dream. Death will be an eternal dream; we will be free-floating, vaporous, helpless to ward off the malevolent forces, the bogeymen and demons and made-up creatures. Dead, there will be no sitting on the shore with Noel, the dazzling clarity of the late August light, the gold that rims fire at the meniscus of darkness. Her minutes with him, her minutes on earth, ticked away by a savage clock.

But she is alive, at least for now. She knows she will wake in the morning, she will come to some accommodation with herself, she will smile into her own sorrow, they will sit together on a piece of driftwood looking at the lakes and she will tune into the frequency of his body, thinking how perfect and simultaneously mauled life can be.

∾

The door opening and closing, the cold slinking in on the heels of the guests like a furtive animal. Wreathes with a single electric candle in the centre hang in the living-room windows, casting red-yellow shadows on the snow outside.

"Well, if it isn't Herself," someone shouts.

She is upstairs, looking down into the pantry through the register. Bottles of Captain Morgan's Dark are lined up, as usual, on the counter.

The pantry door opens. She recognizes the top of her mother's head from her straight middle part, a milky line of scalp cutting through two wings of auburn hair. She wears her hair long, folding down over her face in two neat sheaths — mid-to-late-Seventies hair. On her feet, platform boots, coffee-coloured with a black panel down the middle. Outpost fashion.

She sees the top of a man's head. He is the beautiful man she has seen from time to time, sometimes in their house but more often at parties like this one. She is only eight years old but she knows he is handsome. When she looks at him she feels the precursor of desire. It feels like a small animal rummaging in the pit of her stomach.

He is her mother's second cousin, that much she knows. He has brown eyes the colour of good champagne, but she does not know this yet — about good champagne. She does not know much about anything, it is true, but on some level she is storing away understandings far beyond her years; even now she knows she must bury them.

This man has prominent cheekbones from which his face falls like two elegant sails. Years later she will remember overhearing gossip about him: *Women just flocked to him. They couldn't help it. He couldn't help it himself.* Someone — her father's sister, maybe — will say, *They were never brought up together, never played as children. If they had, it would never have happened. They would have been like brother and sister.*

Everyone knows they would never have been brother and sister. It is so unusual and disruptive, that register of feeling — call it what you will, passion, besottedness, terror — that people insist in smudging it, rubbing it out.

Smoke so thick it forms a veil. The ripe smell of rum, women's perfume, men's aftershave — a rich fug that hastily absorbs the astringent fume of winter on people's clothes.

He says something, she can't catch what, but his voice is thick, supple, yet stretched, it has the sound of good leather gloves embracing knuckles. She watches as the tops of their heads draw together and meet and stay.

A crack of sound — someone opening or closing a door — and their heads separate.

Her father is in the room with them. Tinsel dangles above his head — one of those red-and-gold star decorations, left over from the Fifties. She can't see his face at all.

She hears her mother say, "We're going down to the Irving station to get some smokes."

"Can't you bum them off someone?"

"I like Craven 'A'. They're all smoking Rothman's."

The beautiful man's voice is different from anyone else's she has heard: medium-pitched, tense. He doesn't sound at all smooth or persuasive. His voice is strung with honesty.

Her mother's voice is more strident. It has the sound of need.

"The road is all iced up," her father says.

They leave the room, followed, a beat too late, by her father. She hears doors opening and closing, the start of a car engine.

An hour and a half passes before she hears her father say, *I'm going out to look for them.*

CHAPTER 20

The rain of the previous night had abated; it hadn't been enough to soak the earth and the land was still kindling dry. She had woken that morning to a radio news bulletin that a single lightning strike up Cape North way had sparked a full-blown forest fire.

Her father was preparing their eel supper.

"Shouldn't you put a real grill on, Dad?"

"They cook just dandy on this. You'll see."

He laid down a grill made from the chicken wire strung around the garden to keep the deer out. He set the wood alight and lay down thick fillets of eel. They soon began to blacken, seared in hexagonal shapes by the wire. Fat hissed and dripped into the fire.

Her father laid aluminum plates with buttered slices of bread and quartered limes. With a blackened fork he speared strips of eel. Noel sat across the fire from her, next to her father.

"Ready for your first eel?"

"As ready as I'll ever be."

They ate with the plates balanced on their knees. Noel chewed slowly, a thoughtful look on his face. "It's oily," he said, after a while. "Meaty. But fishy, too. I think I like it."

Her father nodded his approval at this description. "There's two things I always wanted to make: eel stewed in Madeira wine, and eel with Málaga grapes. I read the recipes somewhere and forgot to write them down. Can't for the life of me remember where it was I saw them."

Málaga. Her father had said the name correctly, the stress on the first syllable. Where had he learned to do that?

"Have you ever been to Spain?" Noel asked.

Her father shook his head. "Never set foot off of this continent."

"You should go."

She watched her father give Noel a transparent, unblinking look. She recognized it, had used it herself for years on American tourists who voiced similar opinions about travel and experience: *You think it's that easy?* Did he picture it as he said it, she wondered, the purple mountains, Alpujarras, the ceramic light of the Mediterranean. She had seen these things with her own eyes.

"Look," she pointed at the hill. Gossamer trails of slime appeared in the grass, gradually illuminated by a wan crescent moon, until they looked like giant stitches in the land. "They're on the move."

Her father nodded. "It's not a bad night. Could be a bit more cloud. That's what they like best."

"So you'll be going out tonight then."

"No, I won't."

"Why not, if it's a good night?"

He gave her a watery, transparent look. "Because I'm not."

"I'm going back home, Dad," she said. "In a couple of weeks."

Her father continued chewing. "I know."

"I don't know what else to do. The doctors say there's nothing medically wrong with you."

He speared another piece of eel.

She drew a breath. "I have to go back, you know. It's not just about money. I have a life there now."

"You're talking to me like I'm asking you not to go. Don't worry about me. I'll make do."

I'll make do. No-one had likely laid a hand on her father in desire in more than twenty years. What would that be like? Flesh needs the invitation to touch. It needs to be welcomed, held. Life was just a remorseless, feral narrative. Of course, it could be kind, too, but not, generally, to people who kept pickups running beyond their prime, people who could barely afford to keep up their insurance, people whose wives loved other men.

You can make another choice, she reminds herself. You could stay. Money will be a problem, it will mean the end of her marriage, but these things might be necessary sacrifices, at this juncture in her life. She had no children to school and clothe, no profession, no friends — somehow they had all forgotten her. The last friend who called her on the phone in the cabin was a month ago. All she had said was, *When are you going to get email?*

Yes, she could stay. There would be the winter, the wind carving through Clam Harbour, gale-born waves slapping the sides of the wharf. Days like empty drawers.

"We'll build you a new house in the spring, Dad. With central heating and everything."

"With whose money?"

"I can make money."

"You think you know best, because you've been out in the world. But that doesn't mean you know what's best for me. Or for Duncan or Anita for that matter."

"I never tried to tell Anita what to do. I would never make that mistake."

"Well then, don't make it with me either."

"I'm just trying to help."

He reached onto the grill and speared another piece of eel. "Well, do me a favour, don't try so hard."

There was a steeliness, a resolution in his voice that she had rarely heard before. Maybe she didn't know him at all. Then again, why should she? There were long years when she can only remember him as a figure asleep on the sofa in the afternoon, after the schoolbus disgorged her. Those years he had worked in the woods to support them, also part-time in the steel plant in Sydney. In the summers he'd moonlighted for the Department of Highways repairing the Trans-Canada at night, coming home in the morning with his face smelling of smudge pots and hot asphalt.

Who's yer father, dear? She sees people recognize her father's name, sees the crochet of relatives and ancestors they seem to have, ready-knit, in their heads. Of course, that's who she is. She is Alistair's daughter. The daughter of Ann who was killed with her second cousin in that tragic accident. Although God knows what they were doing out together in the dead of night.

It didn't matter; she will never be from the island again. *You have your freedom, and guilt is the price.* For years, that was everything Anita said to her, in a nutshell. But did freedom always have to have a price on it, she wondered. Couldn't freedom be free?

She looked at Noel, across the fire, chewing on his oily eel. By the weekend he would be gone. Then she would begin to pay another price, although she couldn't yet read the amount on the tag.

Her father rose. "Time to go to work."

"But you said you weren't going fishing."

"I'm not." He made toward the shore. After a few paces he stopped, turned around. "Are you two going to give me a hand or wha'?"

"Give you a hand with what?" She had started to clear the plates.

"Leave that stuff. The raccoons can have it."

They followed her father through the moonless forest. He needed no flashlight, of course, didn't even look at the path, while Eve and Noel had to keep an eye on the ground to avoid tripping over roots and falling flat on their faces.

They arrived at the river mouth. Before she realized what was happening her father was on his knees and pulling at the trap doors.

"Dad, what are you doing?"

He didn't answer.

"I said what are you up to?"

He stood up, dusted his knees. Behind him a sluice of eels headed into the open water. "I'm finished here."

"What do you mean, finished?"

"Are you two going to give me a hand or do I have to do this by myself?" The expression on his face was the one she had seen in the auto-portrait photos. Uncomprehending, exposed, but resolute.

In another second she understood what he meant to do.

"Just help me," he said.

She had to use all her strength: the river was high and the water murky. They tugged at the ropes attached to the flood-gates. One by one they came up and their cargo of live eels flooded into another holding pen until she reached the last one and, with a tug that wrenched her shoulders, it was open. She watched them spill downstream, then into the ocean. A thousand, two, five, ten thousand dollars, swimming busily away.

When she looked up, her father was standing above the tank where he had kept Harold for ten years. He reached inside and picked up the eel. Harold was so accustomed to his touch he allowed himself to be picked up without a squirm. He held him in both hands, Harold's head resting on his shoulder. He walked to the river and bent down.

"There you go, buddy. You can go now."

The eel convulsed with the shock of being in open water, and then disappeared.

A few traps remained, and she released them herself. Inside, the eels huddled together, ravenous for proximity. On the lip of a grand voyage, delirious with reflexes, their caustic skin, their eyes turned blue, flattened into saucers. The traps were littered with globs of their Vaseline-like slime and bodies of dead eels that have been crushed or strangled by other eels. In their zeal to leave they asphyxiate each other.

She stayed that night at Noel's. She didn't even try to hide the fact from her father. They did not talk about what happened that evening, nor did they talk about the future. Between them the future was suddenly demarcated, ringed with a cordon of mines.

So they spoke about the past, how they had been too-bright fifteen year olds on the road to becoming valedictorians if they weren't careful, shy and resented by their classmates apart from a few other misfits, then university, trying to mount a production of *Six Characters in Search of an Author* or serving as Secretary-General of the model UN — it didn't matter, their goal had been the same: hide your idiosyncrasies, grip the world, assign identities. This was another reason why she loved him, she realized. They had been the same person.

In the dream everything is on fire. The mare's shrill whinny, the chemical fume of melting paint, creosote, varnish. Flames leap above the treeline.

She snaps herself awake. The clock says two-thirty in the morning. But awake, the smell remains. The hiss of burning wood.

With a yelp she is out of bed and running.

The cabin was alive with flames. It was changing shape, expanding and contracting, then imploding as it allowed itself to be consumed.

She stood transfixed. It must have been burning for at least half an hour already. There was no entering that burning mass. If he was in there, then he was gone. She stood impassive as a beam-sized piece of burning wood whizzed past her head.

A tug on her arm. She whipped around to see her father, his face streaked with charcoal.

"Get out of here."

A shrill sound, half-human, came from the field. The mare was tethered to a tree within range of flying debris. She bolted for her. She untied the horse from the tree, hit her on the rump. "Go, get out!" The horse bounded down the road from which she had appeared.

Noel came from the other direction, running at full speed down the path. She saw him dodge a flying spear of burning wood.

They ran for the shore. Halfway to the woods, she suddenly stopped, stricken by a sudden paralysis. She inhaled the caramel smell of scorched blueberries. Her mother's journal, the photographs, her own journal. She made to turn around and run.

"For Christ's sake." Her father locked her arm in a callused grip.

They reached the shore and he slid the rowboat into the water. They rowed into the water, her father hauling the oars, Noel in the bow, her in the stern, watching. The water scraped at the oars; it sounded viscous and scratchy, like taffeta. The burning cabin was a distant flare in the darkness, although it sounded as if they were inside it, the hiss and crackle rang in their ears. The water and the sky were navy and there was no line between them. She watched as flames leapt from the pile of wood that had been their home. She never thought anything burning could be so beautiful. She thought, this is the beginning of forever.

When they were half a mile out into the channel her father hauled in the oars. He reached inside his jacket and took out an envelope.

"I saved these for you."

She looked down to find him holding her notebooks, her mother's ledgerbook and a long envelope full of photographs.

"There's something else." He handed her a legal-sized envelope she didn't recognize.

"What's this?"

"The tests. You should have a look."

"When we get back on shore."

"No, now." It was again the steely, tensile tone. Her father took a flashlight from his pocket and shone it over the envelope.

PET, SPECT, EEG. Each had a form attached on the front with "normal activity" ticked. Beneath these was another sheet. This one sported no acronym, no ticked form.

In the darkness of the lake water she could barely see his face. "What's this?"

"Another test."

Her eyes scrambled over the sheet. *DNA. Correlative. Paternity. Then a figure: 98.8 per cent negative.*

Her mind refused to think. She was gripped by a horizontal vertigo. She wasn't falling through space as much as across time, waiting for it to catch her. But time was in collusion with space; it let her plummet.

She ripped the piece of paper from the envelope and flung it in the water. It buckled, flooded, and then disappeared beneath the surface.

His face was a mirror of her own: alarm, real panic and dread.

"You can do that," he said. "But it won't change the truth."

They all slept the rest of the night in John Rory's house, although she lay awake for a long time, Noel asleep beside her, her father in the adjacent bedroom.

She tried to think but her thoughts were smooth and treacherous. A fey, evasive fog stole between them, filling every crevasse, just like the icy fogbanks that loitered off the coast in the summer, causing June temperatures to plummet. For the first time in her life she found she could not think. Thinking was useless, and dangerous, and a lie.

She allowed her mind to drift in and out of random memories, as if scanning a globe for the outlines of familiar countries. She remembered that in a week it would be her birthday. Her birthday lay on the meridian from summer to autumn. On the island the season changed overnight and without warning. One day the skies were coated in summer haze and the next they were glassy and sharp.

The years she turns eleven, twelve, thirteen, her birthdays are identical: bonfire, cake, midnight swim. Anita was married and gone, now it was just her father and her. Each year he hosted a birthday bonfire on the beach below the cabin. All the neighbours would come. Her father would bring wieners, marshmallows, hot dog buns for them to roast, skewered on the ends of sharpened alder branches. The dogs would bask beside the fire, their golden fur melting to amber in its light. Even though autumn was in the air they would all go for a swim in the warm black water beyond the fire's halo. She remembers the nights were still warm enough, but in a few days they would be cold. She remembers swimming in an ocean warmer than the air.

⁓

Orpheus journeys into the marine underworld, quelling his fear with desire. His fingertips burn to touch his wife; concern turns to impatience, fear to a glittering point of happiness when the waiting will finally be over.

He prepares to launch himself into the unreality of the void, into another cunning infinite night. He has lived with this extreme tension for years, so that the longing has become a necessary part of his life, a reflex action that keeps him alive, like breathing.

Next to the yellowed copy of *Sonnets to Orpheus* lies the *Selected Poems of Rainer Maria Rilke*. This volume is fronted by an introduction. These poems are addressed to an impossible interlocutor, the introducing professor writes. To a person who, if he deigned to answer, would finally grant the understanding the poet is seeking.

The task is to bring love into light, the introduction claims, to give it reality in the world. Orpheus was willing to defy the laws of the night, their banishings, to find his wife, to have a chance again at her love.

The boundless, imprudent drive, this impulse to... to what?

She didn't mean it. She wanted them to live. But the power of her anger surprised her, and surprise came so quickly. By the time she thought to correct it, it was too late.

Her mother has underlined some phrases of the introduction

in pencil. The critic writes of Eurydice's "diurnal truth, her everyday charm."

The everyday charm of a wife. Like daylight.

He is back for Christmas, but something is wrong. She kisses him and feels it immediately: the withdrawal in his mouth, a fear and caution that have never in all these years made an appearance. Gone are his colossal kisses, the way his tongue used to meander searchingly about her mouth, tracing the ridges of gums on her palate, her small, perfectly formed teeth.

She is stranded in the desert she has known all along was her habitat, but his love has so far protected her against the scavenging night creatures, the manic bats, their little garnet mouths. A new sound starts up inside her, the shear of despair. There is nothing she can do to drown this desolate symphony. The sun is square, a yellow tile in the sky. She can hear the universe scraping round, nudging people onto their separate tracks. It is ready to deliver another of its spiteful epiphanies. It knows full well that some separations are impossible to bear.

The violence of the place she has arrived at shocks her. She inhabits a castle where all the rooms are torture chambers. She is in one of them, a live carcass flicked on a hook, her back cut open on an obsolete link. She despises herself; she wants ridicule meted out upon her. This is what she deserves. Black-robed figures swish down dank hallways, trailing bloodied sacks behind them. She is in a fable, a conspiracy. What is that smell, oily and animal?

She tries to wake up, but she is already awake.

In life he requires normalcy. He behaves as he always has. At social gatherings she watches his eye drift toward other women. For her, he holds rebuff at the ready. It is a plate of dark glass in his eyes. In them she sees the black stride of disaster horses. Their plum mouths. Cassocked figures from the castle. Seekers—

* * *

A week before Christmas her mother has a dream. It is the only dream she records in the ledgerbook.

She is at a circus. Half-animal, half-human creatures are in the ring. The audience urges them to do degrading things; people jeer, throw stones. The creatures look confused, but keep to their routines.

Suddenly he is there, sitting beside her in the stands. He takes her hand and says, "Let's get out of here." She starts to cry. "Thank God," she says. "I thought I'd lost you."

Eve is getting a feel for this man, now, after reading so many urgent pages of wonderings and entreaties and curses to him, written in her mother's strangled hand.

He has woken up in a dark wood in the middle of his life. He betrays his wife physically twice a season, he betrays her more often in his heart. The depth of the mystery is beyond him; he is so clearly not a man built to have a fractured heart. All his life he has been pursued by women and it has made him vigilant of his own desires. But this accentuates his attractiveness, the agile tension so visible within him, the wiry sense he emanates, of a man who has to hold himself in check. But he is not someone to wilfully live in the realm of the enigmatic, emotionally. He is a conventional soul; he doesn't want his heart to be a place of shadows.

He has one rule: He never thinks of Ann when he is with his wife and his family. He waits until he is stuck on some airplane for ten hours, or during his half-hour commute from home to the office. He will only think of her when he is in transition from one place to another.

She forces him to realize how colourless most of his dealings with other people are, how much about outcomes and practicalities, and how haphazard his friendships. Most of life goes on like this — meetings, obligations, resentments. Then you meet someone and it is like having floodlights switched on inside you. *Oh, it's you,* you think. *You've come.*

He knows they are linked, and he doesn't like it. Ann is one of those curious acute affinities that erupt in life and that one ought not to accommodate. He searches himself for love. It is there, but it is a wolf, prowling the perimeter of his understanding, hungry and unpredictable. He already knows what he must do; he will hunker down in responsibility and its satisfactions. He will demolish his feeling for her, plank by plank, if necessary. For the rest of his life he will feed off the strength he has found, the strength to forsake love. He may not even know it as love, after a time. He will tell himself: I was able to do that. No-one has dominated me.

Sound travels much farther at night. As the ground cools a temperature gradient forms in the air. Sound waves move obliquely upward through this gradient and are refracted downward, turned back toward the ground as they move from the slow cold air to the fast-moving hot air.

The night is cold and still. In the lee of the lakes there is not much wind. The scrawl of braking tires is loud, as is the sickening slide, the low grunt of rubber trying to get a grip on asphalt.

There is a moon, it is almost full, but for a minute it is obscured behind one of the few ragged clouds in the sky. If they had come upon the patch of ice one minute sooner, or later, they would have seen it clear as day.

There are times when we feel ourselves to be inside sound, not just listening to it. Humans can navigate by sound even more than sight, but we have lost the ability, we rely too much on the eyes. In moments of terror things slip away in front of our eyes too quickly, streaks and blurs, intense and ribboned. But the sound — in our emergency we are inside it.

To their ears the crash sounds distant at first, even though it is happening to them. But then it rushes, headlong, at supernatural speed. It has begun somewhere very faraway and is travelling toward them with the velocity of a bullet.

No-one lives very close to where the car goes off the road, but there are one or two houses a quarter of a mile away. One old man, a Donald MacDonald, said it was one of the loudest and most terrible sounds he ever heard: the brakes like a woman's scream, the squeal of tires not unlike hysterical children, the cymbal smash of metal and glass. Then silence. That's the terrible thing, he will say to her aunt at the funeral — the silence after it. A hissing sound, he says. Like one of them cassette tapes after the music stops.

It is the days before people are obliged to wear seatbelts and they hurtle unrestrained through the windshield. They are tossed onto the rocks in a flurry of glass. The stones receive them, their jagged arms ripping into bone and flesh. The car follows them, nose down, and lands on top of their bodies.

The reason Eve doesn't see her father in the days after the accident is that he scrambled down the rocks after them and gave himself a three-inch wide gash in his leg. Anita will tell her, years later, that he had to be sedated. I don't know what they gave him, she will say, but he was out of it for two days. When he finally comes round he gives the nurse a look of supplicating dismay. His first words are *Please Lord God let me die.*

Look what I've forsaken, her mother writes, before they have become lovers. *My husband, my peace of mind. For what? A warm look, a smile, an embrace on the dance floor.*

Where are the dead? Eve wonders. And how, once so thoroughly banished, can they ever hope to get back home?

She dreams she is held hostage in an underwater palace where she is fed on lupines and deliberately frightened by giant puppets. Lupines are psychotropic; her mind is lit, as if from behind, so that everything is cast in silhouette. Luminous, marbled palaces, the marine stare of their windows. Chandeliers made of eelgrass dangle upward.

She is sure the gods are toying with her. They are playing with her heart and her soul and she is no match for their seigneurial unconcern. What gods have ever been undone by love? She can't meet the challenges of darkness, can't confront the problems of rescue. She is no longer living in a world of God's design. The world is full of shadows and she herself moves among them like a ghost, a conspiracy of liquid tones.

She reads her mother's counsels to herself. *You are in a spiral, the deepest point of a spiral, that is all. Stay there for a while, and then you can move up again.*

That morning, at four-thirty when she found her mother smoking on the beach, a blanket thrown around her shoulders, baleen scattered in strips on the shore. She knows now, she has read her entry.

Her mother had awakened at three-thirty, catapulted out of sleep by dread. What is she doing in this life? Her body does not feel welcome in the world, sleep is forbidden. She can't imagine another man ever touching her. Why sleep if she cannot wake into a day when she will see him? These occasional angels have visited her, and they are called joy. She tells herself: don't crush them with reasoning and control and regret. Most of what is meaningful in her life will be delivered to her in this fluttering and compromised manner. At least she has been happy. At least she has known this.

But no, there is the desert. It stretches before her, gleaming its barren utopia.

Eve remembers the expression on her mother's face that night, when she came upon her, bleary-eyed, still in her nightdress. It was as if she were willing herself away, far from the dawn lakes, the wool mist that obscured their surface, the distant bridge like a toy, the bucking skies patrolled by eagles. A flat in Dartmouth, perhaps, because she can't afford to live in Halifax. Somewhere near the ferry terminal, one of those second-floor conversions that were more corridor than anything else. Working in a bank or a school as a secretary. Or waitressing in a truckstop diner full of men somewhere in the marshy woods of New Brunswick, dressed in orange hunting gear, dead deer strapped to their pick-ups. *Get me another coffee, will you darlin'?*

The scuff of her feet on stones, announcing her presence. Her mother whips around.

Eve. What in the name of God are you doing here?

I couldn't sleep.

Well, how did you get here?

I walked.

You walked, my darling. She scoops her daughter up in her arms.

Where can she go?

Orpheus lived the rest of his life in blue shadows cast by the death of happiness. His wife, her beauty, the things they would have done together: cracked open an egg, her arm casually flung across his shoulder as she sleeps, her cool, small fingers entwined in his, also the dark sexual hunger. It is there even now, eight years after they met, seven years after they first made love. So that she still wants to bruise his lips, knock teeth. She wants to take hold of him, hard, by the waist.

From the beginning she has known instinctively what it takes to make him smile. She doesn't need to think about it. She makes jokes, languid sorties into his understanding, she takes minor risks that only he will be able to identify as such. And he lights up, he unfolds like a Spanish fan. She is responding to a taciturn hidebound quality in him that suggests he needs liberation. She never knew she could be this playful, this mischievous.

Other things in her journal tell Eve that her mother is learning: that she needs to feel romantic about a man, she needs him to capture her imagination. She didn't know that when she married Alistair. Not that she doesn't love her husband — she does, dearly.

She learns that loving two people at once means being two people at once. She learns that she needs aggression, but not violence, in sex. Not only for it to be meted out upon her, but that she also needs to be allowed to be an aggressor. She admires his attack, but she also needs to go on the offensive. This is how she discovers that she is more powerful, more commanding, than she thought. She is learning to trust her instincts, to trust what she feels, and this seems to her the most valuable thing that love has to teach her.

She wonders which came first, the fascinating features and their *pas de deux* of opposites, or the tensions being played out inside him, which rise to the surface. For seven years she watches him speaking to his uncle, unpacking picnic baskets, fixing cars, and never loses her fascination for his face. So severe with its drastic slopes, hollowed eyes, slightly hawkish nose and full, mobile lips. His lurching smiles, his attacks of bashfulness, his stuttering boyish delight.

Oh, he is so beautiful, this man, so thin and acute and restless. Look at his lean, intelligent face, his oyster eyes, the eyes of a gorgeous censor. The man is a blade. Turn him on his side and he disappears.

CHAPTER 21

At seven in the morning the remains of the cabin were still smoking. Eve and her father stood together, their shoulders nearly touching, outside the perimeter of ash and scorched grass.

"I took some of your things," her father said. "That poster of yours, *Horse and Train*. Your clothes, too. I've got it all in the truck."

She turned to look at his profile. It was still the same mild, harmless face she had seen all her life.

"It was an accident," he responds, to her unspoken question. "The candle caught the curtain. I had time to gather your things, that's all."

The shed is full of other things he had saved. She had risen from her sleepless bed at four-thirty that morning and gone to look at the ruins of the cabin. On impulse she'd opened the shed door and found a pile of his clothes, his barometer, a stack of magazines that only the day before had sat beside the kitchen table. He'd even saved a few spice bottles and the ancient Scrabble games.

He gave her a private, shy smile. "You know," he said, "I used to drive all night. Just get in the truck and go. I'd drive across the causeway, past the toll booths. At the time I used to argue with the poor guys, why the Jesus do I have to pay two dollars to drive onto my own island? But I miss them now, I don't know why. At dawn I'd stop at some truckstop outside of Antigonish or New Glasgow, eat breakfast and turn back. Cost me a fortune in gas and tolls. At first I used to stop in at the restaurant where she worked. They fed me on the house. Then there came a day I couldn't face it anymore."

"Why did you do that, go driving halfway to Halifax?"

"Because I thought I would go insane if I didn't do something. It was all I could think to do."

She pictured him driving alone at night, his face lit by the dashboard. Passing the abandoned farmhouses that littered the island, alders and birch growing up around them. Their dark bedroom windows like the eyes of abandoned children.

"Noel's leaving tomorrow. Where are we going to stay when he goes?"

"We'll stay in the house. Get the key off him. The sisters won't mind. I'll talk to them."

The trees closest to the cabin were shorn of their needles on one side where flames had licked them. They smelled of scorched balsam. Down the hill the grass was stained black with melted blueberries. Fire had transformed their land. Suddenly she was standing not in the home she had grown up in, but somewhere exotic, a place of threatening flowers and unidentifiable birds.

She made to pick up a piece of wood that had flung itself out of the flames.

"Don't touch that."

"Why not?"

"Leave everything as it is until the insurance people get here."

"But you didn't have insurance on this place."

"Of course I did. Here, give this guy a call." He handed her a business card with a Sydney address and number. He turned and started down the hill.

"Where are you going?"

"To the shore."

There's nothing there anymore, she wanted to say. All the eels are gone.

She watched him walk down the hill until he had disappeared into the woods.

* * *

It is their last night together and they go out driving. They are all staying at John R's now, and the only way they can be alone is to go out in the truck.

They drive to Indian Bay, and then pull in at Duncan's gas station, closed for the night. They sit in the truck with the radio on low.

"Your father knows how to set fires so that it looks like an accident," Noel says.

"I know."

He gives her a searching look, which she returns to him. The look says, there is nothing I can do about it.

"Why did you throw that piece of paper in the water?"

"When?"

"Last night, in the boat."

"It was something I didn't want to know." She turned away. "We'd better be getting back."

A mile from the turnoff to Clam Harbour they see him, the kamikaze moose, standing sentinel near the MOOSE CROSS-ING sign. He has grown into his legs; he is no longer an adolescent but a fulsome young bull. He has enough bulk now to destroy a car.

Saucer lights in the rearview mirror. An unbroken stream of cars ribbons behind them.

It is a simple turn, right-hand; they don't need to cross the lane of oncoming traffic. Just as Noel swings the truck around the corner, the moose vaults into the road.

They lock eyes through the windshield: the coal eyes of the moose, lit from within by a sharp seam of alarm. Their faces, the dashboard night. She tears a look at Noel from the side and sees alarm, fear. The lack, the secrecy, emerging in one last reckless look at the beloved's face. The car skidding, there's no point trying to steer. Brakes only take it to the opposite bank, a twenty-foot drop to the rocky shore below.

I can't do this anymore. I'm married. I have two children.

Seen from the side his face is the same face, largely

unchanged, that cut though her like a knife the first time she saw him more than seven years ago: an intelligent, austere face. She has run her lips along that cheekbone, taken his earlobe in her mouth.

I don't love you anymore. I can't.

You don't or you can't? They're two different things.

It should make a difference: *don't, can't.* All these years she has understood perfectly well why he couldn't love her in the open, but she knew that the feeling was there, that he loved her.

You don't want my love. What she means is, you don't *need* my love.

He knows this, because he replies, *I am loved. I have the love of my wife and my children and I don't want to lose it. I have enough love.* He pauses. *You do, too.*

The cold compassion in his voice slices into her heart slowly, a casual knife. Why bother telling him that she doesn't, in fact, have the love that she needs? That from the first moment she saw him she knew that it was his love she wanted, and needed. She has had a version of his love, yes, among the rebukes and the flirting and the desire. She has also had more of him than he will ever know.

She could try to manipulate him; she could try guilt. But then she would lose any esteem, love's residue, that might remain in his heart.

In the kitchen the women say: *He's had his fill of her. He'll have another one on the go in that town where he lives by the fall. If he doesn't already.* The relatives imagine things they have only seen through photographs: massive station wagons cruising eventless streets, the thick soundless houses on either side of them, women wearing lime green pantsuits, their lipstick a red slash on their faces. *You mark my words. Men like that.*

Ahead of her, there is snow and time. Blasts of wind. The protean body — a living, squirming thing — of his absence. She has no other life, apart from her life with Alistair, her daughters, the island. He does; he will travel to Zambia, to Qatar, to Borneo.

She sees his life, the future of it swallowing her memory, enveloping him in a knit of circumstance and desire — for his wife, for fly-by-night women perhaps, as he ages, women who he can take and leave in one go — sees her touch on his skin being erased as efficiently as if she had never run her tongue over his lips, never held him by the waist.

She considers telling him, but she knows that even what she has to say will not bind him to her. She is not being chosen. She is the one who will be left behind.

More terrible, though, is that he will no longer tell her the truth, she can sense it. As long as she has known him he has been honest with her. But now that he has chosen, and chosen for his wife, he will lie to protect her, lie to protect himself. She is losing not only a lover, but her partner in truth, her kindred spirit. Her kin.

The bottom of a spiral is a centrifugal force. Farther down is the underworld with its grey personnel. Orpheus wading though dead faces, looking for the face of his wife. Suspended there, out of touch, alive among the dead.

I hate to think of you going to waste in a place like this.

For the first time she thinks truly ill of him. He has used her; he has only been flexing his muscles with her so that he can see himself to still be that lethally attractive man. What does he know of the deserts she has inhabited, how she has wanted everything from him — to stay at least one night with him, to be able to curl herself into his sleeping body, lay her head on his chest, for his voice to be the first thing she hears in the morning.

We have lied to each other and to the people we love, for this love. We have been unloved, and also too well loved. The surfeit, the lavish oasis, and the desert. There is no love like this love, an outsider wandering a scoured landscape, an ingenious torture, but also a ripening in the dark.

A reckless second. Her mother's small hands on the steering wheel, she sees the lure of the precipice, the soft verges of dread. An inch to the left, to the right. With ice, that's all it takes.

Them sitting in the car afterward, breathing hard.

Why the hell did you do that? We could have gone over.

I don't know. I feel so desperate. I'm sorry.

His dread cancelling his waning love for her. After that, he will never come to her again. He will be afraid of her. He will never again see her as that surprise thrown up by the casual slipstream of events, but as a ghoul, someone who will deprive him of his family, his wife, even his life. He will fear her. She can already hear him in years to come, talking of her to a very few choice confidantes, referring to her as *my narrow escape.*

She counsels herself: Keep your love like a gift held underneath a table. Out of sight. But she can't. It is there, standing on the table, as garish as pain.

The moon takes temporary refuge behind a cloud.

Her rebellion is rash, and childish, and total. Even as she performs it she feels she won't be able to recall the gesture, to recast the lethal order of things. It would have to be final. There could be no survival, because to survive without his esteem would be worse than death. Banished from love she hardly knows who she is, who she will be. Her husband, her children — no-one will help her bear the haggard promise of tomorrow.

Fear nearly blots out the thoughts skittering through her as they go over, the vertigo, just like those dreams when you step off a cliff and are falling. In the moment of her death her thoughts fracture in the same way as when she falls asleep.

Things I have left undone, my child, my lovely breather, these random strandings life forces upon us, the passion of the outcast, I will never see the desert now, the hum of happiness, sitting next to your face which I love. And at last, the stillness.

They came to a stop. Ahead the moose scrambled, his dinnerplate knees uncoordinated, up the bank.

Eve turns to Noel. She thinks she can see the hollows and clefts his face will assume in ten, fifteen years from the broken nights attending to crying children, the ravaging winters of upstate New York.

They are both breathing heavily.

"I never want to see that moose again," he says.

"You won't." She turns away from him and looks out the window, but there is nothing to see.

At dawn she takes up a vigil position by the kitchen window, not knowing what she is waiting for. It is September and dawn comes late now, at 7 a.m. The morning is cloudy and the rising sun is only a calico smudge on the horizon.

She has been looking out at these lakes for so much of her life, waiting for something, some message, a crucial piece of information, perhaps, something that is rightfully hers and which has been taken away to be returned to her.

They come first in individual blows that make pockmarked sounds as they hit her skin, then in waves, until she can no longer distinguish them. It is like being stoned.

She will never know her mother, she will never hold her hand, wrap her hair around her finger. Such a simple thought, and yet in all these years she has never allowed herself to think it, even though she has been tracing the outlines of this outrage, unwittingly, all her life.

Her mother is shredded. Nerves, tendons, the eelgrass that rises in undulating threads from the lakebed. She doesn't know this from seeing her — both wakes are closed casket, unusual in Cape Breton, but necessary, considering the circumstances.

She is eight years old when she is told, and not all that gently, by her aunt and Anita, that she will never see her mother again. Although she already knows; the pulpy feeling in her stomach tells her. Anita and her aunt Maureen are both stern with mission. There is no point telling the child fibs, no point making it easier on her. She listens to them, her hands clasped between her knees.

She has a sense of it then, how for the rest of her life she will wonder about togetherness and apartness, how in the second her mother — the person who put her on this earth — ceased to be in the world, she had no idea. She was upstairs, lying in a heap on the floor. She had fallen asleep next to the register, waiting for her mother's return.

Later that night, after her father has returned with the news and the ambulance and fire crews have been summoned, someone — an aunt, a cousin, a friend of the family — will scoop her up in their arms, cover her with a blanket, and put her to bed.

Christmas is cancelled that year. At first this is what puzzles her most. The turkey that had been put to slow-cook on Christmas Eve stays in the oven and burns dry before someone remembers it. The carcass sits on the counter all day, a shrivelled brownish lump, mocking the proceedings.

Drawn-faced women appear from town — distant relatives she has never seen before from Sydney, Glace Bay, Halifax. They wear magenta nail polish and smoke and pace in the kitchen, people bring bannock, giant dishes of lasagne and scalloped potatoes and trays and trays of squares: date squares, Nanaimo bars, raspberry crumble squares, cheesecake. Unusually, no-one tries to stop her from eating too much, and after her fourth Nanaimo bar she throws up.

On Boxing Day someone manages to get hold of a bunch of lilies. She has never seen flowers before, not like that: in a vase, on the table. It is strange to see flowers in winter.

Whenever she tries to speak to an adult they all look at her with a distracted manner, and then their eyes well up with tears. What's wrong? What's wrong? She means to comfort them, but at the sight of her they start to cry.

It is Christmas Day, 6 a.m. The house is thick with sleep. Eve alone is awake, sitting by the tree in the darkness, waiting to open her presents. She had asked for a Sno-Kone machine.

She sits in front of a pile of unopened presents in her nightgown, scratching away at the wrapping paper. She looks up into the branches and is dazzled by ornaments — angels, scarlet apples nestling in the branches, fat golden geese.

No-one stirs until eight o'clock, when her aunt appears. Her eyes are ringed with ashen circles.

Can I open my presents now or do I have to wait for Mommy and Daddy?

Anita appears. Her face looks smudged. Anita and her aunt approach her with an expression on their faces of the kind she has never seen before. She bursts into tears. *I didn't do it. I didn't do it.*

She sees her aunt's face falter, but Anita's expression remains fixed. They sit her down on the couch, between them in her nightdress. Each takes one of her hands in their own. She stares at the Christmas tree, dazzled by its multicoloured population of tin angels. A turquoise angel, a purple one, and, hidden on the inner branches, her favourite — tangerine.

The nights are full of people crying. They shut themselves away in bedrooms upstairs. She hears only ragged snatches of muffled sounds. She hears the words *destiny, comeuppance, God's punishment.* After a few drinks the wailing starts. *Please, Lord. Mercy. Their souls.* It sounds like church, she thinks.

In the middle of the night she pads downstairs and turns on the Christmas tree lights. Someone has left the kerosene heater on by mistake and the window streams with condensation. She stands on the chair and looks out into the night. It is snowing. She watches the flakes hit the window with a delicate, silent flap, meet the window's heat, then disappear.

It is fourteen years since she has spent a winter on the island. She can barely remember what it is like — the lakes half-frozen, a skein of treacherous ice, crows curling in the sky. The silent impassivity of the land that has so recently absorbed two lives. How, in winter, you feel it most, the island's tenacity, the isolation and separateness that is not so much geographical — only a mile separates it from the mainland — but of its spirit.

On Boxing Day black ragged streaks unfurl in the sky — wood fires from the neighbours, tendrils of dark cloud. She puts on her snowshoes and takes the dog for a walk in the woods. The dog gets lost — this is what everyone assumes — but she knows better. He has run away, he wants out of this house of sorrow. He shows up two days later, the glint of hunger in his eye.

No matter what your father tells you, this is where your mother is, now.
   Up there with God?
Her aunt nods. Eve doesn't believe her for a second. Her mother is somewhere, that's for certain. But where? For weeks she wanders the shore with the dog for miles and miles, scrabbling in and out of coves, brackish suds, dead seagull, his eyes plucked out, looking for her.

Her father is putting her to bed. It is a year later, they have moved to the cabin. He tells her the story about the creatures that came from a long time ago, from the bottom of the world. Rising and rising until they were on the surface. There they float, too insubstantial to do anything else. They grow, thickening, until they arrive in their lakes. They are so tough, these creatures, with their rubber hide, their toxic blood. They stay underwater for years, her father tells her. But when they are required to surface they find they can breathe air, too.

Upstairs in the attic at John Rory's, she stands looking out onto the lakes. The sheer curtains that so entranced their disabled son billow in and out in the breeze.
   She is thirty-four years old, the age her mother was when she died. She can remember thinking, ten, twelve years ago: some things you just have to turn your back on and walk away. She has dropped her mother, and the memory of her, as you would let a heavy shoulder bag fall to the floor, and moved on. The lightness she felt afterward, the dislocation.

And now how late and how useless, her love and pity for her mother, her belated understanding of her life. She can see it all, like a story she has read in a novel: the mother's sheltered farm upbringing, early marriage, immediate pregnancy. Then this ambush, the terrible conviction of love. Eight years of guilt and yearning and separation, picking her way though a minefield of emotion she hadn't been brought up to hope to feel.

She realizes she has always been afraid of the lakes, and this is why she has swum wearing goggles all her life. Who knew what she might see if she opened her eyes in the depths? Her mother floats there still with the shreds of whales' skin, the eel-grass and the jellyfish, residual molecules, filaments of hair wrapped around a rock.

He can't love me, my love. I am drowning in this life once so much mine.

It is disquieting, even ghoulish, to read the sexual despair of her own mother. She is afraid for her mother; she wants to save her, even though she has been dead these many years. Her mother's words make her afraid, too, of how despair can verge on rapture.

She is sinking inside herself. She will come to rest on some soft underwater verge covered in silt, inhabited by starfish, glow worms. From there she will write occasional dispatches to the person she once thought herself to be, the woman whose father fished eels and made do in Cape Breton, whose mother was killed in a tragic accident. The person who fled, convinced a terrible fate awaited her if she stayed.

She is afraid for Noel, too, diligently trying to separate out truth and lies, to reconstruct fault, or at the very least identify cause and effect. All because he felt stripped. He felt himself to be exposed and bare, and needed to show kinship with others who were even more vulnerable in the face of malevolent events that swirled around them like djinns.

What is truer for each of them is simply a mackerel sky laced with cloud, her father's memories of moonlit nights camping out up Cape Smokey, Noel's velvet nights, families cooking in cement-block houses on charcoal fires whose smell is the smell of memory. Each of them alive, caught in the vicious grasp of ecstasy.

Her mother and her father are not among them. They are not in any other dimension, they are not in the eelgrass, not in the rocky plummet where the car went over, not in the carmine soil of the land. They are simply gone.

Her lips against the glass window, Eve faces the lake and mouths, but does not speak, the words she has not dared utter to her mother since that Christmas Eve. It was her bedtime and she had gone downstairs to say goodnight to her mother, fighting her way through clumps of adults in her nightdress, they pat her head. *Merry Christmas, Eve, hello darlin', what are you doing up at this hour?* until she finds her mother and clasps her calves, which are encased in those terrible boots, her head reaching the bottom hem of her mother's miniskirt, to say goodnight, Merry Christmas, and that she loves her.

The man — he is somewhere close by. She can feel him.

CHAPTER 22

They do not say goodbye. Later, she will not be able to remember what they substituted. Safe drive, perhaps. Have a good trip.

They hug — a ragged, substitute gesture that they both disengage from too soon.

She watches the car drive down the road in a haze of red brakelights; they illuminate the thrusting Statue of Liberty on the licence plate. She watches it accelerate down the grey denim road. She watches it turn the corner.

Water tank, septic tank, foundations — everything left of the cabin was underground. She spent an entire day filling out reports: police, insurance. The insurance man from Sydney was in the middle of a family crisis. His brother worked for Shell in southern Nigeria and he and a group of Germans and British engineers had just been taken hostage by Islamist rebels. She told him how forgetful her father was now, the stove. She showed him the tests.

The insurance man nodded. She watched her reflection bob up and down in his sunglasses.

"You know your father has secondary insurance on the place."

"What's that?"

"It means the insurance covers the cost of rebuilding." He rifled at the folder of papers in his briefcase. "He's covered for three times what that place was worth, that's for sure. He should be able to really go to town."

The insurance man's cellphone rang with a call from Ottawa. Someone from External Affairs, an urgent call about his brother.

Everyone came to see the damage, neighbours, people she and her father knew and some they didn't, stepping delicately around the charred timbers, shielding their eyes from the sun. That's some fire, they say. We could see it all the way down the point. Thank the Lord you got out.

At night she went for a walk down by the ferry. In a reprise of a game she played as a child she walked the fading yellow meridian in the road, one foot in front of the other, keeping to the line, like a tightrope walker. Then she went to sit on the driftwood logs ringed around a pit of carbonized wood — the remnants of Bob and Celyn's bonfire. On the way back to John Rory's she picked blackberries, savoured their sweet-acid crush.

The following afternoon Celyn came to the door.

"It's Anita on the phone," she said, her still-pretty face uncharacteristically drawn. "You'd better come."

On the 19th of September she sits in the same departure lounge on the same vinyl bench Llewellyn had occupied only three weeks before, in what seems now like another dimension.

People congeal around her, pensive men in bomber jackets off to autumn contracts in Alberta, British Columbia or even farther afield — Borneo, Papua New Guinea.

Scattered among the bomber-jacket men are well-groomed women on their way to regional management conferences in Halifax or Moncton, students returning to university who had, like her, been caught in the chaos of the last few days. These people glance nervously at her dark glasses, her overpercolated coffee, her hand shaking ever so slightly as she brings it up to her mouth.

She tries to read the newspaper. Although the paper carries the odd wire-service piece about the attacks, most of the news is local. The island is gloomy with its own future. Articles quote ministers and scientists who talk of "the collapse." It's been so much worse for Newfoundland, everyone says. To her it seems clear that the death of the cod implicates everyone:

Newfoundland, Cape Breton, Labrador, Greenland and Iceland, the Spanish and Norwegians and Russians with their marauding trawlers — they are all responsible for the death of plenitude. They had been there for so long, the cod. Not quite as long as the eels perhaps, but so much longer than humans, thick in their underwater phalanxes, nourishing their secret lives.

FENCE TO BE ERECTED AT TABLE HEAD AFTER TEENAGE TRAGEDY. The headline and article were tiny, sandwiched between blaring articles about Saudi Arabia and airport security.

In the last two weeks she had watched as her sister acquired the terrible majesty people who go through tragedy are doomed to gain. The whole experience presented itself to her in atomized moments, split into granules: shuttered faces; cucumber and cream cheese sandwiches; getting gas for Anita and Lloyd because they can't face it, of course they can't, putting the nozzle in and filling the tank. The newspapers full of alarm, exploding airplanes, mug shots of a determined-looking, thin-featured man. This is wrong, everything looks wrong. The gas is too yellow, like apple juice, the trees are wrong too, her credit card looks like one of the tarot cards the dream-demons dealt her. Anita's house, the faucet taps on her bathtub, the floppy houseplants, the uneaten piece of toast at breakfast, Kelly's bedroom door. They lose the significance of objects, they all have the same void-born name: not-you, never again you. *Never.*

She is sitting in a departure lounge, waiting for a plane that will take her to Halifax. There she will take another plane to Toronto. She tries to read the newspaper, and then gives up. The events of the last ten days flutter in her memory like banners set back on a distant perimeter, whipped by the wind.

All day Anita can't speak. Her face is a television left on overnight; floods of static, sudden thrashings into a blurred image as it picks up a random signal. She merely nods, looks around in an animal confusion. The torn look in her eye is frightening.

Anita ripping the casket top open and kissing her daughter once on each eye, or what she thought were the eyes. The face was like a stone that had been split open, and the sockets were empty. Her husband moaning at the sight. The other mourners plucking at their fingers, sitting on their hands, eyes averted, out of respect.

She and Anita sit outside on the back porch, smoking a cigarette. Anita is woozy on Valium. There is a half moon and the stars are very bright. Some of them are not stars at all but migrating planes, heading to England, Germany, France.

The drugs have loosened Anita's tongue. She speaks with an uncanny dreamy intensity, her voice not more than a whisper. Eve hasn't heard this voice since they were children and lay in their bunkbeds at night, reading books by flashlight, Anita whispering the words as she read.

"You barely knew what it meant, her dying," Anita said. "But you got all the sympathy. They expected me to bear it, but I was the one who cried. You never seemed to cry. I missed her so much. I knew from the first minute what it meant, that I'd never see her again. I knew it even before they told me."

Anita took a drag on her uncharacteristic cigarette, coughing as she exhaled. "I wanted to be married so badly, as quickly as possible. I wanted to be protected." Anita threw the cigarette a suspicious look. "You know I haven't smoked since I was eighteen and I've lost heart. I can't even smoke anymore. When I married Lloyd he made me give it up."

Eve stared out at the night. In the past days her sister's face had changed more than it had in ten years together; it took on a new urgency, had acquired a sharper aspect of the compelling beauty of their mother's face.

"When I got pregnant the first time I wasn't sure I wanted it; but I was married, and that's what you were supposed to want, so I went ahead with it. That was Kelly." Anita swallowed, a choked, gurgling sound, fragments of disbelief loose in her eyes. "But even when it happened again and again, I didn't know. I just went with it. I thought, this is all I can expect from life, for things to happen to me and for me to make the best of them. Didn't he always say that, Dad? It's not the cards you're dealt, it's how you play them."

Anita didn't wait for an answer. "It happened at dawn. I thought she was in bed. I watched the sun come up." Her sister's voice was a slurry whisper. "I thought it was just another day."

I dare ya. Go past the fence, around the side of it. Go as far as you dare.

As for Kelly, she does not think herself invincible, but the idea of boundaries excites her. These days she is driving too fast, driving with people who are drunk; she went swimming in the Mira in June, just after graduation, and at night to boot. It was so cold she thought she could feel her head seize up. She is hungry for experience. It is a kind of passion.

The ground is soft with moss. It absorbs her steps. A crescent moon is rising over the Atlantic. She will go one more step, maybe two. Then she will start back. But the moon slips behind a cloud and as she turns around she is suddenly uncertain of the way she has come. Her friends, stupidly drunk, their voices sound so faraway now, like distant pulses. *I dare ya, I dare ya.*

But she doesn't want to go farther. She wants to turn around and walk down Timmins Street, through the gate in the backyard, and right into her mother's arms. Kelly is so sorry, suddenly, for the peculiar games she has been playing with her, proffering her affections, dangling them in front of her, only to withdraw them when her mother reaches out to her. She is drunk and cold and the wind harries her back, or forward, she doesn't know which direction. *I'm so sorry, Mumma. I'm so sorry.* She will say this, and then she will tell her mother she loves her.

Then she is plummeting through darkness, just as people will, in a few days' time and in a distant city, hurl themselves from tall buildings into daylight, waiting for something to catch them. Kelly will scarcely believe her own impotence, that she is not God. That at no particular point could she have paused the tape, put happenstance on hold, and prevented it from occurring.

As for Eve, it is the first day in her life that feels like the Christmas Eve her mother went out and did not return. She may have lived through years and years of days since then, but it is always this night. Over the years it has accumulated on her skin, droplets of rain turning jade, then sapphire.

She is getting closer; soon she will understand the nature of error — true error, the kind you make only once or twice in life. Nights when the cabin shook with wind, animals — raccoons, squirrels — snuffling for scraps of food underneath the floor, their rummaging. Taciturn nights, trying to wring love out of her heart. The day she and Lew get married her hands look different. They are a wife's hands. Her hair, too — the hair of a wife. She has changed state, composition. *The hot pearl sting of his lips.* New museums sprout every spring. The island is becoming a live museum to its own heritage. When places become full of museums she has the feeling that time is over, there are no memories to be enacted anymore. Her father too has reached the stage in life where memories are no longer recollections, but a deconstruction of certainties. Look at that fat liquid moon, orange and hazy, an August harvest moon. The kind of moon that draws eels to their destiny. It's not clear that her father is not ill. He is lonely and depressed; he has come to the end of himself. This is as much an illness as anything that assails the body.

And Noel, his work has been a lament. But for what, for whom? He is so tired of rebuking himself. He has spent his professional life poised on the brink of error. In his work, mistakes costs lives; mistakes of judgement are the ultimate failure, and so a constant temptation. The gawky cawing of crows, the land unclenching the fist of winter. She has only this, and the ribbon of asphalt that divides her from him. She has two daughters who don't know who she is, whose relentless demands exhaust her, make her feel older than her years. Looking at them she thinks, they will love men who are free to love them, they will have better luck. They will not make the mistakes I have made. But she thinks this not with hope, with love, but with jealousy and resentment, even hatred, and it frightens her.

Truths that have to grind their way through you before you register them as such. Can it really be a force for good, love? How it changes all the meanings so recently arrived at, all the accommodations and the satisfactions. *What makes you think you can walk in here and change everything?* She had thought herself happy: a husband, a daughter. But she is not; instead she is only another piece of crockery in this cabinet of grotesque inevitabilities called life. It takes a certain courage to say: This is the way it is, this is the man I love, I don't care if other people think me depraved and pathetic, and go forward into hopelessness. Sitting up late at night, squandering precious sleep by writing pages and pages of urgent entreaties to fate. *My deepest impulse toward you is sexual. I am absorbed by your beauty. For ten minutes of your love I would give, for your love—*

Her mother stops writing abruptly. Some raw scavenger darts underneath the floorboards, startling her.

CHAPTER 23

She called him on September 9th, a Sunday, five days after he had left.

Rachel answered.

She took a breath. "I need to speak to Noel. Please."

"He's not here. Can I give him a message?" It was impossible to read anything from Rachel's voice. Only that it was the smooth, calm voice she remembered, the voice of a serious, well-educated woman.

"He left a book."

"Oh, sure. I'll tell him. What's it called?"

"Human Rights: Culture and Context." She made up the title on the spot. "Could you tell him something else: Kelly's dead."

"Who's Kelly?"

"She was my niece. Noel knew her."

"What happened?"

"She fell from a clifftop. They'd been drinking. She was only fifteen."

"I'm so sorry." She could hear it in Rachel's voice, the gravitas of real sorrow. Although behind it, as if kept hidden by a thin curtain, so that its outlines are visible, her condemnation. Eve is a marauder of other people's happiness. This is what will give Rachel the moral sanction to not tell Noel about Eve's call. She will never give him the message.

Of course, Eve could write to him at his work email. But she can feel his will holding her at a distance. He needs a woman he can do things with more than a woman he can talk to. He will choose Rachel for this reason. Perhaps this is how all men choose their wives.

She will not stop loving him for this, even though part of her thinks it a cowardly decision, really, not one she would allow herself to make, were she a man.

"Thanks." She hung up and the world swirled, coalesced into bunches of blackberries. She watched the blackberries ripen, and then she passed out.

As she fell into unconsciousness she had a sense, fleet and breathless, of how much she had wanted to hear his voice again. That note of judgement, the unforgiving tone that hovered inside it, but which he balanced, ingeniously, by generosity. The conflicts within him, his surface tensions — they were so audible in his pleasant, entirely common light baritone that tended toward honeyed notes in its upper reaches. His voice was the first thing she missed.

That Tuesday she went kayaking in Bob's boat. She wanted to skim the coastline, the peninsulas, Seal Island, the hidden coves. She wanted nothing in her mind but the sound of water sliding from her paddle.

It was a cloudless mirror morning. Light bounced from the lakes like individual knives. She didn't know why, but something urged her to look up into the sky. She saw a plane, very high, arcing gracefully, trailed by two thin streams of vapour. She watched as two, three, four more planes performed the same parabola and headed back out over the ocean, toward Newfoundland.

As she neared the tip of Seal Island she was waved over by two campers. Local people, by the look of it; a couple in their fifties or sixties sitting on the beach in plastic lawn chairs, a six-pack of beer open at their feet. A radio fizzed beside them.

The woman called to her. *Did you hear about those planes in the States?*

From Celyn's phone she tried to call him at work, but she couldn't get through. The recording of a woman's sanguine voice told her that all lines were busy. What did they mean all lines — what was the point of fibre optics? She dialled and redialled and it was just like those nightmares she had when Noel was still there beside her and she was trying to reach him. Telephones that wouldn't work, misdialled numbers, clogged lines. She might be trying to call a world that no longer existed.

His office wasn't that far downtown, she reassured herself. She knew New York well, had been to New York fashion week a dozen times. But right now she can't picture the city at all.

Noel left the NYU subway and headed toward the deli where he habitually picked up his morning coffee. He looked casually, automatically, at his watch. 8:30 a.m. The sky was a clear, soldered blue. The day would be hot and dry; the thunderstorm the previous night had sieved the air of its late-summer humidity.

This was his favourite time of year — the lavish, even grandiose autumn of eastern North America. This kind of early autumn always made him think of that luxuriant phrase, *Indian Summer*, of the plenitude of the Huron and the Iroquois who once occupied the Hudson Valley, a glut of partridge, persimmon, blackberries.

A year from now he would, all being well, be installed in a college town. He could already picture it: the mist of a cold night fringing the town, smoky and damp, soon burnt away by a powerful continental sun. He will watch from his office as children of new technology oligarchs are delivered up curving drives to brick buildings and step delicately from the safety capsule of their parents' SUVs. He sees himself delivering lectures. *In human rights terms,* he intones to a room of languid young people, mostly women, *the 1990s was a decade of despair.* He hears himself broadening out the discussion to encompass the new political economy of human rights. Hears himself using terms like "fallacy of composition" and "neoliberal multiculturalism."

Some of his students' eyes will go quite dewy with the double impact of desire and the threat of his knowledge.

He was seized by a curious solemnity, he couldn't say why. Everything was going his way; he felt back on track. But the tension came with a pungent impatience verging on disgust and that frightened him. In the five days since he had come back from the island he constantly felt like standing up and shouting. Back in his office for the first time the day before, a Monday, he had spent hours wading through his accumulated email, buckets of spam — Feeling depressed about the size of your..., Your confidence and self-esteem will..., Your Help is Highly Needed. Among this dross of supplication and bullying something was radically missing. What was it? The message that would change his life, that would deliver his fate to his doorstep, for once. But what would that be? He knew where he was headed; he needed a miracle or deliverance less now than he ever had.

Then, after work, dinner with their best friends Arturo and Sue, to welcome them back to the city. It is a close, humid night. At ten o'clock spectacular thunder and lightning storms will move in, but the air will not be rinsed of its humidity.

Arturo is assistant professor of political science at NYU, Sue an editor at Oxford University Press USA. Another couple Noel and Rachel have not met before have been invited, Jason and Angelique. As her name suggests, she is French. She has a full lower lip prone to quiver that reminds Noel deliciously of Juliette Binoche. Otherwise though she has a poised, alert quality that dissuades him from attempting much conversation. Jason is a colleague of Arturo's, a wry Southerner.

Arturo wears a short-sleeved shirt in a shimmering jade colour that suits his honey-and-avocado complexion. Sue and Rachel both wear tiny cream-coloured dresses. Noel has come straight from his office and wants desperately to put on a pair of shorts.

Arturo raises a glass. Here's to Noel's return to the land of the living.

"I wasn't aware I'd been dead."

"Not dead," Sue smiles. "Just off the map. On your island retreat."

Rachel groans. "Was it ever off the map. I really thought we'd fallen over the edge of the known world. Like in those *mappae mundi* with icebergs and dragons in the margins. It actually made me *long* for Manhattan."

A round of laughter follows. It makes Noel think of thinly iced ponds.

"I would have loved to see the island. I've heard it's like Maine, but emptier."

Rachel's glance at Sue confirmed what she had already told him, that his friends were hurt not to have received an invitation, not to have been given an escape from the steaming city. Although they did escape, renting cottages in Vermont, a seaside house in Nantucket.

"I needed to be alone." He can hear the sullenness in his own voice.

Sue gives him a smile of sly tolerance. "We would have left you alone."

"I can't believe you two aren't going to come live in the neighbourhood," Arturo says.

"There's this great organic bakery that's just opened on our corner," Sue adds. "They do these amazing juices."

Arturo nods. "It's a great neighbourhood now."

"Hey," Sue says. "What do you think about Elvira?"

"As what?" Noel asks, a little obstreperously. He knows very well that Sue is trying to get pregnant. Or maybe she is now pregnant, and this is her overture to delivering the news.

Sue gives Rachel a quick glance that says: *poor you*. To Noel, she rolls her eyes fondly. "As a name for a *girl*."

"You've got to be kidding," Arturo groans. "Too Alabama trailer trash."

"I like the idea of naming against the cultural elite. It's counterintuitive."

"Does that mean trailer trash families are naming their children Oliver and Amelia?" Jason interjects.

Sue gives an exasperated wail. "Trailer trash is *cool* these days."

"It might not be cool in twenty years' time when she's trying to get into college."

Another ripple of content laughter follows Noel's comment, although Noel understands this response is less unthinking than everyone would have liked — they have made a conscious decision that he meant to be funny. He catches Rachel's eye. *Leave them alone. Can't you see they're not serious?*

Noel kept protocol after that, keeping his mouth and mind shut for the rest of the conversation, observing Sue, allowing his impressions of her to congeal. She is an utterly pleasant woman, he decides, the happy possessor of a steady disposition. Not dull or uninspired, necessarily, but unperturbed. There is no sign of conflict within her, no edge apart from the niggling dissatisfaction of not having gotten precisely what she wanted from life.

The rest of the evening they talked about the Bush Agenda, the curious national amnesia that allows everyone to forget that electoral fraud is the reason their current president holds office, the exhaustion of the democratic process. The faces around the table display an instant childish disgust at having this bogus gargoyle president. *What can you do?* they laugh. *We tried to vote for someone else.* Arturo and Jason debate the electoral congress system. *Proportional representation is a fiction in this country.*

Normally Noel would be right in there, but he chooses instead to eavesdrop on the parallel conversations taking place. While the men talk politics, Sue, Rachel and Angelique discuss relationships. Now there's a gendered dinner party for you, Noel thinks, in the wry voice that has cropped up in his head lately: world-weary-Noel-talking-to-ingénue-Noel, even if he is neither jaded nor innocent. The voice is beginning to worry him. It must be age, or maybe disappointment. Before, he has only observed and absorbed what is going on around him. Now he seems to need to feel complicit with his own observations.

"I can't really think about it. Jason and I have only been together six months," Angelique is saying. I never wanted to be one of those women who starts writing out the wedding invitations and naming the children after the first date.

"But the way I see it, that's six months of womb time," Sue says.

"Oh God. Tick, tick," Rachel laughs.

"I know," Sue says. "I never thought I'd think this way. I feel like I'm being brainwashed, but I don't know by whom."

A black cloud rises from that place he thought he had abandoned, the interior pantanal, the giant swamp and its terrestrial anacondas. He looks around the table and sees six serene, accomplished young people gearing up to reproduce. But at the same time he perceives a certain emotional itinerancy in them that suggests they might be less secure in their relationships than they think, that they might — a decade more will tell — be part of that emotional army of individuals who move on when the going gets tough. Their entire conversation is designed to guard their values, and what they have all achieved. In secret they tell themselves: *You're not doing a good job in particular, but you've got your place.* They are content to be heading for a routine eternity.

Noel wonders what would happen if he opened his mouth right now and said: I need love. I need to keep taking risks. I need to get beyond things we merely want, beyond family, even. I still need to go out into the world. There's so much to learn. If he opened his mouth and said what it was he needed? Stony silence, or embarrassment? It would make him the rebel among this complacent intelligentsia, with their benign and squalling observations.

Will they move away from him when they realize he is not, after all, one of them? When they come to perceive his weakness, that he will not necessarily pursue his own interests with the requisite ruthlessness? That he does not see life as a personal treasure chest, its contents to be siphoned at will to feed his desire. His friends will see him as a challenge to their own integrity. Not that they will be obvious about it, for Rachel's sake. A coffee date missed, a carefully inserted insinuating comment that Noel will take as snide, and for which Rachel will dismiss him as "paranoid." A dinner party that goes slightly awry, with Noel — the expert on human rights after all — finding his incursions into the conversation rebuffed. Evidences will accumulate. Meetings with their friends will become a trial, although no-one, including Noel, will be quite sure why. Neither is any of this programmed or inevitable. Most of it will happen at the level of the unconscious. Even so, it will rob Noel of the friendship and belonging he once so much enjoyed.

It occurred to him he might not have been rigorous enough in his friendships, he might not have kept the right company. Too bad, he instructed himself. It's too late now. It's not as if you can just go out at your age and get a whole new life. But the right company. Who would that be? People who did not view love as an artefact, goods to be possessed, who were comfortable with the idea of love dispersing itself in themselves, and in the world.

"I've heard wheatgrass and beetroot juice, for the first three months anyway. You feel so tired, your blood pressure drops."

Purple cabbage steams on the stove. Its humid, ferric smell fills the kitchen. Arturo is chopping basil at the table, a roll-up cigarette in the ashtray beside him. He inhales the swirl of three different women's perfumes. There is no love or understanding, Noel is suddenly completely convinced, no chance of even the possibility of it. A ravenous and mechanical element is at work in life, something truly cruel. He will not be exempt; he is also a person who will cut people out of his life no matter what he feels for them, bar them access to his heart, if they don't fit with his *plans*.

"So, have you told work yet?" Arturo asks.

"That I'm leaving? I'm going to tell them tomorrow."

"How do you think they'll react?"

"I suppose they'll affect sadness for an hour, and then get on with finding my replacement."

Arturo is looking at him oddly. He knows Noel has worked at Global Witness for six years, that he is a valued member of the team. It's not the kind of organization anyone leaves easily, or without regret.

"You'll need to set aside next summer at least to do your lecture notes," Arturo counsels. "No more sitting in remote farmhouses for you, Assistant Professor."

This is said jokingly, but it is also a threat. Noel knew his friend thought that he was perhaps making a mistake. Arturo is in the thick of academic ladder-climbing, organizing workshops, attending conferences, running an Activist Academics group, involved in political documentary film-screenings. At the same time he is scathing about his colleagues. They dine out for years on their initial research, he tells Noel, endlessly repackaging it, ploughing their furrow.

"That's right," Noel agrees. "No more farmhouses for me."

He watches Rachel automatically brushing the crumbs scattered across the table from the *pain au levain* into a napkin. Rachel had been distant, at first. She had drifted around the house, briskly arranging flowers in vases, puzzling over what picture to put above the fireplace. He had expected as much. It was a rebuke for him overstaying in Clam Harbour, for not wanting to rush back. He couldn't really blame her.

Eve. He has not thought even her name since he left. When he really needs to shut something out, he can make himself feel utterly indifferent. He has been swayed by gusts of emotion in the past, of course, but this time he's not letting it happen.

Sue picks at olives, sucking her fingertips. Everyone apart from Angelique, who retains the alert posture of the outsider, sits slumped down in chairs, legs open, feet planted wide on the floor, or hooked on the undercarriage of the kitchen table. The smooth, lithely muscled arc of the women's upper thighs, sides of small breasts exposed by the tiny dresses. They laugh elongated, mouths-open laughs, a perpetual sigh in their voices.

He looks at the women and cannot stifle a faint disgust. Women are lying to themselves, he thinks, or at least they aren't being fully honest, when they claim to want a sensitive man. They want resoluteness, even ruthlessness. They want a man who will be admired and wanted by other women, who will be active in the world and who will protect them, who other women will want; he will have to disappoint these other women, their names and the word *wife* fresh on his kissable lips. The slumped lissom women around him are fatally relaxed, gorging on obscure satisfactions, now that they think they've found such men.

He is going to have to live in that world, whether he likes it or not, Noel instructs himself, where there are only appropriate and inappropriate feelings and anything outside of these bounds is punished by a strict, inhibited lore older than him, better than him. He has been bested.

Why don't you leave, then? Just turn your back on the whole thing. The new wry Noel-voice interrogates him. But both he and the voice already know. He doesn't want to be alone, cast out. He doesn't fully possess the sad recklessness of the outsider. He will stay because like so many people, having wandered into love he finds it hard to find his way out of this maze — of sympathy, understanding, contentment and yes, of convenience. If someone showed him an easy exit and shoved him through it, he would probably go. It occurs to him that you could spend the best part of a lifetime like this, seemingly content while actually scouting for an exit. He had enough sense to realize that he ought to have been shocked at this decision he seemed to be making. He was, after all, a man who responded with all his heart.

Above him the sky was sheared open by a deafening whine. Noel looked up, coffee in hand, to see a plane, a few blocks to the east. It looked so close, like a hologram, a projection from another dimension: outsized and far too low. The morning sun glinted off the fuselage's silver belly.

A thrill born in some black unvisited place inside him unravelled itself, setting off goose pimples. *It's going to crash.* Then another, more humane thought intertwined with the previous one, like a helix. *Don't be stupid. Planes in Manhattan fly low all the time and don't crash. It's just circling for La Guardia.*

The sound was less an explosion than the lead timbre of metal on metal, followed by an aural waterfall of smashing glass.

He kept walking, head down. *I'm sure that plane didn't just crash. Something else must have happened. It didn't sound like a plane crash. The earth didn't move underneath me.*

A sudden symphony of sirens. Fire trucks charged from the fire station next door.

From this point on, things happen in the present tense. He is trapped in an insoluble now.

Chinatown mothers are taking their daughters to school. The girls are cute in their checked cotton uniforms and black patent shoes. Occasionally the mothers turn to look over their shoulders at the thick spiral of black smoke that is beginning to gauze the pure sky. A delivery man loads sides of meat into a restaurant.

Noel is heading to his office at the end of Broadway. He is worrying about that day's meeting with his new boss (although not for long, he thinks — he will hand in his resignation straightaway), the Head of Americas, a guy who's come from a lobbying background in Washington. He doesn't like Washington people for all the usual reasons: too much proximity to power, praetorian self-importance, grassroots instincts corroded by hobnobbing with the exact foreign policy makers his organization criticizes in its reports. You've got to learn to speak their language if you want to influence them, they say, which is code for: You've got to dumb yourself down in order for thick Republicans to get it.

There he is, freshly showered, sunglasses shoved onto his head. In a remote province of his brain lives the thought, *a plane has just crashed into Manhattan.* He forces himself to look up and there it is, a gash, a jet-sized tattered hole. The charcoal stain has spread across the sky so that it partially blots out the sun. He blinks, closes his eyes, opens them. It's still there.

On impulse he changes course and jogs down to the corner of Canal and Lafayette. He has a clear view now. He can see people leaning from the lower lip of the gash. From the ground they appear as sticks, almost indistinct from the torn epidermis. Then, very slowly, the stick figures tip, hovering, poised on the edge. Then they fall; one or two are on fire. Tongues of flame flare from the window where they were balanced a second, grasping, as if furious to have missed their bodies.

Another plane appears, suspended in the canyon between two skyscrapers. It looks small, but improbably close — another visual puzzle. The plane disappears. From the time the plane disappears from his view, hidden by the tower, to the explosion, Noel finds himself counting the seconds, although very slowly. One, two, three, four, five—

The explosion shakes every bone, every cell. The sidewalk trembles. He feels a blast of air, like a convection current, then an unidentifiable smell. He starts to shake, although lightly, as the fireball vaporizes above him.

Debris falls from the edges of the fire; odd-shaped bits of metal, steel columns, sheets of glass. He distinguishes one or two ragged shapes that are definitely bodies — *people,* he corrects himself. They might still be alive as they fall. They will not be bodies until they hit the ground. The flames change colour from bright orange to the livid red of Chinese silk.

He breaks out in an instant filmy sweat. He stands on the sidewalk, transfixed. He doesn't know how long he is there — five minutes? Three seconds? Before he shakes himself out of his stupor and sprints to the office where he meets colleagues running in the opposite direction, down the stairs. Don't use the elevator, they shout. Get out of lower Manhattan. We're all going to be killed.

He doesn't think to ask, what's going on? Whatever it is, it is lethal. He can figure out the exact nature of it later, after he has fled. While he has been out in the street his colleagues have been logging onto the Internet and watching the news. They flew two planes into the Trade Center, they yell. One's gone into the Pentagon. There are other planes, they don't know where they are. Who's *they*? No-one answers. His colleagues have PhDs in politics, in history, so they don't jump to the instant apocalypse conclusions he will hear in the next hour on the street, from van drivers, bike couriers: *It's World War Three, isn't it?*

His colleagues spill out of the building. He stands in the lobby, watching them stream by. Where did he put his coffee? He can't remember leaving it anywhere, but it's definitely gone. A woman who works on Indonesia — Harper, Morgan? One of those women with surnames for first names — comes up to him and takes him gently by the arm. He has seen her in meetings, in bars after work when ten or twenty of them have gone out for a drink, she has shot him feathery, embarrassed looks. This woman whose name he can't remember is in love with him, and he hasn't taken this seriously at all.

"We've got to get out of here."

Again he jolts from stasis to frenzy, without any transition. He is out on the sidewalk and he is jogging. Harper or Morgan is gone, he doesn't know where. He jogs uptown out of instinct but really he doesn't care where he's going. One thing makes itself clear: if he is going to be killed, then he wants to be moving when it happens.

Thousands of others have the same idea. On the street two rivers entwine: people rushing toward the burning buildings, screaming someone's name, and stone-faced office workers, identity passes flapping on their chests, heading north. The office workers are calm, resolute, a silent marching army. No-one is talking to each other — so eerie in this city of spontaneous zest, of casual street conversations. Although a bike messenger says, to no-one in particular, *It's terrorists, isn't it?* Drops of sweat bulge on his forehead. *The Palestinians.*

He is just above Union Square when he realizes he might pass out from the heat and his sprint up Manhattan. He buys a banana — the only food he can stomach — and a litre bottle of Poland Spring water. He emerges from the store to find that the radios delivery-van drivers have going at full blast in the street emit only static; the announcers are speechless. One is groaning, actually grunting, over the airwaves. People are running, panic blaring on their faces. Noel's first thought is that they can see another plane so he runs too, it doesn't seem to matter which direction.

He runs up the middle of Broadway, spewing water from his Poland Spring sport bottle behind him. He is met by a young man with dreadlocks marching purposefully down the middle of Broadway in the other direction and yelling at the top of his lungs. The cocksuckers! The cocksuckers got the World Trade Center! A middle-aged black woman wearing bright red lipstick and gold jewellery falls to her knees, then flat on her face in the middle of Broadway, moaning. No-one tries to help her.

He realizes that people are screaming because the North Tower is falling. Suddenly he is a structural engineer with opinions: it's too soon; that building should stand for at least a few more hours.

He watches as it is swallowed by a cement-hued cloud of dust. The cloud billows, then crawls sideways toward them, and they all start running again. He doesn't feel panicked so much as claustrophobic, caught in cement canyons and wind-tunnels with a disaster-sized rubble cloud sidewinding toward him. He is intolerant of the products of panic, of screaming and shouting and cursing and moaning. He wants to tell everyone to pull themselves together.

The street is lined with people three and four deep talking on their cellphones, tears coursing down their faces. Silent queues form at public phones, one person after the other making short calls in consideration of the dozen people behind them and which he overhears in snatches. I'm fine, they say. I'm okay. I'm going to try to get home.

He hasn't called Rachel. In fact, he has forgotten about her, and it is not just a temporary omission. For the hour or so since it happened he has actually forgotten her existence. She is upstate today, he remembers, in a reclaimed wood showroom buying hardwood floors for their new house.

She answers and without drawing a breath she says, over and over, "Why didn't you call? Why didn't you call me? I've been calling you on your cell but I couldn't get through." In her voice is the same panic he saw in the eyes of the black woman who pitched forward on Broadway.

He can feel the distance between them multiplying, until it is so many more than the thirty-five miles between them, until it is dimensionless. He might never see Rachel again, just because he is in Manhattan and they are all under attack and she is in a hardwood flooring showroom upstate.

"What are you going to do?"

He will continue uptown, he tells her. Maybe sit it out at Mark's office if he's still there — Mark is a friend of his who works in a radical publishing firm in a nondescript midtown building. I don't think I'm going to be able to get out of the city today.

Rachel's voice is shrill with fear. "Why not?"

"They're closing it down. All the bridges, all the tunnels. There's no trains out. I'll stay with Mark. I'll call you later, okay?"

He remembers he has a camera in his knapsack. He takes a photograph hastily, guiltily, of the ash cloud and of the remaining South Tower, which is still burning. As he snaps the shutter he imagines, for the first time that morning, the people in the buildings, clumped in stairwells, sweating, trapped uselessly in elevators, or on the roofs, where they must have fled to escape the smoke and heat. He experiences an overpowering feeling of reality and unreality intertwined, so that the moment becomes hyper-real, unnegotiable. It requires him to seal his mind shut and submerge his thoughts deep inside him, as in a bathysphere.

Everyone repeats the directionless running when the South Tower falls. Afterward he stares at the piece of sky where the towers were. Apart from the radios and the symphony of emergency vehicles, there is curiously no sound: the city has fallen into a silence threaded by shrieks.

"Come on in, we're watching it on cable. Channel Seven got knocked out when they hit the second tower." Mark greets Noel as if he has just dropped by for a coffee.

"Can I stay here? I'll even stay in the office. I just don't want to go back downtown."

Mark gives him a curious look. "Sure."

This is the first time Noel has seen Mark in three months, and he seems to have aged over the summer. They were at college together. Somewhere in the ten years since, Mark became gay. At college Mark had been serially sexually successful with women; Noel had even inherited one of his girlfriends. Noel isn't sure if the gay issue is why they see so little of each other these days — different social circles, different interests — if he is skittish at the idea of changing your sexuality halfway through adulthood.

Out of nowhere Mark says, "This has nothing to do with me." His voice is offhand, as if he is already tired of the subject. "In another month this won't even be in the newspapers."

Noel nods dumbly. "Can I make a phone call? I can't get a line on my cell."

Mark's office is on the tenth floor — not high in Manhattan, but high enough to make him keep one eye peeled for a plane slicing through the window.

He manages to get an international phone line by redialling constantly. The number rings and rings. Then a recording in a flat Canadian tone informs him the number is out of service or does not exist. Of course, he's dialling the cabin. The cabin no longer exists. Had he forgotten? He realizes he doesn't have another phone number for Eve; he doesn't know how to reach her. There was no landline in the house he and Rachel rented for the summer.

"There are other planes unaccounted for," a colleague of Mark's announces, to no-one in particular. "They're tracking them on radar; they're coming toward the east coast."

A searing noise as the sky is zipped open. He looks out the window expecting to see another avenging metal angel, and catches sight of a fighter jet cruising low over Fifth Avenue.

For the next hour they sit in Mark's office and watch cable TV. It is soothing, being around faxes, computers, listening to people talk about how they are planning to get home. He over-hears Mark on the phone to a colleague on the West Coast. "Well, I guess we're not going to get much work done today, let's pick up the price issue tomorrow." He says this wearily, as if they are experiencing a public-sector strike, or bad weather.

Eventually, Mark announces they should go home to his place in Hell's Kitchen. "Then how about we go for a walk in Central Park? It's gorgeous this time of year."

Noel gives him a glassy stare.

Later that afternoon they walk across the Meadow. Women in bikinis are sunbathing; a couple of guys slice a Frisbee back and forth. Noel ducks away from it, as he will shy away from any flying object for months to come. It is the end of a late-summer day, still hot, and a golden halo surrounds everything; even the edges of buildings are trimmed with a shimmering light.

"How about a drink?" Mark proffers. "I know this bar that should still be open. It's got a real zinc counter."

The bar/restaurant is on Columbus Circle. It is hardly full, but it isn't empty either. A blond woman in a pale green linen dress plucks at an oyster. The wait staff are all well turned-out Hispanics. Noel wants to speak to them, to ask them, *Qué hacen aquí? Qué estamos haciendo en esta ciudad?* The interior is a lush, faux Rococo, gold and nymphs wrapped around marbled columns.

As Mark promised, it had a real zinc counter. Noel thinks of the Periodic Table of Elements, the temper and properties of zinc, of aluminum. How he had seen reinforced concrete and steel falling away like melting plastic, and the airplane that buckles, aluminum too, because he is a frequent flyer and knows it was a Boeing and they are still built that way and not with composites, as Airbuses are, the way it was absorbed so neatly into the building, so cleanly, the gash retaining its general shape, so that he half-expected to see it emerge intact from the other side.

Mark drinks a Martini; Noel downs a beer in three gulps. He tries to talk about what has just happened, about what he saw, but after a few seconds Mark looks away, annoyance rippling across his face.

"Could we change the subject?"

"Sure." Noel pauses. "What do you want to talk about?"

Mark inclines his head in the direction of Lincoln Center, which is just across the street. "How about opera?"

That night in Mark's apartment Noel wakes up at two o'clock in the morning with stomach convulsions. He was dreaming that he was vomiting, but not just the contents of his stomach emerge, also its lining, then intestines, then lungs. It all comes up in a red adipose slop. Soon all his organs are in the bowl.

He forces himself to sit up, even if he is afraid it will make him puke. He steadies his stomach and looks out the window. First he has to pry open his left eye. It has been like this all day, tacky, kept half-shut with an unknown substance.

The downtown core is draped in a veil of dust. There seem to be floodlights, too, although he is not sure where they are coming from. Helicopters buzz through the sky at the tip of the island. Otherwise it is a preternaturally quiet night. He has the impression of a city holding its breath.

He can see the shape of things to come: the state of emergency, a haphazard response, lashing out somewhere in the Middle East, a nation in panic, suspension of civil liberties.

More flesh will be burnt, more kerosene expended, and it will all happen on beautiful early-autumn days, or spring, or summer. Just as the Huron and the Iroquois had been slaughtered under these same skies, flies will go on buzzing, bees humming, blueberries ripening in their contented bogs; just as in Rwanda people try to disappear into the folds of hills and plead with the moon to save them. It all happens under the same spectacular insolent sky.

His heart pounds, exploding into a full-blown panic attack; within a second he is hyperventilating. His thoughts flare into a lurid mosaic.

The whine of the engines of the first plane. *This day matters.* The plane that turns into a fireball. *I have lost something. I have let it slip through my fingers.* The deserted streets draped across the island, so that he can see so clearly the arc of the island, its delicate camber. *My family is complacent, they transmit arrogance. They think they are geniuses, they can do anything. They have all the bravado of intelligent people whose bravery has never been tested.* And then, *I'm one of them.* A weird soundlessness, so that in the moment he can't hear anything — the explosions, the rumble of falling buildings, although later he will remember the entire experience in sound more than in vision. *I need real happiness in my life, not just the absence of need, the absence of pain. Is this what most people think of as happiness?* He doesn't even know where these thoughts are coming from, except that he may be at the end of his life. Perhaps these are the things people realize, just before they die.

He looks out the window onto his city, as it has been for years, even before he came here to work. The New York of the late 1970s, him agog at the Puerto Rican kids on a dim, lime green subway, taking a break from popping gum bubbles to kiss each other, their mouths ravenous. His parents saying something about taking a cab next time, the city has changed, winos on every corner. Their innocent outing to the Natural History

Museum or children's musicals. Then a teenager, coming into the city with a posse of friends, unaware or painfully aware of how square they looked, slumming it to dance at dank Bowery clubs in the 1980s. Now suddenly it is the twenty-first century and his city has been spirited away, deposited in some other realm, and he is left in this garrison of alarm.

He thinks of Eve on her depopulated island like an index finger pointing into the Atlantic. Has he really done it? Used her as a decoy for his own personal study: minerals, natural history, fish of the Atlantic. Used her as a conduit to the next stage in his relationship with Rachel, in their life together. The intimacy he built with Eve might have been born of the gaps in love they both felt in their families; perhaps they encountered their disappointment together in that gap, rather than each other.

He couldn't deny that with Eve he felt the tug of another spirit, just as he felt with Rachida, and that he hadn't been able to resist. They were connected in some way; how else to explain the strange companionship, as if they had merely resumed something that had been curtailed in the past, but which they had both forgotten. With her, he could feel the shimmering complexity of another soul. The ice-cream cones eaten together on he boardwalk in Indian Bay, the Scotland-shaped clouds forming and dispersing in their eyes at Grove's Point, the dark purple of the flames in the shore bonfires, a boat rowed into an ink lake, their urgent, exploratory conversations. In all of this lay the colossal accident of intimacy, of understanding. They had looked at each other from the beginning and saw the exact mix of hope and fear mirrored on each other's faces. Wasn't that love? Wasn't that intimacy? And if that wasn't, what was?

A siren sounds on the street below. He remembers that something extraordinary happened in a yesterday only a few hours old, that he saw thousands of people die. Even stranger, there is something familiar about what happened that day, as if he always expected to live through such an event, albeit against a different backdrop, in Rwanda, Colombia, the Middle East. He is a dangerous person and he has always expected catastrophe to catch up with him, he supposes, to claim him as one of its own. He feels dispossessed, betrayed, as if he never knew anyone; deposited alone on a remote citadel where the only sound is the sound of the wind blowing.

CHAPTER 24

Landscape whips by: black spruce unfurling into the blue of hidden lakes, flashes of red and orange — the leaves of maple trees. Her thoughts feel like this, too: ribbons torn from the edges of a mind, not hers, someone else's — someone who left in a hurry, who left them behind for her to collect.

Her father is driving. He pipes up. "Did I ever tell you how we met?"

She shakes her head.

"At a dance. Not very original."

He is twenty-three, Ann is twenty. She is flanked by an imperial guard of sullen, wise-cracking, less pretty friends. The first second he sees her pandemonium breaks out inside him: a shrill wind of panic, a sudden swamping fever, his heart tumbling over itself in a strenuous bid to keep beating. He's never much thought about it before, but now he definitely believes in love at first sight.

Ann in her emerald dress, honey hair spiralling from her shoulders. A tectonic shift takes place inside him; he can feel his heart as he has known it slipping away, all its motivations, ineptitudes and irregularities are reformed in a single seismic moment, all it has embraced and contained: his mother, father, brothers, wet boots by the stove, coal smoke, the little statues of Mounties his mother placed for decoration on an heirloom-free mantelpiece, all going away, becoming irretrievably *past*.

Two years after that dance and he is twenty-five, Ann twenty-two, and they are getting old by the second, their youth ignited then consumed immediately by Anita, then, much later, by Eve. They look at their daughters with the same incredulity. *Look, Alistair. There's two kids in our kitchen. How did they get here?*

The day after Eve is born he drives to fetch Ann and the new baby. A late-summer storm perches on the horizon, one of those fierce September squalls that are remnants of some hurricane or other that has drifted up from the Caribbean. They are in the hospital in North Sydney, Northside General, a lime green sentinel of a building perched on a rocky headland facing a stewing sea.

They all squeeze in the front seat of the truck: Ann, Anita, him, the new baby who they haven't even named yet. Anita wants to call her Laura; Ann wants a good Scottish name — Kathleen, he thinks it was. He has chosen Eve; he likes it because you can spell it forwards or backwards, he jokes. Ann and Anita shake their heads, but let him name her in a gesture of mollification. Poor girl, he thinks, looking at the baby on his wife's lap. You've got my stamp on you.

He looks at her unblinking filmy eyes and the studs of squid ink hair — black like his father's hair, also his grandfather's. None of the men on his side had gone grey until their seventies, and even then only at the temples. This girl might be of their line, those reserved, intense men who lacked the hard veneer of the adventurer, who were too easily moved.

And now that he knows? He scours himself for rage, surprise, disappointment, for a sharper version of that hollow cheated feeling he has already nursed through years of days. But — and it is so simple it feels like a trick of some kind — he doesn't feel differently about his daughter at all. He has absorbed her, and she him. They understood the delights of restraint, with their shared vague dispositions, dreamy and intense. They both shied away from the emotional truth of any given situation, at least at the beginning, whether out of any real denseness or a talent for evasion he didn't know. They avoided thinking of the injuries they had inflicted on others, but nor did they go around showing everyone their bruises. She is his daughter, still.

He still could not believe that this ended for him that night. Yes, he had two daughters, but his life had stopped that

Christmas Eve, and been rewound — not only to its beginning, but to some murky and irresolute time before, to some other life in which he is still standing behind the car — he will be there forever — bathed in the red reflection of the taillights, gulping his breath and expelling it in ragged clumps of steam. As they drive away he sees Ann turn around. In his memory it happens slowly; a deliberate, stiff gesture, as if her limbs are gelid with fear. She looks at him through the rear windshield. Despite the night and the dim reflection of the lights he can see the expression on her face clearly. Her face is contorted with alarm and dread. It is as if she knows what is going to happen.

They arrive at the airport and walk to the check-in desk. There are two flights going at the same time, and the check-in area is full.

They have never been people for hugs. At the most, the gestures of parting had been hands left lingering on an arm or a shoulder for a fraction of a second longer than necessary.

She tells her father, "I'll be back." And she would be, at Christmas; she will be back in the spring too, to help her father start building his new house where the cabin had stood.

Her father is walking away from her with his skittering step like a stone skipped across water. Then he is turning around and coming back toward her where she stands by a square pillar, holding her ticket to her chest.

Announcements on the loudspeaker; percussive voices careen off edges of concrete, steel, so that she almost doesn't catch what her father is saying to her.

"I went out to try to talk to them. He'd been drinking, the roads were iced up. I went out and tried to talk to her but she didn't want to see me. She wouldn't even roll down the window." Her father takes a breath, held it, let it out.

"I never stood a chance against that man. I'd never seen anyone like him before and I haven't since." He purses his lips, drops his eyes to the floor in a strange duet of shame and respect. "He would come to the island in the winter tanned from some place he'd been working, some place I knew I'd never set eyes on in my life. He was the kind of man who was always on top of other men, y'know, always in charge, but it was natural in him, he was relaxed. I could never hate him, although I tried. He was a serious-minded man. I could see why she loved him."

Her father peered at her — no, through her; his gaze built to go a distance, as if he might see this man in the back of her eyes, or in the furthest regions of her mind.

"But why—"

"I don't want to think in *whys*. Why didn't I try harder to stop them, why didn't I...," he shook his head. "All these Jesus years I've had to stop myself thinking, *why*, every single day, just stop myself from going stark raving mad. There was something between them, something unusual. I don't know what you call it. They had a connection—" he raised his finger, put it to his temple "—*here*. I could see it, everyone could. It was the strangest thing."

In her father's voice she heard the note Noel had described in the massacre survivors: a childish wonder and delight at having survived.

"Did you ever read her diary?"

He shakes his head savagely. "I didn't want to know a Jesus thing about any of it. If I did I might not be able to go on living. I wanted to try, to stay and fight. I wanted to stay in life."

And he had stayed. How could she have thought him a mild character all these years, she wonders, a harmless man? She sees now that he is so angry, angry enough to want to go out and stun the world.

A stark charge of love and rage zings through her deep inside, on an amphibian level. She has never received a look from the man who was her father and thought, *He is my father and he loves me.* Running alongside it is an equally powerful current of shame, which she would feel so deeply for a man she never knew, who was never as much her father as the man standing in front of her. Still, she wants to ask, *What was my father like?* But it is too grotesque: she wants to hear about her father from her father.

She would like to say, now that she knows: I knew it all the time. That man she died with was my father, you are someone else. You are the man who brought me up. I knew it, but I didn't know it. But this would not be true. That he is not her father in those terms — glucose, proteins, amino acids — this should all either be a devastating surprise or an enormous relief. But she does not feel particularly surprised, or relieved. Instead, a nameless weight — she could call it fear, or dread, or something entirely opposite, like salvation — blots out everything.

"She was pregnant when she died," her father says. "The autopsy showed it. Not much; eight or nine weeks. She might not even have known."

She stares at her father. A feeling of complete familiarity, of predictability, overtakes her, as if she has been expecting him to utter these words all her life. The question careening through her suddenly oxygen-less, dizzy brain. Pregnant *with* whom? Who would that person have become?

Her father raises his hand and brushes her hair behind her ear. "I don't want you to worry about any of this. You've got everything I could give you."

She is tiptoeing into his room at night, she's had a nightmare. He let her sit on his knee through card games, playing with friends until one or two in the morning, roll-up cigarettes, shot glasses of rum, tapping them on the table, running her tongue around their insides to collect the dark nectar. Even when she inadvertently gave away his hand, he'd let her stay. She is hunting with him in the fall, bullets heavy in her palm, ricocheting off each other. They bring home the dead deer together, strapped it to the roof with ropes, its black tongue lolling from its mouth, flapping in the wind. His trips to the brand-new North Sydney Mall to buy her children's jeans and wine-coloured sneakers in

Zellers, in Woolco. The stricken look in his eyes when he sees her stiffen with horror. She will wear them on the schoolbus and change in the bathroom at school, for fear of hurting his feelings.

She watches her father walk down the corridor with his slightly stiff gait, knees thrown out, faded jeans, shirt peeking out of his belt at the small of his back. He walks out the automatic doors of the airport and into a blare of sun.

Her flight is called. With the other passengers she shuffles, a vague dread slowing her step, toward the door. In another day the mining engineers will be in Borneo, the oil men on drilling platforms off Aberdeen, the students in their wan residence rooms at Simon Fraser, at McGill.

The Dash-8 gleams on the tarmac. Soon the bright ocean of the stratosphere will slide across their eyes, just as below eels are being hurled by the grip of currents toward their final home. They have left the gouged coastline of the peninsula province and have entered the deep waters of the continental shelf. It is nearly over, this life they have lived as a symphony of convulsions sparked by instinct. They are never going to know how it feels for their desire not to be the same as their will.

The night before Kelly's funeral she and Anita stay up all night. They listen to the marine forecast, the radio announcer's voice seductive and reassuring as she performs the nocturnal recital of the ragged islands and peninsulas in their corner of the world: Anticosti, Gaspé, Fundy, Grand Manan, Sable.

The day of the funeral is spectacular. The sky is a cloudless blue, the air is sieved of summer humidity into a spare clean heat, as hot as at the apex of summer. The island has emptied of tourists; camper vans and trailers and motorcycle touring groups are dispersing across the continent. The trees are fringed with the rust of autumn, pumpkins ripen, mourners dressed in black jackets shake them off outside the church, fling them over bare forearms and squint into the sun thinking, summer is nearly over now, but it does not feel like a season in decline.

Afterword

This is a work of fiction. Some of the place-names used in this book do not exist in Cape Breton, although they can be found elsewhere in Nova Scotia. There has been no significant eel fishery on the island since the eels' migratory route was interrupted by the building of the Canso Causeway in 1955, although eels are still found in the lakes and waterways of the island.